MIDNIGHT RENDEZVOUS

Whitney waited until her parents had retired, then slipped out of the house to the meeting place. She knelt before the huge cottonwood and searched with her hands behind a flat rock where letters were to be hidden, but again there was nothing. Then the snap of a twig told her she was not alone. Fear paralyzed her for a moment, until she heard the familiar voice.

"Will I do as well as a letter, Whitney?"

"Mitch," she gasped. He stepped from the shadows and in a moment she was in his arms.

He kissed her feverishly and for a while they could only hold each other.

"I had to see you. I couldn't stand it any longer."

"I'm so glad you're here."

"Whitney, I have a feeling it will be a long time before we can see each other again. Slipping across enemy lines is getting harder. We're moving north fast."

"Oh, I hate this war," Whitney cried as she tightened her arms about his waist and pressed closer as if she could keep him from danger. But he was more worried about her. He knew what might be coming and felt she was in more danger than he was. At least he could defend himself, but Whitney was vulnerable.

"Mitch, will you keep writing, even if you can't get back here for a while?"

"You know I will."

"It's just . . . your letters . . . they're all I have of you, and I miss you so terribly."

"No, Whitney, they're not all you have of me. You have all I am or ever will be. Don't you know by now that you're my life?" He lowered his voice tenderly. "Or must I prove to you again that we are always a part of each other, no matter what happe

"Yes," she murmured as h

"Yes, tell me again . . . agai

SYLVIE F. SOMMERFIELD

Love's Stolen Promises

PINNACLE BOOKS
WINDSOR PUBLISHING CORP.

For Carin Cohen Ritter

—and the beginning of a new and promising relationship. My thanks for making the transition so easy and for always being there when I need help. I hope this book marks only the first of many we will do together . . .

PINNACLE BOOKS

are published by

Windsor Publishing Corp.
475 Park Avenue South
New York, NY 10016

First printing: August, 1992

Printed in the United States of America

Prologue

The moon was high and full and no clouds barred its rays as it bathed the land below in a soft white light. Cottonwoods rustled under a gentle breeze and cicadas sang softly. It was a miraculously beautiful night, a night meant for lovers, and the two who met beneath the dark shadows of the cottonwoods were indeed lovers . . . forbidden lovers.

He had been standing alone for some time, alternately afraid she would not come, then afraid that she would and her coming would do her harm. Even in the shadows, it was easy to see he was exceptionally tall and broad-shouldered. He leaned with his back against the tree, his arms folded against his chest, obviously deep in thought.

Then suddenly he heard a sound and saw her running toward him, a whisper of white in the darkness. He pushed himself away from the tree and ran toward her. He caught her up in his arms, spinning her around until her skirts swirled about them like a cloud.

Her laugh was warm and bubbly and she threw her head back in the sheer joy of his embrace. When he set her down his hands reached for her thick unbound hair and buried themselves in it as he lifted her face to his.

She made an inarticulate sound of intense pleasure as his mouth took hers in an all-consuming kiss. Her body arched against his and her slender arms held him close. They swayed together, his strong arms holding her as if she answered his every prayer.

5

When he let her go they whispered to each other and laughed softly with youthful assurance. They were sure that even though their love was forbidden, they had found a way to be together now and they would find a way to be together forever.

But after a while the whispers and the laughter were not enough. They turned to each other for a deeper fulfillment, and to make their final commitment. She whimpered in surrender as his hands slowly and gently began to disrobe her. She met his gaze with pride, reveling unashamedly in her womanhood . . . and his desire. He was all she had ever wanted. Her eyes were smoky with passion, dark and glowing as she stepped closer to lend trembling fingers as he, too, cast aside his clothing. Then they embraced, wordlessly surrendering to each other. He kissed and caressed her feverishly, savoring every inch of her slim, silken body. He kissed her temples and eyelids, then nibbled softly down her throat and over each aching breast, then drew her slowly down to the warm grass.

As she lay against him, he worshipped her with his fingers — tracing the soft curves, exploring every inch as if he had to discover with his mouth and hands what his senses already knew.

His mouth skimmed down her body to trace kisses from her slender ankles to her soft thighs. He held her gently while his mouth sought her honeyed, eager core. He knew the joy of creating deep pleasure as he felt her convulsive trembling. He stroked gently as she moaned softly and reached for him, alternately torn between ecstasy and the blazing need to feel the hard thrust of his maleness.

Her hands closed about his hot shaft and she could feel the throbbing life. She knew without any doubt that he and only he could cause this desperate, mindless craving. She drew him to the hot, pulsing entrance and was rewarded by a deep groan as he filled her. Now their need became primeval. She arched to meet him and he struggled to keep his fulfillment from coming too soon.

6

He gentled her with his hands, grasping her hips and slowing his thrusts, keeping a slim margin of control so he could be sure the full pleasure would be hers first. He moved in slow, gliding strokes, enjoying her mindless surrender. Her slim legs gripped him and her hands held him tightly. Her head tossed from side to side. Finally, sensing that she was nearing the brink, he increased his rhythm to the frenzied, ecstatic thrusts that brought them both to a convulsive climax. She was clinging and shivering as he murmured her name and held her close.

She lay against him and his hands caressed her lightly, sharing the gentle peace of knowing that what they had just done had been exquisite, and theirs alone.

They were satiated and exhausted, yet still they clung together. Only then did they remember that their love was forbidden.

She lay with her body still singing from the magic; both were torn by the knowledge that they had so much to give each other.

He spoke bitterly about what he wanted her to have and she soothed away his frustration with gentleness and loving.

He made the promises of a lover who wanted the one he loved to have everything she deserved. He spoke of wanting to share the rest of his life with her, of wanting them to be together always. She gave her promise that she would be his always—that nothing, no power in the world, could separate them.

They sealed their commitment with warm kisses and gentle touches until passion ignited once again. Their lovemaking was gentle this time, meant to seal their love forever.

Then the time came to part. The moon was already descending toward the horizon. He rose, reluctant to let her go, and helped her dress; then she helped him. They walked slowly through the trees, hating the moment of separation.

When finally he had to let her go, he reminded her of

their pledge: they would let nothing or no one separate them; they would fight for their love. She smiled, kissed him goodbye, and swore the pact would be honored. He watched her disappear in the pale mist, fighting the urge to go after her and take her away to a place where they could claim each other before the world. Then finally he turned toward home, holding their promise deep in his heart and praying that the misgivings he felt were only his fear.

But far away from where the lovers had met, something ominous was taking place. A fort sat silent as men watched from the ramparts with bated breath. There was fear across the land, fear that the peace was about to be shattered — and that the wound would be irreparable.

Then it happened. The cannon roared and the lovers would feel its impact to the depths of their souls. Fort Sumter had been fired upon and the war had begun. Men would be tested, and so would the promise two lovers had made beneath a peaceful moon.

One

The huge spiral staircase of the Clayborn plantation dwarfed the young black girl who walked slowly up. Her hand slid along the gleaming polished wood and she hummed softly to herself. She had just put her foot on the top step when a sharp voice from below made her spin around, her eyes wide with respect — and fear.

"Girl, yo' keep a-pokin' along an' ah's gwine kick yo' tail fo' a mile. Now yo' gets to Miz Whitney's room right quick."

"Ah's gwine fas' as ah kin. She doan be 'wake anyhow. Yo' knows Miz Whitney likes ta sleep 'til noon."

"Yo' go lay out her clothes an' tell her her mama want to see her quick as she can. Now scat!"

Addy sighed and hurried until she had rounded the corner. Only then did she have enough courage to defy Berdine. It was commonly known that next to Ethan and Hope Clayborn, it was Berdine who ran the big house. But Addy felt smug this morning because she knew a secret nobody knew, not even Berdine. Wouldn't Berdine just turn inside out if I told her what I saw last night, Addy wondered gleefully. But she wouldn't tell nobody. She wouldn't tell because she liked Miss Whitney so well and it would sure cause her no end of trouble.

Addy kind of liked that young man, too, that Mitchell Flannery, even if he came from poor folks who hardly had a place big enough to feed the family. That Mitchell, he was always lookin' at Miss Whitney, Addy pondered. But last night was the first time she knew for certain that Whitney Clayborn was sneaking out late at night to meet Mitchell Flannery down by the river.

She knew for certain because she had seen them. She herself had been doing exactly the same thing. She sneaked out to meet Priam because he'd begged her to. One kiss and some laughing and fumbling was all they had done — she had gotten scared and left. It was on her way back to the big house that she had seen the glimmer of white. At first she thought it was a ghost and had been terrified. Then she had seen him step from the trees and catch her up in his arms and spin her about. Then they had walked into the shadows together and Addy had run on home.

Addy opened the door of the semi-dark bedroom and went inside. She crossed the room and opened the heavy drapes to the bright morning sun, causing the girl in the huge bed to stir, groan, and open her eyes slowly.

"Oh, Addy," she said in a sleep-drugged voice. "What time is it?"

"It's most onto eight-thirty, Miz Whitney."

"Eight-thirty! Why are you waking me up at this ungodly hour?"

"Yo' mama want yo' at de breakfast table, Miz Whitney. She say she want to talk wif yo' an' it's real important. Yo' is to come quick as yo' kin."

At this the girl in the bed sat up abruptly. Wide violet-blue eyes looked intently at Addy. She was very alert now, and somewhat frightened.

"Has something happened, Addy?"

"Happened? Ah doan know. Ah ain't heard 'bout nuthin' special happenin'."

"Nobody . . . nobody's come to visit or sent any notes to Mama or anything, have they?"

"Ah doan know, Miz Whitney. Yo' knows Berdine doan let me do nuthin' but work in de kitchen or come up here to help yo'. Ah doan know 'bout visitors, or notes, or nuthin' like dat."

Whitney was already tossing the blanket aside and

swinging her long, slender legs out of the bed.

"Get me a dress, Addy, quick. Is there water for a bath?"

"Yessum."

"Good. Help me. If Mother has something important to say I'd best hurry."

"Yessum," Addy agreed. But she knew the real reason for Whitney's fear—the remote chance that someone else had seen her nocturnal rendezvous.

Whitney Clayborn had celebrated her eighteenth birthday five months earlier. Only five months, she thought, five months since she had seen Mitchell for the first time. Oh, not the first time, for they had known each other as children. But he had gone away to school early and she had not seen him again until five months ago.

It was like being born again, she thought. She had looked into his smoke-gray eyes and instantly lost her heart. He too had been unable to keep away from her. They were not allowed even to speak to each other, for she was the daughter of a wealthy family in Holly Hill, South Carolina, and he was the son of a poor dirt farmer without a dime and little prospect for improvement. But she *had* spoken . . . she had watched his quick, heart-rending smile . . . she had kissed him and known in the deepest depths of her heart that she would always love him.

He had struggled, but the Flannerys had very little chance in a society already turned against them.

If her parents had one glimmer, she would be sent away and most likely never see him again. She couldn't let that happen. She was terrified to face her mother.

She hurried as fast as she could, tying back her flaxen hair with green velvet ribbon because she didn't want to spare the time to do more. She dressed hastily and in half an hour walked into the breakfast room to face her mother.

Hope Clayborn had the same blond hair her daughter had inherited. She also had a porcelain complexion and

11

sea blue eyes. Her appearance was rather fragile, but Hope was as far from fragile as anyone could be.

She had married Ethan Clayborn first because he was extremely handsome and second because he was extremely wealthy. Ethan had been the most eligible and sought after bachelor at her debutante ball, where Hope had first met him. Tall and well built, he had the most remarkably penetrating blue eyes she had ever seen. His hair was light brown, nearly blond, and his strong, chiseled face was softened by a heart-melting smile. Hope may have been fierce and determined, yet in her own way she loved Ethan. She had come to the Clayborn plantation as a bride and had ruled it with an iron hand from that day on. She had decided when she was very young that she would marry well and once her mind was made up, she always carried out her decisions.

She had given Ethan a daughter and a son and had made certain plans for them. Whitney would marry well . . . and *well* meant a great deal of wealth. Hope and Ethan had spoiled Whitney, giving her every luxury.

Hope, groomed carefully and looking her very best, had come downstairs early to share breakfast with her husband, something she rarely did.

"Hope, my dear," Ethan had said, pleased at her presence, "how good to have you with me for breakfast."

"Ethan, there's something we must discuss."

"Dear?"

"I've heard some startling gossip and I must say it has upset me."

"What is it?" Ethan smiled tolerantly. He would do whatever was necessary to make Hope happy.

"We allowed Whitney to go to that play in town with the Waverlys."

"Yes?"

"I was told that one of those atrocious Flannerys actually had the nerve to stop Whitney in the lobby at intermission and speak to her, with dozens of our friends there."

"Did she speak to him?"

12

"Ethan! I'm sure she had better sense than that!"

"Hope, aren't you being a bit of a snob? I hear the boy has gotten himself a fine education. I've even heard he earned his own money for school."

"Would you really want your daughter to be ostracized? My heavens, Ethan, you can't envision your child ending up with a man with nothing! They live in a hovel. Would you subject a girl with Whitney's upbringing to something like that?"

"I'll talk to Whitney."

"Don't bother. I'll speak to her at breakfast."

"Breakfast!" Ethan laughed. "With Whitney you mean lunch, don't you? So what is it you want me to do about this?"

"Speak to him. After all, the Flannerys are indebted to you, are they not? You practically own the land on which they live."

"Speak to him . . . or threaten him?"

"Whatever it takes to keep him away from Whitney."

When they married Ethan had turned most family concerns over to Hope. She had done well and he had come to trust her judgment. Even though he loved Whitney, he did not understand her so he especially trusted Hope's judgment in regard to her. He would keep Mitchell Flannery away from Whitney.

Ethan rose and kissed Hope's cheek. "Well, I have to be on my way. I'll see you at dinner, darling."

"You'll talk to that young man?"

"Yes, I'll talk to him. I must admit," he said with a grin, "the boy has excellent taste in women."

"Ethan, this is not amusing and his taste is not in question. We have to protect Whitney from money-hungry rakes. She's young and vulnerable and we can't let her be foolish enough to fall into the arms of the first handsome face that comes along. I will not allow my . . . our daughter to marry beneath herself."

"Calm yourself, Hope. I'll talk to the gentleman in question and put an end to it."

"*Gentleman,*" she scoffed. "Offer him a decent sum and

see how quickly his ardor cools."

"Maybe you're wrong and all of this is foolish gossip."

"Let's not take any chances, Ethan. Better to be careful than to have regrets."

"I'll do what I can today." Ethan patted her arm consolingly and left, quite unaware that Hope watched him with narrowed eyes. In her estimation Ethan was too gentle and this made him weak.

Ethan had hardly left the house when Whitney entered the breakfast room. Since breakfast was always served from the sideboard and the family usually served themselves for the informal meal, Whitney walked to the sideboard and picked up a plate. She moved from chafing dish to chafing dish, lifting each lid and taking a bit of food from each. Sausage and eggs, biscuits and fruit. As she sat she smiled at her mother.

"Good morning, Mother. Addy said you wanted to see me."

"You're not usually so chipper so early in the morning, Whitney. I'm surprised."

"I don't like to get up in the mornings, but since you wanted me I hurried. I know I'm spoiled, Mother."

"You sleep late in the day because you like to play and dance all night," Hope replied. She was pouring herself more coffee and did not notice as Whitney's face grew pale and her eyes widened in fear.

"What . . . what made you say that? Mother, I don't . . . *play,* any more than any other girl my age."

Hope looked at her daughter intently. "It's high time you stopped wasting your time frivolously and started learning the ways of a lady and a wife. You should soon be considering marriage. It's one thing I wanted to talk to you about."

Whitney's hands trembled so that she couldn't lift her fork to take another bite. Her heart pounded. She knew her mother well—there was something important she meant to say. Whitney was terrified that someone had seen her meeting with Mitchell. She remained quiet, praying silently.

14

"I know you have a great many friends, Whitney. Do you favor one or the other as a prospective husband?"

Was her mother baiting her? She knew! She had to know! And she was most likely furious.

"No . . . no, not really."

"There are a great many wealthy young men for you to choose from."

"Wealthy. . . . Mother, is wealth that important?" Whitney asked quietly.

"Don't be foolish. It means everything."

"I'm not so sure it's all I want."

Again Hope's hand paused, then she laid her fork aside as another thought struck her.

"I've had a nasty piece of gossip brought to me, and I hope your last remark has nothing to do with him."

"Him?" Whitney asked speculatively, hoping she was wrong.

"Mitchell Flannery. Now don't deny he had the effrontery to speak to you."

"No, I won't deny it. But what's ever been wrong with a gentleman being polite?"

"As long as that's all it was and all it will ever be. I forbid you ever to allow him to speak to you again."

"Forbid! Mother, I just can't be rude."

"He *has* nothing and he *is* nothing! I will not let you even consider such a creature." Hope sat back in her chair, surveying Whitney carefully. What a beauty she was, Hope thought with pride. Her eyes were as blue as summer violets, her hair like cornsilk. She was tall, like her father, willowy and delicately feminine. She would be a prize for a man with a purse who could keep her in the luxury she'd known all her life.

Whitney knew she should do battle and proclaim her love for Mitchell, but her courage never held up before her mother. She had to think of another way. Maybe she could bring Mitchell to see her parents and then they would know how wonderful he was. They would see how much they loved each other and allow them to marry.

"He's not a *creature*, Mother, he's a man."

15

"Yes, I'm quite sure—and the poor wretch is smart enough to sniff out a golden opportunity."

"You make me sound like a commodity to be bought and sold."

"But at a rare price, my love," Hope chuckled. "You were born to live a life of luxury."

"There are none I would choose, Mother," Whitney said obstinately, using every conscious effort to return her concentration to her food and away from her mother's intense gaze.

"Well, you'd best choose," Hope said in a voice that would harbor no argument, "because if not, very soon your father and I will choose for you."

Whitney was shocked into complete attention.

"Choose for me?"

"Your father and I want you happily settled, Whitney, and you are now of marriageable age. You choose or within three months we will choose for you."

Whitney stood up abruptly, completely shaken by the resolve in her mother's voice.

"I will *not* marry a man chosen for me!" she cried angrily. "That is out of the question."

"No, I'm afraid not, my dear. It's quite an acceptable thing. Many families have joined in fortuitous marriages."

"Well, I won't! I won't."

"You're as wayward and stubborn as your brother," Hope replied. She stood, her voice calm. "But neither of you is going to disgrace this family by dallying with riffraff. We're a family of position."

"I have no intention of disgracing you and Father and I'm sure Keith doesn't either. But neither of you can be serious about this. I won't believe it." Whitney turned and ran from the room.

"Mitchell Flannery," Hope muttered. "Well, he'd better not get in our way, my girl. You'll take up with the likes of him over my dead body." She sat slowly back in her chair with two questions in mind: would Ethan really speak to the man in question—and how was she to make certain her children didn't slip from her control.

Whitney returned to her room, closing and bolting the door behind her. She was in a state of panic. Who had told her mother? How much was really known? Worse — what could they do to stop her from seeing Mitchell again?

She knew Mitchell's fierce pride. If he had to face her parents and their demands she knew the anger and hurt he would feel. She had to see him and tell him. In desperation she ran to her desk and grabbed a pen, hastily writing a note. She folded it and put it in her pocket as she left the house and almost ran to the stables. She searched until she found the person she sought.

"Lazarus!" The huge black man who had been currying a horse turned to grin at Whitney. He'd known and loved her from the time she was a child.

"Lazarus, I need you to deliver a message for me."

"Miz Whitney. Yo' sho' yo' wants me to do dat? Ah doan want yo' to have no trouble."

"Please, Lazarus. This is really important."

"Miz Whitney, it ain't fittin' fo' yo' to be sendin' letters to dat po'-white trash . . ."

"Stop it, Lazarus," Whitney said heatedly. "You just do as I say and keep your mouth shut." He began to walk away. "Lazarus."

"Yessum," he replied, turning to look at her.

"I'm sorry. I'm just a little upset. I didn't mean to shout, but you don't know him. He's not like the rest. Tell him to hurry, Lazarus . . . please."

Whitney was certain that despite his disapproval, Lazarus would do as she asked. She watched him leave, then started back toward the big house.

Why was everybody against Mitchell Flannery because he had no money? It was unfair, she thought. But she didn't care! He loved her and she loved him and they had made a pact. If they had to stand against the world, they would.

17

When she walked into the house, she smiled to see her brother, Keith, as he came down the stairway toward her, tall and blond with the same blue eyes. He was just over a year older than she was. He seemed extremely upset.

"Keith, why are you so excited? It looks like you're in a hurry. What's happened?"

"It's what you get for sleeping half your life away. You don't know what's been going on. Well, there's going to be a war, sister dear, and I'm already enlisted in Jeb Taylor's cavalry."

"A war! Keith!"

"If you paid attention to any of your beaus that have been coming around, you'd know what's been going on. It won't last long, Whitney, so don't worry. We'll lick those Yankees inside of a month."

"But . . . a war! Keith . . . all the men . . ." Her words choked her. Mitch! He would go, too. He would fight, maybe even die. The thought was so terrible that she was speechless.

"Whitney, don't worry," Keith misinterpreted her pale-faced silence. "I'm telling you it won't be long and just think of all the parties and the uniforms and parades. It'll be fun. You'll have more men at your feet than you ever did."

She tried to smile to keep him from seeing the fear in her eyes.

Once Keith had gone she fled to her room where she could get away from the prying eyes of people who wanted to destroy the beautiful thing that existed between her and the only man she would ever love.

It seemed as if time dragged interminably, but she had to be alone. She was obsessed by the fear that someone would read the truth in her face and stop her from leaving with a barrage of questions she would never be able to answer.

But the questions swirled in her mind like dry leaves in an autumn wind.

He must promise her he would return. She was sure

her life would end if he didn't come back to fill it. The minutes moved slowly . . . slowly into hours, hours filled with doubt and fear.

Two

Mitchell Flannery straightened up and drove the pitchfork into the ground, then stretched to ease his aching muscles. Shirtless, he worked with his father and brothers in the fields of a farm that yielded barely enough to keep the family alive.

He hated it. He hated the barren existence. But worse, he hated the fact that his poverty stood between him and the woman he loved and wanted with every waking thought and, he smiled to himself, with every dream as well.

His body was lean and bronzed from the sun that glistened across his broad shoulders. Strong muscles, well used to hard work, rippled beneath his skin. The same black hair that matted his muscular chest grew like a thick wayward mass on his head. A little too long and unkempt, but it gave him a rugged look. His face had known harsh reality. His eyes were like a storm-filled sky, gray and moody. His mouth was wide and sensual, the only thing left untouched by anger and pain. When he smiled it was like a ray of sun on a rainy day.

With grim determination he kept his mind off Whitney . . . Whitney. Even her name excited him. He loved her so deeply he couldn't imagine the rest of his life without her. Yet he knew in his heart that the odds against them were astronomical.

He gazed up at the sky, wondering if some great event could occur that would allow him and Whitney to be together. But it was wishful thinking. He would have to convince Whitney to run away with him. He would make her happy and maybe someday her parents would forgive them. Maybe when they met again he could convince her. He'd tried many times, but her beauty and his love for her were so powerful that all he could do was love her in the rare moments they had together.

"Mitch."

"Huh?" Mitch's attention was drawn to his father who worked a short distance from him.

"We've got to get this field done today, boy."

"I know, Pa." Mitch grinned and reached for the pitchfork.

But he felt his father's worried gaze on him. He watched for a few minutes, then walked to Mitch's side.

"Mitch?"

Mitch turned to look at him. "Yeah?"

"You came home real late last night."

"You keeping track of me, Pa?" He smiled to keep the shock from his voice. "I thought I was getting too old for that."

"Not usually. I just don't want to see a son that turned out as well as you have run across any problems."

"I'll be careful," Mitch said solemnly.

"Got news today."

"What kind?"

"Something to set off your touchy temper again, I guess."

"What's happened?"

"There's really going to be a war, son. I know. . . . I know how you feel."

"We're wrong and you know it," Mitch said firmly. "If we fight a war, Pa, we can't win it."

"Mitch . . . most folks around aren't too reasonable in times full of fire like this. Your sympathies are

21

somewhere else and folks are going to take offense. They can get real radical . . . maybe violent."

"What are you suggesting?" Mitch asked quietly.

"I'm suggesting that for the duration of this war you ought to pay a visit to your Aunt Martha in New York. Then . . . if you do join . . . if you do fight . . . you'll be where you want to be."

"I don't agree with our neighbors and friends about the war . . . but I'll stand and fight with them. After all, it's my home. You and my brothers, Pa. Do you actually believe I'd do that?"

"I . . . I just wanted to give you the chance, boy. It's hard to fight for something you believe in, let alone for something you don't."

"I believe in our family, our land, and our people. I don't always believe in the ideas that lead to war. If we divide this country in two we're open prey for any foreign country that wants to grab us. We have to stay united."

"Maybe. Maybe I even believe that, too. But that don't change what's happening."

"Then beliefs or no . . . . I'll stay and I'll fight if necessary."

Stuart Flannery sighed deeply. He loved this second son, maybe more than he loved the others, although he would never admit it. He also knew how Mitch felt about Whitney Clayborn.

"Mitch, I know what's holding you, too, and I have to tell you it can never work. The Clayborns would never let a Flannery marry into their upper crust family. They'll stop it, and all you can get is hurt. And if you keep shouting that the North is right and slavery is wrong you're going to have a whole mess of trouble down on your head . . . and down on your family."

"I'm not running, Pa. I believe I know what is right. You and my brothers can get that through your heads right now. I'm not running. I'll stand and fight with my own . . . for what I want."

Stuart looked into Mitch's steel-gray eyes and knew without doubt he meant every word.

"Okay, boy," Stuart said softly. "I just didn't want you to be the one paying the price for all this. The Clayborns are not to be played with."

"I know."

"Do you?"

"What does that mean?"

"It means the Clayborns can ruin us."

"How?"

"He holds the mortgage on this land."

"Are you behind?"

"No . . . but this war could do it."

"We pay our way. If you're not behind, don't worry. He can't hurt any of us."

"I hope you're right, son. But I have a feeling it's just beginning."

Mitch watched his father move away, uneasy that he had the same uncomfortable feeling. After a while he went back to work.

When they stopped to eat the midday meal, they were gathered about the table when they heard a knock. Mitch was the closest so he rose and opened the door.

Ethan Clayborn stood with his hands clasped behind his back. A formidable presence, he exuded a sense of power even when he stood silently, smiling politely.

"I hate to interrupt your lunch, Mr. Flannery. I was riding by and since I wanted a moment to speak to you, I thought I might just stop."

"Of course," Mitch replied, knowing the visit was not an accidental thing. "Come in, Mr. Clayborn."

"I would rather speak to you in private, if you don't mind."

Mitch nodded, stepped outside, and drew the door closed behind him. Inside, the rest of the Flannerys looked at each other in silent surprise.

Mitch and Ethan walked slowly a little distance from the house, then Mitch broke the silence.

"There was something you wanted to talk to me about, Mr. Clayborn?"

"Yes." Ethan stopped and looked intently at Mitch. Despite all his thoughts and his wife's anger, he liked what he saw.

"I want to talk to you about my daughter, Whitney."

Mitch gave a nervous half-laugh. "You certainly don't beat around the bush, do you?"

"Not where my daughter is concerned. I think it's better to come directly to the point. My daughter has been raised with every luxury. Marriage to someone . . . ah . . . out of her class can only bring her unhappiness. I would not be much of a father if I stood by and let her be subjected to a life like that."

"Don't you think Whitney should have some choice in the matter?"

"She's young and innocent and sees the world through romantic eyes. We know life is not like that, do we not, Mr. Flannery?"

"You can't stop us," Mitch said in a voice soft but filled with promise.

"Can I not? I should hate to have it come to that. But if it does I shall remind you of a law I think you know nothing about."

"Such as?"

"Such as your father has a mortgage on his home."

"Paid to date," Mitch retorted quickly.

"Yes, but if you read it, Mr. Flannery, you will see that I can demand payment in full at any time . . . any time I choose to. Is that clear, Mr. Flannery?"

"Why can't you try to understand how we feel?"

"I do understand. But if I loved someone, Mr. Flannery, I would not want to ruin her life and force her to a life of little more than nothing. No, if I loved someone I would want her life to be full and happy. I would not cheat her. So you see, my boy, you have to decide

24

if you really love her or not."

Ethan walked away, leaving Mitch with a blinding fury and nothing to fight against. He knew Ethan Clayborn spoke the truth. He could promise Whitney nothing. His love was not a lie, but his love would offer her a life so very different from anything she had known. There was so much he would be taking away.

Slowly he walked back to the house. He had hardly returned to his seat at the table when they heard the sound of a galloping horse, then another knock. This time it was Mitch's father who answered the door to admit a young neighbor, panting in excitement.

"Jake, what's wrong?" Stuart questioned.

"The war, Mr. Flannery, it's started. We done fired on Sumter last week. They're calling for volunteers and every man jack is goin' in to sign up."

There was silence for a moment while the shattering news sank in. Then both of Mitch's brothers were on their feet. The excitement was electric as Stuart and Mitch exchanged glances. As far as Mitch was concerned these were words of impending doom. There was no way he could escape what had to be faced and no way to bring a new wife into such a situation.

Mitch had never felt more defeated. The world seemed solidly against him, and he had to tell Whitney he was leaving. Would she wait for him, even though she knew how he felt? Could she understand that he was doing the only thing possible? Would she give him the chance to build a new life for them?

The afternoon was filled with tension so strong it felt like an electrical current.

Mitch was still in the field, trying to drown himself in work, when he saw Lazarus making his way toward him. Neither man spoke, and Mitch could read Lazarus's disapproval in his stony silence. He couldn't understand the black man's hostility. He wanted understanding from this man, some kind of acceptance.

25

Slavery was ingrained in Lazarus, and Mitch was angered that even a slave didn't approve of a relationship between a Flannery and a Clayborn.

Lazarus handed him the note in cold silence, and Mitch took it the same way. If he thought he saw a touch of sympathy in Lazarus's eyes it was fleeting. Lazarus turned to go home and Mitch read the note swiftly and stuffed it in his pocket. He worked with an angry vigor. He would show the world and one day he would have Whitney, he promised himself grimly. She loved him and he knew in his heart she would wait. Tonight they would confirm their pact, and the pledge that would carry them through the dark days ahead.

Mitch tied his horse beneath a huge oak so he couldn't be seen and made his way to the place he and Whitney had considered theirs for so long. He stood beneath the moss-hung trees and waited, trying to form the words in his mind that would ease his leaving. But very few words came to him. He could only tell her that he loved her now and would love her always, that he would come back and change their lives. He would also tell her that he desperately needed to know she would be waiting when he returned.

He knew he was much too early, that Whitney might not be able to slip out. But the anxiety of waiting in a home so divided was more difficult than finding some escape in riding.

Whitney could not bear the lonely hours either, and long before he expected her he saw her half-running through the darker shadows of the trees.

He took several steps toward her and in moments, with the soft sound of his name on her lips, she was in his arms.

He could feel her body tremble as she clung to him. It told him without doubt that she knew as well as he what must be. When he released her he caught her

26

face between his hands and kissed her with a feverish passion.

"Mitch . . ."

"Shh, don't talk now. Let me hold you." He drew her into his arms again, afraid of the words soon to be spoken.

"I'm afraid," she whispered.

"Not of me, love, never of me?"

"Of being without you, of losing you."

"You won't lose me. We must face our problems head on. We won't be beaten. Maybe . . . maybe we just have to wait a while."

Whitney stepped back and looked up into Mitch's eyes.

"Whitney, don't look at me like that," he said miserably. "Do you think I want any kind of separation? I love you. But I can't . . ."

"Can't what?"

"Can't hurt you by forcing this, then leaving you to face it. I can't destroy my family by deserting those I love, the land I love, and . . . I have to join the South even if I feel it's a terrible mistake."

Whitney strangled a sob. "You're going away."

He nodded silently.

"Mitch, you can't, you can't."

"I have to. Whitney, I can't take you away from what you have to . . . nothing."

"I don't care!"

"I do. Where can we live? With my family? In a house so crowded where it's hard to put enough food on the table? Or your house, where everyone would be against us? I'm asking you to understand. Give me a chance to provide something worthwhile for us both."

"We could go away."

"Where? Where, Whitney, where? You tell me. What do we live on?" His voice was angry for the first time and his misery even more evident. Whitney turned from him and began to cry softly.

27

He closed his eyes for a minute, regret filling his being. Then he came up behind her and wrapped his arms about her, burying his face in the fragrance of her hair and rocking her lightly. "I'm sorry, love, I'm sorry. I didn't mean to take all my frustration out on you." He turned her gently in his arms and tipped her face up so he could kiss her tear-moistened lips.

"Can you trust me, Whitney? Can you trust our love to be strong enough to carry us through this?"

"Where will you go?"

"I'll join up tomorrow. Stanton's Cavalry, I hope. I'm a good rider. When this damn war is over things will be different."

"Promise me that, Mitch," her voice was pleading. "Promise me you won't let anything happen to you, that you'll come back to me."

"I'm lucky Irish Flannery," he joked, trying to laugh. "Nothing will happen to me. There's only one thing in my life, one thing that makes it all worth it and that's you. I'll find our way, Whitney, and I'll come back for you. The question is, will you wait?"

She reached up and took his face between her hands. "I'll wait, Mitch. I'll wait forever. My dear sweet love, there's only one man in the world for me and that man is you. Come back for me. Let's make a solemn vow before God. We'll have our love . . . when this war is over. And we'll seal the pact," she whispered.

"Yes," he replied softly. "I swear before God, Whitney, that you are my wife now and you always will be. I'll come back."

"Husband . . . I will be here. When I hear the war is over I will come to our place . . . here . . . every night until you come."

"Whitney." He said her name with a kind of awe, reaching another plane of his love for her and knowing he could put no words to it. He drew her into his arms and kissed her.

The kiss lingered and grew. Embers of a fire banked temporarily caught again. He needed something to take with him, something only Whitney could give. And she needed a part of him to serve as a shield against the barren loneliness she would know when he was gone.

He undressed her as if it were the first time, devouring her loveliness, aching to make love to her. But he was deliberately slow, caressing her soft skin and memorizing every line and curve.

They surrendered to a magic heightened by the knowledge that they might not be together for a long time, and the surrender sealed their mutual promise. When she lay in his arms, sated and calm, he held her in momentary silence.

"Mitch?"

"Yes?"

"Write to me. Tell me where you are and what you're doing."

"Of course. But what will your parents say?"

"I don't know. What can we do?"

"Maybe I could find someone to send them to who would bring them to you. Christ, I hate this plotting and sneaking around."

"I do, too, but we have to. I might have to do without you for a while but I'll die if I don't have any word at all. At least I must know you're well."

"I'll find a way."

"Mitch?"

"Uh-huh?"

"What . . . what about others?" Her voice was tight with strain.

"Others? What do you mean *others?*"

"Other women," she whispered. "You'll be gone a long time. I don't want to lose you."

For the first time his laugh was genuine and he rolled on his side to look into her worried eyes. "I've been as close to heaven as a man can get without dying. I have no intention of losing you. You're all I need, Whitney. There's no reason to look at any other. What about you? There'll be a lot of handsome uniforms running around here shortly."

"I couldn't fall in love with a uniform, Mitch. I already love a man who doesn't need any finery."

"Damn!" Mitch exclaimed, and suddenly scrambled to his feet. He dressed swiftly and walked to his horse.

"Mitch?"

"I forgot. I brought you something." He fumbled in a sack hung from his saddlehorn and took out a square object. He returned to kneel beside her and handed it to her. In the pale moonlight she could make out a small wooden box, elaborately carved with roses and twining vines. Then Mitch lifted the lid and she could hear the soft tinkling sound.

"A music box! How beautiful."

"While I'm gone, I hope it reminds you that my thoughts are always with you."

"It will. Wait, let me . . ." her voice grew thick with tears. She handed him the box, then lifted her fingers to loosen the fine gold chain about her neck. It held a tiny gold cross. "Let me give you this. It's so small, but maybe if you wear it close to your heart it will protect you." She placed the cross and chain in his palm and he carefully put it inside his shirt. Like all lovers, he was sure he could feel her warmth on it, and always would. He held the box out to her.

"I shall cherish it always," she whispered.

He tilted her face once more for his kiss. "And I shall cherish you," he murmured against her lips.

For Whitney, the new day dawned with a feeling of desolation. Mitch must already be gone, she thought as she stood by her bedroom window holding the softly playing music box. Although she couldn't see Mitch's house she could imagine it and knew those who lived there must be as unhappy as she was.

Her mother stood in the bedroom's open doorway, knowing Whitney was unaware of her presence. She took in the unhappy look of longing and the direction in which it was cast. She also saw the music box and heard its love song. Her expression reflected anger mixed with grim determination. There would be no more contact between Mitch Flannery and her daughter. One way or another, she would see to that.

Three

The excitement spread like wildfire as young men answered the call with the mistaken idea that this "small confrontation" would end soon. Whitney's brother was one of the first and the entire family was proud of him, resplendent in his new uniform. Her father, called upon personally by General Lee, was given a commission.

There were balls and parties, for very few took this gentleman's war too seriously. Although Whitney attended the parties, her heart was always filled with thoughts of Mitchell. Where was he now, she wondered. Was he, well . . . was he thinking of her as she was thinking of him?

Mitch and Whitney had made arrangements for his letters to be sent to a friend of his in the city who would see that they were delivered to the secret meeting place. It was nearly three weeks before Whitney received the first, telling her he loved her and missed her, where he was stationed, and that the military might promise him a better life than the farm. He found himself adapting well and hoped to save all his money so he could claim her when the war was over.

It was such a relief to hear from him that Whitney sat down immediately to pen an answer.

The first months of the war seemed dominated by the South as they won battle after battle. The letters came about twice a month and because of her fear of her mother, Whitney would slip out at night to retrieve them.

Then came four long months of no word at all, nothing, and Whitney became frantic with worry. Every night she would slip out to search for a letter and every night she would return home with a heavy heart.

Tonight she waited until her parents had retired, then slipped out of the house to the meeting place. She knelt before the huge cottonwood and searched with her hands behind a flat rock where letters were to be hidden, but again there was nothing. Then the snap of a twig told her she was not alone. Fear paralyzed her for a moment, then a familiar voice made her heart nearly cease to beat.

"Will I do as well as a letter, Whitney?"

"Mitch," she gasped. He stepped from the shadows and in a moment she was in his arms.

He kissed her feverishly and for a while they could only hold each other.

"I had to see you. I couldn't stand it any longer."

"I'm so glad you're here."

"Whitney . . . it will be a long time before we can see each other again. I have a feeling there's going to be a lot of changes in this war and slipping across the lines will get harder. We're moving north fast."

"Oh, I hate this war," Whitney cried as she tightened her arms about his waist and pressed closer as if she could keep him from danger. But he was more worried about her. He knew in his heart what might be coming and felt she was in more danger than he was. At least he could defend himself, but Whitney was vulnerable.

"Mitch, you will keep writing, even if you can't get back for a while?"

"You know I will."

"It's just . . . your letters . . . they're all I have of you, and I miss you so terribly."

"No, Whitney, they're not all you have of me. You have all that I am or ever will be. Don't you know by now that you're my life?" He lowered his voice tenderly. "Or must I prove to you again that we are always a part of each other, no matter what happens."

"Yes," she murmured as his lips lightly touched hers. "Yes, tell me again . . . again."

He tasted faintly of whiskey and tobacco — compellingly male, just as she had always remembered.

His tongue outlined her lips, then silkenly pried them open and entered her mouth. She uttered a small, whimpering gasp. He took control, twining their tongues together while he explored the sensitive insides of her cheeks, running across her small even teeth. His lips brushed and pressed, caressed and heated, until she was mindless and breathless, melting into him, returning the kiss with abandon.

He pulled her down with him in the tall grass, and they lay still for a moment. Then very gently he touched her, caressing her with infinite tenderness. Slowly he undid the buttons of her blouse and dropped it off her shoulder. The straps of her chemise followed and she felt the tender strength of his hands against the soft flesh of her body. It was like a current moving from him to her as he kissed her again and again. First her cheeks, her throat, then the softness of her shoulders, then lightly the tips of each breast, touching them with his tongue until he felt them swell and rise and harden with passion. He removed the rest of her clothes and ran his hands over her, enjoying the warm feel of her body. Then he rose and removed his clothing. She watched him, enjoying the sight, absorbing everything about him. He was like a young god, she thought. His body was long and lean with tightly pulled muscles. His stomach was flat, and the black hair on his chest grew downward into a long line that ran down his belly to the pubic hair. His manhood was large and throbbed with a life of its own. The delicious pain of desire overwhelmed her, and she lifted her arms, whispering his name. He gathered her tightly against him as hunger for her throbbed with every beat of his heart. Then he took her mouth again in a kiss that left her breathless.

"You're so beautiful, Whitney, and I love you so very much."

She laid her hand against his cheek. "I know," she whispered, "and I love you, Mitch. I do love you."

She melted into his arms. Their lips blended in a long, slow kiss that sent quivers through her. Mitch was magic for her, his hands gentle and seeking, his body warm against hers.

He let his hands skim over her as if discovering for the first time the sweet feel of her flesh.

Slowly his lips caressed her mouth. Tenderly, gently he kissed one corner then the other. Her lips parted to taste his and it sent a current through him that quickened his loins. His mouth was possessive now, his tongue probing deeply, answered by hers. He sucked gently, nibbling her softness until she felt weak and feverish. Then his lips left hers to travel the soft smooth flesh of her throat and shoulders. They burned a path that made her gasp, seeming to scorch her flesh wherever they touched.

He buried his hands in the mass of her blond hair and his desire grew hot and sweet as he sought her breasts and their sensitive crests. The buds hardened and she arched her body to meet him, feeling the rough texture of his hands against her skin as he teased and taunted. He tasted one nipple hungrily, then the other, teasing with his tongue, sucking

35

gently until he could hear her soft throaty purr of passion.

Ripple after ripple of delicious pleasure coursed through her as his mouth sought her most sensitive places. There was not a part of her he didn't savor—the small valley between her breasts, the soft curve of her waist, the flat, taut plane of her belly.

Now he was above her again, tenderly observing her surrender. He was filled with an exaltation that turned his blood molten and set his heart pounding. She would be his forever. The thought made him wild with need, but he held it back . . . a while longer. He needed all of her, for only together were they whole.

He stroked her gently, feeling her quiver with ecstasy. His fingers found the center of her need, and his strokes were even and sure as he felt the tremors of passion begin.

Whitney's hands roamed over him, touching with sensitive shyness at first, but never ceasing their quest to know him as intimately as he knew her. Every inch of him would belong to her and she was greedy to possess him. Her hands slipped from his hard muscled shoulders to his broad chest, then down to the hard, flat belly. He was breathless with her fiery touch and filled with joy that she wanted him so completely.

Her hands gentle and teasing, they gripped his shaft softly at first, then firmly as they began a rhythmic movement. He closed his eyes and immersed himself in the fiery swirl as her lips encircled his flesh. She teased, nibbled, and tormented until he groaned with delicious agony. Then the softness of her lips kissed him, tasted with her flicking tongue, then closed about him. His breathing grew ragged and his body tensed with sheer ecstasy.

He moaned soft words of love as she took him beyond any pleasure he had ever known. He was blinded by delight until his entire world was Whitney and Whitney alone.

As he neared the brink of release, he pressed her to him and began to brand her flesh with hot kisses until she cried out in delight.

His lips moved over her, searing a path and searching for the sweet center of her. Gasping and clinging, she cried loving words of loving abandon as his tongue stroked and pressed deeply.

Their bodies throbbed with an almost violent passion. Gently he held her thighs apart and drove within, sinking to the warmest depths of her.

She could no longer breathe, only cling to him and sob in sheer pleasure as he thrust again and again.

Now it was sweet violence as he caught her to him and moved faster and faster, building to a climax that exploded in passion and left them clinging helplessly to each other.

Whitney rested against Mitch as he rolled from her, his arm still binding her to him. She nestled into the curve of his shoulder and rested her head against his broad chest. He stroked her hair gently and she closed her eyes, basking in the gentle aftermath of their love.

"Oh, Mitch, why can't I go someplace near you? I hate your having to go so soon."

"No more than I hate to go, but there's no other way, Whitney. Listen, I've been saving all my pay, turning it to gold. It's the only safe thing to do. By the time this war is over I'll have enough saved to give us a future. That way no one will interfere anymore."

"I'm so glad you're here tonight. I know how hard it must have been."

"I might not be able to do it again. There's a

change in the way the war is going. Anyone who isn't blind can see that. It scares me to death to think we'll be so far apart. I don't know if I came to give you courage, or if I needed you to give it to me."

"We need each other, Mitch," she said softly. "We always will."

"Yes . . . always. Whitney, be careful. There's a lot of trouble coming. See that you take care of yourself."

"I will . . . I will."

"I have to go," he groaned, feeling both angry and miserable.

"So soon?"

"It won't be easy to get back."

They rose, but neither could find the strength to let the other go. They clung to each other, kissing gently, sensitively. Then, with all the strength he had, Mitch moved Whitney away from him and began to help her dress. She helped him as well and amid soft whispers, loving touches, and tender kisses, they finally stood together . . . unprepared to part. There was no way to prolong it. They parted with a renewal of their promises, both unaware of the dark eyes that watched.

Hope Clayborn paced the floor of her bedroom. She had known full well that letters were passing between her daughter and Mitchell Flannery. But she didn't know how. For weeks she had had her spy watching Whitney's every move. Soon there had to be word about how correspondence was getting through.

One way or another she meant to destroy any contact between Whitney and Mitch. She could not allow a nobody to spoil all her plans.

Angrily she flung herself down in a chair. Surely some word would pass between them soon. All she needed to know was where he was stationed and who carried the letters. From that time on she could hire those she needed to take care of the problem.

She was about to go to bed when a timid knock sounded on the door.

"Come in," she ordered bitingly. Addy slipped inside and stood with her back pressed to the door. No matter what information she had that she knew Hope would want, Addy was still terrified of her mistress. She had felt Hope's wrath before. She hated to betray Whitney, but her fear was great and she could not gather her courage to defy Hope in any way.

"Well, girl, don't stand there like a nitwit! You have some news?"

"Yessum," Addy mumbled, already trembling.

"Must I drag it from you? There's been a message sent?"

"Yessum, dey been letters."

"Letters. Delivered how? . . . Where?"

" 'Neath de old cottonwood down by de river." Addy was not going to tell Hope she had seen Mitch with Whitney that very night.

"And who carries them?"

"Young Mistah Wakley from over to the village smithy. He done bring 'em. He's a friend to Mistah Flannery."

"Very good, very good," Hope mused. She intended to make sure Carl Wakley did not carry any more — she had enough friends to see to it. The next messages would all end up in her own eager hands. She looked coldly at Addy who began to sweat in fear. "You know what will happen to you if you breathe one word of this to anyone? I will personally see there is no flesh left on your back before I sell

39

you to some powerful slavemaster who will see to it that the rest of your days are spent in the worst misery you can imagine. Do I make myself clear, Addy? Do you understand me completely?" Hope's voice was soft, but Addy felt a terror unlike any she had ever felt before.

"Yessum, ah understands. Ah won' say nuthin' to nobody."

"Nobody," Hope said firmly. "If I hear one whisper of this among the slaves I will know you talked. Then your days will be numbered."

"Ah won' say nuthin', Miz Hope. Please, Miz Hope, don' hurt me. Ah swears ah won' say nuthin' . . . nuthin' to nobody."

"Remember well, Addy. I hear everything. Now get along and go back to bed. I'll take care of the rest of this little farce. Mitchell Flannery will not destroy Whitney's chances to make a fine marriage. Not even if I have to . . ." She looked at a wide-eyed Addy again, "Get out, Addy, and keep your mouth shut or I'll do it for you."

"Yessum," Addy muttered and grasped the door handle quickly. She could not wait to get out of Hope's presence. Terror followed, and well it should have for Hope knew quite well Addy was a weak link in her plans. She intended to eliminate that weakness as soon as she found a way to do it, but for now she had to concentrate on other, more pressing, matters.

The next morning a note was sent to town by messenger and late afternoon brought a large man to a meeting in the study with a well-prepared Hope. She had made her plans during the night.

They spoke for almost two hours. Then money exchanged hands and the man left. Hope sat back in

40

her chair, relieved that any further messages would find their way to her first. Then she would make sure they were taken care of in a way that fit into her plan.

The man left the house and returned to town. He laid his plans well, finding out all of Carl's movements. Then, knowing letters might come at any moment, he rehearsed all of Carl's routes until he knew them by heart.

Carl Wakley moved through the night shadows without knowing he was being followed. He had no idea that all the man following him needed to know was what happened to Whitney's letters after he picked them up and how he received Mitch's letters. The chain could not be broken or it might bring Mitchell Flannery back before Hope could realize her plans.

Carl rode slowly along a rural road and the man who followed watched closely. He arrived in a stand of trees and dismounted, then walked to a tree. The man could make out a box, wedged in the crook of the limbs. Carl looked inside, found no letter, and left.

But the man stayed. He camped for over a week because he had to be first . . . and he had to be sure. The letter came and minutes after it was put in the box he removed it. Then he waited for Carl. This time he would put an end to all the problems.

Carl came the next night.

He took the letter to Hope, who read it and cursed. She started to put the letter in her jewel box, then realized she and Whitney often exchanged jewelry. An idea struck her. She took a pair of scissors and loosened the satin lining. Then she put the letter in it and reattached the lining. In minutes it looked as though it had never been touched. It was a large, elaborate box and would conceal many letters. Pleased, she replaced the jewelry and closed the box.

A few days later a letter written to Mitch from Whitney was taken from its hiding place again and brought to Hope who read it and put it safely away. She still had time, she thought. She would find the right marriage for Whitney. Then she would pen letters of her own that would put an end to the affair once and for all. Whitney would soon forget, Hope smiled to herself. When she had made an advantageous marriage she would finally see what a mistake Mitchell Flannery would have been. After all, this crazy war would be over soon and she was responsible for Whitney's future.

Four

For the next three months the lovers' letters were intercepted and placed in Hope's hands. Whitney worried that there was no word from Mitch and begged him in each of her letters to find a way to tell her he was well and still loved her. It was the same with Mitch, who was frantic wondering why Whitney no longer wrote.

But the war had turned. The North was becoming more aggressive and the lack of preparation was beginning to tell on the South. All of this made it impossible to return home. He could only worry and continue to write, trying to convince himself that no news was good news. But it didn't work. He was suddenly frightened—a sixth sense told him something was drastically wrong. He prayed for the war to end quickly so he could find out if something had happened to Whitney. She meant everything to him and he could hardly bear the thought that someone or something had made her change her mind about their life together.

But a new kind of fear had entered Whitney's life. She held the reins in trembling hands and guided the carriage toward home. Through tear-blurred eyes she found her way down the tree-lined drive. Once in her room she sat on the edge of her bed and struggled for the proper words to write Mitch. After long hours her tears dried and she went to her desk and sat down to write.

Dear Mitch,

I haven't heard from you for months and don't even know if your feelings for me remain the same. I must tell you something I feel you have a right to know. I'm going to have your child. The doctor confirmed today what I already knew. Oh, Mitch, I love you and I'm so frightened. If you would just write and let me know that you're well I'll be able to face what is to come. As long as I know you want this child as much as I do I'll be able to find the courage to go on.

Please keep yourself safe and well and come back to me. If the child is a son I'll name him after you. Come for us, Mitch. I love you with all my heart.

                                    Whitney

Whitney slipped out late that night to put the letter in their secret place, hoping she might find a letter already there. But she was disappointed. With a sigh she put the letter safely away, then returned home.

The letter found its way to Hope's hands a few short hours later. She had never been quite as angry in her life. She hated Mitchell Flannery with a depth of passion that surprised even her. That Mitchell Flannery would be the father of her first grandchild was unpardonable! After a short while she controlled her rage and sat to give thought to what she might do.

Hope practiced copying Mitch's writing for three days, until she was satisfied that writing from the chaotic atmosphere of a battlefield would account for the difference. Then she penned a letter she hoped would end it all forever.

Dear Whitney:
   I've given our situation a great deal of thought and now I realize that your family has been right all along. We were young and passionate, but that's not enough to build a future. I know things will be fine for you. I'm sure your family will find you an appropriate husband and you'll be happy.
   Maybe it's better this way. I wish you happiness and I'm sorry for any inconvenience I've caused you.
                    Goodbye.
                    Mitch Flannery.

Whitney knew the secret could not be kept from her mother for long. With her father and brother away and fear running rampant across the land, she would need her mother's love and support.

When Whitney went that night to find if there had been any letters she was filled with joy to find one. She tore it open and read . . . and as she read a pain such as she had never known filled her. Hot tears scalded her eyes and her body shook with anguish.

It had been a game for him—for one of the poor Flannerys to defeat one of the proud Clayborns. All he had said had been a lie. She had been a challenge, a gullible challenge, and now he had no further use for her. The thought nearly destroyed her. She needed someone . . . she needed her mother.

Hope arrived home after a trip to town and was amazed at the panic that greeted her. There was a rumor the Yankees were near, that they threatened to attack at any moment. A wave of fear seemed to engulf everyone. Hope knew there were few to defend her and Whitney; since the slaves had been freed, there were few of them as well. Many had lived in fear of her anyway and had left at the first opportunity. Hope was sure it was just a matter of time until the tides of war changed again.

When her carriage reached the house she saw two horses standing out front. She climbed out quickly and started up the steps only to be met by a wide-eyed and frightened Whitney.

"Mother! There are men inside. They want to talk to you."

"About what?" Hope asked, breathless and aware that something was very wrong. She moved slowly, Whitney at her side. They entered the study and looked at the harassed and war-weary men who awaited them.

"Gentlemen," Hope said, her voice cracking slightly. "Please sit down. I have a little wine left in the cellar. May I get you some?"

"Thank you, Mrs. Clayborn . . . but no. We have to hurry. General Lee has too few men for us to linger."

"You're here for a purpose, gentlemen. Please state your reasons then."

"Mrs. Clayborn . . . ah . . . it's difficult. We don't quite know how . . ."

"It's Keith, isn't it? My son."

"I'm afraid it's more than that, ma'am."

"Mother," Whitney whispered.

"My husband . . . Ethan." Hope had gone pale and her frightened eyes begged to be told her dreaded thoughts were not true.

"Mrs. Clayborn," one man said, trying to control his own grief. "I'm afraid Major Clayborn is dead and your son, Lieutenant Clayborn, is reported missing in action."

"Oh, God," Hope whispered. Before Whitney's stunned eyes her mother seemed to wither, then slowly crumple to the floor.

Week followed week of fear and dread. Hope Clayborn seemed to close herself off from the world. She was like a broken doll.

The war grew worse and worse and as Whitney's body grew larger, her world seemed to grow darker and darker.

Now there was only Addy, Berdine, Lazarus, and Josiah to help her continue the struggle.

Addy could see the disaster that had befallen Whitney. She had also seen the change in her and knew Mitchell Flannery was not coming back. So she kept Hope's dreadful secret, not wanting to cause Whitney any more grief.

Then the Yankee threat became a reality. Whitney was eight months pregnant and it hurt her friends to see her struggle to get enough to eat. She was thin and gaunt and cared for her mother as one would a child.

Hope was seated on a chair on the front porch, and Whitney and the others were in the kitchen trying to scrape together a meal.

The soldiers who attacked the house that fateful day were the dark kind that lusts for blood, drunk with the destruction they were wielding.

Whitney had just walked from the kitchen and up the stairs to her bedroom. Addy had gone with her to get Hope a shawl, when they heard the sound of thundering hooves.

Both Addy and Whitney ran out into the hall just as Lazarus came up the stairs two at a time.

"Lazarus, what is it?" Whitney cried.

"Yankees, Miz Clayborn, renegade Yankees. They

be burnin' de Morgan place. In a hour dey be here. Dey gonna burn us out. We gots to get you an' yo' ma outten here afore dey gits here. Josiah, he done go fer yo' ma. He'll take her out to de woods."

Whitney was so frightened she was momentarily paralyzed. Then Lazarus and Addy thought she had lost her senses as she ran back into her room. It would be hard even for Whitney to say why she did what she did. She ran into her room and snatched up the music box Mitch had given her. Clutching it close, she ran out into the hall again.

"Addy, Lazarus! Go into Mother's room and gather whatever is left. Get Mother's jewelry, we might need it. Don't forget blankets and Mother's sewing kit. Hurry!"

They ran into the room and Addy and Lazarus gathered everything they could carry, everything they thought could be used. Addy grabbed up the wooden silk-lined box on Hope's dresser. She never knew of the letters hidden in the lining. If she had, she might have been too frightened of Hope to save it. The sound of horses outside the front door gave flight to their feet as they ran down the stairs, leaving through the back door at the same moment the front door was slammed open.

Whitney could not move as fast as the others and after a while Lazarus gave his bundle to Josiah and swung Whitney up into his arms. Hope stumbled along in silence. They reached the safety of the woods and sank down, gasping for air and listening to the wild and uncontrolled looting of their home.

Whitney had no way of knowing just how long she had lain in the dirt before she saw the first of the flames lick through the windows. Stricken, the group watched the renegades ride away. Whitney's face was streaked with dirt and tears as she watched her home slowly burn to the ground.

"Miz Whitney."

"What, Lazarus?" Whitney replied, her voice full of quiet misery.

"Dey's dat cabin down by de bend in de river. It's only a good day's ride. Iffen we kin make it, it'll be safe fo' a while. We kin get dere real soon if we starts now. Ah kin make yo' a safe place. Seems like dey's another kind of storm comin'."

Whitney looked up at a sky filled with black rolling clouds.

"Yes, Lazarus," she said as she struggled to her feet and felt a sharp pain in the center of her back that made her gasp and reach to rub it. Addy and Berdine exchanged a look of fearful understanding. It was too soon for Whitney's baby, but they both knew the multiple shocks she had borne could well bring the birth on. What worried Lazarus was that there was still a good distance of rough terrain before they would reach the cabin.

The storm struck when they were a little over halfway there and so did the fierce, tearing pains that made Whitney clench her teeth and gasp for breath. But she struggled on. She knew what was happening, but she was grimly determined her child would not be born in the rain and mud. A seething anger grew within her. Anger at the war and at the twist of fate that made her family victims. But a deeper and more lasting fury was growing into something even more powerful, directed at Mitchell Flannery.

They reached the cabin near midnight — bedraggled, wet, and cold. The cabin was dark and dirty, barely offering shelter from the storm. Addy and Berdine laid the blankets on the floor after making sure there was nothing alive besides the human occupants. By the time Lazarus and Josiah managed to build a fire in the small fireplace, Whitney was already in deep labor.

Hope was put on a blanket and covered, then all attention was given to a weeping and struggling Whitney. The storm grew in intensity, as if it meant to match the white-hot pain that seemed to tear her apart. Her sobs and cries were all that could be heard above the rumble of thunder and the crash of lightning.

Dawn brought a stillness as rain dripped from the trees and the world seemed to be washed clean of the evil that had raged the night before. The early quiet was cut by the hearty wail of a new life.

But grief had not dealt Whitney her last blow. During the night Hope's heart could take no more strain. She died while another life struggled to enter the world, and no one knew of her passing until the battle was over.

When Whitney finally had to be told, she stared at Berdine in disbelief. Could the heavy hand of fate deal her any further hurt, she wondered. She took the news dry-eyed and listless—there seemed to be no tears left. Both Berdine and Lazarus knew it was all dammed up and needed to be released, yet Whitney seemed incapable of responding.

The next day Lazarus carried Whitney outside and sat her close by for the burial of her mother. Berdine and Addy wept, but still Whitney remained dry-eyed. When they carried her back into the cabin she sat before the small fire and gazed into it in silence.

Whitney's mind was in a turmoil of disbelief and anguish. Her world had disintegrated before her eyes. Everything she loved had been snatched away, leaving her empty and desolate. Mitch's betrayal had been the first and maybe the worst. Her body, sapped of its strength by the difficult and lonely birth, trembled under the stress of knowing she faced a world without those she loved and filled with nothing except more of the same for the future.

The mixture of emotion swirled within her like a black cloud consuming all thought except the one that battered her most. Mitchell . . . Mitchell, who had vowed to love her always. Had he read the letter about the child and laughed at her? Had he been as her mother had said he was, a rake and a weak, undependable man? She would never be such a fool again. Slowly an insidious anger began to blossom into something darker and much more lasting. As it grew, Whitney could not seem to overcome it. She seemed filled with a darkness that threatened to suffocate the very life from her. Her breath was ragged and tears began to come. After a moment they overwhelmed her, and she wept with an agony that tore at the others who could only watch helplessly.

She cried until she seemed an empty shell, but Berdine in her wisdom knew she needed one tie to sanity before all was lost. Berdine knelt before Whitney and put the baby in her arms.

"Chile, yo' done 'nuff grievin'. It has its place but now it's over. Yo' chile needs his mother. He's a hungry babe an' he only gots yo' in dis dark world. Now yo' take de boy an' yo' finds yo' gots mo' strength than yo' knows." She thrust the child into Whitney's arms and for a moment Berdine was frightened that Whitney had lost her senses. But after a few minutes Whitney unbuttoned her dress and the baby, hungry and seeking, nestled against her. Whitney could feel his small mouth sucking at her and his tiny fist against her flesh. Slowly her tears dried and she looked down at the only ray of light in her world.

"Yo' ain't named de chile yet," Berdine said softly, hoping to keep Whitney's mind on something beside her grief.

Whitney thought of how she had wanted to name

51

the child after Mitchell if it was a boy. But she couldn't. Mitch had given up his right to the child when he had denied his paternity and their love. She would never let him know about his son, never. The baby was hers and hers alone. She looked up at Berdine. "His name is Jonathan," she said softly.

"Dat be a right fine name."

"Jonathan Clayborn," Whitney added. For a few minutes Berdine looked into Whitney's eyes. Then she nodded. Whitney had some right to her bitterness and anger.

"Yessum . . . Jonathan Clayborn."

Whitney reached out and put her hand on Berdine's arm, her eyes relentlessly holding Berdine's.

"Berdine, swear to me that no one . . . . no one will ever know who his father is."

"But, Miz Whitney. He be de boy's father."

"No! Berdine, you swear to me," Whitney's hand tightened. "Jonathan is mine and mine alone, and I don't ever want his father's name mentioned to me again. It will never be spoken again, do you hear? Now swear! Swear!"

"Ah swears, Miz Whitney. Ah swears," Berdine said unhappily.

Whitney returned her gaze to her son who slept contentedly.

"He's all I have, Berdine," Whitney said in a half whisper. "Don't let him come back here and take him from me. He's all I have."

"Yo' thinks his daddy come back here?"

"I don't know. I pray he doesn't. I don't even know if any of his family is still here. Even if he does come back we are far enough from the plantation that he might never find us. I don't want to see him ever again, Berdine." She looked down tenderly at her son. "You're mine, Jonathan, and I love you. We'll be fine, you and I . . . just you and I."

Slowly Whitney regained her strength. Lazarus and Joshua trapped and fished to keep food on the table. Whitney knew quite well all four of them could have fared much better without her, yet they remained and she understood their love, loyalty, and devotion. That and her son got her on her feet and helped her gain strength.

Lazarus was good with his hands and Whitney made him go back to the burnt-out plantation to see if any of the old tools could be rescued. There were no carriages or horses so Lazarus had to walk. And he was lucky. Amid the rubble of the destroyed plantation and the surrounding cabins he found a smattering of tools — enough to give him a start on rebuilding the cabin into something more substantial. It took a long time, even with Josiah's help, to bring all he could scavenge back with him. When he returned Whitney was overjoyed.

"Miz Whitney, why doan we all go back an' build by yo' old house? Seems to me nobody evah gwine know where yo' is. Dat land sho' looks deserted."

"We're never going back, Lazarus," Whitney stated firmly. "We'll watch over the land, and one day we'll sell it, if anybody in the south ever has any money again. This cabin is still on my father's land. I don't want anyone knowing where we are."

"Yessum," Lazarus replied, not quite able to understand. He was more than willing to build something for Whitney as well as himself and the others.

The days were a physical struggle as Whitney did things she never thought she would ever do. She worked beside Berdine and Addy to clean the cabin while Lazarus and Josiah felled trees and cut wood to make rough beds and tables.

When Lazarus brought her the cradle he had fashioned from a large tree she could barely contain her tears. If Jonathan had been born amid the love

53

and care of her family and a loving husband, he would have had the best of everything. Here he had a rough cradle built with loving hands and a patchwork quilt to cover him. They had made his clothes and diapers from her petticoats.

Jonathan began to thrive. He was a healthy and happy baby, cared for by five pairs of loving hands.

Slowly the cabin changed from one dirt-floored room with a leaking roof to a snug four-room house nestled in a grove of trees. It was far enough away from the burnt-out plantation that memories did not haunt them and secure enough to keep anyone from finding them easily and causing problems. Whitney seldom smiled—it was usually Jonathan who could bring a smile to her lips. She never mentioned Mitch's name again and after a long while the others forgot him. If he lingered in a quiet part of Whitney's mind or occasionally appeared in her dreams, she kept it to herself. Her world circled around Jonathan and their life together. She was determined Mitchell Flannery would never have the pleasure of having Jonathan in his life. He had made his choice long ago; now she had Jonathan and he was enough. She began to look toward the future for the first time in a long, long while.

Five

Mitch groaned and tried to move to a more comfortable position, but the wound in his lower right side protested painfully. He conceded to the pain and lay still as he had for over a month and a half. He was still amazed that he had survived his stay at the field hospital after they had brought him in so severely wounded. His infection and fever had brought him to death's door. After the field hospital came the excruciating pain on the trip back behind the lines to the camp where prisoners of war were held.

For the past three days they had been helping him to his feet for a few minutes each day and his strength was slowly returning. He had struggled to get on his feet as quickly as he could.

Today he had sweated through that routine with the hope that a visitor he expected soon would bring him the words he needed to hear.

From private to sergeant to lieutenant, Mitch had worked his way up through the ranks displaying bravery and leadership from battle to battle. He had saved every cent he could get his hands on, keeping his dream of Whitney and their future before him.

He had carefully gleaned all the information he could about the area in which he had lived. Bribery and promises had gotten him threads of information

that had scared and puzzled him. Whitney was alive
. . . then word came to him that her father had
been killed in action and her brother was missing.
Once he had even coaxed a friend to search for letters left by Whitney but there were none.

Today he waited for word. It had been weeks and
he'd heard nothing. But today he had been told to
expect a visitor. He had made a motley group of
friends, among them a young man posing as a newspaper correspondent who was really a courier. He
knew his friend would be here soon and he prayed
this time the word would be something he could
cling to — something that would help him keep up
hope that this nightmare would soon be over.

He'd written letter after letter and had them delivered by the same method but no answers had come.
He needed one grain of hope that Whitney had not
forgotten him.

He closed his eyes, thinking that it had been
Whitney and Whitney alone who had carried him
through everything. He knew for certain his letters
were being delivered to the same secret spot, but
there had been no answer for months. He sighed,
hoping the man would come soon. The waiting was
nerve wracking and only seemed to make his pain
worse.

The raspy clearing of a throat brought Mitch's
eyes open quickly. He looked up at the man who
stood by his bed.

"Lieutenant Flannery, sorry to wake you but you
said you wanted news as fast as we could get it."

"I wasn't asleep, just lying here worrying." Mitch
tried to smile, but the shifting of the man's eyes and
the still-grim look on his face bled the smile from
Mitch's lips. "Phelps, what is it?"

"I sure as hell would like to bring some good
news, Lieutenant, but I'm afraid there just isn't any."

"You delivered my last letter?"

"Yes, sir."

"And?" Mitch prompted.

"And there still isn't any reply."

"That isn't all your news, is it?"

"No, sir."

"Come on, Phelps, don't make me drag it out of you. What have you found out?"

Phelps sighed and sat down on the empty cot beside Mitch. He clasped his hands before him and held Mitch's eyes with his. "Well, sir, after all the things you told me I made a couple of decisions on my own. Since there weren't any letters where there should have been I decided to swing off and drop around by Clayborn's plantation. I figured maybe there was something wrong, and she couldn't get the letters to you."

"So?" Mitch prodded impatiently.

"Lieutenant . . ." Phelps hesitated.

"Go on, Phelps, damn it!"

"Clayborn's plantation is burnt to the ground. From what information I could get, the old man and his son were killed before and the women were there alone. It wasn't Sherman. It was a bunch of rough riders. Anyway . . . it looks like there's nobody from Clayborn's plantation still alive to tell the story. I took a couple of days to search. They ain't nowhere. I honestly think they're dead, Lieutenant. If they were alive they'd have to be somewhere and they're just not. I searched every town around and every place else I could think of. These things have happened before. They're dead and the place is nothing but ashes."

Mitch's face had grown grayer and grayer with each word. A pain he would never have had the words to describe clutched his breast, cutting off his air and making his heart pound as if he were dying.

57

"No," he rasped, struggling to sit up. "It can't be. It can't be!"

"I'm afraid it's true, Lieutenant. I've seen the place with my own eyes. It's nothing but a pile of ashes. And I've searched for the girl until I was sure. They're gone, sir . . . I'm sorry."

"God." Mitchell lay back on his pillow, sweat slicking his brow, his fist clenched. "I won't believe it unless I see it with my own eyes."

"You sure aren't in any shape to try anything foolish, Lieutenant. You can't go out, and you can't go looking. Most likely it will be months before you can. The war's getting hot. You won't be able to get there."

"I'll find a way. I have to know. I have to see."

Phelps rose and looked down on Mitchell with a look closely resembling pity. "I wish you luck, sir, I really do. But I think it would be best if you prepare yourself."

Mitch was silent, his mind filled with images of Whitney and the destruction of her life. He never even heard Phelps leave. For long hours he lay so, deep in a misery so indescribable that he could not find the strength to fight it.

Mitch was to find out Phelps had been right. It was weeks before he could move about freely and by that time the South was on fire and there was no way for Mitch to get news.

Blake Randolph was a Yankee. He was also Mitch's best friend. As a prisoner, Mitch had been befriended and cared for by Blake, who hated the war as much as Mitch did. It had grown into a strange kind of friendship, beginning with Blake finding Mitch wounded and taking him back. He had been the difference between life and death for Mitch, who had never forgotten it.

Blake was a tall, slender man of deceptive

58

strength. His hair was usually tousled, its brown, golden depths unruly. His eyes were hazel, his mouth wide, and he smiled easily.

Mitch watched the war grow worse and worse for the South, and he suffered the tortures of the damned as his imagination filled with the horror of the stories that seeped from camp to camp. The aristocracy of the South was being swept clean and Mitch could hardly face the despair of the endless waiting. He drank too much, ate too much, and grew so testy that few intruded on his private misery.

Blake was worried to death about Mitch's sudden retreat from life. He had literally forced the information from him and then began to wonder what he could do to help retrieve Mitch from the brink of self-inflicted death.

He felt as if fate had given him the answer when he was invited to the home of Major Kingsly by his son, Stephen, who had recently become a friend. It was the first time he was to meet the wealthy and very pretty Cynthia Kingsly. Silently he prayed he could maneuver a meeting between Cynthia and Mitchell. He was certain the antidote for the poison that was slowly eating at Mitch could be Cynthia and the promise of some kind of beauty in his life.

Blake was reasonably free to come and see Mitch whenever he chose. He searched for a way to get him out of the hospital for a few days to break the gloom of defeat that gripped him. Some well-placed money gave him a pass to remove Mitch to his home for "special care" for his wound; it also gave Blake enough time to bring Cynthia and Mitch together.

It would have been perfect, for the lovely Cynthia found Mitch more than attractive. Her smile held great promise, a promise that said there really could be a future in which Mitch too could smile. It would have been perfect if Mitch could have gotten the ghost of Whitney Clayborn out of his mind and his heart.

Even Blake would have had to admit that Mitch tried. For several days he tried as Blake kept his fingers crossed and prayed. He was sure time was on his side, for the war still raged. But Blake was too pleased too soon, for he didn't count on one thing: the end of the war. The South surrendered with Lee and Grant's meeting at Appomattox and with a sinking heart Blake saw Mitch's eyes turn toward home. Cynthia seemed to know it as well. She was never able to solve the mystery she saw in Mitch's eyes. She wanted him to stay, to respond to the feelings she had for him, but she did not know Mitch had already packed for the trip home. They walked together in the garden of the Kingsly home.

"Mitchell?"

"Yes?"

"You're extremely quiet tonight."

"Maybe it's because I'm finding it very difficult to say what has to be said."

"Then don't say it," she said softly, a note of pleading in her voice. They stopped and turned to face each other.

"You and I both know it has to be said. I'm leaving tomorrow. I'm going home."

"But why, Mitch, why? You have so much opportunity here. The South is a disaster. There's nothing for you there but struggle." Cynthia had hoped Mitch would stay until their short acquaintance could grow into something more promising, but with a sinking heart she knew he had never meant to.

"Cynthia, you're one of the loveliest ladies I've ever known. You're much too fine for me ever to lie to you. Neither of us could bear that. There . . .

there's someone I must find."

"I see . . . is she pretty? Tell me about her."

"She is . . . was . . . everything to me."

"Was?"

"I . . . I don't know if she . . . survived."

"Mitch . . . please tell me about her."

They walked for a time in silence while Cynthia let him struggle with his painful memories. He began to speak, to open the doors and let his thoughts run free. As he spoke, Cynthia's hope melted into pity.

"But surely, Mitch, they wouldn't lie to you. Her home and family are gone. She's dead. What good is it to search for a grave when you can stay here and build a full and happy life."

"I can't accept that!"

"Can't, or won't?"

"I won't. I'll believe she's dead when I see where she lies and not until then. I don't expect you to understand. No one does. Sometimes I don't even understand myself. I only know if there's a thread of a chance that she still lives I must find her."

"You love her that much?" Cynthia whispered.

"Yes, I do."

"I envy her. It would be wonderful to have a love like that. It's been four years and still your heart is there. Yes, I envy her."

Mitch bent to kiss her cheek lightly and for a moment she clung to him.

"Mitchell, if . . ."

"If?"

"If you find that your dream is gone, will you come back?"

"I don't know," he said honestly. "I truly don't know. I'm afraid I'm trying not to face the fact that she might be dead. I don't know if I could be a whole man for any woman again."

"Then why not bring that half back? Maybe . . ."

"I couldn't do that to you."

"If you don't find your dream, come back."

"Cynthia, I can't promise anything. I don't know where I'm going and I can't offer enough to a woman like you. You deserve so much better. All I can say is I'll try at least to let you know where I am."

"You've told me so much about your past, but do you think your town will welcome you any more than they would before? Why go back to be hurt?"

"It would surprise you," Mitch said bitterly, "the sins that can be forgiven in the name of money. There'll be very little money there now and even if they find it hard to swallow a poor Mitchell Flannery, they'll find it a lot more palatable to accept a rich Mitchell Flannery."

"What of your family, Mitch?"

"I don't know. That's another reason to go home. My father and mother . . . they must be finding it hard if they're alive. My brothers . . . God, I have to know, Cynthia. I have to help them if I can. It was one thing to fight for principles but quite another to desert one's family if they're in need."

"I hope you find your family well and safe, Mitch." She kept to herself her hope that the girl who held Mitch's heart had somehow found someone else and Mitch would be free. Yet, when she looked up into his eyes again, the force of the truth was almost too much to bear.

There was no more to be said and they both knew it. He bent to kiss her lightly and whispered an almost inaudible "Goodbye."

Cynthia sank to a bench and turned her face away, trying to contain her tears. She could hear the sharp click of his boots against the stone walk as he left. Then there was nothing but a deep, aching silence.

Mitch had been smart enough to turn all his Confederate paper money into gold long before it became useless. He had put it in hiding carefully. It was a godsend, for he would be going home with enough money to rebuild. He prayed his family was safe. Knowing that would give him the courage he needed. He knew he was still planning on building for Whitney. He would never believe she was out of his life forever. Somehow he knew he would sense it if she were. He was wholly devoted to finding her.

When Mitch returned to Blake's home he found Blake there and was surprised to find three large suitcases beside his. Blake was seated comfortably, his feet propped up on a table. He smiled when Mitch came in.

"It's about time you got here. I'd almost given up hope that you'd be home tonight."

"What do you think you're up to, Blake?"

"Taking a trip with a friend."

"That's unnecessary and you know it. You've got your own life to take care of."

"Look, Mitch, I'm . . . sort of at loose ends. I guess it's hard to pick up the pieces. Everything around here seems to have rolled right along without me. At the moment I don't fit and it makes me jumpy. I thought I might go with you for a while, at least until my system gets settled back into peacetime living. Besides, I just thought you might need help finding your way back here . . . just in case you lost your way or something."

"Or something," Mitch repeated with a smile. "You're not my keeper, Blake."

"No, but you see, there's an old Chinese proverb

that says if you save a man's life you're responsible for him and since it was me who dragged you in half dead I feel it's my duty to see you get straightened out."

"It seems you've been maneuvering my life quite a bit lately."

"Cynthia?"

"Cynthia. That wasn't the easiest thing in the world to do."

"Maybe it was a mistake," Blake said gently.

"No, trying to deny what I must do would be a mistake. I guess it's almost impossible to make anyone understand."

"Well, maybe I don't need to understand, my friend. Maybe all I need to know is that in the near future you might need a little help. And maybe I care enough to want to be around just in case."

Mitch gazed at Blake thoughtfully for several moments, realizing his friend wanted to be beside him in case what he found when he got home was too much to handle. He could find no way to refuse, so he smiled.

"Thanks."

Blake shrugged and chuckled as he rose. "That's a relief. I thought I was going to have a hell of a battle on my hands. Let's get going. By the way, just how are we traveling? From what I hear most of the trains aren't running."

"We'll buy either a coach or a few horses."

"I'll take the horses," Blake replied. "Being a cavalry man, riding in a coach just isn't my style."

"Horses it is."

The next morning the two men bought four horses—two to ride and two to carry their belongings. Mitch was sure his father would have use for the horses . . . if the farm was still there.

He was grateful for Blake's company during the

long trip home. It kept his mind from the darker thoughts about what he might find when he arrived.

Much as he would have liked to search for Whitney upon his arrival, he knew he couldn't. He was tired, the wound in his side ached, and he needed information. So he decided it would be best to go home first and find what was left of his family.

He and Blake rested the night in a boarding house run by a woman who had seen better days, as had her home. When he paid her with gold her eyes widened in surprise. Money was rare, most of it paper. He knew she could buy much more with the gold coin and he wanted her to be grateful enough not to ask questions he was not yet ready to answer.

As they rode along the next day, both were silent. They could see the destruction of war all about them. Mitch's heart felt like lead as he grew closer to home. What would he find? Would his parents be well? Would Morgan and Shawn be alive . . . uninjured . . . home? He prayed as he had never prayed before.

His heart began to thud furiously as he saw the fine wisp of smoke, then the welcome sight of his house. He was still a good distance away when the door was thrown open and his mother ran out on the porch.

No one could have made Caryn Flannery doubt that the tall, square-shouldered rider coming toward her was anyone other than her son. She would have known him in the dark of night.

She spoke his name softly as he kicked his horse into a run, leaving the packhorses for Blake. Mitch was out of the saddle before his horse came to a skittering stop in front of the porch. He took the steps two at a time and caught his mother up in his arms and whirled her about. Both were half-laughing and half-crying. When he stood her back on her feet she could not seem to let go of him.

"Mitchell! Oh son, I'm so glad you're home. You're well? You're not . . . ?"

"I'm fine, Mother, just fine, now that I'm here. Where's Pa?"

"He's out back. We have such a small garden now and he likes to work in it."

"Morgan and Shawn, Mother?" he asked in a quiet voice filled with fear. "Are they both . . . ?"

"Morgan was wounded at Chancellorsville, but he's all right now, and Shawn came home without a scratch. This family will always be together. We love each other, Mitch, and right or wrong we'll stick together. Do you understand me?"

Blake had arrived by then and Mitch introduced him to his mother, then he left Blake to unpack while he walked around the house.

He could see his father, hoe in hand, working the small garden. Nearby his two brothers were talking to each other. None of the three heard him approach. He was within a few feet of Stuart when he spoke.

"Pa?"

The hoe froze, then dropped from trembling hands. Slowly Stuart turned. He had seen two of his sons come home safely from a disastrous war and prayed daily for the other. Now his prayers had been answered. He took a step or two toward his son, holding out his arms in welcome. The sound of tears thick in his throat, Mitch took the last few steps and threw himself into his father's arms.

Six

Whitney sat on the top step of the porch and watched Jonathan at play. Could he be over two years old already? Time had flown and she had found a different kind of love in the nurturing of her son. If there was a dark, hollow place deep inside her, she had locked it carefully away.

She laid her head against the pillar of the porch and thought of the changes in her life from the moment Jonathan had been born — born in the midst of the conflict when the world had turned dark. How they had struggled the last two years of the war, fighting off those who would have stolen what little they had, fighting to keep body and soul together. Even when peace had come there were dangerous ragtags and renegades.

Now they had two small cabins, one for her and Jonathan and one for Berdine, Lazarus, Josiah, and Addy. Despite the fact that Whitney had insisted they all continue to live in the original cabin and make it larger, Lazarus made it clear that such a thing, if found out, could only make life more difficult for her and Jon.

The war had been over for almost eight months . . . . and now she was certain that Mitchell had never intended to return.

The cabin was comfortable, and if Whitney ever had the inclination to go back to the shell of her former home she repressed it. Lazarus had told her of its total destruction and she didn't want to see it.

She had gone into town a few times with Lazarus or Berdine and was amazed to see so many strangers. Many of the other plantations had been destroyed and the families and friends she had known were mostly gone. No one knew where she was and Whitney preferred to keep it that way. One day the land her home had stood on would be Jon's. Maybe he would want it. It was the only material thing she had to give him except a few pieces of jewelry . . . and the music box. Would Jon ask questions about his father she would never be able to answer? He was already following Lazarus about, longing to relate to a masculine personality. This frightened her as nothing else could, and it did not take long for Berdine to verbalize her fears. Whitney closed her eyes at the thought of her last conversation with Berdine. They, too, had been watching Jon at play.

"Dat boy gwine be right tall like his daddy. He be right handsome, too."

"Yes." Whitney tried to deny Jon's resemblance to his father but that was very difficult since the resemblance was so clear. The same thick black hair and the usually smiling, always questioning, cloud-gray eyes pierced Whitney's heart.

"Dat boy, he need a daddy."

"Don't start that again, Berdine. I have no intention of marrying. Many men died in the war so there'll be a lot of children without fathers. Jon will just have to learn on his own. Maybe it will make him a better man than . . ."

"Den his daddy was?"

Whitney cast Berdine a defiant glance. "I'm going to make him a man to be proud of, Berdine. A man who would not casually destroy another just for his own desire. I want him to be a man of honor. Is that too much to ask?"

"Ah din't say that. Yo' got de right ideas 'bout raisin'

68

him. It's jes' dat it be a hard job to do. Havin' a husband an' a father would make it easier."

"And just how am I supposed to get this husband? Are you suggesting that I just grab the first man who comes by? I've seen that caliber of man. Ragtag, landless wanderers. Is that what you want, Berdine? Would one of them be a good father for Jon?"

"Ah din't say dat neither. What ah said was dat yo' should have some life. Yo' should go into town, mebbe do some work fo' de church. Yo' kin meet a lot of nice people dat way."

"Oh, Berdine . . . it . . . it sounds like I'm on the hunt for a man. I can't do that. My parents would have been scandalized."

"Yo' parents lived in a diff'rent world den yo' has to. Yo' ain't de rich an' powerful Clayborn family no mo'. Yo' had 'nuff backbone to fight fo' survival de way yo' did, now yo' gots to go on. Yo' gots to fo'git what yo' pretty face an' yo' money could buy yo' befo'. Yo' gots to think 'bout yo' boy an' his future."

"My clothes are so . . . so plain."

"Yo' won't be out of place. Most folks don't have much now. We can git some cloth an' make yo' some dresses. We kin make do. Clothes ain't de problem, yo' backbone is."

"I feel like I'm competing in a contest to grab some unsuspecting male," Whitney moaned, laughing uncomfortably.

"Yo' fightin' fo' yo' son's future. What's too much to ask fo' his life? How yo' gwine git him schoolin' an' mebbe a chance to meet an' marry a fine girl? Yo' gots to git out of dis cabin once in a while. Yo' ain't bein' fair to Jon either. He don't have no friends."

"I feel guilty enough, Berdine. Don't remind me."

"When Lazarus came back from town de other day he heard de church is havin' a basket social. Ah kin rustle up a fine basket of vittles. Yo' takes de boy an' go."

Whitney was silent for a long minute, then she spoke quietly. "I'm frightened."

"Ah knows," Berdine said softly. "But yo' been frightened befo' an' dat never stopped yo.' Yo' gots to think of de boy's life, too. He needs friends. He needs to play . . . . he needs to learn dere's a world to laugh in."

A world to laugh in. She sat and watched Jon, thinking about those words. Could she find Jon a world to laugh in?

Berdine was preparing the basket and Whitney knew Lazarus was already hitching their only two horses to the wagon. They had sold the other two to buy seeds and other necessities.

She was dressed in a deep blue cotton dress, made by Berdine. Far from the finery she had been used to, but flattering to her blue eyes and light hair. Addy had done her hair carefully and Whitney realized it was the first time since Jon's birth that she had worn it in anything but a long braid. There was no mirror to look into but by the look in Jon's and her friends' eyes she felt suddenly pretty . . . and very, very vulnerable.

Berdine carried the basket out of the house and placed it in the wagon that Lazarus had driven up before the porch.

Jon was playing in the grassy area that bordered the woods not far from the house. Whitney called to him and watched his quick smile as he ran to her on sturdy legs. She caught him up as he got to her and listened to his delighted gurgle as she swung him up. His arms about her neck filled her with a sudden possessiveness. Was it wrong for her to raise Jon alone? Why couldn't she be enough for him? She could teach him to read and write and do sums, since her education had been so thorough. She made a silent vow that any man she met would have to really love Jon and want to be his father before she would ever consider marriage.

Always afraid to go into town herself, she had sent Lazarus, Berdine, or Addy to get supplies. She was amazed at the changes war had wrought. New businesses with new proprietors existed where old friends had been. Yet the bustle of the town intrigued her; it seemed so alive. After all the destruction she felt she would never see such life again. She searched the crowds in vain for faces of old friends. Perhaps she would see some at the church bazaar.

When the wagon stopped before the church she could see the crowd gathered on the green grass on the side of it. Lazarus helped her down, then lifted Jon out along with the basket. While Whitney walked toward the lawn with Jon's hand in hers, Lazarus followed with the basket.

At first no one seemed familiar, then someone called her name. "Whitney! Whitney!"

She turned quickly and found a small group of people headed toward her. A young girl, running well ahead of her parents, was about fifteen. She had been a visitor in her parents' home many times. When she reached them she grasped Whitney's hands in hers.

"Oh, Whitney! How wonderful to see you!"

"Emily Britton, it's nice to see you again. You've grown a great deal since I saw you last."

Before Emily could speak again her parents joined them.

"Mr. and Mrs. Britton," Whitney said, smiling. She was pleased at the look of warm friendship in their eyes.

"My dear Whitney," Ralph Britton said. "We had heard that everyone . . . I mean that your home was burnt."

"It was destroyed," Whitney said quietly.

"And your parents?" Mrs. Britton questioned.

"Both dead, I'm afraid."

"Your brother?"

71

"I don't know. He was reported missing. The war has been over so long but I . . . I don't want to give up hope."

"Oh, my dear child, I understand," Mrs. Britton said softly. "We have all lost so much . . . so very much."

Whitney remembered another member of their family. "Rodger?" she asked hesitantly.

"At Gettysburg, so long ago."

"I'm so sorry."

"Well," Ralph said, "welcome to the gathering. It's time we put aside the darkness."

"Thank you," Whitney began, but Jon was tugging on her hand, anxious at finding himself surrounded by so many strangers. "All right, Jon," Whitney murmured. She lifted him and handed him to Lazarus, whose strong, familiar arms made Jon much more secure.

"What a lovely child. Such remarkable gray eyes. Are you caring for him? Whose child is he?"

Whitney was momentarily stunned and knew what thoughts would fill their minds when she claimed Jon as her own. But she loved him too much not to.

"He's my son," she said quietly, waiting for their cold withdrawal. But it never came. Instead she saw understanding on their faces.

"We have all passed through such trials," Mrs. Britton said, her voice filled with sadness. "But at least you have a great reward. I wish I were in your place."

For a moment Whitney's eyes filled with tears, then Mrs. Britton put her arm about her shoulder. "Come, let's join the fun."

That was the beginning. In the next few weeks Whitney found herself involved in a whole new life. She began visiting new friends and a few months later the Brittons invited her to a party in their home. With Jon safely tucked in bed under the watchful eyes of Berdine and Addy, Lazarus drove her to the Brittons'.

"Good evening, Whitney," Ralph said as he welcomed her. "You do look lovely tonight."

"Berdine is quite handy with a needle."

"And you wear it well. Come, I have someone I want you to meet." He drew Whitney with him as he crossed the room.

The man stood with his back to her, and as they neared she could sense a kind of power. Obviously, from the fine cut of his clothes, he was quite wealthy. That alone was a rarity. But, as he turned to face her at the sound of Ralph's voice, she could see he was quite handsome as well.

"Whitney, my dear, I would like you to meet one of our most prominent bankers, Trent Donnelley. Trent, this is Whitney Clayborn. She's from one of the very best families."

"How do you do, Mrs. Clayborn. It's my pleasure. And Mr. Clayborn?"

"Mr. Clayborn," Whitney said honestly, "was killed. He died honorably. I'm very proud of him."

"As you should be." His eye appraised her, liking what he saw. "And I'm sure he would be quite proud of you as well."

"Thank you."

"Please do get acquainted," Ralph said, "while I see to some of the other guests."

When Ralph left there was a moment of silence. Then Trent smiled. "Do you feel as if you're on display?"

"A little," she laughed.

"Suppose we get away from the crowd and do these introductions over again." She nodded and he took her elbow. They made their way to the patio.

He's tall, she thought nervously. His hazel eyes were tinged with humor and his smile was quick. "Now," he said as they reached the patio and he turned her to face him. "Suppose we get past the initial snobbery. I'm more than just a prominent banker."

73

"And what *are* you, Mr. Donnelley?"

"For one, I'm deeply appreciative of beautiful women, and you're one of the prettiest I've seen in a long time."

"Thank you," she murmured.

He laughed aloud. "You're not one bit impressed. How refreshing."

"Am I supposed to be impressed?"

"Well, I'd like you to be. I certainly am."

"Really?" she asked suspiciously.

"I most certainly am."

"Why?"

"Straightforward."

"And interested in an answer."

"Because you're not . . . ordinary," he replied earnestly.

"What does that mean?"

"You're not defeated in any way. I can see fire in your eyes. That's rare today."

"I'm afraid I've seen my defeats as well as all the others."

"You just don't let it stop you, do you?"

"I can't afford to."

"Why?"

"I have a son, Mr. Donnelley."

"Trent, please."

"Trent. I have a son, Jon. He's a little over two years. I can't afford to be defeated when he depends on me."

"A lady of courage as well. I should really like to get to know you better. May I call on you, Whitney?"

"Yes."

"It must be difficult for you. Our hostess said you came from one of the finest families. You're not related to the past owners of the Clayborn Plantation, are you?"

"That was my home."

"I'm sorry. I heard it was lovely. Where do you live

now?"

"I don't see that you need that information on such a short acquaintance, Trent."

"Well then," he said quickly, smiling the same charming smile, "suppose we go back in and join the dancers and make the short acquaintance longer."

Whitney was hesitant at first, but the dancing was fun, the kind of fun she had not experienced in years. And Trent was handsome and interesting. That, too, was something she had not experienced in years. But she refused to be caught by his charm alone. She was wary and Trent knew it, but he was more than intrigued.

It did not surprise Whitney to find Trent at every occasion to which she was invited. Still it was almost three months before she agreed to let him escort her to an affair.

He came for her in a carriage that bespoke his wealth. He said nothing about the small house in which she lived. She did not invite him in when he came to pick her up nor when he brought her home. She knew she was afraid. He was handsome, rich, and charming—but she had been a victim of another man who was handsome and charming and she was not about to fall into the same trap again.

They were riding one day, and enjoying themselves. Whitney savored the pleasure of every moment, knowing the future could be as brutal as the past. They walked side by side leading their horses to let them rest.

"You're not being very fair to me, you know," Trent said quietly.

"Fair? I don't understand."

"You're keeping a barrier between us. We've known each other for weeks, yet you refuse to acknowledge how I've begun to feel about you."

"I'm not ready for that, Trent."

"Will you ever be?"

"I don't know," she said honestly.

"Whitney, if you could tell me everything about your past you might feel better. You hold something inside, away from me. How can I fight that?"

"All right." Whitney didn't know if what she felt was fear or anger. "You want the truth, I'll tell you the truth. I was never married. The Clayborn who died was my father. I was in love with a man who deceived then denied me . . . me and his son. Is that enough truth for you?" Her eyes blazed defiantly like twin points of blue fire.

"And this is what's keeping us apart?" Trent asked gently. "This thing that should never be a barrier has kept us from finding happiness together? Whitney, do you think I'm some kind of judge and jury about the terrible and bitter things you've gone through? I'm not. I'm falling in love with you and I want you to forget the past . . . and I want you to marry me."

"Marry . . . I . . . I can't . . . . I don't know."

"Don't decide now. Think about it. I'm throwing a big party in two weeks. I would like your permission to announce our engagement then. Will you think about it?"

"Yes, Trent, I'll think about it."

"Wonderful," he said softly as he bent to kiss her gently. Then he rode home with her, kissed her again, and left.

Dismounting before his house, Trent was smiling as he took the steps two at a time and entered. A man sat in his library, a whiskey in his hand and a smile on his lips.

"Mason, what are you doing here?"

"Just checking to see what progress you've made."

"Considerable, my friend," Trent replied as he tossed his jacket and gloves on a chair and poured himself a whiskey. "More than considerable."

"You'd better before that little filly finds out what you're really after."

"Don't worry, Mason. She'll be eating out of my hand. I've just proposed marriage to my little Cinderella."

"And she accepted?"

"She will, my friend, she will."

Mason rose and he and Trent touched glasses. "Here's to a very large profit for us both."

"I shall enjoy both the lady and the profit," Trent retorted as their laughter mingled.

After two weeks of very serious thought Whitney decided that a marriage like this would be the best thing for Jon's future. If she did not taste true passion on Trent's lips it was all right. Something deep inside told her that flame would never rise again.

When Trent came the night of his party he brought her an extravagant gift. She quietly accepted his proposal. Trent was delighted.

When they arrived at the party Whitney was at once surrounded by both Trent's friends and hers. It had been agreed that Trent would announce their engagement mid-way through the party.

She danced the first waltz with Trent and when the music finished he tucked her arm in his and they started to walk from the floor.

Then Whitney grew paralyzingly still. Her face paled and she felt as if she couldn't draw another breath.

In the doorway, frozen as motionless as she, his eyes filled with disbelief, stood Mitchell Flannery.

Seven

Mitch had reveled in the sheer joy of his parents' welcome. Nothing mattered to them except that all three of their sons were home and safe.

What distressed Mitch was the defeat he saw in the eyes of his older brother, Morgan. He had been wounded but not as badly as Mitch. They had talked over the supper table and Mitch could feel a barrier, a withdrawal. It scared him in a way the war had never done. He had to find a way to shake Morgan out of his darkness.

He spent that night, after the others had gone to bed, talking with his father.

"It's been hard for you, Pa," he stated quietly.

"For a while, I guess it was for everybody. But when the boys got back safe we managed. Morgan, he got a pension of eight dollars a month because he was wounded. We've been getting by. Now you're home and we're all together again. The good Lord's been good to us, boy. Some others don't have no sons coming home."

"Pa, I'm worried about Morgan."

"Worried? Why?"

"He's defeated, angry, and hurt. It's time to pick up the pieces and try to forget our anger."

"Morgan needs time, Mitch. He needs time. You and him have been closer than most boys. Hold on, Mitch, and he'll come around. Just give him time."

"I suppose," Mitch agreed reluctantly. "Pa, what happened around here? All the families, everything seems so changed."

"It is. Most were run off. Some women, when their men were killed, went off to relatives. Others just lost too much and moved out lookin' for something new."

"Some of the big plantations around were hit hard."

Stuart Flannery looked at his son closely. "You haven't forgotten the Clayborns, have you?"

"It's pretty hard to do that, Pa. You don't really know how it was between Whitney and me."

"Ain't none of them around anymore, Mitch. You have to accept that."

"No, I can't. I can't."

"Look, son, Ethan Clayborn died in the war. His son was reported missing at the same time. If he isn't back by now he's not coming."

"And Whitney?"

"You need to forget, Mitch."

"What about Whitney? I have to know."

Stuart sighed. "All right, I'll tell you all I know. The night the Clayborns were hit it wasn't a battle, it was a bunch of renegades killing and robbing. I was outside when I saw the flames. By the time I got there the whole place was just a smoldering ruin. The women . . . well, they must have either been killed in the house or dragged away. There's no way of ever knowing, Mitch. Not you, me, or anyone else is going to be able to find out. You have to accept the fact that she's dead . . . or worse, and too far away for you to find."

Mitch's heart had grown heavier with each word, but despite this he knew he would have to see for himself. He had to keep looking. He could not let her go, not without trying.

"This friend of yours . . ." Stuart began.

"Blake?"

"Yes. He's concerned for you. He says you're getting . . . obsessed with this ghost from your past."

"Blake is a friend, but even friends have to know when to mind their own business."

"What are you going to do, Mitch?"

"A lot of things, I hope. Make peace with my family. Help us start over. I have money, Pa. We'll build a nice house and get more land."

"And that's all?"

"No," Mitch said quietly. "I have to know, Pa. No matter what you or anyone else says or thinks, I have to know. If she's dead I have to know that, too. I loved her, and despite what everybody believed, she loved me."

"I suppose you're a Flannery and you won't stop your hard-headed Irish ways until you're satisfied."

"Somewhat like my father," Mitch said with a smile.

"I wish you luck, boy, but I hate to think of the heartaches you're causing yourself."

"I guess I'll just have to face that."

"So, what are your plans?"

"I'm riding over there tomorrow and look around. Then I'll check every official record I can get my hands on."

"Well, there's nothing more to say. I wish you luck, and I hope you're strong enough to take what comes."

Mitch reached out and placed his hand on his father's shoulder. "Now, Pa, who always taught me not to accept defeat?"

Stuart laughed and shook his head as they walked back into the house.

The next morning Mitch refused Blake's company and rode to the burnt plantation alone. After a long ride, he arrived around the noon hour. He rode through the cottonwoods, poignant memories plaguing him. He could see Whitney behind every tree and the pain was as fresh as the day he had heard of her fate.

As he approached the place where the once magnificent plantation had stood, he saw only rubble, darkened by a long-dead fire. He could envision Whitney here that long and terrible night. He groaned aloud as he thought of what must have happened. Defenseless . . . hurt . . . needing him. His whole body shook with rage.

He tied his horse and walked through the destruction without heeding the passage of time. He called up every vision of Whitney he ever had. He knew he couldn't afford despair or defeat. He had to try to re-live that night and find out what happened. Then, he had to have proof that she lived . . . or that she was dead.

Where could she have gone if she had run, he wondered. It was a great distance to town. Surely she couldn't have made it on foot. The pampered Whitney couldn't have stood that. But if she had managed an escape someone would have found her. If she had not . . . then where had they taken her? And who were they? He intended to write a lot of letters — someone would have the official record.

He sat on the stump of a burnt tree and tried to block out everything but ways to begin. It was a long time before he rose and walked to his horse and rode away.

He left without knowing about the man who stood beneath the trees and watched him. Lazarus's face was cold and angry. This man had hurt Whitney too much. Now he had come back, and he could only hurt her again. Lazarus had no intention of telling anyone that Mitchell Flannery was back. Maybe, he thought, their paths would never cross again. Whitney had a right to some happiness after all she had been through. One way or another he meant to keep these two apart.

When Mitch arrived home it was late afternoon. His mother was preparing dinner and his father and brothers had just come in from the fields.

"Where's Blake?" asked Mitch.

"He rode out about an hour after you did. Said he was going into town and might not be back until tomorrow," Shawn replied.

Morgan had remained quiet, which concerned Mitch. As they sat down to the evening meal Mitch could sense Morgan's withdrawal. They ate in silence because Mitchell and Morgan refused to talk about the war in front of their mother. But after the meal, when Morgan went to the barn, Mitch followed him. He found him tossing hay into the cow's stall.

"Morgan, it's time you and I had a talk."

"What is there to talk about, Mitch? We were dirt poor before. This war doesn't really change much. People still look at us as white trash Flannerys."

"So, we have to prove them wrong."

"How do we do that?"

"By making something of ourselves and not lying down and quitting."

"Do you think I'm quitting?"

"Aren't you? Pa needs us, the South needs us. We lost the war. Let's not lose the peace. We can make something of this family. We have the opportunity now."

Morgan was miserable and confused, and Mitchell knew why. He knew because he had been suffering, too.

"Morgan, for God's sake . . . for our parents' sake . . . for our sake, let's pick up the pieces."

"I'm trying . . . but . . ."

"But you don't know how. And I don't know how. But maybe if we take one day at a time we can build something strong enough to last."

"One day at a time?"

"That's all we can handle."

"Maybe if you could tell me why, Mitch, maybe if I could understand, it might be easier."

"Who knows why in war someone wins and someone loses. There are no answers."

The brothers stood looking at each other for a silent moment. Then they embraced.

"Come on," Mitch laughed shakily. "I'll help you find the rest of the stock."

They set about their work without speaking until they had their emotions under control.

"Mitch?"

"What?"

"I've been home quite a bit longer than you."

"So?"

"So I've been into town a lot, I've been around the countryside a lot. I know most of the new people and some of the old ones who are still around."

"What are you leading up to, Morgan?"

"That I know the Clayborns were wiped out. There's no trace of them. She had to have died that night, Mitch."

"Maybe you know all these things, brother," Mitch said softly, "but I don't, and I won't until I know in my heart that it's true. Can you understand?"

"I could understand if you had a chance in hell, but you don't. Where do you go, Mitch? Where do you start? And I have one more question. Will you ever know when to stop or will you spend the rest of your life looking for the ghost of what might have been?"

"I don't have the answers—and I have too many questions of my own."

"You're going to get hurt again, Mitch."

Their eyes locked and both understood that those words were probably true.

"Then help me, brother. Don't make it any harder. I might need a lot of strong people around me."

When Mitch stopped speaking, Morgan put an arm around his shoulder. "Let's go back in the house. They're probably worried about us."

Mitch nodded and they walked back together.

The days moved on and Mitch continued his search. His family watched the heartbreaking process — he refused to believe that Whitney was really lost.

Blake rode with him, searched with him, and continued to coax him from his self-destructive path.

At dawn Blake and Mitch rode toward town. In response to Mitch's many letters, they had gotten a message from the authorities that it might be possible to get a list of men and officers who had been in the area at the time in question.

"Mitch, these men could be scattered across the country. You can't find all of them."

"I don't need to."

"What are you going to do then?"

"Find the ones who were here and ask them questions."

"But . . ."

"It only takes one man with a good memory, Blake. One man to tell me the truth."

"And the truth will be that she's dead," Blake said brutally, hoping to shock some sense into Mitch.

"Then," Mitch said quietly, "I want to know where she's buried and who buried her. I want to know who killed her and how, and I want . . ."

"Good God," Blake breathed, "you want to kill someone, don't you? If she is dead you won't be satisfied until someone pays for it. I'm right, aren't I?"

"Maybe."

"Maybe hell, I'm right! God damnit, Mitch. You can't do this!"

"I haven't done anything."

"But you plan to."

"They're your words."

"I know you, my friend."

"Then as my friend, quit trying to stop me."

"Someone has to before you destroy your whole family. Your folks love you and they've just gotten you back. Do you want to stop that, too?"

"You want to leave, Blake?"

"No, I want to help you, but I don't want to help you destroy yourself."

"Let it go, Blake. With or without you and with or without anybody else's help, I'll do what I have to do."

Blake sighed. It was useless to argue. He really did know Mitch well, well enough to know that Mitch was telling the truth. He was the kind of a man to see anything he undertook to the end. He just hoped the end would come soon before his friend started falling apart.

They dismounted in front of a building that served as a jail and courthouse. An appointment had already been made so they wasted no time. Major Paul Ryan was a Union officer in charge of the occupation forces, an astute man who kept his fingers on the pulse of the city. If there was a record to be found Paul Ryan knew where to find it. He greeted both men at the door of his office, extending his hand.

"You're Lieutenant Mitchell Flannery."

"Just Mitchell Flannery now," Mitch said with a smile.

"Come in, gentlemen, come in."

"How did you know about me . . . my rank,

85

I mean?"

"I know a great deal about you, Lieutenant . . . ah, Mr. Flannery, I've heard a lot of good things."

"Thank you."

"Now, what can I do for you?"

"I'm interested in an incident that occurred close to here, Major. I need the names of the men who were here at the time."

"There's someone particular you're looking for?"

"Yes," Mitch said softly, "the woman I had planned to marry."

"Good God," Paul Ryan whispered in shock. "Suppose you tell me what happened and I'll do everything I can to help. Union or Confederate, it's beyond conscience to make war on women."

Mitch told him everything he'd been able to find out. The major listened intently, anger and disgust written clearly on his face.

When Mitch finished, Major Ryan nodded and rose slowly from his desk. "All right, I think I know enough. It shouldn't be too difficult to find the men who were here. I'll have a list for you in a couple of weeks."

Mitch shook his head. "I'll be very grateful, Major."

"No problem. Mr. Flannery, you were born somewhere around here?"

"Yes, it's rather a long story."

"Would you and your friend be my guest at dinner tonight?"

"Thank you, we'd be pleased. We had planned on staying the night anyway."

"I know an excellent restaurant, Delmonicos. Suppose we meet at eight?"

"Eight will be fine."

"Good. You can rely on me," Paul said as he walked with them to the door. "I'll find your names."

"I know it might be difficult, but if you have any

information about deserters or renegade groups and their leaders it would be of immense help."

"I should like to think it was that kind of element that did the horrendous thing and not the kind of men we've fought shoulder to shoulder with."

"War does terrible things to a man," Blake said solemnly. "It changes some of the best into some of the worst. I've seen it happen. There has to be some understanding."

"Understanding! For men who destroy for the love of destruction? For men who loot, pillage, and kill? No, my friend," Mitch said coldly. "There are no excuses for men like that. They ought to be hunted down and slaughtered like the animals they are."

Paul and Blake exchanged glances, but in the face of Mitch's fury, neither of them said any more.

Dinner that night was an enjoyable interlude as the three men exchanged stories of the past and shared their hopes for the future.

"We've got to help with the reconstruction of the South," Paul stated. "This country has to be healed before it falls prey to foreign powers."

"I agree," Blake said, "but where does a man start?"

"I would say," Paul replied, looking astutely at Mitch, "with taking an interest in the running of his city . . . or his state."

Mitch smiled. "Political office. I'm not the one to tell others how to run their lives when I'm having a hell of a time with my own. Besides, I have a job to do and there's no time for anything else until it's done."

Once again the huge wall of bitterness rose between Mitch and those who would turn him from his chosen path.

The discussion led to late drinks in a small bar-room. Blake, more drunk than sober, assisted a completely drunk Mitch to their rooms. But the night was not to end so easily. In his intoxicated state, Mitch talked more than he ever had before. It was the first time Blake truly understood the details of Mitch's lifelong battle. He saw Whitney as Mitch had seen her, a woman of tender love and understanding who had inspired Mitchell Flannery to want the kind of life he could be proud of. Blake could see what was in Mitch's heart and realized that in Whitney, Mitch had found his one true love. He was scared for Mitch, because even if he found the men he sought, even if he killed them, what would he have then? He wouldn't even have hatred to hold him together.

Blake and Mitch remained in town for several days. Paul was doing his best to introduce them to every important person he felt might encourage Mitch to run for office. Most of them found Mitch promising in his attitude, strength of character, and personal magnetism; and they felt he would be popular with the public. But Mitch was not interested.

He stood before a mirror dressing reluctantly for a party. Paul had done so much for him that he could hardly refuse his invitation.

"A very influential banker who has political aspirations himself," Paul had said. "He's been seeing this lovely creature for some time. He sure has an eye for women. She'd make a wonderful Governor's Lady."

Mitch was not interested enough even to ask her name. He planned to make his appearance, stay for as short a time as possible, and leave. Blake was ready and waiting.

"Looks like this banker is going to announce his engagement tonight. Rumor has it the lady is really extraordinary."

"Let's go, Blake. The sooner this is over with the

better. If I didn't need Paul's help so badly I wouldn't even be going."

The carriage ride to Trent Donnelley's home was short and quiet. Blake had no idea what Mitch was thinking and for some reason he was more than usually hesitant to ask.

They were met at the door of the elaborate home, its design and decor reflecting the affluence of its owner. Dancers whirled about the floor as Blake and Mitch stood in the doorway looking about for their host.

Then the music stopped and a couple who had been dancing turned toward Mitch and Blake.

Mitch was so stunned he couldn't breathe. He felt as if a great hand had closed about his heart and was squeezing the life from it. Across the room, her blue eyes wide with shock, stood Whitney Clayborn.

Eight

Whitney and Mitch stood frozen as memory swept them back into the painful past. He absorbed her like a man seeking the rays of the sun to ward off the frigid cold. He could think of nothing but that she stood before him—more beautiful than he ever remembered.

His broad shouldered form seemed suddenly to fill Whitney's whole world. So handsome, his gray eyes seeking hers with their well-remembered warmth. Her body trembled with memories buried, but never forgotten.

Neither of them noticed the spark of recognition in Trent's eyes before it was quickly camouflaged.

"Whitney," Mitch breathed softly, almost painfully. Reality had suddenly begun to crash around him— *Whitney was not dead!* Blake was open-mouthed at the sound of her name. He tried to put a restraining hand on Mitch to no avail. Mitch moved toward them, his eyes still locked with Whitney's.

She uttered Mitch's name with a touch of anguish that wasn't lost on Trent. The trembling of her body and the paleness of her face assured him of the power wielded by this man. He didn't know how they knew each other but he meant to put a stop to it.

Whitney could feel the heat of Mitch's gaze as he

moved closer and closer. She seemed rooted to the floor, unable to move, almost unable to breathe. She struggled valiantly for control. This was the man who had ignored her, denied her. This was the man who had even abandoned his own son. She could not let him enter her life again, not when her world was beginning to be safe. When he got within inches of her she was powerless to speak.

"Whitney?" he repeated, a disbelieving expression in his eyes. "I thought you were dead. They told me . . . everyone told me you had died the night your home was destroyed." He struggled to keep from taking her in his arms. "I didn't believe it! I knew. . . I knew it couldn't be true."

My God, she thought, the agony of the idea tearing through her. Was he telling her *he knew? He knew of that night? He knew of the death and the burning and the disaster and still he had not come?* It was as if he had struck her with all his might. She couldn't allow him to cause her further misery.

"Mitchell Flannery," she said, smiling the coldest smile she could muster. "It seems the war is making even our poorest feel they're as good as their betters."

Her words were as cold as her eyes. Mitch and Blake could feel antagonism emanating from her like a primal force.

Mitch couldn't believe his eyes and ears. This was Whitney, his Whitney, the woman he had always loved!

"I don't understand." Mitch was unable to associate this behavior with the girl he remembered — and loved. "Whitney, I have to talk to you. I have to know . . ."

"Whatever you have in mind, my friend," Trent said firmly, moving between Whitney and Mitch. "It seems my fiancée is not in the least interested.

Now, if you'll be so kind as to desist, I don't want to embarrass her."

"Fiancée?" Mitch repeated. "She can't be. Whitney, this is impossible. Talk to me!"

"I see no point in talking to you. It might be better, Mr. Flannery, if you just went on your way." She put her hand on Trent's arm but her eyes were on Mitch. "There is nothing . . . nothing left to discuss."

Mitch was gripped by an almost blinding rage. He reached out toward Whitney's free arm.

"The hell there isn't," he said grimly. His voice was low and didn't carry, but she saw what was in his eyes. "Dance with me . . . now, or I'll cause a scene the likes of which you've never seen."

He meant it and she knew it. A scene might cause repercussions in her son's life. That was the last thing she needed. If one dance would rid her of him she would do it. She began to move toward him.

"No, Whitney. You needn't lower yourself," Trent said arrogantly. Mitch's eyes blazed with a threat that terrified Whitney.

"It's all right, Trent, I don't mind. Maybe after our dance Mr. Flannery will remember how to be a gentleman."

Trent and Blake could do little more than stand and watch as Whitney and Mitch moved away toward the dance floor. Then they exchanged looks.

"Your friend is going to find more trouble than he bargained for," Trent said coldly.

"Mitch can take care of himself. Maybe . . . the trouble won't be his."

Blake half smiled as he moved away, threading his way through the crowd. There was a great deal of information he might be able to gather that could come in handy later. Trent watched the dance floor with a closed look on his face. He would find a way to put an end to Mitch's interference.

Mitch could feel Whitney's body trembling as they moved to the pace of the music, but his eyes would not release hers.

"You have to tell me what happened, Whitney. I've been frantic since I got word."

"You got word, and when was that?"

"What?"

"When did you find out that my home had been destroyed? That my whole life was nothing but ashes? Just when did you find out?"

"A year ago."

"A year," she repeated scornfully.

"Why didn't you write to me? Why did you stop?"

"Oh, Mitch, please. Don't try to blame me for your tricks. It was you who refused to honor our pact. I suppose when you decided to go off to fight your honor became just a word to you."

"That's unfair, Whitney. If you had written that you needed help I would have found a way."

"Well, I don't need help. I don't need you, or the past, or memories! And more, I don't need to pretend. It's just a little too late."

"You can't marry him!"

"I can't?" She laughed harshly. "I can marry whom I choose."

"You can't, I won't let you."

"You!" Her anger flared. "You walk away from me for years. You refuse to write, refuse to acknowledge . . . all my letters. How dare you tell me you won't let me? You have no say in the matter."

"Is that what your promises mean? Is this the way you keep your word?"

"At least do me the honor of letting me forget my young and foolish indiscretions."

His arm tightened on her waist and she gasped at

the blaze of passion in his eyes. "An indiscretion! Is that what we were? Those nights together, were they a game for you? The lady of the manor having a fling with the poor boy?"

She wanted to cry out and tell him no, but she didn't dare. Whitney was wise enough to know about a man's power in society. Since it was obvious that he had not gotten the letter about his son . . . or had been too busy and careless to bother to read it, she had to keep Jon a secret. Society would allow him to snatch Jon from her and Jon was her life.

"You may think whatever you choose. But I know what happened. My letters meant so little to you that you never even bothered to read them, let alone answer them. Whatever you think we had, Mitch, it's gone. This is our tomorrow. Let it go."

"But I can't, Whitney," he said gently. "I can't. Shall I tell you that every dream I've had since the day I left has been about you? Shall I tell you that the only thing that kept me going, kept me alive, kept me struggling, has been you? You and our promise to each other."

She fought for control. How she wanted to melt into his arms, to taste the sweet passion on his lips. But they were only words, sweet words she could not believe because the price was too high. She didn't dare trust him again. She had struggled through too much pain and grief, to allow him to wreck what little peace she had been able to find.

"No, Mitch," she said softly. "No more sweet words. After tonight, we won't see each other again. I intend to marry Trent Donnelley."

The music stopped and they stood looking at each other.

"No," he said quietly. "You can lie to him or yourself all you want. I'll make you another promise, Whitney. You'll never marry Trent Donnelley. I'll do everything in my power to stop you."

"Mitch, don't do this," she moaned. "Just go away, go away."

He was about to answer when Trent appeared at their side.

"You've had your dance, my friend. Now it's time for you to leave. I would advise you to go quietly because I'd like nothing better than to throw you out."

Trent had a half-smile on his face as he spoke, but when Mitch turned to him the smile dissolved. There was fury in Mitch's eyes—he felt as if he had been struck by a sledgehammer.

"Please, Mitch," Whitney said. Her voice was filled with tears, and they never failed to reach Mitch.

"This isn't over, Whitney, that I promise." He turned to Trent and smiled. "If it weren't for Whitney, I think your trying to throw me out might have been rather interesting. We might just get to it one day." Mitch walked away and Trent watched him go with a sense of relief. He wasn't sure Mitch wouldn't become a serious problem. He'd have to see that he never got the chance.

Mitch walked over to Blake at the edge of the dance floor. He had a smirk on his face and Mitch was pretty sure he knew what had happened.

"You've got a story to tell, buddy boy."

"The story doesn't have an ending yet, Blake. There's a whole lot that just doesn't make sense."

"Well, maybe I can help you out a bit."

He had Mitch's full attention. "What are you talking about?"

"I'm an avid listener," Blake grinned. "I just happen to know where the lady in question lives."

For the first time in a long time Mitch smiled. "You do?"

"Yep. Seems she has a small place a few miles

95

from here. Shouldn't be too hard to get to. It might be best if you talked to her alone instead of in the middle of a crowded dance floor."

"I always knew our paths crossed for a purpose," Mitch replied with a chuckle. "So tell me where it is."

Blake described the location of the house. Since Mitch knew the area so well he was surprised he hadn't searched in that direction.

"Maybe," Mitch said quietly, "you just ought to stick around and see what else you can dig up."

"And you?"

"Me?" Mitch laughed softly. "I'm going to take a little ride. This time I'll find my answers."

"Walk carefully." Blake nodded toward Trent. "He doesn't look very forgiving."

"Don't worry, this isn't the time to handle him."

"Uh-huh . . . . I'll bet you have the time planned though."

"That I have, my friend, that I have."

"Where are you going?" Blake asked as Mitch started away.

"I'm going for a ride. See you later."

"Mitch, be careful. This might cost you more than you bargained for."

"The way things were, Blake, I wasn't living. Now, now at least I see a light in the darkness."

"Mitch . . . what if it was . . . the truth? That she forgot you as soon as you left. That all of it was . . . nothing."

"Then I have to know that, too, don't I?"

"Yes . . . I guess." Blake watched Mitch move through the crowd and vanish. He prayed Mitch wasn't going to be hurt even more. But either way he knew Mitch was right. In his place Blake would want those answers as much as Mitch did.

Trent had danced with Whitney again to keep Mitch from cornering her in a place where she could not protect herself . . . or, more accurately, where he could not protect his interest.

Whitney tried to keep her mind and eyes on Trent, but they refused to cooperate. She searched the faces as they danced by, but Mitch seemed to have disappeared. It was for the best. She didn't want to face the fact that he still had such an effect on her. Even after all the misery and the hatred something had come alive in her. She couldn't dare let him into her life again, not after what he had done. And Jon! Good God, Jon. He could be taken from her. If Mitch thought she had used him and thrown him away he might just take her son to get revenge.

"Whitney?"

"Yes, Trent."

"This has obviously been very difficult for you. Can you tell me why this man had such an effect on you?"

"I . . . I don't want to talk about it, Trent."

"Whitney, I want you to be my wife. It's not fair for you to keep secrets from me, especially since all I want to do is help."

"I know." She tried to smile. "Trent, would you take me home . . . please?"

"Then we cannot make the announcement tonight?"

"I really don't feel up to it. Can we plan it another time?"

He knew he couldn't push her any further without making her feel too much pressure and begin to wonder why he was in such a hurry.

"All right, my dear, I'll send for the carriage and get your cloak."

"Thank you, Trent."

Whitney had never felt so nervous and upset. Her greatest desire was to get home and hold her son. She had to find a way to protect Jon from Mitch. Maybe marriage would be the way, but she couldn't make that decision tonight.

Trent returned with her cloak and placed it about her shoulders. "The carriage is ready, my dear."

They walked out and got into the carriage as Trent gave the order to drive to Whitney's.

Mitch had no trouble finding the two houses nestled so carefully in the shelter of the trees, but of the two he had no idea which one was Whitney's.

As he looked closer he realized how humble the houses were. Whitney had gone from the lap of luxury to this. How difficult it must have been. But he still couldn't understand her guarded fear of him— and fear it had been. He had seen it dance in her eyes.

He breathed deeply and chose one of the houses. After tying his horse securely he moved slowly through the shadows to the back of the house. He found one window slightly open and raised it higher and climbed inside. Slowly he walked through the rooms. There were three downstairs and, he imagined, the same above. The moonlight filtering through the windows lent a semi-light to the rooms. They looked so . . . comfortable. How would it be to share this small, comfortable place with Whitney? He smiled. He had enough money to do so much more. The shoe seemed to be on the other foot now. He began to think again of Whitney's reaction, accusing him of not responding to letters he never received. Yet, never answering his. Never leaving word where she could be found when he came back and, worst of all, her denial of him and being in the arms of another man.

As Mitch thought he moved about the room slowly, his hands brushing objects until he found the music box. He looked at it, lifted it, and held it, remembering the night he had given it to her. She had kept it, kept it when everything else was lost. Another question that needed an answer.

Mitch was trying to keep his mind from what Whitney could be doing at the moment. It might be hours before she returned. Reasonably sure the other house was occupied, he couldn't light a light and there was little use exploring an empty second floor. He had no idea his son slept there with Addy on a small bed next to him.

Finally he sat in a comfortable chair with the music box on his lap, his fingers gently caressing it, and waited.

Trent drove the carriage down the tree-shadowed road to Whitney's home. Lazarus and Berdine were in their cabin waiting to be sure of her safe return. When Lazarus heard the carriage stop he listened, certain that Whitney would not invite Trent in.

"Thank you, Trent. I'm so sorry the evening ended like this."

"Nonsense. I just don't want you to be upset. Now, go in and get some sleep. Tomorrow evening I'll ride out and see how you're doing."

"That's fine."

He bent to kiss her gently. Too many memories crowded Whitney's mind for her to even try to respond. Trent climbed down from the carriage and helped her out. They walked to the door together, neither of them aware that Mitch was inside listening.

"Good night, Trent, and thank you again for being so understanding."

"Why should I not be understanding? I love you, Whitney, I want to marry you soon. Don't keep me waiting too long."

He kissed her again and inside the house Mitch's imagination filled the silence.

"Good night, Whitney."

Mitch listened and heard Trent cross the porch and go down the steps. Soon the sound of the departing carriage would be heard. He waited, but the door didn't open. Quietly he moved closer to the door. He was ready to open it just to see what Whitney was doing.

She had walked to the edge of the porch and was gazing up at the gold-white moon. As she began to turn around, the door to Lazarus's cabin opened and he walked across the open space between the two.

"Miz Whitney?"

"Lazarus, you're up late."

"Yo' home a lot sooner den we suspected yo' to be. Dere ain't nothin' wrong?"

"No, Lazarus, nothing wrong. I just . . . wanted to come home."

"Yo' aw right, Miz Whitney?"

"I'm fine, Lazarus. Go on back to bed."

Mitch could feel Lazarus's resistance and he wondered if he was sensing something he just couldn't put his finger on. He waited in breathless silence.

"Yo' wants me to come in an' make sure yo' gets settled aw right?" Mitch held his breath.

"No, really, I'm fine. I'm going in right now. Get some sleep."

"Aw right. G'night."

"Good night."

Mitch backed away from the door and watched the latch lift and the door open. Whitney walked in.

100

She gasped raggedly, then stood completely still. If she screamed or ran, Lazarus would be here in seconds. But it also might wake Jon. She gathered her courage and swung the door shut. He was not going to intimidate her.

"Mitch, I should have guessed you might be here." She spoke quietly and with enough control that Mitch was taken by surprise.

"You know me so well," he replied in the same velvet-touched voice.

"Oh, yes, I know that when you want something you won't let anything stand in your way. I guess that was how it was from the start, wasn't it? I was a challenge you just couldn't let slip through your fingers. Well, it's time you know that you can't always get away with it."

"You belong to me, Whitney, and I won't accept what you say unless you tell me why you betrayed me."

"Betrayed *you?* Get out! Get out!"

Mitch reached behind her to slide the bolt home. "Not now, Whitney. You and I . . . we have a lot to say to each other."

Nine

Whitney was panic stricken. Suppose their voices woke Jon? She had to get Mitch out of her house. Yet she knew he had no intention of going unless . . . unless she could find some way to answer his questions and convince him she wanted to be rid of him.

"Mitch, this is useless. Time has made too many changes in our lives. It's too late to go back now. We were young, children."

"That's not true and you know it. We were in love. We made a promise and swore never to break it. How do you justify what you've done? By just saying we were young, forget it?"

"What do you mean *justify what I've done?* It's you who ran. At least I have an idea why you went. The game you were playing with me was over and you needed an escape route."

Mitch looked at her in total shock. He couldn't believe what she was saying.

"You said I refused to answer all your letters. How could I answer what I never received?" He could see in her eyes that she didn't believe a word. "Whitney, you've got to listen to me. We can't lose what we had. I have enough money to make everything easy for you again."

"That's all that's ever been on your mind, isn't

it, Mitch? Money! Well, I don't need your money. Nor do I need more promises. I've picked up the pieces of my life and I intend to live it my own way by my own rules."

"Damn it, Whitney! You accuse me of not answering your letters, but it was you who stopped writing. What happened? Did you meet someone you wanted more than me?"

"You make me sound like . . . like . . ." She was enraged and without thinking she struck him. For a moment they were both caught in an unnamed fury, then suddenly he reached out and caught hold of her arms, pulling her against him.

His eyes were brilliant with anger, and glowed with something more deadly than that . . . remembrance. What was worse was that the old familiar feelings were sparking to life in her wayward body, betraying her struggle for control.

She could feel the solidity of his body pressed intimately to hers and she trembled with breathless expectation.

"Don't . . ." She barely had time to gasp before his mouth found hers in a kiss that tore at her resolve, battered her walls of defense, and sought entry to a place guarded from hurt for so long.

"I'll make you remember," he whispered against her throat. His voice was thick with passion and the need to find a way to convince her.

Memories flooded her mind—against her will she felt her senses answer his. It was as if time stood still. She felt herself entwined in tendrils from the past. Her mouth parted to accept his and for this one forbidden moment she allowed her emotions to reign.

His hands released her, only to pull her closer, wrapping his arms about her and crushing her to

103

him as he had wanted to do when he saw her in the ballroom. The ache of his need brought tears to his eyes. Feeling her body molded to him and the softness of her lips against his was almost painful.

He held her and could not let her go. He had thought to kiss her just to prove how wrong she had been, but it had slipped beyond his control.

Through a whirling mist of passion Whitney struggled to regain her senses. It took every ounce of her strength to push herself away. They stood inches from each other, breathing raggedly, standing on the brink of a chasm too wide for either to cross.

"You can't do this to me," she half sobbed. "You can't come back out of nowhere and just walk into my life. What are you trying to do?"

"I'm trying to make you listen to me. Whitney, we have to give ourselves time. We have to talk. You just can't marry him. I'll stop you, any way I have to."

Whitney's mind leapt to Jon. Of course he could stop her. All he needed was to say that Jon was his, and there could be no denying it. It would ruin every plan she had for her son . . . her son.

"Please . . . . please go away," she whispered.

"I can't, Whitney . . . I can't. And if you stop lying to yourself you'll admit I'm right. We meant too much to each other. Your words might be able to go on with the lie, but your lips and your body say something else."

Mitch set the music box on a table close to them, backed up a step, and reached out to open the lid.

Soft music filled the room. Whitney turned her face from him lest he see her tears and her fear.

104

Was she a fool, a child, to fall into the same sweet trap that had nearly destroyed her?

"Remember, Whitney," he urged quietly, "and remember this as well." He drew his shirt open to expose the thin gold cross and chain. "It was all I had of you." His voice was thick with emotion.

"No, I don't want to remember," she half whispered.

"Then why did you keep the box?"

"I . . . kept a lot of things."

"I don't think so. I went to your home. I saw the ashes. I don't think you had much time to save too many things. But I think you kept this because it was the memory you held dearest. I think you kept it because the promise that went with it was one you can't forget."

"What do you want from me?"

"Tell me when you changed. Tell me why you decided to throw away what we had. What was it that made you change and quit writing to me? There had to be something . . . someone. Is that what it was, Whitney? You didn't want to be tied to me any longer?"

Whitney gathered herself together. She clasped her hands before her to ease their trembling, then walked past him and stood some distance away. In the shadowed room she was a pale ghost-like glow, and despite his urge to go to her, to possess her, he waited.

Slowly and softly she told him of the attack on her home, of the long days of battle and the longer nights of despair and loneliness. He could feel her anguish, taste her pain.

"I looked for letters from you," she finished softly. "I used to dig in the ground for fear I'd missed one. I prayed for letters, I cried and I

105

begged God to let them come. I needed your strength, Mitch, but it just wasn't there. Then I finally learned it wasn't ever going to be there. I needed to find my own strength." She whirled to face him. "And I found it," she said defiantly, "and I'm not going to let you walk back into my life so casually and destroy it."

"But I sent letters, Whitney. I had everyone taking my letters to you. But I never got any in return."

"If your men . . . your friends, had come they would have found my letters, Mitch. It does no good to lie now. I just want you to leave. Let me forget a past too painful to remember. I've learned to forget. You must do the same. You advised me in the only letter I got that it would be best to forget you."

"That's not true!"

"Why do you lie when I have proof?" She walked to her desk and removed the letter she had kept only for the purpose of maintaining her hatred. She threw it at him and it struck him on the chest and fluttered to the floor. Mitch reached down and picked it up . . . and read words he had never written.

"I don't know who wrote this, Whitney, but I didn't."

"Please don't try to make me look like a gullible fool. I know your writing."

"I didn't write this. I never would have."

"Mitch, leave me alone! Go away. I'm tired and I don't want to fight with you. You were out of my life for a long time. I've made a new life and I'm not going to let you spoil it. Go away! Just go away!" Her plea ended in a choked sob.

Mitch heard the echo in her voice of something

106

he had not paid attention to before. There was more than the letters, more than the supposed lies. Whitney was afraid of something. His eyes narrowed as he watched her intently. It was in her eyes, in her defiant carriage, in her nervously clasped hands. There was something about this tragedy that Whitney was not telling him.

Whitney sensed his curiosity; she had known this man, known his every thought. Now he instinctively knew that she was keeping something important from him. He also had the feeling that his life depended on information only she could provide.

"What is it?" he questioned softly. She shook her head and backed away a step or two, but he moved closer. "Whitney, what are you keeping from me? A lot more happened here, didn't it? A lot more I should know."

"No." The whispered word was weak and uncertain. She backed away further.

"What is it, Whitney . . . what?" She continued to back away and he continued to stalk her, his eyes relentlessly holding hers.

She backed as far as the small cabin would allow, then she uttered a smothered cry as he reached for her again.

"There's a secret in your eyes, Whitney," he said softly. "You never were one for keeping secrets or telling lies."

"Mitch, please. For God's sake, just go."

He held her close, feeling the rapid pounding of her heart. Like a frightened bird, he thought. Indeed, there *was* a lot more here than he knew.

"Not until you tell me what it is behind those eyes that makes you so afraid."

"I'm not afraid."

"You're shaking like a leaf in a storm."

"You're holding me too tight. Let me go."

"It's not because I'm holding you, it's because you're scared to death that I'm going to find out something you'd rather keep hidden. You might as well tell me because I'm not going to go until you do."

"I could scream. Lazarus is right across the yard."

"You could. But it would be foolish if you did."

"Lazarus could break you in two."

"He probably could. But then there would be a great deal of confusion when your ex-fiancé found out about my being here."

"You wouldn't!"

"Wouldn't I? Scream and see."

"I was right. You are a scoundrel."

"Why, because I want answers I feel I have a right to?"

"You gave up your rights to . . . to everything a long time ago. Why do you feel you can just appear and everything could be just like it was? Things change with time. I did, and you did."

"Things change and people change, but facts never do. Somewhere there is something so important you're afraid of me finding out. Well, I'm going to stay here until I do."

"You can't mean that. You have to leave, you have to!"

They stood in silence. His hold on her was relentless and the effect he was creating just as relentless. Her whole body felt as if it had been ignited with a teasing flame. She had never been more aware of him than she was now.

There was no doubt that Mitch had no intention of leaving. Every moment that he remained increased the danger of Jon or Addy waking. If Jon awoke, he would call out for her and she knew it. She thought of the turmoil and confusion Mitch could cause, and in the end he could be the only winner. She was desperate and her mind searched in panic for a way out.

Mitch stood between her and the door. Her only escape was to get to Lazarus and Berdine. Would Mitch really let Trent know he was there? What would Trent believe? Either man had only to look and they would both know who Jon's father was. She had to have time—she had to maneuver herself closer to the door and Mitch far enough away from it that he could not stop her flight. It was calling his bluff and she knew it, but she had no choice. Certain that if he remained much longer he would have every answer he ever wanted and more than uncertain what his reaction would be, she knew she had to take action somehow.

"Let me go, Mitch. We can talk."

"We can talk without me letting you go. It's been much too long, Whitney. I find it very difficult to let you go."

"I can't concentrate if you continue to do so."

"So," he said softly, "what was between us was not just in my mind. You have never forgotten either. That's good to know."

He released her slowly and quite obviously very reluctantly. She stepped back, breathing a sigh of relief and praying she could find her way out of this.

"Even if," she began, "if we did want to . . . to . . . renew what we had, it can't be like this, Mitch."

"I don't understand."

"This has been such a shock after all this time. You've got to give me time to get myself together,

109

to understand all that's happened." As she spoke she began to casually move away from him. He turned with her, his eyes following her movements, but seemingly unaware of her plan. He seemed intent on what she was saying and not what she was doing.

"I guess we do need to talk. I'm sorry I was so rough with you. It's just that it's hard to see a dream evaporate before your eyes. I don't know what happened to the letters, Whitney, but I did write them, at least up until the time I was wounded. For a while I was incapable of writing. I would have given my life for one of your letters then."

"Wounded?" she repeated, surprised at the pain that thought brought. "How badly were you hurt?"

"Badly enough to keep me out of circulation for a while."

Whitney kept moving slowly, circling Mitch, who still seemed engrossed in her words. His back was to the fireplace and she stood within five feet of the door. Still, the distance seemed too great for her to cross before he could get to her. Her heart was pounding, partly because of her position and partly because of the intensity of his gaze. He seemed to be memorizing everything about her.

"Even though you said you wrote . . ."

"I did write."

"Even though you wrote," she repeated, "it's too hard to forget everything we've been through just like that. It's unfair to expect it."

"Whitney, let me tell you something," he replied, his voice deep and resolved. "It was our dream that kept me alive. It was knowing I could come home to you that gave me enough courage to stand what had to be stood. Look at me, Whitney."

She had turned her head away from the brutality of his gentleness. Now she lifted her eyes to his. "Do you think I want to hurt you? I don't. I love you and that's the God's truth. I only want to try to pick up the pieces."

"Maybe," she said softly, "there are too many pieces to put together. I've made a promise to another man. Is it fair just to walk away?"

"You don't believe for a minute that I'll just let him have you?"

Whitney moved another step toward the door, but she quickly saw the glint in his eyes. He crossed the area between them in a few steps, then stood towering above her. His eyes were gentle.

"Don't run from me, Whitney. It's no way for us to settle anything."

She knew she had to stand her ground. "All right, Mitch, I won't run. But you must respect my wishes as well. I'm exhausted and confused. I need time to sort my thoughts, time to make decisions about what I want to do. I'm asking you to go now, to give me the time I need. And . . . . I'm asking you to honor whatever decisions I make."

"I can't agree to all of that. I'll go, if I have your promise you won't hide from me. If winning you back is what I have to do, then I'll do it. I won't honor any decision that takes you from me. I'll fight because I can't afford to lose — the loss would be too great."

"You have my promise that I'll talk to you again."

"When?"

"Soon."

"When?" he insisted.

"Mitch!"

111

"No halfway answers."

"All right, in a week."

"Here?"

"No! No!" she realized at once her sudden fright had alerted him to her desire to get him away from this house. She saw suspicion in his eyes.

"All right," she added quickly, sure she could get Lazarus and Addy to take Jon away for a day. "We'll talk here."

"I'll be here."

She sighed with relief. She had a week to regain her control, to fortify herself against the effect he had on her. She had to find protection against the magnetic power he seemed to have over her.

Her tangled thoughts had consumed her mind, and she hadn't realized Mitch had moved closer until his arms encircled her again. This time they were gentle.

"God, Whitney, I've missed you so much. It's like part of my own body has been gone. I guess maybe I can understand your reaction. It was a shock to see you tonight. I had been told you were dead, killed the night your home was destroyed. I saw your face in every woman I met. Something deep inside told me you were alive. I would have felt it if you had been . . ." his voice lowered, "I'm glad you're alive . . . warm, beautiful, and alive."

His mouth found hers, but this time the kiss was gentle and delicate, and it tore at her more deeply than any force he could have used. For a moment she clung to him, then she pulled away.

"Please go, Mitch . . . please."

"One week, Whitney, remember that. And remember this." He kissed her again, then reached for the music box. He wound it carefully, then as the music again filled the air he placed it in her

112

hands. Their eyes met. "Remember," he added softly. Then he turned and left, closing the door quietly behind him.

Whitney stood immobile, suddenly overwhelmed by all that had happened. Her life had been reasonably organized. If it wasn't romantic and exciting, it was at least settled and secure. Now, like an earthquake, Mitch had shaken her foundation. He had asked her to remember the good times, but the painful memories returned as well. It was impossible to believe that none of her letters reached him; it was also impossible to believe that none of his could reach her. She remembered so well hiding the letters herself. No one knew their secret place, no one. And no one could have found them. Why would Mitch insist he had sent them if he hadn't? Why did he expect her to be the naive girl he had left behind? Was she expected to believe that all those months after the war was over he was trying to find her? He had not expected to see her, he had not been searching for her. She was so confused and frightened. She had too much to lose and as far as she could see, very little to gain.

Slowly she went up the steps and into the room Addy shared with Jon. She walked to his bed and sat on the edge. He slept, like a tiny angel, his dark hair tousled and his breathing slow and rhythmic. She reached out and held one of his small hands. He was hers! He was all she had that was not a terrible memory from her past, and she was not going to let Mitch or anyone else take him.

She walked to her bedroom and undressed slowly. In bed she lay stiff and cold. She had to find the best way, and maybe the best way was to tell Trent she wanted to move their wedding day up. Why did they need a long engagement? It was an answer . . . but was it the right one? Would Mitch leave her alone if that was what she decided?

She tossed and turned for hours and finally fell into a restless sleep, but her dreams plagued her more than all her waking problems. They were filled with confusion and angrily flashing pictures. She finally was wakened by one and remained awake the rest of the long hours until morning.

Ten

Mitch felt wedged somewhere between total euphoria and abject despair. He found it hard to believe that none of Whitney's letters had reached him if she had written them, and that none of the letters he *knew* he had written had reached her.

He was quite aware of her singular need to get him away from the house. At first he attributed that to shock and her initial fear. But now, considering it more deeply, he began to wonder just why she didn't want him to return. Something was being hidden from him, and he made up his mind to find it out.

Now that he knew Whitney was nearby he could hardly bear the fact that he had actually agreed to wait a week.

"Very poor strategy," he muttered to himself. A good move would have been to press his advantage when he had it. But on the other hand he couldn't see forcing himself on her in the state she was in.

Awakened by the warmth of a vitally alive Whitney, the doors of memory opened, allowing his mind and senses to fill with thoughts of her. The miracle of the love they had shared in the weeks before the war was as poignant now as if it had happened yesterday. The sweet taste remained with him during the long ride back home.

Despite the late hour he found Blake still awake and waiting for him, anxious to hear all the news.

Mitch was silent for so long that Blake became even more impatient.

"All right, friend, stop looking like the cat that just lapped up the last of the cream. What happened? I can see you didn't get shot. Can I hope that all is healed and forgiven?"

"Not quite that easy—not that I wouldn't wish there could be a wedding tomorrow. No, I'm afraid I've got a fight on my hands."

"This gets worse by the minute. I thought just finding her alive would be enough to solve everything. Then I see her greet you with sparks in her eyes and all her claws bared."

Mitch threw himself down on the bed and laced his hands behind his head.

"A lot of things went wrong." He went on to explain about the letters.

"You mean she claims to have answered yours?"

"No, not answered mine. She says she continued to write even after I had stopped."

"But you never stopped. While you were in prison, I can attest to what a curse you were to live with when she never wrote."

"I don't think she's prepared to believe me, you, or anyone else, for that matter. Blake, something else is wrong. She seems to be blaming me for something a whole lot worse than the missing letters."

"Like what?"

"Damn if I know."

"But you intend to find out?"

"As sure as I'm breathing."

"So if you left on less than friendly terms, how do you think you're going to find out anything?"

"I don't know who stayed loyal to her through everything, but I know Lazarus has."

"Lazarus?"

Mitch went on to explain that Lazarus was the

only one who had known about his correspondence with Whitney. "Old Lazarus disapproved of me."

"So maybe he put a stop to the letters."

"No. Reluctant though he was, he would never have done anything to hurt Whitney. He worshipped her. I guess that's why he stayed on to help. Blake, it must have been incredibly hard for her. I suppose if Lazarus hadn't stayed she might not have made it."

"What do you plan to do?"

"I haven't figured that out yet, but I will. I only hope Lazarus doesn't attack me when I try to talk to him. He's big enough to tear me apart."

"And that fellow at the party, Trent Donnelley. I've been told they're engaged to be married." Mitch turned to look at Blake, who laughed and threw up his hands in mock surrender. "I didn't say it, I just heard it."

"There's something about him," Mitch said vaguely, searching his memory. "I have a feeling I've seen him before. Someplace he didn't belong."

"That doesn't make sense."

"I know. But I've still got the feeling I should look into Trent Donnelley."

"Look into or get rid of?" Blake asked, grinning.

"Well," Mitch replied, his chuckle wicked, "you don't think for a minute I'll let him stand in my way, do you? Whitney might be confused, but somehow I'll work it out. I'm not letting her go again."

"She's a beautiful creature, Mitch. I can see why you fell in love with her. The rest of this mystery . . . well, I hope for your sake you can solve it."

"Yes," Mitch replied softly. The room grew silent, and after a while both men slept.

If Mitch was thinking about Trent, it was no more than what Trent was doing about him. Trent re-

117

turned to the party, said goodnight to his guests, then went into the study to brood over a brandy.

Anger filled him. He knew Mitch was a threat to him and Whitney, but he also knew Mitch was another kind of threat: a threat to his goals, for Mitchell Flannery knew something that could ruin Trent's political aspirations completely. Mitch knew things he most likely didn't know he knew. The confrontation had been so short. Mitch had been a prisoner until the end of the war. He and his Yankee friend, Blake, had met in prison.

As a spy, Trent had moved often from South to North, acquiring large amounts of money. To the South he was a hero; in the North, only a few knew he was an informer.

They had met in a dimly lit tent and he was only face to face with Mitch for minutes. But had those minutes registered in Mitch's mind and was he already comparing the face he saw then to the one he had seen tonight?

He knew tonight's confrontation had been shattering for Whitney and Mitch's full attention had been on her. He had to know more about that as well. He was certain of one thing: somewhere along the line it would be necessary for one Mitchell Flannery to meet with an untimely and very fatal accident. Trent could not afford to wait until Mitch's memory returned. Not now — there was too much at stake.

There were many questions he wanted to ask Whitney, but he knew he would have to be subtle and move slowly. He had no intention of frightening her away. Somewhere in her possession were letters, letters from her brother. Obviously Keith Clayborn had died without reclaiming them and their secret. He had to have them and Whitney was the only one who could give them to him. She was a Clayborn and her family's reputation would make her an asset with voters. And even more important, she still owned one of the largest tracts of land in the county. He could rebuild the house and the added prestige of a well-honored name would make him a power in the county, then the state, and, hopefully, one day in the country.

The next day Trent rode slowly toward Whitney's home. He could not understand her insistence on living in such a secluded place. Once they were married he would begin work on the house. After all, the land would then be his.

He thought of her son, a child he had only seen at a distance and really preferred not to see any closer. Once they were married there would be servants at first, then boarding schools and other ways to keep him from interfering in his and Whitney's life.

Whitney had just given Jon his breakfast and Addy insisted on taking him for a walk along the river.

"He sho' like to play in de mud."

"You'll be very careful, Addy?"

"Now yo' knows ah won't let him anywheres near de water. Ah'll be careful like he mah own."

"All right."

" 'Sides, in a couple hours he be hungry again. From de way he eatin' an' growin' yo' gonna have a hard time keepin' him in shoes an' food."

"I'll fix a big lunch for us all. Maybe we can eat out under the trees. It's such a nice day."

"Dat sound good to me."

Addy bent to lift Jon and Whitney followed them out onto the porch. She shaded her eyes with her hand and watched until they disappeared. She was about to go back into the house when she saw Lazarus approaching.

"Mornin', Miz Whitney."

"Good morning, Lazarus."

119

"Addy take de boy to play?"

"Yes, I told her I'd make a big lunch and we could all eat under the trees."

"Dat sho' sounds good to me. Sho' a fine day fo' it."

"Are you going into town, Lazarus?"

"Plannin' on goin' tomorrow. Is dere somethin' special yo' needs?"

"I thought I would go into Magruder's store and see if they have some nice cloth. I think it's time I made a wedding gown."

Lazarus gazed at Whitney closely with a look in his eyes she could not understand.

"Miz Whitney?"

"Yes?"

"Yo' happy 'bout marryin' dis man?"

"Why shouldn't I be, Lazarus? He's a fine man. He can provide a more complete family life for Jon, give him all the things I probably never could."

"Sho' he a fine man, an' he rich. But are yo' marryin' him fo' yo' . . . or fo' de boy?"

Since Lazarus's devotion had been so absolute she had begun to think of him as family. He had been invaluable with the land and the houses and with Jon, and a never-ending source of strength for her. This was the first time she could not answer him honestly.

"For both of us, I guess," she said softly, but her eyes avoided his.

"Ah don' 'spect guessin' is a good 'nuff reason fo' marryin'."

"Lazarus, I'm a little past worrying about love and romance. That died with the war. Now I have to be sensible and logical and do what's best for the future."

Lazarus seemed to be on the verge of saying something, then he clamped his mouth shut and turned

120

from her to look out over the clearing.

"Lazarus . . . you don't approve of this marriage, do you?"

"Hain't mah place to approve or not. Yo' makes up yo' mind what yo' wants."

"But you think I'm wrong?"

He remained silent, and Whitney walked down the three steps and stood beside him.

"Lazarus, you're more than just a friend. Without you I wouldn't be here, maybe I wouldn't be alive. I don't think I could have survived, and I certainly could not have done this," she added, sweeping her arm to encompass everything around them. "And Jon, Jon could never have survived those first days if it hadn't been for you. After all that, don't you think it's unfair to keep secrets? Don't you think you can tell me what you really think?"

Lazarus *was* thinking. He thought of seeing Mitchell Flannery at the burnt-out plantation. He knew that Jon was Mitch's son—it was impossible for the father to be anyone else. He was confused, trying to sort out what was right and wrong. Mitch had hurt Whitney, and for that alone he deserved no kindness or consideration. Yet Jon needed a father and Lazarus wasn't certain Trent was the man for that job. A man had a right to his son.

"Lazarus?"

"No, ma'am, ah hain't gwine say one way or t'other. Yo' decides what yo' wants to do an' ah stands wif yo' when yo' does it. But ah doan make dat kind of decision, no way."

"You'll stand with me," she repeated softly, "but you really don't approve."

He turned to look her in the eye. "Miz Whitney, yo' a fine lady. Ah knowed yo' since yo' was a child. Yo' grown from a sweet girl to a woman any man would be proud to have fo' a wife. Jus' yo' remember,

121

yo' did de growin'. Yo' didn't need no man to help yo' wif dat, an' yo' don' need no one to help yo' decide what to do wif de rest of yo' life an' yo' boy's life."

"Lazarus, is there something . . . something else bothering you?"

"No, ma'am. But . . . maybe ah should . . ."

Before he could finish the sentence the sound of an approaching carriage could be heard and Lazarus and Whitney turned to see Trent driving toward them.

"Ah gots things to do," Lazarus muttered. Before Whitney could protest his leaving so quickly, Lazarus walked away. Whitney watched him, feeling her uncertainty grow. She sighed and turned back toward Trent. She would go to their cabin and talk to Berdine and Lazarus later. There was something on Lazarus's mind and she valued him too much to let him be upset if she could help it. Besides, she had a feeling he was trying to tell her something.

Trent jumped lightly from the carriage, tied the horse, and walked toward Whitney with a smile. When he reached her side, he bent to brush her cheek with a light kiss.

"Good morning, my dear. You look lovely as usual."

"Trent, what are you doing here so early in the morning?"

"After your delicious company last night I couldn't wait to see you again. It's a lovely day. What do you say to a nice leisurely ride? I have something I'd like to ask you."

"I'm sorry, Trent, really. But I promised Jon a picnic under the trees, and I just can't go now. Come in and I'll make some tea, then we can talk."

Trent was disappointed, but he smiled and followed her back into the house. From some distance

122

across the yard Lazarus watched them. He couldn't fight the feeling that Trent was wrong for Whitney. He also couldn't bring himself to tell Whitney that he knew Mitchell Flannery was home. She had a right to know but he didn't know what kind of problem it would cause and hurting Whitney or Jon was more than he could bear. He shook his head and went about his work.

Trent attempted to take Whitney in his arms but she moved gracefully away, unsure of why she didn't want his display of affection.

"Now, my dear, can't you cancel your picnic for one day? What I have to ask is really important."

"It's not fair to Jon, Trent. I promised, and he has so little to look forward to. Besides, I hate to break promises."

Trent smiled, but inwardly he resolved that once they were married this kind of thing would not happen. Whitney set about making tea while Trent sat down at the table.

"There was something you wanted to ask me?"

"Whitney . . . the gentleman who was so rude last night, did you know him before?"

For a moment Whitney's hands froze, then she continued preparing tea. She could not tell him everything, and she wasn't too sure of what Trent already knew.

"Yes."

"How?"

"I knew him before the war. He . . . he used to live a short distance from my home."

"Did he mean something to you?"

"Why do you ask?"

"I rather disliked the way he looked at you. He's somewhat arrogant, isn't he?"

"I don't really know, Trent. I only danced with him once."

123

"But what about . . ."

"Trent, is this a cross examination? Am I on trial for something? If I am, please tell me what's on your mind. I have no time for games."

"Darling, don't be so touchy. I suppose it's just a bit of jealousy on my part. I apologize, but . . . it's made me do a lot of thinking."

He rose and walked to her. This time he did not touch her but his eyes held hers intently. "Whitney, I love you and I don't want to lose you. You never agreed that I could announce our engagement, but this time I'm asking for more."

"Just what are you asking, Trent?"

"We could be married in my home in two weeks. It would be an exciting surprise. There's no real reason for a long engagement. We know what we want from life and we're strong enough to get it. All you need do is say yes, and I'll make all the arrangements."

"Two weeks," Whitney protested nervously.

"Two weeks. You need not make a gown. I can buy you the very best. We can go on a nice long honeymoon and . . ."

"Even if I agreed, I couldn't go away, Trent. I wouldn't leave Jon that long. After all, I'm all he has."

"But he'll have a father once you're my bride."

In the few months Trent had known Whitney, he had never really seen Jon. When he had come to take Whitney out, Jon was usually asleep or Addy had him playing somewhere nearby. Whitney was suddenly stricken with the thought of what would happen when Trent saw Jon. He had already seen Mitchell—the resemblance was so obvious.

Whitney felt as if the walls were closing in on her, torn between two suitors, neither of whom was the man she needed. But what did she really need? A

124

man who could offer a reasonably good life . . . Trent. A man who could see that Jon got all that he deserved . . . Trent. A man who was honest, and who could be trusted not to desert her when she needed him most . . . Trent. And a man who would be a barrier between her and the blackness that hovered in the dark . . . Trent.

"Whitney?"

"Oh, Trent, I need to think. I . . ."

"But you've spent too much time thinking already. I'm thinking of you, how you've worked and struggled alone. Now, it's time you had some help. I can make you happy, Whitney."

"I know you're thinking of my welfare, Trent, and I appreciate that. But I have to consider Jon and what I'll do with the house and . . . so many things. Berdine and Addy have looked forward to making my gown. I can't disappoint them. Those two, and Lazarus and Josiah, are about all I have left of my past."

"Whitney, as my wife you'll have to be mistress of my home. My suggestion is that you sell the land and give your friends some money to tide them along until they find a new life. You're not responsible for their future."

Trent realized he had made a mistake seconds after he said it. Whitney's eyes widened first in surprise then in growing anger. "I would not do that to the people responsible for saving my life. If anything, I would give this land to them."

"One does not just give land away, Whitney."

"It is mine to do with as I choose, and Lazarus, Berdine, Josiah, and Addy deserve it."

He clenched his teeth, keeping his smile intact. "Of course it is," he said, patronizingly enough to set her teeth on edge. "Whitney, you're too tense to make decisions now. Will you share dinner with me

125

Wednesday night?"

"The day after tomorrow?"

"Yes, I'm having a few guests in and I'd like you to meet them. If you need a new gown . . ."

"I'll manage," Whitney retorted, her cheeks flaming. She did not want Trent buying her clothes. It felt as if he were getting a hold over her. "I'll come."

"Good." He lowered his voice. "What about us?"

"I don't know, Trent. Two weeks is so fast."

"But you'll think about it?"

"Yes."

"Can I expect an answer after the dinner?"

"I won't promise. But I'll think about it, and I'll really try to give you an answer."

"It isn't as though we weren't planning a future together. This only makes it a little sooner. I'll give you everything you've missed, Whitney. It'll be like it used to be. Please remember that I love you very much."

"I will."

He kissed her again, then left. Soon she heard the sound of his carriage fading away.

She sat slowly down in a chair and clasped her hands before her. Never had she been in such a state of confusion. Trent seemed to be the answer to all her problems, but if he was, why did she feel such a sense of misgiving?

Mitch would return in a week and expect some kind of answer. She owed him nothing, yet was it fair to keep Jon a secret from him? If she married Trent, Mitch just might do something drastic.

She was frightened again, for the first time in a long time, and the taste of it brought the old terror back. How would she ever decide . . . . what would she decide? For a moment she allowed the tears to come, then she firmly brushed them aside. This was no time for tears—this was a time for decisions.

Eleven

Blake and both of Mitch's brothers watched Mitch carefully for the next two days, making wagers on whether he would really last the week out.

At first his family had been shocked to find out Whitney was alive. Then, when Blake had explained to them in more detail, they began to worry. They knew that Mitch was not one to put aside something he wanted as much as he wanted Whitney.

They all waited breathlessly—and they were right: Mitch lasted two days, then made the decision to see and talk to Lazarus. He had to know everything that had happened to Whitney. He also decided to find out all he could about Trent Donnelley. The vague whisper of memory still plagued Mitch's mind—had he seen Trent somewhere before?

Mitch waited until dark, then slipped out and went to the barn to saddle his horse.

He rode easily, remembering how many times he had done so before and the beautiful nights he had shared with Whitney under the cottonwoods.

He arrived at the two secluded homes very late. He dismounted, tied his horse carefully, and started to walk toward the clearing. A sound drew his attention and he stepped back into the shadows.

It was an open carriage and Mitch, who would have recognized Whitney anywhere at anytime, saw her clearly in the moonlight. Her companion was recognizable as well. He waited . . . and watched

. . . and grew angrier by the minute. He wasn't going to stand by and let the only thing he loved be stolen by someone else.

Trent assisted Whitney down and walked to the door with her.

"It was a lovely evening, Trent. Thank you."

"You needn't thank me. It's a pleasure to spend an evening with you. Whitney . . . have you given some thought to what I said before?"

"Yes, Trent."

"And have you decided?"

"I need more time, Trent. You promised."

"Yes, I did, and I'll honor it. But you can't blame me if I'm impatient."

"No, I suppose not."

"I am impatient, you know. I would like nothing better than to start preparations."

"I'll give you an answer soon."

"I can count on that?"

"Yes."

"Good," he said gently. He put his arms about her and drew her to him. The kiss was more passionate than she was prepared for. Her need for love and her resistance were at war.

"Good night, Trent."

"Good night, Whitney. I'll see you over the weekend."

"Yes."

"Whitney . . . you won't be making a mistake, you know. Outside of the fact that I love you, I can provide the security you need. This place is not good for a woman alone."

"I'm not alone," she reminded him gently. "These people were with me when the days and nights were truly lonely."

"I know . . . I know. But I want to give you so much more."

128

"You've been kind, and you deserve an honest answer. And I'll give you one . . . as soon as I know in my heart what it is."

"All right." He smiled, adding, "Again it's temporary surrender. But I won't give up."

"I'll remember that. Good night."

He kissed her again, wanting so much more, then turned to leave. Whitney stood on the porch for a moment then walked inside. Neither was aware of the anger-filled eyes that watched.

As the carriage disappeared, Mitch walked to the porch and silently moved across it to the door. He rapped lightly.

Whitney had just laid her shawl aside and started upstairs. She turned and smiled. Obviously Trent had forgotten to tell her something, or just wanted to say good night again. She walked to the door and opened it. Her smile faded.

"Mitch . . . . what are you doing here?"

His broad shoulders and tall body were enough to move her aside as he strode forward. He pushed the door shut and for a moment leaned against it.

"We have to talk, Whitney. This can't go on any longer."

"What do you mean *this can't go on any longer?* You promised . . ."

"To hell with that kind of promise. I stay away and act honorable and that . . . that sweet-talking scoundrel comes in and steals what's rightfully mine."

"Rightfully yours? How can you be so . . . so overbearing and conceited? Nothing is rightfully yours. You gave that up a long time ago."

"We're not going into all the ugliness of the past. Not tonight."

"What . . . ?" But her question was never finished. She recognized the look in his eyes and her heart skipped a beat.

129

"Tonight we look for the truth, Whitney . . . the truth we knew before and deserve to have again. Our own truth, Whitney."

She backed up a step or two before he reached out and gripped her waist, drawing her against him. Her hands futilely pressed against him but he was much too strong. Slowly his head bent to hers and he heard the whispered, "No," as his mouth took hers.

For a moment, one brilliant moment, she was swept up in the memory of their searing passion. Then she used all her strength to push herself away.

They were only inches apart, breathing in ragged gasps. Whitney's eyes were wide with fear. Not fear of him, but fear of herself: she had felt the raw, burning passion that had nearly destroyed her before — the lure of danger mingled with the heady scent of a need she had tried so hard to deny.

"Mitch, go away. This can't be, not now. You said . . ." She inhaled deeply. "Is this the way promises are kept, as they were in the past?"

"I didn't come here for this," he admitted.

"Why did you come?"

"Actually I wanted to talk to Lazarus."

"Lazarus? Why would you want to do that? Lazarus has not exactly been a friend of yours."

"I know . . . but Lazarus was with you all that time. He knew . . . I wanted him to tell me the things I should know, and that I was sure you would never tell me."

Lazarus! she thought in renewed panic. If Lazarus were to let her secret slip, if Mitch were to continue to come here, eventually he would know of the child! Maybe he would even see Jon. Then all would be lost.

"Let the past go, Mitch. I've done that. It's best to take each day as it comes."

"You can't kill the past by just pushing it away.

130

What we had was too important for that."

"Yes," she laughed bitterly, "so important it left your mind the day you rode away."

"That's not true. But no matter what you believe, Whitney, you can't deny what has always been between us."

"Not enough to build a lifetime on, Mitch. I need . . ."

"What?"

"I need something more . . . secure."

"What are you afraid of?" Again he sensed something bigger and stronger than anything he knew.

"You wouldn't understand."

"Try me."

"No . . . Mitch. Leave me alone."

She turned away, hoping to blot out his presence as she was denying the intensity in his eyes.

He grabbed her again and spun her around. Before she could fight back or protest he was holding her tight against him.

"What can I say to let you know how sorry I am for all that's happened? You can't do this. You can't just let go. You have to face the truth."

"Please go, Mitch . . . please! This is the way it has to be."

"We'll see," he said softly. He bent his head to kiss her gently, softly, and she uttered a sound of sheer panic and tried to escape, but his arms refused to release her. His lips played gently across hers, drifting across her cheeks and back to her lips to taste and taste again until she could have fainted with the sheer pleasure that began to fill her.

"You belong to me, Whitney . . . you belong to me, and I'll prove to you what I already know: we love each other and there's no room for anyone else."

Painfully conscious that her body was throbbing with a growing passion as he pressed her close to him, Whitney desperately tried to control her responses . . . but her control was rapidly slipping away.

Slowly his kiss warmed her. He refused to release her lips once he had captured them. Their mouths lingered together first gently, slowly turning savage and fierce, drowning all her thoughts. Tongues met as their mouths slanted across each other's in hungry impatience.

Something wild splintered inside of her and began to grow to an indescribable pleasure. She cried out as she wondered if she could bear more of this rapture.

When she could finally gasp out a word it was a trembling refusal. She had so much more to protect than he would ever know and she meant to do that with everything she had. She could not let Jon become a victim . . . but would that make one of her?

Even when he came to try to be fair, Mitch thought, her delicious body and inviting lips seemed to destroy all good intentions. Combined with the challenging coldness in her eyes, a coldness he wanted to change to the look of love he had seen before, he found it impossible to keep good intentions in mind. He came to try to talk . . . to explain, to reach her somehow. And now he wanted her so badly that his blood sang in his veins, and his senses were tangled around her slim, lush body like vines about the trees in the forest. The sheen of her skin in the mellow lamplight was like burnished gold, reflections of the same mellow light that danced in her blue eyes. Her body was warm and pressed intimately to his; he could feel her sensuous curves, combined with the trembling that made him want to hold her even closer. He wanted the trembling to cease and a loving response to replace it.

Reluctantly, Whitney was just as aware of the virile strength of the hard, taut body pressed to hers, awakening sensations she had tried in vain to forget. No man seemed to have the power to awaken in her what Mitch did. He was the one man she could not afford to respond to. Nothing could come of it but disaster, for their lives had gone in such different directions. Both wanted . . . needed different things . . . didn't they? This was obvious to her even now, as her body quivered with desire and her mind struggled to deny it.

"I cannot stand this, Mitch," she whispered. "I want to be something special to someone. You're a man who takes things casually and smiles as he waves goodbye. We're worlds apart."

"We're not worlds apart! We're only as far apart as the barriers you put between us."

"Barriers you set as well. I'm not insensitive about what you've gone through but you don't seem to think I feel. This is not the 'truth' you seem to think I feel. This is not the 'truth' you seem to be searching for."

"On the contrary. I believe you feel everything. But there's more to truth than simply feeling. Just as there's more to this. At least face one thing, Whitney," his voice lowered to a softly breathed whisper as his lips gently brushed her cheek, then slipped to her soft, half-parted mouth. She inhaled with a startled gasp as his embrace tightened and his mouth seared hers. She felt as if the core of her was melting, flowing into her limbs. Her knees almost buckled, and she clung to him with the overpowering sense that she was drowning, and he was the only stable thing to which she could hold. Her heart raced, sending her senses reeling, and he could feel the heat that matched his. Her mouth was soft, moist, and pliant beneath his, and he absorbed the sweet taste of her like the taste of water in the barren dryness.

133

One arm held her bound to him until she felt she must break, yet her body strained to his. His other hand skimmed down her back to pull her even closer.

By the time his mouth released hers, they were both breathless and caught beyond their depth in a surging river of scalding passion. Neither had the strength to escape their overwhelming need, the silent call that broke down all barriers.

Mitch caught her face between his hands, threading his fingers in her hair. With infinite gentleness he kissed her forehead, her eyes, her cheeks, then sought her mouth again. There was a soft, inarticulate sound from her depths as his mouth closed possessively over hers. No thoughts of right or wrong, or the wisdom or foolishness of what they were doing was allowed to affect their need to travel this road to the summit.

Whitney prayed that this was different, that it meant more to Mitch than before. He told her there was truth in this, and this time she wanted desperately to believe that he would know as well as she that there had to be more than passion alone.

She had only to cry out and this overpowering moment would end. But she couldn't. A flame beyond her control had melted her defiance to a need that echoed in every beat of Mitch's heart.

Nimble fingers found the hooks at the back of her dress and released them, and the thin material beneath was little barrier to his seeking hands.

Her breath was coming in ragged gasps as she ran her fingers through his thick, dark hair to press him closer. The dress slipped to the floor, and his hands caressed her warm, pulsing flesh.

Again he stopped the kiss, but only to let his lips press against the throbbing pulse at her throat and burn in scalding kisses along her shoulders and the soft flesh of her breasts. Caught in the magic, she hardly knew when he tore off his clothes.

Mitch swung her up in one fluid movement and took a step toward the couch.

She was suddenly frightened and aware that this was wrong, but he could see the pulse at the base of her throat beating frantically.

The pressure of her hands was not enough to keep him from taking her. She could feel the lean muscle of his chest pressed intimately to hers and the arm about her felt hard and strong.

An inner voice shrieked a warning that this was a trap but his mouth was already claiming hers. He took possession of her in a way that almost frightened her. She was aware of a deep, all-encompassing hunger that pulled at her, body and soul. It was almost as if she might disappear into him. She felt the edges of her being soften and dissolve.

His hand caressed the length of her body, reverence and intensity in his touch, as if he were a sculptor, intent on molding them into one.

Somewhere in the back of her mind she could almost hear a small, despairing voice asking why . . . why could she not end this . . . why could she not battle the feeling that she was drowning in his warmth?

Mitch was immersed in a seething cauldron that was rapidly melting the bones within him until he felt as if he could flow into her.

The world seemed to rock and sway as he let his mouth roam from her lips to her cheeks and throat.

His hands moved over her breasts and down the length of her body, exploring every inch of her. With her mouth still clinging to his, Whitney's mind realized dimly that she had wanted him to make love to her from the minute he had walked into the room. But none of her memories of his touch and none of her imaginings had ever been like this.

135

She felt his mouth on her breasts, lips, and tongue, teasing her nipples until she groaned, a muted, strangely incoherent sound. At the same time his hands moved lower.

"Whitney," he half-groaned as with silken body and bold seeking hands she stirred to higher heat the fury of their passion.

His tongue traced patterns on her flesh, sending a tingling shudder through her with his feather touch. Lower and lower he moved, nipping gently at her flesh with his teeth until she wanted to scream.

Gentle hands parted her thighs and suddenly she felt the piercing heat of his seeking tongue and her hands caught at him and tangled in the thickness of his hair to urge him on.

Suddenly he was above her and her body arched in shock as with a deep thrust he embedded himself in the depths of her.

She began to move, inexorably and steadily. Her body quivered with delight. Her breath came in short gasps and soft moans escaped her. Prisoners of unexplained enchantment, they moved together, her slim body arching to meet each driving thrust and her hand moving over his body, digging into the muscles of his back, sliding down to the hard, muscular hips to urge him deeper. Each was hungry for fulfillment, each was aware of the other's needs, giving and taking, lifting higher and higher until his mouth was all that silenced her cries of ecstasy as they soared to the pinnacle and beyond.

The pale gold glow of the candelabra put the area where they lay half in shadow, half in light.

Mitch gazed down at Whitney, mesmerized by the beauty of the pale light against her skin.

No woman had been able to enchant him as this one had. But at the same time he was reveling in the magic of loving her, he saw tears escape from beneath her closed lids. They hurt him as no wound ever had.

He sat up, drawing her up beside him. Then he lifted her chin and forced her to meet his eyes.

"I don't want to hurt you, Whitney. Why do you think I do? What is it that keeps you from seeing what we have?"

"Maybe," she said softly, "I haven't yet been able to put the bad memories away. Maybe I never will be able to."

"We all suffered from the war and the way it tore our lives apart. But you hold it, and everything that happened, like a wall between us. If you don't talk to me and tell me what it is, how can I fight it?"

"I don't want you to fight it. It's not your battle to fight, it's mine. I can't lie to you after tonight and tell you that I no longer respond to you physically. But I can't base my future on physical love. I did that once before and the price was too high. I have a responsibility to . . . others as well as myself. I cannot allow this to change my mind."

"What others? Lazarus? Who else lives here with you?"

She grew cold with renewed fear, but determinedly held her voice steady.

"Berdine, Addy, and Josiah. They helped with the work, nursed me like their own child when I was . . . sick. They knew that I suffered when your letters no longer came. They even helped me through that. I cannot just discard them when you return with your sweet talk and your promises and your kisses. I cannot forget. I'll make my own decisions . . . in my own time."

"Sweet talk, promises, and kisses. Is that all this was for you? What am I to believe, Whitney? You respond with a passion beyond all my dreams. Yet you deny me and our future."

137

"I must plan my own future."

"Without me?"

"If that's the best way."

"I won't let that happen, Whitney. That's one promise you can count on. I still think there's a whole lot more you won't tell me."

"What more could there be?" She rose and began to dress, avoiding his eyes.

"I don't know."

"There's no more. The past is too hard to forget. I have to face the future knowing I won't be hurt like that again."

"There's pain in everyone's future one way or the other. There's no escaping that. No one can see ahead or plan a life that's all sunshine and roses. But at least if you have someone to face the rainy days with, it's easier."

"I thought that once, but the storms came and I was alone."

"Whitney, I never stopped loving you."

"Don't, Mitch. I'm so confused and exhausted. I don't want professions of love. I simply want to be left alone to make my own decisions."

He sighed and stood up. No matter how he tried he could not seem to get through to her. Nor could he wipe from his mind the thought that there was still a secret holding them apart. He had won a battle, but the war still raged and it was a war he couldn't bear to lose. Sometimes, he thought, strategic retreat was the better way to ensure another confrontation.

He needed answers she would not provide. Lazarus and Berdine and maybe Addy were the other links in the chain. He would retreat, but speaking to Lazarus was still his next step . . . and he intended to take that step when Whitney was not here to stop him.

"All right, Whitney. I guess you're right. I forced something tonight that I shouldn't have. I'll go . . . but I won't give up."

She was so relieved at his willingness to go that she barely heard the rest of his words or the vow that he would return.

"It's better this way. Believe me it is. Whatever I decide, I'll talk to you myself."

"Before you do anything else."

"Yes. Before I agree to marry Trent Donnelley."

"Whitney . . ."

"No, no threats, Mitch."

He moved closer. "Then I'll go. But not before I kiss you again. I need it to remember . . . just in case."

"It's not wise. I . . ."

His arms were around her and his mouth stopped her words. The kiss told her more than anything he could have said. "Good night, my love," he whispered. "But not goodbye . . . never goodbye."

Then he was gone, and Whitney slowly sat down in a chair. She knew with certainty the biggest battles of her life were yet to be fought.

Twelve

His confrontation with Whitney did not stop Mitch's desire to talk to one of the four people who had shared the traumatic experiences with her — experiences that had closed her mind. He was fighting ghosts and, from the look on her face when he left, he was losing the battle.

This, of course, brought his thoughts back to the biggest thorn in his side, Trent Donnelley. The uncomfortable feeling returned and he was sure it was somehow important to find out a great deal more about the man.

Obviously he had been good to Whitney yet she was having a difficult time. But if she cared deeply for this man, why was she having such a struggle? If she loved Donnelley, why allow another man in her life at all? This thought intrigued him and the longer it lingered the more he liked it.

She had been content with Donnelley until he had returned. His stepping back into her life had disturbed her a great deal, and the only answer to that was she really didn't love Trent. The memories he had revived had destroyed her new-found security.

But why the battle? Why not pick up where they had left off? Why the barrier? No, there had to be another reason, one he still didn't know. But he intended to find out.

He spent the next two days watching the house,

leaving at dawn before his family rose and arriving home late at night while they were asleep.

He was rewarded the third day when he saw the carriage before Whitney's door. She had to be leaving. He watched to make sure which of her friends would accompany her.

He watched Whitney leave the house and stand by the carriage. He was prepared for many things, but not for what he saw. A child!

The boy ran out onto the porch and Mitch could see Whitney turn, laugh, and stretch out her arms to catch him as he leapt fearlessly into her arms. The shock was staggering. There was no doubt the child was hers, and that he was most likely the problem that had been troubling her. Someone had comforted Whitney in his absence, and the child was the result. No wonder she was afraid of him. He was filled with a surge of jealous anger.

He had one of his answers, and it filled his mind with stinging questions. Who? And why? And worse, how long had she stayed faithful to him? It couldn't have been long—the child looked somewhere around three. It must have happened at nearly the same time he had left for the last time. The agony of another question filled him. Was she seeing this . . . intruder at the same time she was with him? Had it all been a kind of game for her . . . playing with the life of someone she was sure was no threat to her affluent life?

Though he tried to deny it, pain twisted within him like the blade of a knife.

The carriage rolled away and for a long moment he was tempted simply to leave and never return. What was left to say? She wanted him to go and, if he had any pride or sense, he would.

But Mitch's stubbornness held him on his course. He would talk to Lazarus and seek more information. Whether he would ever go to Whitney again was a question he would decide after some very careful thought.

When the carriage was gone from sight he mounted his horse. From his vantage point he could see Lazarus walking into the woods, an ax on his shoulder. Mitch urged his horse forward.

He crossed the clearing and entered the woods as he began to hear the sharp sound of the ax. When he soundlessly approached, Lazarus had his back to him. Mitch watched the strong arms swing the ax easily.

Within a few feet he stopped his horse and dismounted.

"Lazarus."

The ax froze in mid-swing, then Lazarus slowly turned. Mitchell Flannery was the last person he expected to see. Lazarus felt filled with disdain. This was the man who had caused Whitney such agony.

"Mitchell Flannery," he said coldly.

"Yes."

"What yo' doin' here 'bouts, boy? Ah thought yo' was de kind to be runnin' to de winnin' side."

"The war's over, Lazarus."

"Is it now? Mebbe fo' sum folks de war nebber be over."

"We have a lot to talk about."

"We," Lazarus mocked, laughing softly. "Ah hain't got nuthin' to say to yo', boy . . . nuthin'."

"No? Maybe we ought to go back to the cabin to talk."

"Mebbe yo' oughta git offen dis land."

"It's yours?"

"Some of it."

"And who else's?"

"Dat hain't none o' yo' business."

"Still think you're protecting her, Lazarus?"

142

He could see the surprise in Lazarus's eyes before they closed against him. "Ah shoulda done a better job of it befo'. Ah nebber shoulda carried dose letters."

"Lazarus, I never meant to hurt Whitney. I loved her."

Lazarus turned his head and spat, then returned his cold gaze to Mitch.

"What yo' know 'bout love, boy? Yo' beds a girl an' dat's given a fine name like love. But later yo' jus' rolls on yo' own way. Why yo' come back here?"

"I came for what belonged to me."

"Nuthin' belongs to yo'."

"Whitney did. Until another came along."

"Mr. Donnelley, he doin' his best to make Miz Whitney happy. Yo' leave her alone."

"I don't mean Trent Donnelley."

Lazarus's face revealed his puzzlement.

"I mean whoever came along after I left."

"Yo' sayin' sumthin' so mean ah don' rightly wanna hear no mo'. Miz Whitney, she a fine lady. She doan deserve no mo' pain den she already had. So speak yo' piece an' git on yo' way."

"Lazarus . . . I'm not going to let Whitney marry Trent Donnelley."

"How yo' gonna stop her?"

"Any way I can."

Lazarus was much more frightened than Mitch could know. He did not know how much Mitch knew—he only knew Whitney was in great danger.

"Why yo' want to ruin her life like dat? She needs some peace, too. Yo' cain't do her nuthin' but harm."

"You seem to know everything that happened, Lazarus, so I assume Whitney has no secrets from you. You've disapproved all along but you were wrong. I loved her then . . . and," he added to his own surprise, "I love her now, no matter what she

143

thinks I've done. Lazarus, I need your help."

"Yo' gots a lotta nerve, boy. Ah hain't helpin' yo' do nuthin' no mo'. Ah was a slave back then. Ah gots a choice now. And ah'll do everything, an' anything Ah kin to make sure yo' don' get near her."

"Maybe you can't stop me."

"Ah'll sho' as hell give it a try."

"All I want is to talk to you, Lazarus. Is answering questions too much?"

"What kinda questions?"

"I was away a long time. I have to know . . ."

"What?"

"What happened. What hurt her, what she had to go through."

"Why yo' has to know now? It's too late to do anythin'?"

"It's never too late."

"Ah doan think Ah kin do dat. Her life's her own. She gittin' over de hurt. Ah hain't doin' nothin' to remind her."

"Then just tell me about that day, the day they burned the house."

Lazarus was perplexed. Why should this man care about the past? Why should it matter how things occurred? They had happened and that was enough. It made no difference anymore. Yet it seemed to matter a great deal to Mitchell Flannery.

"Dey hain't much to tell. Dey cum too fast. We knew we din have much time so we took what we could grab up. Miz Whitney could only save a small bundle of things. Dey done looted den burned de house. It was too much fo' Miz Hope. She done lost all her will when her man, den her son . . . she die later. Miz Whitney, she couldn't even cry no mo'. She bury her ma . . . den she fight . . . fo' a long time she fight. She dig in de ground an' she scrub an' clean an' went hungry sometime. But she fight."

He watched closely. "Dat why she got de strength to fight now. Dat why all yo' big ideas doan mean nuthin' no mo'. Ah said what happened, now yo' go 'way an' doan bring her no mo' heartache . . . or befo' God ah'll see yo' buried, too."

Mitch had been silent, vividly imagining everything Lazarus was saying. He felt the pain Whitney must have suffered. She had lost so much. Then she thought she had lost him. She had stood alone against everything. He was sick with the pictures that flashed in his mind.

"I don't want to hurt her any more, Lazarus."

"Den go 'way."

"I wish you could understand that I can't," Mitch said with a grimace.

"Yo' best," Lazarus said quietly. "Yo' best."

"I don't want to be your enemy, Lazarus."

"Yo' Miz Whitney's enemy . . . yo' mine."

"Damn it, man, things are not like you think."

"Ah doan think 'bout how things are. Ah knows Miz Whitney. Ah'll stand wif her no matter what. So's yo' don' misunderstand. Yo' cum 'round, yo' give her mo' tears to cry . . . an' yo' will wish yo' gots yo'self killed in de war."

"You're a hard-headed man, Lazarus." Mitch's voice had a touch of bitter humor.

"Yassuh." Lazarus's mouth twitched in a responding smile.

"Stubborn."

"Yassuh."

"You think you can stop me?"

"One way . . . or de other. Yassuh. Ah'll stop yo' iffen ah has to."

Lazarus's confidence and trust were two things Mitch would have given his right arm for. He was just as determined to earn that as he was to have Whitney back. But the first battle had just been

145

fought and he had lost it. It was the second time in the past few days he had to back off . . . and he was getting damn tired of retreating.

"All right, Lazarus. I'll go for now. But remember something. This is my home, too, and I'm not leaving. Whitney and I . . . well, we're bound to cross paths again. You can't stop that."

"Where she go an' whose path she cross, dat her affair. But here, on dis land an' in her house . . . yo' ain't welcome."

"Unless Whitney invites me."

"She won't."

"But if she does?"

"Ah'll try to stop her."

"And if you can't?"

"Ah guess," Lazarus said calmly, "ah'll jes' cross dat bridge iffen ah gits to it."

"You'll get to it."

"Yo' so sure?"

"Yes . . . I'm sure."

"Yo' doan know . . ."

"What?"

"Fo'git it."

"I know there's a lot I don't know, Lazarus. But you see, I've got time on my side. One day Whitney will belong to me and you'll be my friend."

"Hain't likely."

"Would you care to make a wager?"

"A what?"

"A bet, Lazarus."

"Ah gots nuthin' to bet." Lazarus's mouth again twitched in an uncertain smile.

"We'll worry about that later."

"Awright . . . so we bet. But what ah said befo' stands. Yo' hain't welcome on dis land. Our talkin's over. Now yo' gits gone."

Mitch sighed. It was doing little good to talk to

146

Lazarus. He was more than certain that Lazarus could and would do just as he said. He didn't even want to try to fight him.

"All right. Lazarus . . . I'm grateful you told me what happened that night."

"It doan make no neverminds iffen ah tol' yo' or not. Ah know de kin' of lady Miz Whitney turn out to be. She was innocent an' trustin' befo' . . . she hain't so trustin' now. An' she hain't gwine listen to no sweet talk agin. She work hard fo' what she got. She hain't gwine give it up easy."

"Even if she marries the wrong man?"

"She hain't marryin' yet." Lazarus looked away as he spoke and Mitch's heart leapt. Lazarus wasn't too confident that Trent Donnelley was the man for Whitney either.

"Have it your way, Lazarus."

"Ah guess dat doan leave us too much to talk 'bout. Ah doan 'spects to see yo' roun' here agin." He put the ax on his shoulder and Mitch had to admit he was a formidable wall of a man and the ax didn't make him any more pleasant.

He touched the brim of his hat in a quick salute. "I'll be around, Lazarus." He started to walk away.

"Not iffen yo' wants to keep on breathin'."

There was little left to say. Lazarus would not let him anywhere near. And Whitney was much too protective to allow Lazarus to be hurt or pushed aside. It was going to be a very rough course.

Lazarus watched Mitch walk away, his brow furrowed in a deep frown. He had told Mitch all he had because he wanted him to understand that Whitney was no longer the girl he had left behind. Mitch's confident attitude worried Lazarus because Mitch was also no longer the boy who had gone off to war.

He knew that Whitney would die before she would allow Mitch to walk back into her life . . . and her son's life. That the boy looked so much like Mitch was another thing that unsettled Lazarus. If Mitch were to see the boy . . . but he wouldn't; Lazarus would see to that.

Lazarus wasn't too sure he should even let Whitney know that Mitchell Flannery had been there. It would unsettle her, make her frightened again, and just when she had started to get some confidence back.

Berdine had always been so much more clever than he about such things. He picked up the ax and started back to the house. He would tell Berdine what had happened . . . what Mitchell Flannery had said. She would know what to do.

Berdine hummed softly to herself as she worked in the kitchen. She was a tall woman, a descendant of the Watusi tribes. She had fine bone structure despite her height and her black eyes bore an Egyptian slant, whispering of an even more ancient ancestry. She had also inherited an awareness and deep intelligence that had little to do with education. Her age was unguessable, for her face bore few wrinkles even though her eyes held many memories. Her hair was just a short cap and her skin glistened ebony in the light of the fireplace.

She looked up in surprise when Lazarus entered. She expected no one at this time of day and she knew Addy, Josiah, Whitney, and Jon were gone.

"What yo' doin' here? Yo' ates 'nuff fo' breakfast fo' two hosses."

"Ah din't come to eat," Lazarus said thickly. He sat down at the table and rested his elbows on it. "Ah gots to talk to yo' 'bout sumthin', Berdine."

"What's botherin' yo' mind?"

"Miz Whitney."

148

"What's wrong wif her?" He could hear the touch of alarm in her voice. Whitney was like Berdine's child and any threat to her was a threat to Berdine.

"Nuthin' wrong wif her. Ah gots to tell sumbody an' yo's de only one kin understan'." He raised his eyes to meet hers. "Dat boy, he back, dat Mitchell Flannery."

"How yo' knows?"

"Ah talked to him. Tol' him git offen mah land."

"He believe yo'? He din't ask no questions 'bout how yo' got land?"

"Berdine . . . he knows Miz Whitney here."

"He know anythin' else?"

"Yo' 'mean 'bout de boy?"

"What yo' tell him?"

"Ah hain't tol' him nuthin'."

Berdine sat down at the table opposite Lazarus. "Now yo' tell me what happened."

Lazarus began to talk and Berdine did not interrupt until he finished telling her everything.

"What yo' think, Berdine? We oughta tell her . . . mebbe even tell him?"

"Ah knowed dis day gwine happen sumtime."

"It ain't fair."

"Nuthin's fair. De Lawd do things his own way. Ain't our right to say what's fair or no. Everybody gets good an' bad."

"Miz Whitney, she had mo' den 'nuff bad."

"Mebbe so, mebbe so. But she have some good, too."

"What we gwine do? We cain't let him cum roun' here. Miz Whitney don' need nebber to know."

"Man's got rights, too, Lazarus. He gots a son."

"He be Miz Whitney's boy!"

"He be his boy, too."

"What yo' sayin'?"

"Ah'm sayin' dat things is in de hans of de Lawd.

149

Iffen he want dat man to know 'bout his boy he guide his feet an' heart. He doan want him to know, he take him away."

"Yo' means we doan say nuthin'?"

"That's right."

"What 'bout iffen he run 'cross Miz Whitney somewheres?"

"Then she tell him what she want him to know."

"What if he see de boy?"

"Lazarus, dat boy his son. Now I love Miz Whitney same as yo', but she hain't always right. Dat boy, he gwine git hungry fo' a man to show him how a man has to walk."

"Iffen she marry dat Donnelley den de boy has a new daddy."

"Ain't rightly de same."

"Ah doan like it."

"Ah doan either."

"Berdine . . . yo' gots to tell her."

Berdine was silent for quite some time, then she sighed in resignation.

"Mebbe yo' right. Maybe ah best tell her. But it sho' gwine make her unhappy. 'Specially since she thinkin' on marryin' wif dat . . . dat other man."

"Yo' doan particular care fo' dat Trent Donnelley, does yo'?"

"Does yo'?"

"Doan rightly say ah does. It jes' . . . well, ah figger if he make Miz Whitney happy den ah keeps mah mouth shut."

"Maybe dis de Lawd's way of givin' Miz Whitney choices. He pushin' her to a corner so's she has to decide."

"She powerful hurt when dat boy run off. Ah heard de night she swore she hate him."

"Dat kind of hate sometime like birthin' pain — yo' forgits it in time."

150

"Or yo' gits stubborn . . . an' Miz Whitney's sho' dat."

"We in de middle. We love Miz Whitney an' we love de boy. We jus' doan rightly know if what's best fo' de one is best fo' de other. Best thing we kin do is tell her an' let her do her own decidin'. She hold dat boy sumthin' fierce. Mayhap she do de right way . . . fo' both of dem."

"Mebbe," Lazarus said, doubt heavy in his voice. "Jes' mebbe."

Berdine watched him as he walked to the door and closed it softly behind him.

"Yo' might be right, Lazarus . . . yo' jes' might be right. Ah sho' hopes de good Lawd is watchin' close. Dat chile gwine need Him."

Thirteen

Mitch rode slowly home, not sure why he hadn't told Lazarus he knew about the child.

"If I had brought that up Lazarus might just have used that ax on me," he muttered.

He thought of all that had been between him and Whitney before the war. And yet she had turned to another man. God, had she just been making a fool of him? And there was a child, a child that belonged to Whitney. He would have given his very soul to have that.

He was so shaken that he could not seem to control his thoughts. What should he do next?

"Whitney," he murmured. He wanted Whitney, and he wanted to heal the past and make a new life with her. Only that wasn't going to be so easy.

But he knew for certain that somehow he was going to stop Whitney from marrying Trent Donnelley.

He had to talk to Whitney again. She hadn't mentioned the child, so obviously she didn't want him to know. But he did, and he felt he had a right to know more.

He had to think, to plan. He knew Donnelley was becoming influential, so he felt it was time he put what money he had to work. Land was cheap. Huge plantations were being sold for the taxes most people could no longer pay. So his first move would be to get his hands on as much land as he could. Then he would build the home he had always dreamed of . . . the home he had once promised Whitney. He'd fought enough battles to know it was always best to meet your enemy on his own ground, so after the land would come seeking information about Trent Donnelley. There was no doubt in his mind that he had seen him somewhere before. If he could just remember where, he had a feeling it might change things a great deal.

He arrived home to find Blake had gone into town, so he threw himself into working with his father and brothers. He immersed himself in the work and the companionship—it was like times past and he needed the temporary escape.

Mitch had not been the only one to feel certain he had seen Trent before. Blake was troubled with the same idea. He knew Mitch was going to talk to Lazarus so he decided a trip to town might be constructive.

He was Mitch's best friend, and he wanted to see Mitch's problems settled, but he was beginning to feel displaced. The war had shaken his life, too. Maybe it was time to go back home and try to pick up the pieces as Mitch was trying to do.

The town was a bustle of construction. The muddied streets did nothing to inhibit the passage of buggies and wagons, and crowds of newcomers milled about on the wood-planked sidewalks. There was a cacophony of sound—pounding hammers, grating saws, and the shouts of men.

Blake let his horse wander slowly down the street, absorbing the noise with half his mind, while the other half wondered what he could possibly find out.

Could he piece together more of the Clayborn story? Surely this woman had friends who still lived here, or had made friends with at least one or two people her age. He just couldn't picture her living out there in such a remote area.

153

There was a lengthy main street with two others that crossed at each end. Between these side streets were several shadowed alleys.

The street was lined with old and new buildings, and Blake could count at least three banks. Someone in the town was making money, he thought. A bank might just be the first place to try. After all, banks handle or know about every piece of property in the area.

He tied his horse to a rail, dismounted, and walked slowly down the street toward the first bank. He had to cross one of the alleys and had started to do just that when the sounds of a scuffle and a muted cry of distress drew his gaze down the alley.

He was startled to see two figures struggling while a third looked for an opportunity to support the more aggressive one. From the flash of white petticoats Blake could tell one was a woman and her position was degenerating rapidly. He could hear the tearing sound of cloth and another cry of distress. She was giving an account of herself but the odds were too much against her. Both men were large and from what he could see she was not much over a hundred pounds.

Blake grasped the situation instantly. He drew his pistol from beneath his jacket, shouted, and ran toward the struggle. The unoccupied man saw him first, took in his size and the pistol, and decided retreat was the better part of valor.

But his friend was too occupied trying to subdue a mass of feminine fury he found harder to tame than he had thought.

Blake wasted no time and slammed his gun barrel down on the man's head. The man grunted and released the girl, who backed against the wall of the building. Then he staggered a bit while he looked around for the source of the assault.

He was a hulking bear of a man and Blake's blow did little to weaken him. Blake was wise enough to know that a physical tangle with this man was insanity, so he simply raised the pistol menacingly.

"I wouldn't, my friend. At this distance I could put a hole right between your eyes, although I doubt if there's much there to stop a bullet."

The man froze for a moment, glaring at Blake.

"Who the hell are you?"

"I don't think formal introductions are necessary. I'm giving you two minutes to get out of here."

The man glared from beneath a neanderthal brow, his beady black eyes slowly absorbing Blake's ultimatum. He cast a quick look at the girl, muttered an obscenity under his breath, and lumbered away. Blake watched him, making sure he left the alley before he turned his attention to the girl, who was quietly regarding him. He tucked the pistol safely away and walked over to her.

"Are you all right?"

"Yes," she said softly as she gathered her torn dress closer. Her assailant had been intent on rape, and had torn her dress in several places. One shoulder was completely exposed and several buttons were torn from the front, leaving it open. She clutched it and looked up at Blake. "I'm very grateful to you, sir."

"That's quite all right. I'm glad I was passing. Can I help you?" Blake was trying his best to keep his eyes from the flesh revealed by the torn dress, but it was very difficult. She was an extraordinarily pretty girl.

Her embarrassment was beginning to show in her flushed cheeks and the trembling hand that held her dress together.

Blake removed his jacket and placed it gently around her shoulders. He realized she was in a state of shock.

"If you'd like I could take you home," he said comfortingly. "Do you live nearby?"

She seemed to be regaining her strength. She looked up at him with great amber eyes, and he could see flecks of gold in their depths.

155

"No . . . no, I was on my way back to the office and I thought I wouldn't be late if I just . . . just," her voice faltered.

"Took a short cut," he supplied.

"Yes."

"A pretty girl like you should never walk alone through a dim alley. There's a pretty bad element in the country right now. It's dangerous."

"Yankees," she muttered with a half-choked sob. "Damn Yankees." Her voice was bitter.

"Wait a minute," Blake replied, still trying to be supportive. "From the looks of the remnants on those two, they were rebs. I'm the one who's a Yankee."

Startled, she looked up at him again. Blake tried a friendly smile, but in the face of her obvious revulsion it was somewhat difficult.

"I'm grateful for what you've done, sir," she replied, her voice intoning everything but gratitude. She took the jacket from her shoulders and handed it back. "I can find my way now."

"You can't go out on the street like that," he insisted, trying to change the subject. "If they see you like this in the company of a Yankee they might get the wrong idea." He handed the jacket back to her. "Please," he said gently, "I'm a stranger here and I don't want to be lynched for something I didn't do."

She knew he was right, that it was the man and not the uniform that made a difference. She had enough conscience to blush again.

"I work very near here. I'll be fine."

"Don't you think I at least deserve to know your name? I'm Blake Randolph."

"I don't think it's necessary since we're unlikely to meet again." She started to move away.

"And I was told the South was famous for its hospitality and its sense of honor."

He knew she could barely keep from striking him. Finally she reached for the jacket and put it around her shoulders. Whatever else she felt, she could not deny she was grateful for the comfort of its concealment.

"You said you work near here? Shall I escort you there, or would you rather go home?"

They both knew he was anxious to find out where she lived, but she had no intention of telling him no matter how gallant he had been.

"I have a packet of needles and thread at work, so I can repair my dress there. Don't put yourself out any further. I can return to work safely on my own."

But Blake wasn't about to give up that easily and was already taking hold of her arm to guide her out of the alley. "No trouble at all," he said amiably. "Just tell me where we're going."

"To the newspaper office," she answered unwillingly. They started to walk side by side.

"You still haven't told me your name."

"Mr. Randolph, I don't see . . ."

Blake was pleased that she had remembered his name even in her state of confusion, and he was determined to know hers.

"Why, I have to know since you don't intend to see me again," he replied. "But you see, you're mistaken. I intend to see you again." He grinned, adding, "So you might as well tell me now."

"You *do* have Yankee persistence."

"Not necessarily Yankee," he said with a chuckle. "But I *am* persistent. Especially if it's important."

"Why should it be important? Do you think the conquerers have subjugated us?" Again there was that flash of cold bitterness. Obviously the war had not been easy for her.

"I'm sorry if I offended you," he said quietly. "I never meant to do that."

"And I never meant to insult a man who saved my honor but it is best, you know." She stopped walking to look up at him and he could do nothing but stop.

"There's no love in my family for Yankees. Nothing will make them change their minds."

"Or you either?"

"I don't apologize for that," she replied stiffly. "I'm only telling you what the situation is, so it's best you go your way with my thanks."

"Grudging thanks. What if I told you that was not enough?"

"You're presuming on my gratitude. It will have to be enough. Please . . . I ask you," she pleaded. She lowered her voice and her eyes grew even wider, the gold flecks dancing. "Leave me here."

"Only if you tell me your name. If you don't, I'll walk right into the lion's den."

"You may be eaten."

"Maybe. What's your name?"

Their eyes held for some seconds and hers were the first to retreat. She backed up a step.

"Noel," she whispered. "Noel Anderson."

She turned and nearly ran from him and he watched until she disappeared into the newspaper office.

"Noel Anderson," he repeated, then smiled. "You haven't seen the last of *this* Yankee, Noel Anderson. Lion's den or no lion's den."

Blake continued down the sidewalk; it was some time before he could force his mind away from Noel Anderson and back to the reason he had come into town.

When Blake got back to the Flannery home Mitch was still out in the field with Morgan. Shawn and Stuart had returned to prepare for the evening meal.

They were standing on the porch before basins of water, when Blake rode up.

"Good evening, Blake. You're just in time for supper."

"Good evening, Mr. Flannery," Blake replied as he dismounted. "I'm hungry enough to eat a horse. Where's Mitch?"

158

Stuart and Shawn exchanged glances. "He's still in the field with Morgan," Shawn answered. "Do you want me to go for him?"

"No, you go on in and I'll go out. I want to talk to him anyway and we can do it as we walk back."

Both Stuart and Shawn watched in silence as Blake walked towards the field.

He could see Mitch and Morgan in the distance. They stood, finished with the day's work but talking. After a few moments they noticed Blake's approach. The setting sun reflected across the land like molten gold bathing the dark forms of the men.

When Blake grew close enough Mitch yelled, "Why is it, my friend, you're always late for work?"

Blake laughed. "Because you're a masochist doesn't mean I am." He grew closer and finally stopped beside them. "Supper's ready and it smells good."

Mitch knew that Blake wanted to talk to him. He clapped Morgan on the shoulder. "Go on in, Morgan. I have a few things I'd like to discuss with Blake."

Morgan nodded and walked away and Mitch and Blake stood together in the twilight for a while in silent yet comfortable camaraderie.

"You love this land, Mitch," Blake said softly.

"Yes . . . I do . . . I had plans . . ."

"Plans for a good life, like we all had."

"I guess so. A lot of dreams have been shattered."

"The war has cost you a lot."

"More than I bargained for. But I guess everyone has suffered the same."

"Yes, I suppose so. Have you settled anything? Did you talk to this Lazarus?"

"Yes, I did." Mitch went on to explain what Lazarus had said. "It's not going to be easy."

"But you won't quit."

"I hope not. Maybe I've finally run across something that threatens my manhood." Mitch laughed uneasily.

"Just what is this . . . threat?"

"She had a baby," Mitch said quietly.

"What?"

"A child, damn it! A child I would have given my life for."

"God," Blake breathed. "Mitch . . . . have you talked to her? Have you let her explain?"

"She doesn't even know that I know."

"What are you going to do?"

"I've been asking myself the same question."

"You love her."

Mitch was quiet for so long Blake thought he didn't mean to answer. Then he spoke softly.

"I wish I loved her less. I wish she didn't own my soul and everything I am. Maybe then I could let her go. But I can't."

It suddenly struck Blake that he knew what Mitch was talking about.

"Let's get back to the house," Mitch said. "My mother gets upset when meals sit and get cold."

They began walking together.

"Mitch?"

"Yes?"

"Did you know a family around here named Anderson?"

"Anderson," Mitch repeated thoughtfully.

"I don't know the family, but there's a girl named Noel."

"Noel! Of course. Noel Anderson. They used to have a big plantation about twenty miles from here. She had a big family — four brothers and a sister, Emma. Noel was pretty if I remember well."

"Beautiful is more like it."

"So you've met her?"

Blake told Mitch what had transpired in town.

"She works in a newspaper office?"

"That's what she said. I watched her go in."

"That's surprising . . . then again, with everything that's happened I wouldn't be surprised at much."

"I found out a couple of things that might be of interest."

"Like what?"

"Like a whole lot of big plantations that were deserted or destroyed are going to face a big problem."

"Problem? What problem?"

"Taxes, back taxes."

"That's ridiculous. Where did these taxes come from?"

"Mitch, there's a lot of northern money . . . and power down here now, not to mention an avid interest in land."

"So what is it you found out?"

"The land your . . . friend owned. It's going to be sold before long."

"How did you find out?"

"A talkative bank clerk who's a sucker for a free meal and a couple strong drinks."

"How many others know about it?"

"I'd say very few so far."

Again they walked in silence.

"Then I think a trip into town is on the agenda for tomorrow," Mitch said.

"What are you going to do?"

"Buy it if it takes every last dime."

"Mitch . . ."

"No warning, friend."

"She might never forgive you."

"It's a chance I have to take."

"But . . ."

"Blake, what if someone else bought it? What if she never had a chance to get that land back?"

"But the house was destroyed."

"Another can be built."

"Can't I dissuade you?"

"No, it's something I feel right about. If I can't give her anything else, maybe I can give her that."

"That's not enough between you and her and you know it."

"Sure, I know it."

"Mitch . . ."

"I know it but she doesn't."

"I hope you know what you're doing."

"I'll give her time to get over the shock, then make sure she knows I'm going to fight like hell to get her back."

"And the child?"

"That's something we'll have to talk about."

"Christ, I hate this damn war," Blake growled.

"And you won," Mitch added softly.

Mitch lay in his dark bedroom unable to find release from his painful thoughts.

Whitney had suffered through things that he could barely imagine. He conjured up his memories: fun loving Whitney, flirting Whitney, laughing and happy Whitney . . . and loving Whitney. If, in despair, she had found a moment of peace in someone else's arms, could he blame her? Could he love the child as if it were his? He loved Whitney and he wanted Whitney. Now he had to convince her he was the best man.

His thoughts finally turned to Trent Donnelley. He had to remember where he had first met this man because, for some reason, he felt it might be his key to winning Whitney.

There was a phantom from the past and he knew he had to shed light on it before Whitney could ever be his again.

Fourteen

Trent sat back in his chair and slowly lit his cigar. Over the haze of blue-white smoke he studied the man across the table. Andrew Crocket was one of the most prominent bankers in Holly Hill, and although his bank was founded under questionable circumstances, he was amassing a great deal of property.

He was one of very few people in the city who knew about the darker side of Trent Donnelley. But it suited him, for he and Trent had the same ultimate goals. They weren't just after money, for each was well off. No, they wanted power, the one thing both craved and would use any measures to possess. Together they meant to own the town and as much around it as they could acquire.

Andrew supported Trent in his bid for political office. He made sure Trent met all the right people at the right functions and had pulled every string, called in every favor.

He was amused to know Trent felt they were peers. When the time came, he mused greedily, even Trent would dance to his tune.

"You've waited a long time to get your hands on this particular piece of land," Andrew began.

"A long time. And then I'll marry Whitney Clayborn. With her name and the land and money I already have, it'll only be a matter of time until I control this whole area."

"Has she mentioned her brother?"

"No, but his letters were one of the few things she saved when the place was burnt. I thought those men had orders to search first."

"They did. From what I gather, the majority of them were drunk. I guess they got carried away."

"Well, at least she saved the letters. It must be in them somewhere and she just doesn't realize what she has."

"Do you ever intend to enlighten her?" Andrew's smile was amused, while his dark eyes glittered with avarice.

"I hardly see the need for that," Trent replied as he chuckled. "She need never know. What she doesn't know won't hurt her."

"And if she did know?"

"I'm afraid it would be costly . . . very costly."

"I see."

"Andrew, are the wheels in motion?"

"For your election?"

"Yes."

"I've greased enough palms. Now you have to get ready. I've scheduled a large rally in two weeks to kick things off. There's no one who can run against you."

"Good."

"Trent, we'll owe a few favors after the election. I've made promises to some very influential . . . and rather demanding people."

Trent shrugged. "Whatever it takes."

"Just so you know," Andrew murmured. Trent paid little heed to the satisfied look in Andrew's eyes. He liked men with big ambitions and little morals. It made his own goals much easier to attain. He raised his glass of wine.

"Here's to your seduction of the elusive Miss Clayborn," Andrew said sarcastically. "It seems you'll also become a father at the same time you acquire a bride."

"Hardly," Trent said dryly. "The brat isn't mine and I certainly don't intend to make him part of my life."

"You'll get rid of him?"

"Of course. There are many ways . . . schools, military academies. One way or another."

"And if his mother protests?"

Trent glared at Andrew. "Once she's my wife Whitney will soon learn to understand who's in charge. Whatever she needs to be taught I'll take great pleasure in teaching her. Eventually she will eat from my hand like a tamed puppy. She'll do a great deal to ensure the safety of her precious child."

"Ah." Andrew's sigh was filled with understanding. He had truly found a man after his own heart—one who would stop at nothing to get what he wanted.

"Trent, what about this Mitchell Flannery?"

"What about him?"

"In the past few weeks he's begun to buy land. More than that, he's ingratiating himself with quite a few people. I just had Stanton Thorpe tell me the other day that Mr. Flannery would make a good representative in Washington."

"Damn!" Trent muttered as he took another quick drink. Andrew could see the hatred in Trent's eyes and couldn't resist prodding him.

"There are also a few rumors about him and your lady. Could there be any truth to them?"

Trent was stunned and tried his best to hide it, but it leapt into his eyes and Andrew didn't miss it. Jealousy could be used like a two-edged sword.

"Mitchell Flannery is no threat to our plans."

"No?"

"No."

"What if he should gain enough support to run against you?"

"He'll never get that far."

"You should get rid of him. If you turn your back on an enemy it might be a fatal mistake. He could

165

jeopardize not only your position but your future . . . plus a great deal of wealth, should he stumble on our little . . . secret, eh?"

"I don't intend to fail because of him," Trent said coldly. "Believe me, Andrew . . . I'll see that he doesn't become a problem."

"Good, good. I can see I made a wise choice. Don't let anything stand in our way. We have too much to lose."

"I told you, don't worry. I'll do whatever needs to be done."

"Well then, all we need to do is look forward to the rally and your send-off. Within a year we should be sending you to Washington. We should also be in possession of . . . everything we need. Make sure you get the Clayborn land and the Clayborn woman. Here's to success." They touched glasses and smiled with eager expectation.

At the same moment Blake and Mitch were in the office of an attorney who had summoned them. He had watched and listened, speaking to many friends about the man he felt they should cultivate: Mitchell Flannery.

Things were in disarray. A strong man, a strong leader, was needed to guide the town and the state out of the quagmire of war and into a future of real promise. Matthew Tyler felt he had found that man in Mitchell Flannery. He had read and re-read his war record, and had seen Mitch emerge as a leader. He had convinced the council who sought a candidate that Flannery was the man for the job. Now he knew he had to convince Mitch.

"You've been a busy man since you got home, Mitch," Matthew said. "You've got some land now, I hear."

"I do. I plan to start building a house as soon as I

166

can. We're clearing some of the trees on my property and curing the wood. I want my house built from my own lumber."

"Your heart's deep in this place, isn't it?"

"It's been home all my life. My parents have been happy here. I like having roots."

"And you'd like to see the city grow?"

"Of course. Reconstruction isn't easy, but there's opportunity too, if a man wants to work hard."

"Sometimes . . . sometimes it's strong leadership that's needed. People who've been defeated sometimes need someone to inspire them, teach them to fight."

Mitch and Blake exchanged glances. Blake already knew what Matthew had in mind. He had heard the whispers and watched as Mitch had cultivated friends and business people with his sincere attitude and honest personality.

But the thought was new for Mitch and he was taken by surprise.

"What are you leading up to, Matthew?" he asked suspiciously.

"Somebody's got to grab up the reins or this runaway team might just be grasped by the wrong man."

"So?"

"I hear," Matthew said quietly, "that Trent Donnelley is planning to grab the representative seat. It would give him a lot of power hereabouts."

Blake could feel Mitch's body go tense, even though his face remained unreadable and his eyes were devoid of emotion.

"Trent Donnelley," Mitch repeated, almost too casually.

"He's got a lot of . . . wealthy friends."

"I didn't know there were that many around here."

"We suspect that some of the money comes from . . . questionable sources. But no one can prove that. The man has a lot of charm and influence. And very few opponents."

"Opponents to what?"

"Running for representative."

"Who's the opposition?"

"Well, the *Holly Hill Sentinel,* for one."

Now it was Blake's turn to be shaken. So his little southern flower was a fighter. The idea pleased him. He knew the only other paper in town was the *Chronicle* and it carried a lot of weight. He wondered if she always chose overpowering odds.

"The *Sentinel* is run by the Anderson family, isn't it?" Blake queried, probing for information that so far had been hard to acquire.

"What's left of it," Matthew replied bluntly.

"So what *is* left of it?"

"They were a pretty big family — four boys and two girls. Out of the bunch there's only two boys and Noel left. Craig was the oldest, then Kevin, and Noel was the youngest. Pretty tragic. The war wiped out the family's home as well, but they're a stubborn, proud bunch. They stand on their own and won't take anything from anyone."

Blake could have asked many more questions, but he didn't want it to look too obvious. Still, he knew if the *Sentinel* and Noel Anderson were to be part of a campaign to elect Mitch, he would certainly be around to help.

"Matthew, all this is leading up to something," Mitch said, smiling. "Something you want from me?"

"Yes, and you've been thoroughly discussed."

"Great," Mitch replied stiffly, slightly annoyed.

"It was necessary."

"I don't know why. My life is my business."

"Up until now."

"What does that mean?"

"We want you to run against Trent Donnelley. We want you to give part of your life to your town and to the people who need a leader they can trust."

Blake remained silent and Mitch whistled softly as

he sat back in his chair, more than surprised at this turn of events.

"Why me?"

"Because we feel you can lead the fight against the dirty politics and shady affairs of the group around Trent. Old Andrew Crocket is the money, but I think the *Chronicle* is the power. It's a hard machine to fight and we need someone with the backbone to do it. Someone we can trust."

Mitch half smiled. How things had changed in four short years. Before the war he would have been laughed out of town for presuming to such a position. Now he was being asked to be a leader by one of the city's most prominent citizens. It shook him, almost overwhelmed him . . . and drove his thoughts to Whitney.

This would have been the answer to their prayers four years ago. Now he couldn't get close enough even to tell her about it. Fate was dealing him a hand that was, to say the least, unfair. He was being offered a great opportunity while at the same time the most important thing in his life was being snatched away.

He knew his battle with Whitney included Trent Donnelley. Maybe . . .

"Think about it, Mitch. Don't make a decision now. They'll be having a big rally in the town hall—that will be the time to challenge Donnelley. Remember how badly you're needed. Donnelley has power and money behind him. I hope we can get someone to put a stop to Andrew Crocket before he gets a stranglehood on this city."

"Matthew, I'm not too sure I'm your man. The old guard around here will still most likely want to protect the 'honest citizen' from the Flannery riffraff."

"Don't go proud and noble on me, Mitch. I know what kind of an education you struggled to get, and I know what kind of a man you are. Do you want to

169

dredge up the past and feel sorry for yourself, or do you want to be part of our effort to rebuild this town?"

"What about the Union occupation force?"

"They'll be withdrawn as soon as we're independent. Let's not make a mistake by holding onto the war and fighting the wrong people."

"You have all the answers don't you, Matthew?"

Matthew smiled. "I had to come here prepared or you would have shot me from my saddle on the first go around. Just think on it, Mitch, that's all we ask."

"All right. I'll think on it. When is the rally?"

"Two weeks."

"You'll have my answer before that."

"Excellent." Matthew drank the last of his drink.

"I think we'd better get going. Blake and I have a lot to do," Mitch said as he rose to his feet.

The men shook Matthew's hand and left. Outside, Mitch stood in the milling crowd in silence for several minutes. Blake could read well the uncertainty in Mitch's eyes. He knew it was a taste of old memories that brought on the beginnings of depression.

"How about a drink?" Blake suggested, hoping an exchange in private might open Mitch up a bit.

"Not right now. Have you set up your banker friend so we'll get advance notice of the land sales?"

Blake knew he was talking about the Clayborn property.

"You'll know a full day in advance. There's no way anyone can beat you to it."

Again Mitch was silent for a while, his eyes studying passing faces as if trying to read what lay behind them.

"So, Blake," Mitch said quietly, "what do you think, my Yankee friend?"

"About fighting Trent Donnelley? It's one way."

"What does that mean?" Mitch asked, turning to face Blake.

170

"It means he's the one that stands between you and everything you want. We've been friends a long time, Mitch. I know about your past problems. But I know you, too. Matthew is right. Don't let the hurts of the past affect the future. You want Whitney and the life you could have together. So fight for it. Be what you always wanted to be . . . and beat Trent Donnelley on his own ground."

"Do you really think I could swing enough votes to send me to Columbia?"

"Why not? People aren't dumb. Stand up and tell them what you want for their town . . . your town. They can make choices."

"Maybe you're right. I've got help with Pa, Morgan, and Shawn . . ."

"And me," Blake reminded him. "And, as Matthew said, it may not be as big as the *Chronicle,* but you've got a newspaper behind you."

Mitch grinned. "And I don't suppose you would want to be the liaison between me and that paper."

Blake laughed softly, "If you insisted on it, old friend, I might be talked into it."

"Oh, I'd insist on it," Mitch said in mock seriousness. Then they both laughed. "Of course, you'll be in dangerous territory. The Union might suffer the final defeat of the war."

"Don't count on it, friend. You give me the means to walk into that place and, by damn, I'll lay siege until they surrender if it takes my last breath."

"You've almost convinced me that even if I do it for the sake of peace between the Union and the Confederacy it might be worth it, just to see if your campaign is successful."

"Just say the word."

"I suppose I should talk to my father, get his opinion. And I think my brothers ought to have some say in it all . . ."

"And . . . you're thinking of Whitney?"

171

"I'd like to have her beside me . . . win or lose."

"What are you going to do about that, Mitch?" It was half question, half challenge and Blake watched his friend's unreadable face for a long, drawn out moment. Then Mitch answered and Blake was glad to hear the determined timbre of his voice.

"Take your advice, old friend. I'll lay siege and fight with every weapon I can find. This is one battle I can't afford to lose."

"Then we're in?"

"We're in. I guess I better go home and warn my family what they're up against."

"Then if I have your permission I'll tell Matthew. Then I'll make sure our friends at the *Sentinel* are aware of *our* campaign."

"Our?"

"Oh, some of them will be well aware that it's our campaign."

"I'll bet you're going to cause some confusion. How can they fight for the rebel and against the Yankee?"

"That's my plan. Enough confusion and I just might pull it off."

"I'd like to see her again."

"First minute she decides I'm no longer the enemy and lets me in speaking range."

"Good luck."

"Yeah . . . for both of us."

"I wonder if the war wasn't easier."

"Easier, but less rewarding."

"I'll see you tonight."

"If we survive," Blake grinned. He gave a jaunty salute and headed down the plank sidewalk toward the *Sentinel*'s office.

Mitch stood, one broad shoulder braced against the wooden post that held up the roof, gazing out over the town.

It was not large and it had suffered from the war. But the bustling activity and the signs of building made him see beyond what it was to what it could be.

Civic duty had not been high on his list of priorities. Yet he knew some of the fault was his. He had never been wanted by his town so he hadn't even considered it. Now it was as if he were suddenly being filled with a kind of raw enthusiasm. The only bleak and lonely spot was Whitney.

He tried to make his introspection as honest as possible, but he could not see himself in such a position of leadership without Whitney beside him.

Certain now that the child he had seen was part of the information she had not wanted him to know, he knew from his sleepless nights and bitter longing that it didn't matter. But how to convince her? There were too many things he didn't know that could only be answered by Whitney . . . or someone close to her. Someone who had seen that their letters never reached each other, someone cold and calculating enough to put his name to a letter he had never written.

Lazarus and Josiah would protect her and Mitch knew there were also two black women who had chosen to stay. One, he was certain, was the slave, Berdine. Whitney had spoken of her. The other he didn't know, but they formed a formidable barrier he would have to break through. Neither hell nor high water would keep him from finding a way to Whitney . . . except a cold refusal from Whitney herself.

He breathed deeply as he stood up straight. If he was making commitments, then he'd better make them complete. He meant well, but he was making a serious mistake. He thought Whitney needed forgiveness and in a magnanimous moment he was preparing to tell her he was ready to forgive her mistakes if she would just remember all he had said and try to understand.

Tonight, he thought, tonight, while the excitement was still bubbling through him. Of course, he would have to slip past Lazarus somehow. The man was a formidable mountain who could tear him limb from limb if he chose. If he had to face Lazarus, he laughed to himself, it would be better to have Whitney between them. At least until he could convince Lazarus his intentions toward Whitney were honorable.

Now, with the possibility of a bright future all he could really think of was making a home and having a family with Whitney. His whole body tingled with the thought of holding her again . . . making love to her. God, the need was so intense he could taste it.

He walked slowly down the boardwalk, listening and watching everything around him with half his consciousness while he savored the vision of Whitney that lingered in his mind. It made him impatient for the moment he would confront her.

He planned all of his life around Whitney and his love for her and the promise of the meeting to come.

As he walked, Blake's thoughts almost paralleled Mitch's. Their friendship had been a quirk of fate. He'd been drawn South to plan his future beside a man he admired and respected, a place where he was destined to meet a woman who would fill his mind and his heart.

He would be walking into a lion's den, she had said, and he might very well be eaten. But he could no more change his course than he could stop breathing.

He didn't worry about other problems but he did worry about the ones that seemed to matter most to her. Her memories, bitter and hard and filled with despair, . . . and worst of all, her hatred for anyone from the North, himself included.

Blake stopped before the offices of the *Sentinel*. Through the front window he could see several people

174

moving about. He watched for a minute, then he saw Noel. Small among the larger figures of the men, she drew his total attention.

He breathed deeply, squared his shoulders, and walked to the door. When he opened it the eyes of the four people inside turned to him. Three were curious, but the fourth was filled with shock . . . and was it wishful thinking, or did he read something more? He hoped . . . then he smiled.

Fifteen

"Can I help you, sir?" One of the men stepped forward—a tall, brawny, and handsome male version of Noel. He wore a patch over one eye and as he moved toward him, Blake could see a slight limp.

Blake was about to speak when Noel seemed to recover from the surprise. She walked over beside her brother. It was a gentle and sweet gesture that made Blake want to hold her close and protect her. It was a move that told him of her own protective feelings, as if her brother had been hurt enough. He was already defensive and he hadn't spoken a word.

"I've come to introduce myself and to discuss political ideas. I believe Matthew Tyler has been talking to you about my friend, Mitchell Flannery." Blake smiled directly at Noel. "But then, I thought maybe you might know about me by now."

Noel flushed, but her chin rose defiantly.

"I've told my brothers about my . . . episode, Mr. Randolph," she said in a formal tone. "You didn't tell me you were a friend of Mitchell Flannery."

"You know Mitch?"

"I knew him . . . a long time ago."

"Noel?" Her brother queried, turning curious eyes to her.

"This is Blake Randolph," she said. "The man I told you about."

Blake's heart skipped a beat. No matter what she

said, she hadn't forgotten him. But he was momentarily surprised that there was no animosity on her brother's face. Then he realized she hadn't told him where he was from . . . that he was the enemy.

"I'm pleased to meet you, Mr. Anderson. I hope we'll be working together."

"My name is Craig."

"But I don't think it would be feasible for you to consider that you will be working with us, Mr. Randolph," Noel said firmly. "I think it would be best for all concerned that we realize that though our goals may be the same . . . . our methods are different. We would do better to work separately."

"Noel!" Craig cried, puzzled at her reaction.

"I'm sorry, Craig," Noel replied softly. She held the pain in her eyes too long for Blake not to see.

"She's trying to tell you I'm a Yankee by birth, Craig. I'm wondering if that makes a difference in what you people are fighting for. If it does, I'm truly disappointed."

Craig's face had frozen in a deep frown. "A Yankee," he said. "What the hell did you expect? You're disappointed? Now isn't that something. Why are you disappointed? Because we're not on our knees?"

"Because you're blinded maybe."

"Blinded to what?"

"To the differences in people."

Craig glared at him. "I think you ought to leave, Mr. Randolph, before I forget the war is over."

Blake was watching Noel, but he was also aware of the silent young man who had stayed at his desk. That he was the younger brother there was no doubt—all the family resemblances were there. He had to do something because he was rapidly losing ground.

"What about you?"

"What about me?" The voice was gentle, sensitive. "Are you asking if I can work with you, Mr. Yankee?

Well, I don't know. I guess I'll have to go ask my ma and pa . . . except the Yankees butchered them. Or maybe I could ask my sister, Emma . . . but she was raped and then killed. Or maybe Charlotte . . . my wife. Yankees killed her, too. My brothers who died, I'll ask them."

The tears on Noel's face were real and filled with misery. Blake felt a sting of compassion. He'd made a mistake. He felt thoroughly chewed by the beast of guilt and regret. He could do one of two things: turn and run, or stay and hope to begin something healing.

"I don't think there is anyone sorrier for all the tragedies the war caused than I am. But there's not much use in all of us spending the rest of our lives hating and blaming each other. You started a newspaper obviously to try and pick up the pieces. From what Matthew has to say, you're fighters. Well, Mitch is a fighter, too, and I'm on his side—and on yours. If you're honestly trying to put everything back together then don't you think it ought to begin by making some kind of peace? I'm willing to try . . . you let me know when you are."

He turned and left the office, amazed at his own emotional and physical reaction. He was sweating and his body was actually shaking from the intensity of the encounter. He wanted to reach out and do something to ease their memories. He wanted to touch Noel. With a kind of desperation he thought of the tears in her eyes and the pain on her face. But he was helpless . . . the next move had to be theirs. He walked slowly down the street toward Matthew's office. He'd told Mitch he would tell Matthew how the meeting at the newspaper had gone, and he would have to tell him that he wasn't sure whether things would work out.

Of course he could forget it all and walk away, but he knew he wouldn't. He'd told them he was a fighter.

Well, he was and he knew damn well what he was fighting for.

He'd only gone a hundred feet or so when he heard his name called out. He spun about and was surprised to see Noel coming toward him. He waited, hoping to see the possibility of something else in her eyes.

"Before you say anything, Noel, I'm sorry. I don't suppose any southern gentleman would have done what I did. But it doesn't change the way I feel. It's time, wounds or no wounds, to look for a kind of peace."

"You can't blame my brothers for what they feel. We've lost so much."

"You're not the only ones who've lost someone. I lost a brother at Chancellorsville. I lost friends, saw them die in front of my eyes. But Noel . . . it's over!"

"I know," she choked. "But it's . . . it's so . . ."

"I know that, too. It's too fresh. But you can't let people take advantage while you sit around and grieve."

"Advantage?"

"Don't you think that's what's happening?"

"My brothers talk about it, but I don't always feel . . ."

"What?" his voice was sympathetic, a sympathy she sensed at once.

"What do you want from us?"

"Mitch needs you, you and your brothers. I want to see him succeed . . . be part of it. Maybe it's my way of paying back. I want to work with you and your brothers. To do that we have to meet halfway."

"It's a lot to ask."

"Depends on what you're willing to sacrifice to put things together again."

"My brothers are strong, decent men. They're also very loyal and dedicated. Don't talk about sacrifices in the same breath."

"Help me, Noel," he said softly as his eyes held hers. "Help me and I'll do everything in my power to make it work, to make things change."

"How can I help you?"

"By not hating me. That's a good place to start. Maybe if you stop hating . . . in time we can teach them to stop as well."

"It's not quite that easy."

"One day at a time. Just one day at a time."

"I won't promise that, I can't."

"Well, there's something I won't promise either."

"What?"

"I won't promise I won't be around every day. Brothers or no brothers, I'm going to teach you to stop hating and start living again."

"Why don't you just support your friend some other way and let us do what can be done ourselves? There's no sense to this."

Again he saw it in her eyes, a fear . . . and an awareness. She was vulnerable to emotions she simply couldn't accept.

"Not on your life, Noel. Don't run and hide."

She hated his ability to reach her in places she thought were well protected and hidden—places she had secured so no one could hurt her again. He wanted to expose the raw pain and she couldn't face it. She turned and abruptly left him.

"Noel!" he called after her. But she paid no attention. He knew it was useless to pursue her now. But he also knew something had begun, and he was not about to give up.

Trent sat in his office, deep in thought. His future was made of gold. He would have power, wealth, and the one woman who truly excited him.

Of course, his meetings with Whitney had not been as accidental as she thought. They were necessary at

180

first so he would have access to her and her home in a search for something of vital importance to him. But so far his efforts had all been in vain. Now he had the added threat of old memories in the person of Mitch Flannery.

His eyes narrowed and his jaw clenched when he thought of Flannery. Trent knew about his past only too well. Wounded and taken prisoner. Championed by that cursed friend of his, Blake Randolph. And part of a prisoner exchange when Trent had the misfortune of being in the wrong place at the wrong time.

As a double agent Trent wore both uniforms, the gray and the blue, when it was convenient. When Mitch had seen him he was recuperating; the meeting had been quick and Trent had easily forgotten it . . . until they met again at the dance.

Heralded as a southern war hero, Trent knew that at any time a flicker of memory might make Mitch realize who and what he was. Trent couldn't afford the problems that could cause.

But he was also aware that Mitch had made a lot of friends since his return home. And Trent was surprised it annoyed him that Mitch had returned with enough funds to make such an impression. If he wasn't careful Mitchell Flannery could pose a problem that would put an end not only to his, but a lot of other, well-laid plans. Mitchell Flannery would have to be taken care of . . . permanently. He wasn't yet sure just how he was going to do this, but he would find a way. The plans for his future were too large, too powerful for Trent to allow someone to interfere.

This town was just a stepping stone. He wasn't too worried about what he could do for the town, but he needed the town to get where he really wanted to go. He could see himself one day as governor . . . senator and . . . maybe even a higher office. He and Whitney. What a first lady she would make, and if he found what he sought there would be no limit to his power. Yes . . . he would have to rid himself of Mitchell Flannery . . . and soon.

Mitch sat across the table from a very proud family. Their faith in him had always been strong, but they had not realized the extent of his ability. Now, they looked at him with admiration and even a touch of awe.

"This war's been a funny kind of thing for the family, hasn't it, son," Stuart said. "It's sure changed everything around."

"For some people, Pa," Mitch said. "Don't get it through your head that everybody's like us. There are still a lot of people who think of us as 'those Flannerys.' I'm going to need everyone's help." They agreed unanimously that every hand would pitch in. Mitch was the only one who noticed his mother's silence.

Late that night, when he thought everyone else was in bed, he stood on the porch and looked up at a night sky filled with millions of silvery stars and a white moon that gave everything a pale glow.

"Mitch?" a voice came softly from behind him. He turned to see his mother standing in the doorway.

"You're up late. Couldn't you sleep?"

She smiled as she walked out and stood beside him.

"Even when you children were babies I couldn't sleep when you had problems."

"Problems? I hope my news doesn't make you worry."

"I'm not talking about your news, Mitch. I'm talking about whatever it is that's keeping you awake, keeping you on edge . . . whatever it is that seems to give you pain."

"It's just the excitement of a new challenge," he lied.

182

"You're one of the Flannery boys," she chuckled. "A challenge has never thrown you off course yet."

"Well," he said softly, "a war could just about do it."

"The war," she repeated thoughtfully. "Mitch, you came home from the war, if possible, stronger and better than when you left." She looked up at him astutely. "I don't think going to war is to blame. I think it's something you left behind."

He looked at her and realized that what she didn't know she sensed. As old as he was, he was her child, and she knew him as very few others did. He wondered what she would think if he told her everything. He considered it thoughtfully and Caryn waited silently. She knew so much more than her son realized. Yet she had said nothing. She would listen to whatever he wanted to tell her and hope she could say something to help him. She waited and almost felt the thoughts churning in his mind.

When he began to speak it was quietly, as if he were seeing into the past, reliving it as if it were yesterday. If she was shocked in any way it didn't show.

He spoke of Whitney and his love for her and the pact they had made at the time they separated. Then for a few minutes he was silent and the call of the cicadas filled the night air.

He spoke again of the pain and anguish of the war and all he had been through . . . then of his return, and finding Whitney. When he told her of the child she caught her breath, but still said nothing. Mitch's soul needed to be cleansed, so she let him continue until finally he was silent again . . . drained.

"Does it change your love for her . . . this child?"

Again he breathed raggedly, "At first, I'll have to admit, I was hurt, but . . ."

"But?"

"But I realized how she must have suffered, too, everything she lost, all the pain. I can't blame her. It

183

was almost too much to bear, and for a woman as delicate and sweet as Whitney it must have been hell."

"Yes, it must have been. I don't understand that dreadful letter, Mitch. Who could have done a thing like that? And the loss of all the letters you wrote and the ones she wrote to you. It all seems so . . . so ugly."

"It is. Whitney doesn't believe I wrote. She believes I thought it was," he shrugged, "some kind of a game or challenge."

"Oh, Mitch." Caryn laid her hand on his arm. "Go to her, tell her the truth. Tell her how much you love her."

"I tried. Don't you think I've tried?"

"But . . ."

"But I can't get close. There's another man she says she's going to marry, and she has a bodyguard."

"A bodyguard?"

"Lazarus. Remember him? The black who was built like an oak and was as big as a house."

"Yes, I remember Lazarus."

"Well, he's a free man now so I've got no power over him. He lived through all this with Whitney. I can't really blame him for not wanting to see her hurt any more. I also can't make him listen to me, so consequently I can't get anywhere near her."

"My, my," Caryn said softly. "I've never known you to be so easily subdued."

"Who said I was?" He grinned at her and she responded with a light laugh. "I just have to find the right time and the right way. I'm not giving up, that's for sure."

"This child, Mitch. You must be sure it . . ."

"He."

"He can't be punished for things he had no part in."

"I know that."

"Then you must be very certain you want him . . . or you must leave Whitney alone. As you say, she's

184

had enough pain. I don't want you to cause her more."

"Believe me, Mother," his voice was tense and thick with emotion, "it's hard just to live day by day knowing she's within reach and hating me. And it's hard to look forward to the rest of my life without her. I can't see the future if she's not in it. She was so much a part of my life and my dreams it's hard even to think when she's not with me."

"Of course. Do you think, my son, you're the first and only person to fall in love? It's sometimes a painful thing, but I have confidence in you. If there's a way to Whitney's heart I'm sure you'll find it."

"You have more confidence in me at the moment than I have in myself."

"Your confidence might be shaken, but you're very much like your father. You'll do fine. Just be careful not to hurt anyone . . . especially yourself. Mitch?"

"What?"

"This political thing, is it something you really want? I've always seen you as a man of the land."

"In time I think I could be both. I'm interested in how my town gets rebuilt, and in making sure that the wrong element doesn't get a hold on it. I'm also interested in having a place of my own where I can grow things. But first things first. If I want to live in peace here . . . with my friends and family, then I have to help do something about it. My town is not up for grabs by any carpetbagger who comes along and wants to snatch it."

"You've said that twice."

"What?"

"*My* town. It wasn't always."

"No, it wasn't. But this is an opportunity to show everyone that 'those Flannerys' are people to be reckoned with. It's sort of a new beginning."

"I wasn't sure of your motives."

"My motives?"

185

"Sometimes, when people are hurt they tend to carry grudges, to find a way to hit back."

"You think that's what I want?"

"Not anymore. I just wanted to hear you say it. I'm very proud of you, Mitch. I guess I've told you that before."

"A time or two," he said with a laugh. "But you're a bit prejudiced."

"I'm not! I just know what a fine person you are . . . besides, I won't have my son maligned."

"It's going to be a long, hard fight."

"Who will be your opponent?"

"Trent Donnelley," Mitch answered. Then he turned to her again. "The man Whitney thinks she's going to marry."

"What kind of a man is he?"

"I don't really know. My jealous side tells me he's a scoundrel. But common sense tells me he's a hard man with a lot of backing. Still . . ."

"Still what?"

"I just have a feeling we've crossed paths before, but I can't place where or when. It's a feeling that seems really important. If I could just remember."

"Do you think Whitney loves him?"

"No!" The answer was abrupt and coldly final, as if he could not allow even the thought to exist.

"What are you going to do, Mitch?"

"I don't know. I'll find a way."

"You know we're all behind you."

"I know. I think you better try and get some sleep. It's awfully late."

"And you want to be alone to think," she said softly, then smiled. "Not very subtle, my son, but very effective." She stood on tiptoe to kiss his cheek. "Good night, Mitch."

"Good night, Mother."

When Caryn closed the door behind her Mitch

186

again leaned a shoulder against the wooden porch support. She had asked him all the questions he had asked himself, and this was the first time he was truly satisfied and secure in his own answers and motives.

There was no doubt he was jealous of every moment Trent Donnelley spent with Whitney, but that was not the reason he wanted to challenge him. The truth made him feel clean and healed. He really did want to do something to ease the wounds the war had brought to his town . . . yes, *his* town. He wanted to be a force that helped move it forward, which had nothing to do with the past, only the future.

Again he thought of the future without Whitney and couldn't picture it. No, he had to find a way and now he was even more determined.

Mitch was still standing on the porch a few minutes later when he heard a rider approaching. When he saw the shadowed form, he knew by the expert way cavalrymen rode that it had to be Blake.

When Blake dismounted he led his horse to the barn, and several minutes later was striding across the open area toward the porch. He paused a moment when he saw Mitch, then continued toward him.

"You're up late."

"You're in late," Mitch chuckled in response. "What happened? Did you get waylaid by a card game or a pretty face?"

"Much as I'd like to get waylaid by this pretty face, what I got was a door slammed in mine."

"And I thought Yankees were invincible," Mitch chided.

"Don't joke, Mitch. This time is the first time I've ever wished I'd been on the losing side. I'd stand a better chance."

"So tell me what happened."

Blake explained all that had occurred after they had separated. "So you see, it looks like I'm going to

187

jam the wheels of progress so far as the Andersons are concerned."

"I don't know, Blake. I can't talk to Noel for you but I sure as hell can try to convince her brothers that it's time to lay down our guns. I never told you it was going to be easy."

"Well, if you can persuade her brothers it will be a big step."

"You can't just forget about her, can you?"

"Not this time. She isn't just another girl. I've seen things in her eyes, Mitch, things a girl her age should never have seen. She's been hurt worse than the rest of them. They've been wounded by bullets, she's been wounded by something else, something deeper, and she's carrying it around like a shield."

"Sometimes wounds like that never heal. Sometimes you just have to know when to let go."

"Like I told you," Blake said quietly as their eyes met, "it's not my choice anymore. There's something else I have to see in her eyes and I won't let go until I do."

Mitch nodded. He understood, and hoped Blake wasn't fighting a war this time that he just couldn't win.

Sixteen

Inside the house Mitch poured drinks and he and Blake sat together to talk.

"I found out some more news in town this afternoon that might be of interest," Blake said with a half smile.

"Information? What?"

"If you can be at the bank when they post the tax sales at eight tomorrow morning you'll be first in line to buy that land you want so much."

"Great!"

"Mitch, are you sure . . ."

"Let's not go through that again. I'm going to buy it, one, because I know she doesn't have the money, and two, because I don't want it to fall into the hands of strangers."

"Rumor has it that there have been inquiries."

"From who?"

"Trent Donnelley and some banker named Andrew Crocket."

"That's number three. I'll do just about anything to keep Donnelley's hands off that land."

"This promises to turn into one hell of a fight. You still think this Donnelley is someone you know?"

"Yes, it's plaguing the hell out of me."

"Maybe in the army?"

"I don't know, but I'll keep turning it over in my mind until I do."

"What's our plan, Mitch?"

"There's a big rally in a week or so. Donnelley will be there to give a speech. That's the time for me to make it known I'm in the race. After that, all hell will most likely break loose. That's when the fight begins. Then we all get to work and talk to as many people as we can — tell them how we feel and what we want to do."

"We start running editorials in the newspaper right away?"

"Not until after the rally. I don't want the paper involved in a fight until we're all ready. You ought to get some editorials ready, though, because when we start we're going to roll."

"I have some ideas already. Hell, who knows more about you and your ideals than I do? I'll get a couple written up."

"Want me to talk to Noel's brothers?"

"No, I've been giving that some thought. This is my fight, too. They have to learn to come halfway if this is going to work. Besides," Blake grinned, "I'll keep walking into the den until those lions decide to quit chewing on me and listen."

"This war's been hard on them."

"I know. I spent the rest of the afternoon and evening walking around town asking questions. I think I know as much about the Andersons as they do."

"I'm glad you're part of my campaign. I sure wouldn't want to work against you."

"I have a lot at stake here."

"You'll stay around . . . go on helping me?"

"I've got nothing to go home to, you know that, and there are things that hold me here. I'll stay."

"I hope it works . . . for both of us."

Mitch touched his glass to Blake's. "So do I, Mitch. So do I."

Pale dawn was streaking the early morning sky when Mitch led his horse from the barn, mounted, and started off to town.

He was pleased with a touch of what he called his Black Irish luck when he dismounted before the bank in time to see one of the clerks come outside and post a white sheet of paper.

There was no doubt in his mind that it was the official notice of the sale. He entered the bank a few feet behind the clerk, who turned when he heard Mitch's footsteps.

"Oh, good morning, sir. You're quite early."

"Yes, I want to see about this tax sale."

"Well, then you want to speak to Mr. Connery."

"Can I see him now?"

"I'll go and tell him."

"Thanks."

"You're Mr. Flannery, aren't you?"

"Yes. How did you know?"

"Mr. Matthews dropped by the bank yesterday to talk about you."

Mitch wasn't quite sure what Matthews had said but the clerk grinned. "They had a drink or two and a few laughs. I heard a bit, something about Irish blarney winning elections. They seemed to be getting on pretty well."

That was a relief to Mitch. "I think there are more forces working in my life than I know."

"I wouldn't be surprised, sir. When Mr. Connery and Mr. Matthews get their heads together a lot of things can happen."

"I wouldn't be much surprised either," Mitch said dryly.

After a few minutes the clerk returned, followed by a rotund, ruddy-cheeked man with crisp white hair and blue eyes that twinkled with intelligent mischief.

"Mr. Flannery, come into my office, please. I'm glad to finally meet you."

"Especially since I've been the topic of conversation for some time now," Mitch retorted with an amused smile.

"That you have, that you have," came the quick and completely unabashed reply. "Your friend has brought me a bit of hope, I don't mind telling you."

"Hope?"

"For our town, Mr. Flannery, for our town."

"My name is Mitchell. We're going to be friends, I hope."

"Most assuredly, Mitchell. Have a seat. What can I do for you?"

"I'd like to buy some land."

"From the bank?"

"No, one of the pieces you just posted outside."

"But . . . they've just been posted. How did . . . ah yes . . . well, what piece are you interested in?"

"The old Clayborn property."

The banker's eyes narrowed as he watched Mitch intently and tried to read his expression. He was unsuccessful and somehow that pleased him.

"You know the house is totally destroyed?"

"Yes, I do."

"The property is quite valuable. Most of the Clayborn family is buried there. It's a real shame when a family gets decimated that way."

"It's more than a shame. The land is fertile and productive. I don't want it to fall into the hands of people who won't appreciate all the sacrifice it represents."

"Will you do a fellow Irishman a favor and tell me why you want it . . . the real reason, I mean."

Mitch felt it was now or never to separate his friends from his enemies. Without taking his eyes

192

from Connery's, he told him he wanted the land because of his opposition to Trent Donnelley and all he stood for.

"So, Trent Donnelley wants it, does he?" Connery said softly.

"He does."

"Well, I just think I'll tweak his nose a mite. The man's a rascal, and I've a mind to be protecting my town from his like. The taxes are almost eight hundred dollars."

Mitch whistled through his teeth. The sum was astronomical since there was very little money in the South that wasn't in Union hands.

"I know it's high, but they've been accumulating since the year after the war started and there have been no Clayborns to pay."

Mitch remained silent about Whitney. It would hold up the sale while her whereabouts were checked into and Trent Donnelley could get it before he could ever explain everything to her. Besides, he thought, soothing his conscience while he counted out the money, the land would be Whitney's again one day anyhow.

They talked about the town's future while the papers were being prepared and both men were satisfied when they were handed to Mitch, who tucked them safely in his breast pocket. There was a knock on the door, then the clerk stuck his head inside.

"Mr. Donnelley to see you, sir."

"Ah," Connery said softly. His eyes sparkled to the point of outright laughter. "Shall we see what the gentleman wants, Mr. Flannery?"

"Might prove to be extremely . . . enlightening," Mitch said in mock seriousness, his eyes gleaming at the thought of a confrontation.

"Show him in, Bently. Show him in, please."

Trent was shocked to see Mitch and controlled himself with a great deal of effort.

193

"Mr. Connery . . . Mr. Flannery." He nodded toward both men.

"Come in and sit down, please. Can I be of help?"

"Yes. I've some business to discuss . . . in private."

"Well, Mr. Flannery was just concluding some business."

"Business?" Trent actually sneered. "Just what kind of business . . . a loan?"

"I hardly think so. He just purchased some land."

"Land?" Trent felt a premonitional chill. "What land?"

"Well, I'm afraid that's private and not my province to discuss."

Trent was deeply suspicious and replied to the banker, his eyes still holding Mitch's. "I've come to purchase some land also."

"And what are you interested in?"

"The Clayborn property. I was told by a very reliable source that it was to be put up for tax sale today."

"Oh dear . . . I'm afraid you're just minutes too late. It seems that's the property that Mr. Flannery has just purchased."

Trent's face did not twitch a muscle, but Mitch could actually feel the hatred that leapt into his eyes. "I see," he said softly. "And just how did he know that the land would be sold today?"

"I should think you would know," Mitch said, his voice matching Trent's in tone. "I imagine the same way you did. You did get advance notice, didn't you? Too bad. Maybe you should have gotten up just a little earlier."

"Damn you," Trent hissed.

"Gentlemen, please," Connery said. "It's only a matter of business. Surely nothing serious. Mr. Donnelley, there's a great deal of land for sale. Another piece maybe?"

"No, not another piece. What did you pay for it, Flannery?"

"Eight hundred dollars."

"I'll give you double."

"No."

"Triple."

"No."

"Name your price," Trent growled through clenched teeth.

"Donnelley, you don't have enough money to buy that land, not if you stripped yourself and all your greedy friends clean. It's mine and you'll never get it."

"So you think you've accomplished something?"

"Maybe."

"You'll regret this. I promise you, you'll regret this." His voice was soft . . . and deadly. He turned and left, closing the door sharply behind him.

"He's a sharp, cold, and very vindictive man, Mitchell."

"I'm sure of it. But someone's got to stop him and I intend to do just that."

"I wish you good luck, my boy, excellent luck. I shall watch this situation with the utmost attention."

"You do that, Mr. Connery. You've been a great help. I would like to promise you that the land will be in the very best of hands."

"I do believe you, and I imagine the fun is about to begin."

Connery escorted Mitch to the door and stood and watched as Mitch mounted and rode away. He was pleased. Things were about to happen.

Mitch was pleased also, but a little shaken. It would not sit too well with Whitney if Trent told her first. He had to talk to Whitney tonight.

Once he arrived home he gave Blake a blow by blow description of buying the land. Blake still had some misgivings about how Whitney would react but Mitch's enthusiasm overwhelmed him.

195

"I imagine Trent was livid," Blake said with a grin.

"That's putting it mildly," Mitch replied.

"If he was upset about this," Morgan offered, "just think of what the reaction is going to be at the rally when he finds out you're running."

"It might be dangerous for Mitch," Caryn put in worriedly.

"I'd say less dangerous, Mother," Mitch observed, trying to soothe her. "For now, I'm an unannounced problem. Later on it'll be public. Once it is, he'd have to be very careful about what happens to me. It might look a bit odd to a lot of people."

"Then between now and the rally you just ought to stay at home," Caryn insisted. They all laughed.

"Mother, if I crawled in my bed and pulled the covers over my head you'd still worry about me."

"I suppose you're right," Caryn agreed reluctantly.

The conversation drifted to plans and strategies, to the editorials Blake had written, then on to what Mitch would do should he really be elected. The time flew and soon Caryn was preparing supper.

As it neared twilight, Mitch was heading toward the barn when Blake called out. He waited for Blake to catch up to him and they continued on together.

"I don't have to ask where you're going." Blake said.

"I'm going to try to clear things up."

"What about Lazarus?"

"I'm slipping over quietly. I've got to reach her pretty quick or she's going to hear the wrong side of the story from the wrong person. It's bad enough now — what do you think will happen then?"

"I wonder what Trent's plans were. I mean, what did he hope to do with that land?"

"Make her a wedding present, I suppose."

"Maybe."

"What are you thinking?"

"He just doesn't strike me as a man who would let his woman be that independent. I'd say it was to have another tie to her. Do you think that land would be a powerful enough hold on her?"

"Sure, she loved it."

"Then I'd believe that, before I'd believe in his generosity."

"Damn, I wish I could label him. It's driving me crazy. Is there any way to find out about his past? School, military records?"

"If he's got something to hide sure as hell he's covered it over pretty good by now."

"Maybe he's made a slip. Let's see what we can dig up. It's worth a try."

"Anything's worth a try," Blake concluded. Mitch had saddled his horse and was curious about the fact that Blake had saddled his as well.

"Where are you going?"

"Thought I might run these editorials into town. See if the 'brothers grim' are still in the newspaper office. If they're not," Blake shrugged, "who knows, I might just drop them by their house." He smiled broadly.

"Not pushing your luck, are you, Blake?"

"No more than you are."

"Just be careful. Some of these war wounds run pretty deep."

"I know. I didn't mean to be funny, but they're certainly not going to come to me, so I'm going to have to go to them."

"Well, let's hope it's a lucky night for both of us."

They rode to the end of the land that led to the house and when they reached the dirt road they went in different directions.

It was hard for Whitney to believe it was Jonathan's third birthday. Berdine had baked a special cake, Lazarus had carved wooden soldiers and horses, and Addy had made him a reed flute. Josiah had given him a leather pouch filled with brightly colored marbles. Whitney had bought peppermint candy, Jonathan's favorite treat. It had been a happy party, until Berdine saw the tears in Whitney's eyes as she watched Jonathan at play with his wooden soldiers.

"What's wrong, missy?"

"His father should have made those for him. Oh, Berdine, I'll never be enough for a boy like Jon. He's so vital, so full of life. He needs a man to guide him, to teach him."

"Yo' quit frettin' yo'self. Yo'll be fine. Dat be one happy li'l boy."

"Now maybe, but who's to teach him to be a . . . a man?"

"Are yo' thinkin' what I think yo' thinkin'?"

"I don't know."

"Yo' plannin' on marryin' dat man jes' to give Jonathan a daddy."

"Berdine, I . . ."

"What about his real daddy? He's not dat far 'way. Don' yo' think he has some right to know?"

"I'm so frightened, Berdine."

"What yo' scared of?"

"You don't understand, Berdine. He never wanted him, but for some reason he thinks *I've* betrayed *him* somehow. The law . . . it sees only men. If Mitch knew Jon was his son, he could just take him. I have no rights and no money to fight him. I couldn't bear it, Berdine. I couldn't lose him, I just couldn't bear it."

"How does yo' know fo' true he do such a thing?"

"It's a chance I can't afford to take."

"Marryin' a man yo' don't love be a bigger chance."

"I have to consider Jon's needs first."

"Jon needs yo' happy, too. Yo' miserable he gwine be miserable, too."

Whitney sighed deeply, silently denying the truth of Berdine's words. She had not been able to sleep and ate barely enough to keep going. She paced the floor at night trying to find some peace of mind. She would give her life to be able to give Jon the future he deserved. She watched him playing, his trusting eyes meeting hers in total confidence. His smile, so quick, so white and a poignant reminder of his father, was enough to tear at her heart.

She swallowed the heavy lump in her throat as she went to Jon and knelt down on the floor beside him.

"Come on, darling. It's been a long and hard day and it's time for bed."

"No, Mummy, no, 'Dine tell me a story." His childish resistance tugged at her. " 'Dine" was the best he could do with Berdine's name.

"Berdine's tired, too. Come along now."

" 'Dine, tell me a story," he pleaded.

Whitney was about to sternly refuse when Berdine spoke up. "Ah promised him a story or two. Why doan ah take him home wif me? Ah'll tell him stories an' put him to bed. An' Addy kin help me. Yo' could use a night fo' yo'self. Have a nice bath an' git some sleep fo' a change."

"Berdine, you're a gem. But you've worked so hard today. I'll just . . ."

"No, yo' jes' have a night when yo' kin pamper yo'self fo' a bit." Berdine walked to Jonathan and lifted the delighted little boy in her arms. He was still clutching one of the soldiers. "Ah'll have Lazarus bring yo' some hot water in dat old wood tub. Yo' kin jes' relax. We's always glad to have de boy fo' a while."

"Thank you, Berdine. I don't know how I'll ever repay the four of you for everything you've done for me."

"We ain't askin' fo' nuthin'," Berdine said perfunctorily. She walked to the door with Jonathan.

Less than a half hour later Lazarus and Josiah appeared at the door with a huge wooden tub. They set it in the middle of the floor.

"Water's heatin'. Ah'll bring it in a bit," Lazarus said.

"Thank you, Lazarus. If Jon gives you any trouble tonight you call me."

"Dat boy ain't no trouble," Lazarus replied, laughter rumbling in his broad chest. "Berdine give him a good washin' an' she was rockin' him an' tellin' him stories. Ah wouldn't be surprised that he's asleep befo' yo' gets outa dis tub."

"I was a spoiled little girl—now I'm being spoiled again."

"Doan yo' say nuthin' to us 'bout spoilin'," Lazarus protested. "Last year when ah got sick wif de fever yo' done nursed me til yo' was 'bout to drop. When Berdine fell an' hurt her back, yo' fetched an' carried fo' us all. Yo' spoilin' us so we spoils yo', too," he added as he left.

He returned a half hour later with two large buckets of hot water, balancing the temperature with two buckets of cold.

"Now yo' enjoy yo' bath. Dat boy most likely be bouncin' on yo' bed come dawn. Sleep well."

"Good night, Lazarus. Thank you."

When he was gone, Whitney returned to her bedroom to get a nightgown. Then she gathered towels and soap and returned to the tub. It was a luxury to enjoy a solitary bath without looking after Jon.

Stripping off her clothes, she tossed them on a chair and stepped into the tub. She sank down in the soothing water with a sigh of pleasure. Slowly and leisurely she lathered herself and closed her eyes, reveling in the sensations. Her tired body relaxed and for a few minutes she allowed forbidden memories to return. It would have all been so different if only . . . It just didn't do her any good to reach for something that had been only a will-o'-the-wisp, a dream that had faded before the guns of war.

She had to make a decision. It was time . . . no,

it was past time. She tried to rely only on logic, locking her heart away. She had made decisions with her heart once before, and the cost had been too high.

She would marry Trent Donnelley. She would give her son the best opportunity for a good future. She would forget Mitch . . . she would. She would never tell Jon the truth . . . and she would never tell Mitch the truth should she ever see him again.

Satisfied with her decision, she rose from the tepid water, toweled herself dry, and slipped the nightgown over her head.

She took up her hairbrush and began to brush her hair. It glistened like pale gold before the glow of the lamps. She was completely unaware of the eyes that watched in utter fascination.

Her skin had an amber sheen and he could remember the softness as if his fingers were touching her. With the night behind him and the light behind her, her body was revealed like a silhouette.

Through the partially open window he had heard the conversation with Lazarus. She was alone. He turned from the window. It was too easy and he meant to warn her about it as he climbed silently and effortlessly to the roof. There he found another window partially open, another thing he would caution her about.

Inside he stood in the darkness, inhaling her perfume—delicate, feminine. His blood raced. He knew it would not be long before she arrived. He licked his dry lips and moved to wait behind the door.

Whitney extinguished the lamps one at a time. She didn't need a light to make her way up the stairs—she had climbed them many times in the darkness of sleepless nights.

As she passed her son's room she paused to push the door open. Sparse in its furnishings, it was still comfortable. But it was not what she wanted for him. Well, she would remedy that.

Slowly she crossed the narrow hall to her door. The bed would be so empty, so lonely. Did she want to share it with Trent Donnelley? Logic said yes, but all her womanly instincts cried out for the man who had first awakened her body.

She sighed and opened the door and stepped inside. At that moment a hand clamped over her mouth and a hard-muscled arm came around to nearly lift her from the floor. She was terrified until a well-remembered voice whispered in her ear.

"Don't be afraid. I won't hurt you."

Mitch . . . her mind breathed his name.

Seventeen

It was early evening and Blake didn't really expect to find anyone at the *Sentinel*. He was preparing himself to search out the Anderson home when a glimmer of light in the window drew his attention.

Someone was there, but the light was so dim they could not be working. He tied his horse and walked to the front window to peer inside.

At the back of the room Noel sat at a desk by the light of one small lamp, engrossed in writing. He rapped lightly on the window and her head jerked up. Even from where she was he could sense her fear.

She peered in the direction of the front window and then he realized that because the light was close to her she could not see who it was.

To Noel, Blake looked like a dark shadow. She lifted the lamp and moved very slowly toward the window.

Blake didn't want to frighten her, so he remained motionless as she approached.

The circle of light moved before her and finally she could make him out. She set the lamp down on a nearby table and came to the door. He could hear the bolt slide open and in minutes they stood face to face.

"Blake?"

Her voice was husky and the dark shadows under her eyes attested to her weariness. Her dark hair had been caught carelessly atop her head in a mass of curls that had gotten beyond her control. Wisps framed her cheeks and several loosened tendrils hung against her back. Her eyes seemed to dominate her face, golden and filled with wariness.

"You're alone?" he queried.

"Just for a while, Craig and Kevin had to attend a dinner for Mr. Donnelley. Some kind of fund raiser, I suppose. Anyway, we had to cover it if we want to stay aware of what's going on."

"Does Trent Donnelley have any idea which side of the political fence you and your paper are on?"

"I don't think he's that careless," she replied, her lips twitching in a half smile. "I'm sure he knows exactly how we feel."

"Look, I need to talk to you, and you definitely need an escort home. Surely you didn't plan to walk these streets after dark alone."

"Well," she answered, then hesitated. "I thought Craig or Kevin would be by but it seems they're caught up in something."

"So you'd find your way home alone?" His voice was sharper than he meant, but he remembered her confrontation in the alley. "You're a little braver than you should be."

"No one is braver than they should be." She smiled, a tentative smile for the first time since he had met her. He had the distinct urge to see her smile again . . . to hear her laugh. "I'll be perfectly safe. It's only a short way."

"I'll walk you home," he said determinedly, "or I'll stay right here until one of your brothers comes."

Noel wanted to argue with him and he knew it. She was worried that one of her brothers would return soon and there might be a confrontation. Or worse, that they would come home and find him there. Her reluctance registered in her eyes.

"Noel," Blake said calmly, "either way I'm not leaving you alone. You might just as well concede."

"Why are you so determined to . . ."

"To what?" he asked innocently.

"To start a problem." Her voice was a touch exasperated.

"I have no intention of starting any problem. I only want to be a gentleman and walk a very pretty lady home. What's wrong with that?"

"You and I both know what's wrong with that. It can only make a very sensitive matter worse."

"As long as these 'sensitive' attitudes remain we'll never be able to heal our wounds. Noel, you, your brothers, Mitch, and I will be working together for the same purpose. Don't you think we ought to try to get along? At least for the sake of Mitch's campaign."

She knew that this was logical, but emotions and logic were two different things. Blake was a threat to her brothers' peace of mind. She concentrated on that, denying his much more potentially devastating threat to her.

"I'd like to be friends, Noel," he added softly.

It was difficult to do battle with him. Had he been the kind of 'Yankee' she knew so well she would have been able to fight him. But how could she keep up a guard against understanding, kindness, and what seemed like an honest desire to help right the wrongs? He knew she was wavering so he smiled his most charming smile.

"Home . . . or here?"

"Home," she said, sighing resignedly, hoping to have him out of the building before her brothers returned. She was exhausted and had been almost ready to leave anyway. She had been filled with trepidation about the walk home, but she would never admit that to him.

He waited, enormously pleased with his minute success. One step at a time, he reminded himself. He had to get past her brothers, then do battle with Noel herself. Bad memories were barriers of steel, and he sensed that was what hers were. He wondered just

205

what it would take to make her look at him as a man and not just as a 'damn Yankee' . . . an intruder, unwelcome and untrusted.

He waited patiently while she made a last-minute check and extinguished the lights. Then they stood on the darkened boardwalk while she locked the door. A few minutes later they were walking slowly down the street.

"It's been a beautiful night," he murmured, seeking to breach the silence.

"It's always pretty this time of year." She was quiet for such a long time that he began to wonder if he was being given the cold treatment. He had no idea of the turmoil within her. She turned her head to glance quickly at him, then looked away as if afraid to let her eyes linger too long.

"What's it like . . . where you live, I mean?"

"Well, Maryland is . . . was my home. It's beautiful, too. It's . . . different."

"How?"

"I don't really know. We lived pretty near Washington so life was a little faster paced. Here everything seems to move like Vermont syrup," he laughed.

"Vermont syrup?"

"My grandmother had a farm in Vermont. We used to go up there in the winter when it was time to sugar off. I guess that's one of my fondest memories. You've never tasted the candy," he sighed, his mind drifting back. "I can remember holding pieces in my mouth, afraid it would melt too fast. We used to skate and ski. Winters were special. The snow and the bonfires . . ." his voice died away with the memories.

Noel watched him with the heart-tearing realization that he had lost memories as well. For too long she had felt that memories were her exclusive domain.

"I've never seen snow. What's it like?"

"Snow?" He laughed. "That's hard to describe. It's like little pieces of your grandmother's lace doilies,

206

only cold and wet. It's really a sight. I'd like . . ."

"What?"

"I'd like you to see it."

"Why did you leave?" She tried to deny his attempt to penetrate her reserve.

"My grandmother died. My father couldn't afford to run both places, so the farm was sold."

"So you spent winters in Vermont and summers in Maryland. What was it like there?"

"My father raised horses, fine horses. I'm afraid this little four-year engagement decimated his stock. He . . . he lost everything because the army just didn't understand about paying on time. All except one horse . . . the one that should have gotten sold."

"I don't understand."

"I used to call him the dragon—a stallion so difficult to handle even the army didn't want him. Can't have your officers being thrown in the midst of battle, can you? Instead . . . instead he killed my father."

Noel inhaled deeply. "I'm sorry."

"It was a long time ago."

"What did you do?"

Blake's laugh was harsh. "I went home and shot him." He waited for recriminations, but none came. "It didn't help. It couldn't bring my father back. It was stupid and I regret it. I guess that's when I learned that no form of revenge makes up for pain and loss. It takes something else to fill the emptiness."

She knew what he was trying to tell her but she was not ready to admit it.

"And your mother?"

"I hardly knew her, really; she died when I was five."

"The rest of your family . . ."

"I'm it, Noel," he said firmly. "The last of the Randolphs." He tried to laugh again to cover his emotion. "And that's just about enough about me. I'd like to know about you. It's only fair, you know."

207

"I'm afraid we're home," she said, as she stopped before a white picket fence that surrounded a small white frame house.

"You don't play fair," he said quietly.

"I didn't know it was a game."

"Noel, even the game of life has some rules. I'm not your enemy. I'm trying to come more than halfway. Maybe you should try to give a little more." It stung her because she knew he was right. But she was afraid. "I could use something to drink before I walk back." His eyes held hers, almost willing her to accept him, at least as a friend.

"All right. Come in."

She preceded him through the gate. Well aware that his heart was thudding rapidly, a wave of pleasure washed over Blake. Round one was his.

She unlocked the cottage door and he followed her into the inky blackness.

"Stand still," she requested. "I know where every piece of furniture is. I'll light a lamp before you fall over something."

He remained motionless, hearing her move about in the darkness. After a few minutes the lamp flooded the room with mellow light.

Blake wasn't too sure what he expected, but it wasn't what he saw. The furniture, although there was very little of it, was rich fine wood that gleamed with care. The floor was polished to a fine sheen as well and an oval braided rug protected it from a large table that sat in the center of the room.

The room was about fifteen by eighteen, with two doors against one wall that he surmised led to bedrooms. The only other room was a small kitchen. He was still gazing at the beautiful furniture in the immaculately clean room.

"It's all we could save," Noel said softly. He looked at her, a little embarrassed that she had read his thoughts so well. "The table was my mother's . . . as was the furniture in my bedroom. I couldn't part with them. My mother had so many pretty things. She . . ." Noel's voice choked to silence and she turned from him. "Would you like some wine or maybe some whiskey? My brother keeps a bottle or two here."

"Whiskey is fine." Blake felt in need of a strong drink. He'd opened a door again and he hated the pain it caused her. Yet he instinctively knew that too much was bottled up inside of her—maybe release was what she needed.

She handed him a glass with a liberal amount of whiskey in it. As he took it from her their fingers brushed and the tingle echoed through him as their eyes met.

Noel was shaken, for her fragile senses could not tolerate the gentleness, the understanding . . . or the faint touch of reined-in passion she saw lurking in the depths of his eyes. With a soft, inarticulate sound she backed away and moved to keep a safe distance between them. He did not miss this—fear was not what he wanted to see in her eyes. He sipped the whiskey, still gazing at her.

"So, tell me about you."

"There's not much to tell. I'll be nineteen in a few weeks. I'm reasonably well educated. I can sew and cook and if I have to say so myself I'm a pretty good newspaper woman."

"That's not what I wanted to know about you, Noel, and you know it," he said quietly.

Her golden eyes were wide and filled with shadows. He could see defiance there as well.

"You ask too much, Blake Randolph," she retorted, her voice distant and shaken.

"Why too much? Friendships begin with knowing and understanding each other."

"Understanding? How could you possibly understand? You don't know how it was before—you never saw or tasted how sweet and good it was. How can you possibly know?"

"Nothing stays the same. Time would have changed it anyway. Life is one continuous change. It has to be."

"Do you think that's an excuse to cause destruction and death?"

"No. There's never a logical reason for that. But don't you think we have to renew our lives and learn to live?" His voice was velvet soft and she refused to look into his eyes. They held questions she had no answers for . . . at least none she could give.

"Blake . . . go away." She stood with her back to him, her hands clenched before her. He could hear the tears in her voice.

"I can't." His voice was just as soft and just as firm. She turned to look at him, her face pale and her eyes so brilliant he seemed to be drowning in them. "I'm not going to let you go on running, denying yourself, afraid to feel anymore."

"Everything seems so simple to you, but I can't forget! I just can't!"

"Have you really tried?"

"What do you mean?"

"Noel, how old were you when the war started?"

"Fourteen. Why?"

"The time when a young girl is aware and very sensitive. Your life must have been so beautiful then." She took a step back as if physically denying what he said. "Your world must have been so complete, so full of love and fun." She shook her head negatively, wordlessly battling him. "Your brothers were your heroes, weren't they?"

"Are you telling me it was wrong to love my family?"

"God, no. It's not wrong. What's wrong is allowing yourself to become a sacrifice to dead memories because you can't let go of them."

"I don't know what you mean."

"You do know what I mean. Noel, there's nothing wrong with sharing the pain with someone who cares, who wants to understand . . . who wants to help."

"You?"

"If you want."

"No. I don't want you with all your answers and all your wisdom. Blake, this is impossible. We cannot work together."

"So you choose to run? Didn't you tell me no one is braver than they should be? I thought you had more courage than that."

He had struck a nerve. Noel and most of her remaining family had lived on little but courage for a long time. It was a blow meant to shake her, and it did. If possible, her face grew even paler. She refused to meet his gaze and turned her back to him. "Go away, Blake . . . just go away."

He came up behind her and took hold of her shoulders, drawing her back against him. He could feel her entire body trembling. "Whatever you've seen, whatever you've felt, it's wrong to hold it inside until it destroys any chance for happiness. Noel, you're a sweet, loving woman, not the child who lived through that terror. You must try to forget."

She tore herself away and spun around. This time anger melded with misery and defiance.

"Damn you!" Tears she refused to shed glistened in her eyes. "I don't know what it is that you think you know, but you don't understand and you never will. I don't want you to understand! I don't want you to care. Do you think you can walk in here and with a few kind words wipe out everything? Well, I don't need anyone to tell me to forget, or to offer me consolation. If it's necessary for the benefit of our town I'll cooperate with Mitchell Flannery. But my life is my own!" She was breathing in ragged gasps and the tears she was valiantly fighting slipped down her

211

cheeks. She looked vulnerable, like a child filled with misery.

In two quick strides he was beside her. Before she could protest he put his arms about her, crushing her to him. A sob seemed torn from her lips.

"I never meant to hurt you, Noel. I swear on everything I am that I won't say or do a thing to hurt you again. I won't interfere in your life. I just want to be part of it."

She looked up at him, doubt clouding her eyes. She wasn't quite prepared to believe him, but their eyes held for just a moment longer than either planned. There was a long, breathless silence.

He couldn't help it anymore than he could have stopped breathing. Her mouth was inches away, and her body was intimately pressed to his. Slowly he lowered his head and his parted lips gently touched hers. For him, the result was electrifying.

But for her it was a threat she couldn't handle. She struggled to get away and at that moment he was tempted to force her to face the fact that the kiss was more effective than she would admit.

At that moment they heard the sound of heavy footsteps and the rattle of a key in the lock. Noel leapt from his arms as the door swung open and Craig and Kevin entered.

Both men were surprised to see Blake, surprised and more than a little suspicious.

"Noel, are you all right?" Craig inquired, his eyes never leaving her face. She looked as if something had really shaken her.

"I'm fine, Craig."

Kevin remained silent, but he had been assessing Blake with a look that was less than friendly.

"And just what are you doing here, Mr. Randolph? It's a trifle late for a social call, isn't it?" Craig questioned.

"I found Noel preparing to walk home alone. Since

the last episode was so dangerous, I escorted her. She should be treated a little more carefully, don't you think?"

"Are you insinuating . . ." Kevin began.

"I'm insinuating nothing. I'm just reminding you that Noel is too important . . . and much too pretty to have to find her way about this very unsympathetic town alone."

"Don't worry about her any longer," Craig said. "We'll see to her safety. What brought you to the paper in the first place?"

"I've written some editorials. I'd like your opinion on them."

"Leave them. I'll read them over."

"All right," Blake said with a shrug. He glanced at Noel, whose gaze seemed locked on Kevin. Blake headed slowly toward the door, reluctant to leave and well aware that what he thought about Noel's self flag-ellation had been right. He would find out why one day, brothers or no brothers, war or no war. "Good night, everyone."

He was stopped momentarily by Kevin's voice, brittle with antagonism.

"Mr. Randolph, there's no reason for you ever to return to this house. You're not welcome and there's nothing here for you."

"Kevin!" Noel was aghast and shamed at what Kevin had said. Her cheeks burned as she turned and walked to her bedroom, closing the door sharply be-hind her. In another moment all three men heard the distinct click of the lock.

"You're a damn fool, Kevin," Blake said softly. "Maybe you're blinded by your inability to rebuild your lives. But that's no excuse for dragging Noel into a quagmire of hate just to satisfy your own stupidity. If I could say or do anything to help her . . . keep her from destroying herself, I would. But she loves you two and she thinks you're all she has left. Well,

213

you're not, and I hope one day to prove it." He turned and left. For long moments both brothers were silent, weighted with emotions they had denied long ago.

"Craig?"

"What?"

"You're not thinking of working with him, of letting him see Noel?"

Craig sighed deeply, his mind deeply weary.

"Noel can make up her own mind, make her own decisions."

"I'm not going to let her forget!"

"And I'm not going to forget! But we have a job to do and for the sake of something bigger than all of us we have to try and work together. At least until the election is over."

"No! No, we can't."

"We will, Kevin," Craig said with finality. Kevin glared at him as if he could force him to rescind his words, but he saw no uncertainty in his brother's eyes. Craig, who had always led them. Who had always been a confident leader, a counselor . . . everything.

With a ragged curse, Kevin went to the door and left the house, slamming the door behind him.

Craig sat down slowly in a chair, favoring his old wound. He felt a kind of despair. He'd worked hard to keep the remnants of his family together. Now Blake Randolph had come into their lives, the biggest challenge they had ever faced.

Questions plagued him — the most important being what, if anything, was between Noel and Blake Randolph . . . and what kind of demon drove Kevin to want to hurt their sister.

Eighteen

"Don't be foolish enough to scream," Mitch's voice whispered softly in her ear. He had no way of knowing screaming was the last thing in her mind. She was grateful that Berdine had taken Jon. He was safely out of Mitch's reach, as he obviously didn't want to awaken any others. She shook her head and slowly he released her.

The room was dark and both of them were silent shadows as she moved away from him.

"What are you doing here?" Her voice was a ragged whisper, and he could sense her fear without seeing her.

"We have unfinished business, Whitney."

"There's nothing between us . . . nothing."

"God, Whitney, there couldn't be more between a man and a woman than there is between us."

"Don't destroy my life again, Mitch. Go away. It's the best thing you can do for us."

"Us?"

"Me," she hastily corrected. He heard a subtle inflection in her voice. It was more than fear . . .

His thoughts went to the child. Maybe it would be better to try to talk about him first.

"Light the lamp, Whitney."

"Why?"

"We have to talk. I can't talk to a shadow." He wanted to see her face when he swore he would love

215

and accept the child, that they could be a family and forget the past.

He heard her move, heard the scratch of the match, and in minutes the room was flooded with amber light.

They looked at each other and Mitch felt as if a chasm yawned between them. He hated the war, the minutes, the hours, the days they had been apart.

She looked so young and so vulnerable. Like the sweet girl he had fallen in love with what seemed like a century ago. But he knew this woman carried bitterness as a shield to protect her now.

He wanted to go to her, lift her in his arms, and carry her to the bed and make love to her until he made her forget the past.

She had no trouble reading his desire. Had she not read the same look in his eyes so many times? But she could not afford to give in to her senses. Too much was at stake.

"There's nothing left for you here, Mitch. Go away, leave me in peace."

It hurt, it was unbelievable how it hurt. How could he make her understand that he couldn't?

"Is it really that easy for you, Whitney?"

"I said goodbye to my dreams a long time ago."

"Well, I never said goodbye to ours, and I won't. Not until everything that's wrong is made right, not until we're together again."

"No, that's not possible." He heard that elusive note of panic again.

"Whitney, what's keeping us apart?" His voice was as gentle as he could make it, considering the tension. "Is it the child?"

Her gasp was half-pain, half-terror. "How . . . how did you . . ."

"I saw him."

"No . . . no one would . . ."

"At a distance. Whitney, for God's sake you could

216

have told me. Did you think I couldn't understand?"

"Understand?" she repeated, stunned that he would say such a thing.

"I can understand loneliness and need when you suffer the way you did."

His words crashed against her like all of her life was crumbling. Obviously he had not gotten the letter about his son. And just as obviously, he believed she had taken another man and slept with him, as if she would give herself to anyone for a moment's comfort.

Her eyes filled with a rage such as he had never seen. She fought it, and fought not to speak the words that would tell him the truth.

"How very understanding you are. How noble to have developed such a code of honor. It seems the war has been generous to you."

He didn't know what he had said that had fueled her rage so.

"I'm not trying to set myself up as something special. I'm just trying to tell you that nothing changes how I feel about you. Whitney, don't let something like this destroy what we had." He had a strong feeling he was making a bad matter worse, but didn't know why. "Whitney, will you listen to me for a minute?"

"Do I have a choice?"

"I mean *listen*," he snapped, his own anger beginning to grow.

"What difference does it make? I'm going to marry another man. The child, *my son*, will have a father so you can keep your nobility to use on some other poor creature. I don't need it." She struggled to hold back the bitter tears.

Her words tore at Mitch. What he had said, intended to say, had somehow been twisted and used against him. Her announcement that she was going to marry another man infuriated him. He knew who

217

she was talking about and he intended to make sure it never happened.

"Trent Donnelley," he said coldly, "you think you're going to marry him?"

"I don't think, I know."

"You don't love him, Whitney."

"You're so certain?"

"Unless everything about you has changed, and I don't think even a war could do that, you're no liar. You don't love him."

"I intend to marry him."

She had not said she didn't love Trent Donnelley. She still wouldn't retreat an inch.

"And I intend to see that you don't," he said just as stubbornly.

"There's really not too much you can do about it," she cried, trying to retain her composure. She could slip and tell him the truth, and she didn't want to make that mistake now that she knew what he thought.

Her heart cried out in a kind of agony. He should have known he was the only one, he should have known!

"I'm running against him, Whitney. I'm going to cut him down to size and keep him from owning and destroying this town . . . and you. That's what he would do, you know."

"Whatever he does cannot be as cold and brutal as what you did. So let me alone. Don't make a mistake, Mitch. He's strong and he knows the right people. You can't win this thing."

"Don't count me out before it's over. The Flannerys aren't quitters . . . not in anything."

Whitney was exhausted, her emotions frayed. She wanted him to leave. She was afraid, and she couldn't handle the fear much longer. Mitch's presence dredged up memories she had tried so hard to forget. How could he still have this effect on her when she had struggled so hard to forget him?

She turned away and struggled once more with her tears. "Please go, Mitch . . . please."

She closed her eyes as she felt him come up behind her. His arms went around her so gently that for this moment she lost her resistance.

It would be so easy . . . but she caught herself falling into the same trap. Gentle persuasion. It could cost her all she loved and all she hoped for. She moved out of his arms and, much as he wanted to, he couldn't fight her.

Mitch was desperate to reach out to her. If he could just get past her self-imposed barriers to the loving person he knew Whitney to be, he could repair the damage.

It was the damned letters. He almost wished they had not decided to write. Then there would have been no chance of misunderstanding. Was this the time to mention the land? He thought carefully then decided to try another tack first.

He raked his fingers through his hair in frustration. "Look, Whitney. When I came back everything was different. Misunderstandings . . ."

"*Misunderstandings?* It's pretty inadequate to use that term, isn't it?"

"No, it's just that you don't want to believe it."

"I can't afford the luxury of beliefs in the past. I have to think of the future . . . my future and Jon's."

"Jon. That's his name?"

She nodded. Her heart skipped a beat. She did not want to talk about Jon . . . not with him. But Mitch felt a throb of something. He was becoming more certain that this boy might still be their common ground.

"I know how important he must be to you, Whitney. I know how hard it must have been for both of you. God, don't you think I understand? I've seen some pain and destruction, too." She turned away

219

from him, feeling the same gentleness that threatened her reserve.

He needed to make her see. He stood close and forced her to look at him. "Look at me, Whitney," he softened his voice so his urgency would not be abrasive. She turned slowly and raised her eyes to meet his steady gaze. If only she could believe what she thought she saw. If only the memories of the pain would not smother the tiny flame that burned deep within her. If only . . . but she just couldn't take the chance. It had never seemed to occur to him that Jon could be his and that she had never lain with another man.

"We've changed, Whitney. There's no doubt about it, this war has changed the whole world. But I swear it hasn't changed the way I feel about you, and if you'll look past the hurt and the terrible tragedies you'll see the truth. Whoever told the lies, whoever kept our letters from getting to each other, shouldn't be allowed to succeed. Try to remember the good things we shared and how it was between us."

"The good things, Mitch? We never really knew what our future would have been. Maybe we were too young and passionate. But the past is gone. So much has happened and we can never go back."

"I don't want to go back. I want to go ahead. I want us to have a future together."

"Even," she said calmly, "if it means you have to forgive me for Jon."

"You're putting words in my mouth. I'm not the one to condemn or forgive. He's your son, part of you, I would love him as if he were my own."

"As if he were your own," she murmured softly. "Mitch, I'm too confused and tired to talk about it anymore tonight. I told you, you have to give me time."

"Time to marry another man. Not on your life. I'm not going out of your life, Whitney. I can't. It would

220

make a shambles of mine. You're looking for a future for you and the boy. I can offer you one, as good as any other man. I'm not the Mitchell Flannery who left here, poor and looked down upon. You might be surprised at the difference in my life now. I can offer you the fulfillment of all the hopes and promises I made so long ago."

"That never really meant that much to me, Mitch, and you know it. Do you think it means that much to me now? I've learned to struggle and to do without. Our positions are switched. If it were not for Jon . . ."

"If it were not for Jon you wouldn't agree to marry anyone at all," he finished for her with a half-smile. "You've become a very independent lady." He was pleased that her first thought was not her love for Trent Donnelley. He felt a new excitement. A marriage of convenience would be no barrier to love if he could reawaken a response in Whitney — the response she was trying desperately to suppress. It only intensified the helpless anger he felt at whoever had intercepted their letters and attempted to destroy everything between them. He didn't know who was responsible, although he suspected her parents. Hatred was wasted on people he could no longer confront and whose crime he could never prove. He had to force these emotions aside, sure that Whitney would reject any recriminations directed at a family she had lost so tragically.

"Yes, I guess I have," she responded cautiously. "And it's something I can't afford to lose."

"You think Trent Donnelley will let you keep your independence?" he queried with a dark frown. "If you do, Whitney, you're making a big mistake. It takes a lot of love to allow the person you marry to remain independent. You don't love him and I'll wager my life what he feels for you is opportunism and not love."

221

"I'll make my own evaluations and my own decisions. Trent has been good to me. I certainly owe him . . ."

"And that's enough to build a life on?"

"Some have built on less."

"Not you," he said quietly. "Not us." He moved to her so quickly she was hardly able to react. In an easy movement he pulled her into his arms. "What we had," he said gently, "was so much more than that. It was a miracle, Whitney. You know it and so do I."

He was right about the magic. It was all around her like a vaporous mist. Her mind shouted a warning her body refused to hear. His proximity was overwhelming and her body remembered his touch so well—her senses came alive with the thought of it. She did know it, but she dared not admit it. All the terrors of the past rose up inside her like a dark and powerful wave. Blind to all but the fact that she could lose Jon, she was assaulted by other memories. The loss of her father, her brother, then her home and her mother. Another loss was just too much to bear.

"Mitch, let me go. This is no way to solve our problems." She struggled to keep her voice calmer than the ragged beating of her heart.

Mitch knew she was lying, but he admired a new kind of strength he saw in Whitney. He couldn't have let her go if his life had depended upon it. Their eyes locked and it became a war of wills and senses, holding them in a whirling vortex above a flame. She was afraid it would consume her and take away the last solid thing she had, and he somehow knew he was losing ground and didn't know why.

He bent his head to kiss her, slowly and leisurely. He savored the taste of her and the softness of her mouth. The kiss lingered, deepened until he pulsed with renewed need. But when he released her lips all he tasted was defeat. Her eyes brimmed and a silver teardrop ran slowly down one cheek.

"Is this what you want?" she questioned softly. "Is your version of love what you can demand of my body? Well, it's not enough for me, Mitch. I put love on a physical plane before, and I won't face the pain it brought me again. If you want to force me you most likely can. But I shall hate you to my dying day . . . that I swear."

Her words made a wound more brutal and painful than any he had received in the heat of battle. He was stung by the truth in them and by the look in her eyes that told him she meant exactly what she was saying. Slowly he released her.

Whitney inhaled deeply. He need not know that her body longed for his touch—and she could feel the emptiness more poignantly than ever.

"I'm sorry, Whitney. You should know me better than that. I've always wanted more than that for us," he said defensively.

Whitney needed the momentary vulnerability she saw on his face. He was hurt, she could read it in his eyes. Torn by the desire to return to his arms and surrender to the need within her, and the selfish fear that all she had could be lost if she made one mistake, she remained still and silent.

"Whitney, I feel I have a right to know what your plans are. I'm a patient man and I can take a lot, but I've warned you: I'll do whatever is necessary to keep you from marrying Trent Donnelley—even if it means dragging you away from here by force and holding you hostage."

For the first time she half-smiled. "Don't be ridiculous. Lazarus would nail you to the barn wall."

He laughed softly. "Lazarus never has approved of me." Then the laugh faded. "What are you going to do, Whitney?"

"To tell the truth I don't know, Mitch. I've been praying that Keith is still alive, that one day he'll come back . . ."

"Whitney, the war's been over for a year."

"I know. But Samantha Nelson's father has just come home. He was wounded and in a prisoner of war camp. It's possible . . . it's still possible."

She sounded so full of hope that he found it difficult to say anything more.

"Sure . . . sure it's possible."

"If he came home things would be different. We could go back to the old place and maybe try to rebuild. After all, our roots are there. It's really all we have."

Mitch saw the opportunity to redeem some lost ground. "Whitney . . . . you've never received any kind of notice about that land?"

"Notice? What kind of notice?"

"About the taxes that haven't been paid for five years."

"No," she said hesitantly, trying to read his expression. "I don't know of any taxes."

"Maybe someone made sure you never knew."

"What are you trying to tell me?"

"That for five years the taxes haven't been paid and the bank has already had a tax sale."

Her face went gray and her eyes seemed to grow wider as the realization seeped in. "A tax sale," she repeated numbly, her every sense attempting to deny her worst fear.

"Look, Whitney, you believe in Trent Donnelley. You think your problems will be over if you marry him. Well, if your knight in shining armor is so wonderful tell me why he was one of the first people at the bank's door this morning intending to pay up the taxes and take over the deed to your land."

"He didn't . . . he couldn't!" she cried in disbelief.

"He could, he would . . . and he tried."

"Tried," she stammered. She was shaken. "How . . . . how do you know?"

"I put a stop to it."

"How . . . why?"

"Because I wanted you to have it. Because I knew what you would go through if this happened. One more blow, one more loss. Think about this, Whitney. I'm going to leave. Not because I want to, for before God what I want is to make love to you until we have what we once had. I want you to love me." He reached out and took hold of her shoulders, drawing her to him. "I want you to say you've never forgotten." He kissed her until his mind spun with the need for more. "I will leave, but I'm going to give you something to think about. Your friend never told you about the land because he wanted it. Ask yourself this: if he loved you, why didn't he tell you? And I'll give you one more thing to think about." He took the deed from his pocket and laid it on a table nearby. "This is your land, Whitney. I bought it just minutes before he did. You see, I know, I remember how you loved it and I wanted you to have it. I'm going, and you can spend the rest of the night thinking about these questions. When you have the answers . . . then tell me."

He put his arms about her, pressing her close to him. With this final kiss he had to remind her that all either of them needed for a bright future was each other.

His mouth took her slightly parted lips with all that he was or hoped to be. With every ounce of love he possessed, from the depths of his soul, he kissed her.

When he released her he backed up a step. Without a word he took the deed from the table and put it in her hand, forcing her fingers to close about it.

"I'll come . . . whenever you want me to," he whispered. "I love you."

He left through the door, leaving a stricken Whitney.

She stared from the paper in her hand to the closed door. It seemed as if her world had exploded and she no longer knew what was right and what was wrong.

Slowly she moved to her bed and sat upon it for several minutes. Then she turned and flung herself across it and cried as she had not cried since the tragedies of the war had frozen her emotions.

Mitch rode toward home slowly, trying to regain control of the storm that boiled inside of him. He'd given her a choice and now he was scared to death she would fling it back in his face and tell him to get out of her life forever.

He cursed himself for his tactless stupidity, and in another breath he prayed that she would understand and ask him to come back.

He thought of the child. Jon . . . . he liked the name. At least there he had not lied. He could love a child knowing it was part of Whitney. That would be enough.

Nineteen

Jon sat cross-legged on Whitney's bed, his box of soldiers beside him. His dark head was bent over the ones he had set up on the squares of the quilt.

Whitney, standing before her mirror, was gazing not at her reflection, but at Jon's. She stood and watched him, a tender smile on her lips.

He must have felt the intensity of her gaze because he looked up suddenly and smiled. Whitney felt a stab of pain in her heart. How could she ever erase Mitch from her life when Jon's clear gray eyes and quick, bright smile were constant reminders?

He looked so much like Mitch that it shook her resolve and frightened her. It also dredged up too many painful memories.

The way his cloud of thick black hair fell over his forehead—how many times had she pushed back Mitch's unruly hair with her fingers? How many times . . . she caught herself allowing the memories to creep insidiously into her mind. She just couldn't afford these thoughts—they were too much of a threat to her resolve.

Nearby, on top of her bureau, lay the deed to her land that Mitch had returned to her. Confusion still filled her. Mitch could have kept it, maybe as a lure to bring her back to him. But he hadn't. He had returned it without regard for himself. She would have to find out what he had paid and return the money somehow. She didn't want to be beholden to him.

Her mind turned to Trent. Why had he wanted her land? To give it to her? If so, why had he not told her? If he meant it for a wedding present, then perhaps . . . but she had not agreed to marry him. She needed to speak to Trent, to see his face and listen to what he had to say. Maybe then she would find a way out of this confusion and find some peace of mind.

Whitney turned from the mirror and walked to the bed. With a loving hand she reached out and brushed Jon's hair back.

"Jon, you must be a very good boy for Berdine tonight."

He looked up at her again, his gray eyes studying her, then he nodded and returned his attention to his play.

Whitney touched the large carved jewelry box that had once been her mother's and the old pain made her sigh heavily. Jon took such good care of the box. He loved it and the store of hand-carved soldiers and horses it held.

One day, Whitney thought, she would have to replace the red velvet lining. It was worn and frayed. She would have to look for some sturdy material that could resist the constant touch of little fingers.

"You know Mommy's going to be away all night?" Again he nodded. "Addy will sleep in your room like she always does and Lazarus will be right downstairs. You won't be afraid, will you?"

It was the familiar tilt of his head, the jutting of his tiny chin, and the gleam in his gray eyes that wrenched her heart.

"I'm not afraid," he replied, his voice belligerent. "I'm a big boy, I don't cry."

"No, of course you don't."

As she sat on the edge of the bed, he lost interest in his toys and climbed onto her lap. His tiny arms about her neck made her tears start, and she hugged him to her almost fiercely.

"Mommy?"

"What, dear?"

"Can I go with you?"

"Not this time, I'm afraid. But if you're a very good boy I'll bring you a present. What would you like?"

"Candy," he said with a quick grin. Mischief danced in his eyes.

"I think I'm being maneuvered, and by a little charmer, too. All right, candy it is."

She stood up, lifting him with her.

"Since Mr. Donnelley is going to be here soon to take me to town, maybe it's best I take you to Berdine and get you settled." She started toward the door.

"My box! Mommy, my box," Jon cried.

"You and that box are inseparable, aren't you?" Whitney said as she returned to the bed. She gathered up the soldiers and stuffed them in the box.

"Someday I'll tell you stories of the lady it once belonged to . . . stories of how wonderful it was . . ." She stopped. Old memories didn't help either of them.

She stood him on the floor by the bed and lifted the box. It was almost too big for Jon to handle, and she knew she couldn't manage it and Jon, too. "I don't know how you manage to carry this thing about like you do. Come on, let's get over to Berdine's. I'll bet she's making those special little cakes you like."

Jon trotted along just ahead of her, bouncing with energy. Her heart swelled with love and pride. He was her compensation, her reward for everything that had gone wrong in her life. The old terror returned. She knew the law. There was no way she could keep Jon if Mitch wanted to take him away from her. Could he do it and justify it somehow? The law was so unfair to women, considering them and the children they laboriously bore and reared as chattel . . . a commodity. Any thoughts she had of telling Mitch the truth were buried beneath that reality. She could not lose Jon. He was her life. He was all she had.

They entered Berdine's small house to the scent of something good baking and the sound of laughter.

Addy and Josiah were seated at the wooden table and Berdine was stirring something that smelled enticing. She stood before the huge fireplace and watched Whitney and Jon enter.

"Lan' sakes, boy, ah come to think dat box is attached to yo'," Berdine called, laughing.

"I swear, Berdine," Whitney laughed. "He won't make a move without it."

"Well, put it somewhere an' come to de table, Jon. Ah made some of yo' favorites fo' dinner."

Jon was quick to scamper to Addy, who lifted him to a seat beside her on the bench. At that moment Lazarus entered.

"Miz Whitney . . . Mr. Donnelley be here."

"All right, Lazarus, I'm ready," she replied as she turned to Jon again. "Now you be good." She bent to kiss him. "And I won't forget the candy." She turned to Berdine. "You know where I'll be, Berdine. At Mrs. Delaney's. I'll be home early tomorrow afternoon. If you need me for anything, just send Josiah."

"Ah'll do that, but ah don' 'spect we'll be havin' no problems. Josiah an' Lazarus gwine take de boy fishin'. Den he be tucked in bed jus' like always."

"Thank you, Berdine . . . but if . . ."

"Now yo' quits worryin'. Ah kin handle one li'l boy. Hain't ah always?"

"Of course you have. I guess I just hate to leave him."

"Yo' go along. Dis rally an' all de parties an' laughin' gwine be fun, an' yo' needs a li'l fun. Jes' take some time to enjoy all de celebration."

"All right." Whitney kissed Jon again and walked to the door.

As she crossed the small walkway to the carriage, Trent watched her. The thoughts that tore at his mind would have shaken Whitney to the core. He smiled, keeping a careful mask in place.

She was beautiful, and he enjoyed her self-possessed stride as she moved toward him. He wanted her. He would have enjoyed throwing her to the ground and taking her. The thought made his loins tighten and swell. He kept his hat on his lap to keep his arousal from showing.

There were many reasons he wanted to marry Whitney, and lust was not the least of them.

"Hello, Trent," Whitney said with a smile as he extended a hand to help her into the carriage.

"Whitney, you look lovely."

"Thank you."

"Mrs. Delaney urged me to hurry. They're planning a lawn supper before the rally, and they want you to share it. I have to go on to the hall, but they'll be happy to bring you with them when they come."

"That sounds fine," she agreed. He climbed into the carriage beside her and picked up the reins. As they rode away from the house, he smiled down at her.

"Excited?"

"Just a bit," she admitted, laughing. "There hasn't

231

been such a celebration since before the war."

"I guess I'm a little excited myself. This has been the realization of one of my goals."

"One?"

"One," he repeated. "Whitney . . . there's little doubt that I'll win this election. As far as I know, there's no one running against me. But I'll never feel I've really won it if I don't have you by my side. Will you reconsider and answer me tonight after the rally? I want my wife to be with me."

"Are you certain you're running unopposed?"

"I don't know of any foolish man who intends to propose himself tonight, but if anyone does, it'll be the biggest mistake of his life. I intend to win."

She was silent for some minutes, knowing Mitch would oppose him but somehow afraid to say it. He would certainly ask her how she knew.

"You haven't answered my question, you know," he reminded her gently.

"The rally is only the beginning. We have so much time. I . . ."

"I'm disappointed, but I'll wait. You're worth waiting for."

"Trent," she began, attempting to keep her voice controlled, "I received a wonderful gift from Mitch Flannery."

Now it was his turn to be silent. When he spoke his voice was firm. "A gift? What could a man like Mitchell Flannery have to give you that you would want?"

"It seems that my father's land had been put up for taxes. I didn't know. He paid them and gave me the deed."

"The man is so clever," Trent said angrily. "Yes, I know about the sale. I wanted to give it to you for a wedding present. Whitney, what is that man after? Who is he and what does he mean to you?"

"I knew him before the war. He gave me back my land and I'm grateful for that, that's all."

"I've made inquiries about him. It seems he's not one of the city's more savory citizens. He was nothing before the war, and he's nothing now. I won't tolerate him interfering in our lives."

"Trent! Why would you make inquiries about him? His life is not your affair."

"Because I don't trust him. His kind won't let anything stand between him and what he wants. I have the feeling I've seen him before, and the situation must have been unfavorable. He's not a man to trust, Whitney. I'm surprised you took that deed without knowing what strings might be attached."

"There are no strings attached!" She was angry and he knew it. He drew the horses to a halt and tied the reins carefully. Then he turned to her.

"Whitney . . . I want you to stay away from this man. He's a clever opportunist, and he wouldn't mind taking advantage of a sweet, caring person like you. What seems like generosity is a ploy of some sort. He's trouble."

"Whatever ploy he has in mind just won't work, Trent. I'm not a child. I don't want either of you thinking I can be taken advantage of so easily."

"I?"

"I don't need protection, and I make my own decisions."

There was a spark of something in Whitney's eyes that made Trent pause. His long-range goals were too important to antagonize Whitney now. There were too many answers she knew to too many questions. He'd slipped, but he was too clever to lose his footing.

"I'm sorry, Whitney. I guess the thought of losing you is more than I can bear. I didn't mean to be so possessive. I love you. Maybe it was more jealousy than anything else. Will you forgive me?"

"Of course." She smiled and agreed, but a small voice in the depths of her had begun to whisper subtle questions. Had Trent meant to give her land back as a wedding present? Or had he meant to add it to his holdings, considering her and all she owned as part of his wealth as well? The thought shook her. Before she had seen Mitch she had had few doubts about Trent. Now she was uncertain.

He picked up the reins and drove on.

"I know how hard it must be for you. The responsibility of your land, your son, and the blacks you harbor. It's too bad your brother didn't survive the war."

"Actually Lazarus, Berdine, Josiah, and Addy have been much more my caretakers than I theirs. As far as Jon is concerned, he's my consolation for all that was lost. I still hope that somehow, some way, Keith is still alive. I never received any final word."

"Surely if he were alive he would have contacted you by now."

"I don't know what reasons he might have. I can only hope and pray."

"Would he not at least write to you?"

"All the letters I have were the ones he sent to Mother and me before . . ." She could not say anything that would make her relive the terror of the past again.

"I'm glad you saved them. At least you have that. I hope one day you'll let me fill the void your losses have caused. Whitney . . . if you do decide to marry me, I would love to read your brother's letters some day."

"Why?"

"Just a way to bring me a little closer to you, I guess."

She nodded, but again the little warning voice stirred. She realized she was growing defensive and was glad she hadn't made a final decision yet.

No matter how she argued with herself she couldn't forget—Mitch had freely given her her land back. Trent had never even spoken to her about her old home and the love she had for it. The question arose in her mind again and again . . . had Trent really intended to give it to her . . . or not?

They arrived at the Delaney home, and Whitney was relieved when Eleanor Delaney came out on the porch to meet them. It put an end to any more conversation, and for a reason Whitney couldn't quite fathom, she was grateful.

"I'll leave you in good hands, Whitney," Trent said. "I must get into town and prepare for the rally. There are reserved seats for you and the Delaneys. I'll see you there. I hope you'll be proud of me tonight. I want you to see what a wonderful future we could have."

"Of course I'm proud of you, Trent. I'll be there."

He bent to kiss her but she turned her cheek. Even though he was aware of it, he acted as if nothing had happened.

But as he walked back and climbed into his carriage, his hatred of Mitchell Flannery was seething. Flannery had been a problem before, but now he seemed to be coming between him and Whitney and that simply could not happen!

Mitch was standing on the boardwalk deep in conversation with Blake and Craig when Trent rode down the street. It was Blake who noticed Trent, but he said nothing. This was not the time for

Mitch and Trent Donnelley to meet. Later at the rally would be much more appropriate and certainly more effective.

"Blake's editorials are set up and ready to run," Craig remarked. "I must say they're pretty damn good, especially for a Yankee," he added, grinning to keep from sounding serious. He liked Mitch and wanted him to defeat Trent. If keeping peace with Blake would do it he meant to bend that far. "Tonight's the kickoff. Old Trent is going to get one hell of a surprise."

"I hope we're not the ones who get the surprise," Mitch replied grimly. His insecurity about his ability to carry the election was clear to both Blake and Craig. Deep inside him was still the 'dirt-poor Flannery' fear.

"It won't be. You underestimate people, Mitch," Blake said. "They're smart enough to understand what you're trying to do and will vote for you to make it happen."

"Be a lot of wasted energy on everybody's part if I lose, won't it?"

"Bitterness and self-pity are too much to carry around, aren't they?" Blake asked ruthlessly, "especially since we're trying to get rid of those same feelings here."

Mitch was struck by what Blake said, as was Craig. He could hear his own bitterness in Blake's words and faced them squarely for the first time in a long time.

Before anyone could speak again they saw Noel walking toward them.

"Well," she said as she reached them, "it's all taken care of. Mitch is registered as an official candidate. I wouldn't be surprised if Trent Donnelley wasn't getting the news just about now."

"I guess the fat's in the fire," Mitch said.

236

"No turning back," Blake agreed. "Come on, we have to go back to the *Sentinel* and polish that speech a bit more. A lot's depending on it."

"Damn," Mitch said laughing. "I haven't been so nervous since my father caught me drinking behind the barn."

Noel laughed, too. "Well, come on, I'll be your audience." She tucked her arm through his. "You don't need to be nervous, Mitch, you'll be fine. The speech is wonderful. I couldn't have done any better myself . . . and I'm the best there is."

"Oh, the conceit of the woman," Blake cried, pretending to groan in pain.

"Not conceit," she giggled, "confidence."

"Well, I could use a little confidence," Mitch replied with a grin. "Let's get on with it."

The four of them walked back to the *Sentinel* office together.

Trent's face was mottled with fury. "What the hell do you mean I'll be sharing the platform with Mitchell Flannery! How did this come about?"

"There was nothing we could do," Andrew Crocket said in a consoling tone. "The man is legally registered and is entitled to run against you. They waited until the last minute to register, possibly because they were pretty sure someone would try and stop it."

"I want him out of my way."

"You'll defeat him."

"You'd better pray that I do," Trent said coldly. The unspoken threat hung in the air between them and there was a thick silence for several minutes. When Andrew attempted to laugh, the sound was like dry leaves before a crisp wind . . .

"Of course we'll see to it that you win. The *Chron-*

icle is behind you. So is a great deal of money . . . and power. Power enough to take care of Mitchell Flannery . . . one way or the other."

"See that it does. I'm sure it means as much to you as it does to me."

"It does. By the way, how is your little romance coming along? I thought you'd have her wedded and bedded by now . . . and have some information for me besides."

"My plans were slowed a little—again, thanks to Mitchell Flannery. You needn't worry—I know for certain she still has the letters from her brother. I just haven't had the opportunity to read them. But I will. They have to contain what we want to know. The kid can't have been so smart he didn't put some information in those letters."

"Just get hold of them . . . or read them."

"I will. She thinks he's still alive, you know."

"Do you?"

"He'd have come around by now. He knows we're after the same thing he is. If he was alive he'd be here. No, I think he's dead. But I still think all the answers are somewhere in those letters. Give me a little more time."

"Oh, I'll give you all the time you want," Andrew chuckled. "Your worries don't come from my direction."

"No . . . Mitchell Flannery. Well, if he wants a fight he'll get it. He'll wish he'd never come back here. So who's behind him?"

"The *Sentinel,* for one."

"The *Sentinel?* That harmless little rag? I don't see what they can do."

"They're a thorn under our skin. The Andersons are a stubborn, tenacious lot. That little girl . . . Noel. She writes well. I have a feeling you're going to see quite a few anti-Donnelley editorials."

"That's your part of the battle."

"Yes, oh yes, I know. You needn't worry yourself on that score."

"There can't be any slip up now. There's too much at stake. We all have too much to lose."

Andrew nodded, but his eyes narrowed with irritation. He didn't like to be threatened. One day Trent Donnelley might just have to learn a few lessons on that score.

Lazarus stood and wiped the sweat from his face with the ragged end of his shirt. The head of the heavy ax he'd been swinging rested on the ground beside the wood he had just chopped into burnable pieces.

He took a deep breath and looked around him. For the past several minutes he had had the eerie sensation that he was being watched. But there was no sign of anyone. Still, the nerves at the back of his neck crawled.

He'd had a lot of strange premonitions lately that rattled his nerves. Most of them had centered around Whitney and Jon.

He'd been their protector for so long that in many ways he thought of them as his. But the threats before had been tangible — solid, visual threats that he could handle.

Now the threat seemed vaporous, a will-o'-the-wisp he could not reach out and touch. This was frustrating, and gave him the first real fear that this time he could do little to protect Whitney from whatever was coming.

He seldom spoke his thoughts, especially to Whitney, but he was worried about the effect Mitch Flannery's return had on her. It was obvious to Lazarus that Mitch knew nothing about Jon . . . or that he was his child. What harm could Mitch cause if he did know? What kind would he want to cause? Trent Donnelley was a problem. If Whitney married him and the truth came out about Jon's parentage what would happen to Whitney then?

Again the sensation of being watched stirred within him. Slowly he scanned the area about him.

He stood in a flat-bottomed gully near a narrow stream. The land on each side slanted up and was heavily wooded. A mist hovered low, sending beams of sunlight through the trees, creating shadows everywhere. But they were shadows he was well used to and could identify. He tried to look carefully about without letting whoever it was know he was aware.

Slowly he let the ax handle drop and flexed his muscles as if he were just relaxing. He saw nothing, yet the uncomfortable feeling remained.

He knelt to pick up the pieces of wood he'd just cut and slowly placed one or two in his arms, using his position to scan the area behind him. He froze as he glimpsed the dark-clad rider sitting on a horse near the crest of the hill.

Both horse and rider were absolutely still and blended so well with the trees that Lazarus had to look very carefully.

The rider seemed to know exactly when Lazarus had spotted him, for in a blur of movement he vanished.

Lazarus was shaken. He was some distance from the house and he knew Josiah was in town for supplies. He reached for a rifle that he had carelessly leaned against a tree . . . too far away to have defended himself. It was careless, and something he promised himself he would not do again.

He loped toward the house in ground-eating strides. When he neared the cabins he could see

Addy on the porch with Jon. He cursed himself for carelessness. If the rider he had seen had been Mitch Flannery, then it made him sweat to think of how helpless Addy and Berdine would have been. Mitch would have known everything in minutes — he could easily have taken his son and the law would have supported him. Whitney would have been more devastated than she had been during the war.

Lazarus approached the house slowly. He didn't want to alarm anyone, but until this question was settled he meant to keep those whom Whitney loved very close.

Twenty

The town of Holly Hill had been battered, but never destroyed. There was plenty of evidence the war had left behind—many deserted and damaged structures were still in the process of repair.

But today the town meant to put on a new face. Election time always created a great deal of excitement.

Red, white, and blue bunting adorned every building, with banners strung across the streets every fifty or sixty feet.

The town hall was also decorated and streamers were hung from every window. That was where the crowd would gather late that night when the excitement of parades and sidewalk speeches were at a fever pitch. Chairs had been set up to accommodate voters who came to hear what the candidates had to say.

On the outskirts of town private celebrations were being held, the Delaneys' gathering being one of them. Their home was a large white frame house on four acres of prime land. Trees sheltered it from most of the town. A large expanse of shaded lawn at the back of the house was dotted with tables that had been set up for a late afternoon and early evening party. Five long tables covered with white cloths groaned under the quantities of food on them.

Whitney was caught up in the fun and happy

memories. How many delightful parties she had enjoyed at home! She helped carry out platters of food, realizing she hadn't enjoyed herself so much in a long time.

She wore a dress of green-sprigged cotton with enough petticoats to be comfortable. Her hair was tied back with a wisp of green ribbon. Her cheeks were flushed and her smile warm.

The Delaneys had proven themselves staunch friends and Mrs. Delaney was trying to take her mother's place as best she could. Whitney was more than grateful.

For this one afternoon Mr. Delaney had opened his home to the townspeople and friends who filled the lawn. Smatterings of conversation and laughter filled the air as men discussed the pros and cons of politics and women discussed the pros and cons of the latest gossip.

It was just dusk when the tables were cleared and men and women began to drift toward the town hall. Whitney stood in the foyer of the Delaney home with her shawl in her hand and waited for her hosts to be sure their children were tucked safely in bed and the young girl watching them had received her final instructions.

"Well, Whitney," Eleanor Delaney said as she came down the stairs with her husband, Robert, behind her. "I'm sorry to have kept you waiting. I'm sure you're excited and want to get along."

"It's quite all right, Eleanor. Are the children all right?"

"Stubbornly determined they won't go to sleep. But never fear, Sally can handle both the little aborigines."

"I imagine she can. You're right, I am a little excited." Whitney laughed as she put her shawl about her shoulders.

243

"If I were going to marry a handsome man like Trent Donnelley, who's about to be our new representative, I'd be excited, too."

Whitney smiled but didn't say anything. There was no way to describe her confusion. Besides . . . she wanted to see and hear what both men had to say.

Robert Delaney draped his wife's shawl about her shoulders. "I think we'd better go along or all the best seats will be taken. I don't want to miss this."

"You're voting for Mr. Donnelley?" Whitney questioned.

"I haven't heard his ideas yet, so how can I say how I'll vote? Fact is, I didn't know anyone was running against him."

"I . . . think he may have an opponent," Whitney replied. Mrs. Delaney looked at her quickly with a puzzled look that Whitney didn't notice.

"Oh?" Robert asked.

"Yes . . . Mitchell Flannery."

"Mitchell Flannery. Hmm, I do believe I've heard the name lately."

"What have you heard?"

"Some talk around town. He seems to have impressed a few people, Matthew Tyler included. No wonder he's been talking so much about the young man. So, he's going to challenge Mr. Donnelley. Interesting. Do you know him, Whitney?"

Whitney was still unaware that Mrs. Delaney was watching her intently.

"Well, I . . . I once knew him . . . slightly, before the war. Since then. . . well, things have been so different. It's hard to pick up the pieces."

Mrs. Delaney felt that Whitney was concealing something, and this surprised her. Whitney was the last person from whom she expected to hear a lie . . . and Whitney seemed . . . it shocked her . . .

244

almost afraid. She could see the faint, lingering fear in her eyes. It would take some looking into. Whitney had become too dear to her to let her go on being afraid of anything.

The three of them walked down the boardwalk toward the town hall amid the slow-moving, bustling crowd. They had just passed the *Sentinel* office when the door opened and Blake and Noel came out.

Blake recognized Whitney at once. "Miss Clayborn, Whitney Clayborn."

Whitney turned around but couldn't quite place the man who had called out.

"Yes?"

Blake took Noel's hand and walked to Whitney.

"I'm Blake Randolph, and this is Noel Anderson. Noel and her brothers run the *Sentinel*. They're campaigning for Mitch, and I'm sort of his campaign manager."

"How interesting," Whitney said. "It's a pleasure to meet you. Noel, I'm sure your paper will be a great help to Mr. Flannery."

"My brothers and I hope so. We've got a lot of competition, but many people have faith in Mitch."

"I'm sure they do," Whitney said softly.

"So, young lady," Mr. Delaney said to Noel with a warm smile. "You're the spirit behind the *Sentinel?* You've given us some provocative ideas with your editorials."

"You read the *Sentinel?*" Noel returned his smile. "I wasn't too sure too many Holly Hill people read it."

"Ah, but I do and as I said, it's very interesting."

"Thank you."

"And you and your paper support Mitch Flannery? Why?"

"Why? Because we think he's the best man for the job. He's honest . . . and he's committed to Holly Hill's progress. Those qualities are so important in the man we choose, don't you think?"

"I concur completely. I shall have to pay very close attention to this young man tonight."

Noel smiled but Blake was watching Whitney's face.

No matter how she tried to mask her feelings there was a look in her eyes that was, for a moment, hard to discern. Then he felt a jolt of pleasure as he realized what he was seeing was a tinge of jealousy. It made him smile to himself as the group continued on to city hall.

The hall was beginning to fill, but Blake found them all seats reasonably near the front. On the wooden stage were two podiums. Blake wasn't sure the affair hadn't been turned into a debate, and he knew Mitch wasn't prepared for that. Of course, Trent might feel he would have the advantage if they did debate. Still, Blake's faith in Mitch wasn't wavering. In fact, he was pretty sure Donnelley was in for a surprise.

Their conversation was brought to a halt when several men came out on the stage and took the row of seats there. But Mitch and Trent were not among them. Blake watched Whitney's gaze grow intent as she watched. He smiled to himself, wondering which man she was looking for.

On either side of the stage, unseen by the audience, Mitch and Trent waited impatiently. They could see each other and both found it difficult to await the coming confrontation.

Finally the hall was filled, every man and woman savored the excitement of the coming battle.

Both Mitch and Trent were introduced and took seats on either end of the dignitaries who shared the stage. Orin McKay, one of the town fathers, had been designated as mediator. He stood and let the applause ripple for a while, then he raised his hands, palm outward, to bring silence.

He began a well rehearsed introduction of both men that amused Mitch, who felt it sounded more like an eulogy. Trent would speak first. He rose, walked to the podium, and waited patiently for the crowd to quiet down.

His voice was mellow . . . and Blake watched his performance and realized this man knew how to manipulate the crowd, how to make people believe him. He wondered how many could see the actor behind the mask. Trent spoke of peace, victories, and goals . . . but it was power he was after.

Blake absorbed every word and not once did Trent set forth any ideas to help the city recover from the aftermath of war. Never once did he offer alternatives, only platitudes to calm—and charm—his listeners. When Blake heard Trent talk he knew Trent's private goals went well beyond Holly Hill. No, this man sought something far greater.

When Trent finished, the applause was strong. He sat down with a satisfied smile.

Mitch rose slowly, fighting his inner turmoil and insecurity. He knew he could not make sweet-sounding promises. All he could promise them was hard work, from them and himself.

Whitney, who chanced to be sitting next to Blake, stiffened as Mitch walked to the podium. Blake watched her from the corner of his eye. Her cheeks were slightly flushed and her lips parted. Something danced in her eyes that Blake could have sworn was a pleasurable excitement. She could lie to Mitch and to herself, but in the moment, unaware that he could see her expression, Blake knew that whatever she had once felt for Mitch was still there. He was

247

as sure as Mitch had been that something else was keeping them apart.

"Friends and neighbors," Mitch began, "we all stood together to fight a war. Now we need to stand together to fight for peace and to rebuild what we lost. I can promise you it's possible. I can also promise you it's not going to be easy."

Blake smiled to himself. Mitch must have been reading Abe Lincoln's speeches, because he came to the audience in the same straightforward, down home way. Mitch continued to speak of the work that needed to be done and how they would have to stand shoulder to shoulder to do it. In simple words he made it clear that he knew them, was one of them, and intended to remain with them. He spoke of fields needing planting, of bricks and lumber needing to be manufactured, of schools needing to be rebuilt and hospitals and doctors. He spoke of town streets . . . and progress that could be theirs if they worked together.

"I've lived my life in Holly Hill," he concluded. "I love it and want to see it grow. I want to live the rest of my life here." His eyes caught and held Whitney's relentlessly. "I want to have my children grow up here. I want to grow old and die here and remain part of the town and this land I love forever. Thank you," he said quietly, and returned to his seat. For a moment there was utter silence, then the audience exploded. Even Whitney rose to her feet and applauded.

Trent continued to smile, but he was barely containing a fury that was directed at Mitch Flannery.

The last of the speeches were made and it was mid-evening as the crowd began to disburse.

"Whitney, will you need a way home?" Blake offered.

"No, I'm staying with the Delaneys tonight. I'll

248

go home tomorrow . . . with Trent."

Her eyes were defiant as they held his for a moment.

"I thought Mitch's speech was pretty good. At least he made the people of Holly Hill understand that he knows what they really need. Mitch will be good for this town."

"That's for the voters to decide," Whitney replied.

"Well," Noel cut in, "we're going to do everything in our power to make this town see just how good Mitch would be."

"Speaking of that, Noel," Blake said innocently enough to keep from arousing Noel's suspicions. "I've left some papers at the office that I really need. Do you mind walking back with me and letting me in to get them?"

"I was supposed to meet Craig here to ride home with him."

"I'll see you get home all right. We'll leave a message for him."

There was little Noel could do without looking to Whitney and the Delaneys as if she were afraid of Blake . . . even though she was. She was about to refuse when Robert Delaney make refusal impossible.

"I want to talk to that brother of yours anyway. If Whitney and Eleanor don't mind we'll wait here for a while for your brother and tell him where you've gone."

"I'd hate to put you out, Mr. Delaney."

"It's no trouble, no trouble at all. Now you two go along and get whatever Blake needs. I'll just tell your brother you'll see him at home."

"Thank you," Noel said finally, unable to think of anything else. Blake would have thanked him much more profusely if it wouldn't have given him away. He took Noel's elbow and very nearly propelled her away from the crowd.

They walked slowly down the boardwalk toward the *Sentinel*. He could sense her withdrawal with every step. With the others Noel had been relaxed and smiling, and he knew it was because she felt there was safety in numbers.

But he had seen a new facet of her that fascinated him. He wanted to hear her laugh —to see that kind of happiness on her face again.

"It's been a very eventful night," Blake began.

"It's been a very eventful week," Noel replied. "Mitch was so nervous until he stood up to talk. Then he was absolutely wonderful."

"I think he made a lot of people take a second look tonight. He looked like a man of the people who meant business. Now I guess it's time for us to get busy."

"Yes . . . I guess it is."

Again there was silence. Neither spoke again until they reached the door of the *Sentinel*.

When Noel reached in her reticule for the key Blake took her hand to stop her. She looked up in surprise.

"I didn't leave anything here," he admitted quietly. "I just wanted to be alone with you for a while. Noel, you've been dodging me for days. I want to talk to you."

"I really don't see the point of this, Blake. We work together for a cause, but that's all we have in common."

"No . . . we have a lot more than that in common. "Noel . . . talk to me. I know there's something between us, something you're blaming on the war. Whatever it is, we can't fight it if you don't talk to me." He reached out and took hold of her arm, drawing her close. Noel was not frightened of

250

Blake—she was frightened of her feelings and the fear she could not hide. He seemed to be tearing down her carefully built armor.

"All right, Blake," she said softly, "you want answers, I'll give you some." She took the key and opened the door and walked inside. Blake followed.

She lit a lamp, then drew the curtains across the front window and turned to Blake.

"You asked me how old I was when the war began. I said I was fourteen, but I was over sixteen when it really got bad for us. Three of my brothers were away, but Kevin was home on a short leave. He had gone to see if any food could be found. I was home, with my sister . . . and Kevin's wife, Charlotte . . . alone when they struck our place. For a while I thought it would be all right. It seemed they only wanted what they could get in the way of food, blankets, and other supplies. In fact, the man who led them apologized for taking what we had. He led his men away after they'd taken everything. But later . . . some of them returned," she nearly choked on the next words, "for what they had left."

For a long moment she was silent as if she was reliving the nightmare. "My sister, Emma, fought the man who was dragging her upstairs. She fell when he lost his hold and her neck broke. Charlotte . . . oh, God, she was so young and pretty, and so fragile. When they left, I held her in my arms . . . until she died, then Kevin came home. Now can you see why Kevin cannot forgive . . . and why I cannot forget? Everyday I look at Kevin and I see Charlotte. I hear her crying . . . begging . . ."

"And Kevin won't let you forget it," Blake said angrily.

"He need not remind me. No one needs to remind me."

Blake watched her. She stood in profile, her hands clenched before her. And at the moment he knew. He knew there was a darker, more brutal truth. He felt her anguish and the helpless fury. He wanted to do something but knew it was futile. Kevin never meant Noel to be free of the memories. His own pain kept the wounds open.

Blake walked up behind Noel, wanting to comfort her somehow, wanting to ease the pain and erase some of the memories. He also knew that some of his battle was going to be with Kevin.

"I know this sounds hard, Noel, but you've got to let go of the past. You can't let your life die with them. You're here, Noel, and you're alive. You've got a life to live."

He saw her body tremble and realized everything was bottled up inside. The door had to be unlocked, but he didn't have the key. He was afraid that Kevin was the only one who did, and it was fairly obvious Kevin hated him. Kevin was clinging to his anger by the only link he had . . . Noel.

"Noel . . . have you ever talked to Craig about what happened?"

"Of course he knows."

"I mean," he added softly, "what happened to you." She turned to face him. "I think Craig would tell you how wrong you and Kevin are. He would say that you have to let go of the past."

Noel buried her face in her hands. "I can't . . . I can't forget, I'll never forget."

Blake couldn't help himself. He put his arms around her, rocking her gently against him, trying to give her some of his strength in any way he could.

He wasn't prepared for the look of sheer terror he saw in her eyes. Her whole body shook and she suddenly struggled so hard he had to release her. If

252

he hadn't known the truth before he did now.

A wave of bitter sympathy swept through him, but he knew she wouldn't want that. Noel had been hurt. Some part of her had been crushed, and Blake grew angry again. Kevin could have eased her agony, but because of his own misery he had kept it alive by nursing Noel's fears.

He had to do something but his uncertainties made it very difficult.

"Noel . . . I want you to know . . . I care. I care about what horrible things you must have gone through. But more than that I care about the strong, sensitive, and very beautiful woman you are, no matter what they did to you . . . to you physically. There's a part of you that they could never have touched. That part of you is Noel, the essence of everything you are. No one has the power to destroy that except you. Feeding the hatred is doing just that. It's hurting you and I can't stand watching you be hurt anymore."

His voice had grown tender, and he reached to touch her lightly. Noel was vulnerable and afraid.

Blake put his arms around her and held her. His strength was more than she had expected and more than she could handle. She felt something inside her stir, the thing she was most afraid of. She had tried to destroy or control her emotions for so long that she was unused to them.

His kiss was gentle, barely a touch, but she felt the old terror swell, and Blake could feel it as well.

"Don't be afraid of me, Noel. I'm not asking for anything. No commitments, no professions of undying love, no promises. All I want is to let you know I care . . . and that I'm right beside you if you want to reach out for someone. You can't go on letting Kevin's hatred run your life. He has to face his own troubles. He has to learn to let go, too."

253

Noel looked up into his eyes. She had been able to handle most men. It was easy to fight an opponent who fought back. But Blake offered gentleness, understanding, and consideration and this she found hard to fight. "I don't understand you, Blake Randolph," she said. "You're supposed to be the enemy."

"So your brothers say."

"They love me."

"If they loved you they wouldn't hold you a prisoner like this."

"Prisoner?"

"What else would you call it? You're locked up tight with painful memories they won't let you forget."

"Craig is not like that!"

"Maybe not, but Kevin is."

"You don't understand him."

"That's where you're wrong. I understand Kevin very well. Maybe better than you know."

"Just what is it you think you understand?" The voice came from the doorway and Blake and Noel spun about. "A very cozy scene," Kevin said coldly. "Just what do you think you're doing, Mr. Yankee? We told you once—Noel is out of bounds for you. Can't you understand plain English?"

"Kevin, don't . . ." Noel protested in shock. She had never seen her brother quite so angry before. She saw anger, but Blake saw something quite different.

"Noel, Craig is waiting in the buggy to take you home," Kevin said.

"Kevin . . ."

"Go on, Noel," Blake said quietly, "it's all right. There won't be any problems."

Noel was wary, but she had little choice unless she wanted to start a confrontation between her brothers and Blake. She cast Kevin a pleading look,

254

then left. Noel climbed into the buggy beside Craig.

"Craig, you've got to put a stop to this."

"Stop to what?"

"Kevin and Blake."

"I wouldn't be afraid for either one. Blake can handle himself, and Kevin has to get it off his chest. Maybe it'll clear the air."

Noel was surprised. Either Craig didn't know the extent of Kevin's anger, or he was blinding himself to it.

Craig slapped the reins and the horses moved ahead.

"I don't understand Kevin sometimes, Craig. I know how hurt he's been, but he seems determined to destroy things. None of this is going to bring Charlotte back. I can understand his animosity to Blake . . . but it isn't just Blake. Sometimes I think . . ."

"What?"

"Sometimes I think it's me."

"Noel!"

"But I do."

"Why in God's name would you think that? Kevin loves you."

"I know," she answered softly, "but I lived . . . and Charlotte died."

Craig absorbed her words and they made him think. Both were caught in their private thoughts until they arrived home, and by that time he had decided to return to talk to Mitch and Blake.

"Stay away from Noel. This is the last warning I'm giving you."

"I'll stay away when Noel tells me to and not until then. You don't own her," Blake said, barely controlling his anger. "What are you afraid of,

255

Kevin? That your sister will fall in love with a Yankee, or that you'll lose your hold and you won't have someone to punish anymore? Don't you think it's time to let the past go and get on with your life and let the rest of your family get on with theirs?"

"Noel will never marry you."

"Noel will never marry anyone if you can prevent it. If she does she might be happy, and you just can't allow that. You don't want to feel your guilt so you make Noel suffer for it."

"Guilt?"

"You weren't there when your wife needed you. But Noel was there. She couldn't do anything to stop it, but in your misery you've let her carry your guilt; in fact, you've been using it like a club ever since. She loves you. She feels pity for what you went through, so she'll carry this load. You're so busy feeling sorry for yourself you never gave a second thought to how Noel suffered, is still suffering. Damn you! She feels guilty if she has one moment of happiness."

"That's not true," Kevin said, but his voice shook and his face grew grim as if he were seeing himself for the first time and didn't like what he saw.

"The hell it isn't. It's not because of the war. It's because you aren't man enough to face your guilt and learn to live with it." Blake moved closer to Kevin. "Well, let me tell you something, Reb. I'm fighting you every damn inch of the way. I'll make Noel happy if it takes my last breath, and I'll do it in spite of you. You'd better face your problems and build some bridges between you and Noel or one day she'll hate you. One day when she sees what you've done, when she understands that it's all right to love someone, you'll be alone . . . then the guilt will eat you alive. Get on with your life, Kevin. Find some love in this world or you'll

256

never have anything at all."

"What do you know? What do you understand?"

"I understand *you*." Blake's voice grew softer as he felt a surge of sympathy. "I understand how you must have felt. But in all your agony did you think to look into Noel's eyes and see what she was suffering, too? No. You had someone to blame."

"I never hurt Noel."

"No? You let her be your whipping boy. She feels she should have died, not Charlotte. Somewhere deep inside you feel that, too. Take it out of hiding, look at it. Maybe then you'll have enough compassion for yourself and Noel to let her go. But until then you're half a man, Kevin . . . and you'll never be whole."

Kevin seemed frozen. He didn't even realize Blake had brushed past him, nor did he hear the click of the door as it closed. He stood still for a long time. After a while he could feel the tears he had denied for so long. He could taste the grief. It overpowered him.

He sagged to his knees and buried his face in his hands and wept. Pent-up emotions broke free and he mourned as he never had before. At that moment he did not know whether he mourned for himself or for Noel.

It seemed like hours before he staggered home. The house was dark and Craig and Noel were in bed. He found his way to his room and threw himself across the bed, where he fell into an exhausted sleep. It was in the wee hours of the morning that he wakened and allowed his mind the freedom to think.

Twenty-one

Mitch had seen Whitney in the audience. In fact, after a while he found he was speaking more to her than to anyone. He was filled with excitement when he saw her stand with the others to applaud. He meant to go to her as soon as he could. But his plans went awry when he found himself surrounded by enthusiastic supporters and after a while they all shuffled off to a dinner and celebration.

There would be very little chance to see her any time during the evening, but he meant to do so first thing the next day. If she was in any way impressed with him he meant to build on the momentum.

When he had returned her land he had meant to leave all further decisions up to her, but now he felt an even stronger urgency. He had to find out what she thought and if all he had said had made any difference.

Matthew Tyler had organized a party and Mitch found himself so involved in political discussion that time passed quickly.

It was some time before Craig and Blake rejoined him. Even then the looks on their faces kept him from asking questions about their late arrival until they were alone. He was curious about why

Kevin didn't come with them, or Noel. These four people were the primary structure of his campaign.

Caught in a conversation with a supporter, Mitch kept an eye on Blake who seemed somehow different. Still, it was the better part of an hour before he could get him alone.

They stood together on the back veranda of Matthew's house enjoying a cigar and a moment's respite from the bustle and confusion.

"It went well," Mitch said. "Much better than I thought it would."

"You're too pessimistic. These people are hungry for a leader. You said all the right things."

"It's still going to be quite a battle."

"Sure. Trent Donnelley's no piker. He'll move heaven and earth to win this. He has high aspirations, I'm sure."

"Blake, what's wrong?"

"Wrong? I don't . . ."

"This is me, Blake, not some stranger. We've been friends too long for you to start lying. Is it Noel?"

"It's that obvious?"

"I know how you feel, how she feels, and how her brothers feel. Since she's not here and Kevin's not either, I'm taking a guess there was some kind of confrontation."

"There was. I was kind of hard on Kevin, I guess. But damnit, Mitch, I'm tired of him using Noel. He's got her feeling so guilty she'd do anything to make him happy."

"Guilty about what?"

"The fact that it was his wife who died, not Noel."

"Good God!"

"I know it sounds odd, but somewhere in his

259

mind he's easing his pain with Noel's guilt." He continued to talk, telling Mitch all of the story. "I'm not letting him get away with it anymore. Noel has had a hard time and it's difficult enough for her to pick up the pieces without pressure from him."

"You think she can?"

"I'm doing everything in my power to make it happen."

"I hope it works."

"What about you and Whitney?"

"Did you see her during my speech?"

"Yeah, she seemed excited."

"And pleased. I'm taking a chance and going out to see her. It might work after all."

"Old Trent will be upset," Blake grinned.

"More than that if I have anything to say about it."

"Mitch . . . I don't have to tell you to be careful. I wouldn't put a whole lot past Donnelley. If he can't get rid of you one way he'll try another."

"I'm pretty hard to get rid of."

"Hard . . . not impossible. Just watch your back."

"I will, I'll be careful. I have a lot to look forward to. I'm not giving up easily or carelessly."

"Well, good luck."

"We'd better get back to the celebration or old Matthew will be upset." Mitch laughed as the two reentered the house.

Whitney had waited for Trent and his friends to join her, then had accompanied them to Trent's home where refreshments and drinks were served. The room was filled with discussions about Trent and Mitch. Though Whitney was silent, she still felt a kind of pride in Mitch. She had listened and knowing him as well as she did was somewhat surprised that she believed what he said. Mitch, who had once felt hatred in his town and hated in response, had seemed so different, so grown-up. She was happy everyone there had responded as they had. It had, she hoped, made Mitch see clearly what she had tried to tell him so long ago.

She knew Trent was unhappy about the turn of events. He had hidden his displeasure behind his charming smile, but she had seen the anger dance in his eyes.

She also knew Trent was not a man to take defeat easily. He was a fighter. Mitch would have a battle on his hands.

Whitney smiled for Trent's guests and played hostess to his satisfaction, but she was gratified when the evening was over. It was nearing midnight when she and Trent rode toward the Delaneys' in his carriage.

"Well, Whitney, what did you think of the evening?"

"It was quite interesting."

"It will get even more so as time goes on. There'll be a great many social events, and I shall have to entertain as well. I really would like your help, Whitney. I need a gracious hostess." He laughed. "In fact, I would really like the woman I love to marry me. It's very good for a man seeking political office to have a helpmate. With you as my wife and partner I doubt if I would lose. You could charm a lot of influential voters."

"I don't really believe a marriage should be based on how many influential votes a 'charming' wife could bring." Whitney didn't mean to sound as annoyed with the idea as she really was, but Trent was tuned into her inflections long ago.

He drew the carriage to a halt before the Delaney home, then turned to look at her.

"You really don't believe that's what I meant, do you?"

"I'm sorry, Trent. I really didn't mean to sound like a shrew. I guess I'm a little tired."

"It's time we talked about it, Whitney. I've been a patient man. Until Mitch Flannery came along and bought your land back I was sure we had a future together. Now, it seems somehow he stands between us. I think I've a right to know why."

"You're imagining things, Trent. He didn't buy my land and return it to me because there's anything between us. I plan to pay him back, whatever the cost. I want no strings between me and anyone. I have to decide what's best not only for my future, but Jon's as well."

"Why can't you believe I can provide a good life for you and your son?"

She knew he was right, but she couldn't bring herself to take that final step. "You hardly know Jon," she said quietly.

Trent suddenly realized what his mistake had been. Success did not depend on wooing Whitney, but revolved around her son.

"I'm sorry, Whitney. You're right. Give me a chance to get to know him better. Maybe this campaign can bring us all closer. I won't insist on a decision now, even though I want to. When the election's over . . . I'm sure you and I'll be together."

"I appreciate your consideration, Trent. Good night."

"Good night, Whitney." He bent to kiss her and

she let him, unsure of whether she was trying to test her emotions or not.

Mitch Flannery was becoming too much of a threat, Trent thought. There had to be a way to rid himself of it and he would find it.

Mitch left town early the next morning. With grim determination he headed toward Whitney's. As he rode he began to wonder if last night's success had given him a new kind of courage, for he was sure to have to face Lazarus somewhere along the line and that didn't make him too comfortable. Still, it didn't stop him either.

He pictured Whitney's face, filled with excitement. Whitney standing and applauding with enthusiasm. He had read a great deal into it, of course, but it had stirred new hope.

He drew close to the two small cabins and reined in his horse. He gazed around cautiously, but there was no one in sight. He urged the horse forward slowly. Within ten feet of the cabins he stopped again. No sign of life from either of them.

With one eye on the cabin that housed Lazarus, he made his way to Whitney's. As he stepped up on the porch he could hear the sound of someone softly singing. The voice was not Whitney's so he surmised it must be the girl that cared for the child when she was away. She had told him of the slaves who had chosen to stay and help her. He continued across the porch to the door that stood partly open. He pushed the door open the rest of the way soundlessly. The sight that met his eyes was enough to stop him in his tracks.

A young black girl sat cross-legged on the floor with her back to him. Before her sat the child he'd seen from a distance. Between them was a large box from which the child was taking some wooden figures.

It was not their presence that made Mitch catch his breath. As he moved slightly the child looked up. The sight of him took Mitch's breath away. It was like looking into a mirror.

It came to him like a thunderbolt. The agonizing truth made him almost groan aloud. That was Whitney's child . . . it was also his.

All the time he'd been so noble, telling Whitney he could accept her child as his own. Telling her he could understand what she'd been through when what she had done was give birth to his child. At that moment he detested himself. Then a question arose: why had Whitney never told him?

Following the child's gaze, Addy turned around quickly. The last thing she expected to see was Mitch and her eyes grew wide. She leapt to her feet, snatched the child, and backed to the furthest part of the room. But Mitch was between her and any chance of escape.

Mitch didn't move. He didn't want to frighten her any more than she already was.

"What's your name?"

"Addy, suh."

"Well, Addy, where's Miss Whitney?"

"She ain' here."

"You mean she didn't come home last night?"

"No, suh, she stay to de Delaneys. Yo' best go now."

He could have smiled, but he was sure she would only grow more alarmed. He moved a few steps in her direction. The child attracted him like a magnet. His son, and he had never known; worse, he had never asked. He wanted to take him from Addy's arms but didn't dare.

"Yo' bes' go now," Addy repeated. "Ah hollers an' Lazarus come pretty quick an' Berdine. We knows Miz Whitney doan want yo' here. Better yo' go now. Miz Whitney, she gwine be mad sumthin' fierce." She was almost begging him to leave, but he couldn't.

This was his child and he couldn't take his eyes from him.

Why had Whitney kept this secret? All this time she had never said anything. Could she hate him this much?

Addy was gathering up all her courage. "Yo' cums one step mo' an' ah's gonna scream. Lazarus, he make yo' sorry yo' doan go now."

"Yes, I imagine Lazarus could do that, but you might just as well scream and get it over with because I'm not leaving until Whitney gets back. She and I have a great deal to talk about."

He watched Addy's frown deepen, then saw her gaze flicker past him so he quickly turned. Whitney stood framed in the doorway, panic and terror combined on her face. The Delaneys had seen her home in one of their carriages, since something had come up to keep Trent in town.

"Mitch . . . what are you doing here?"

"I think we're overdue for a talk, don't you, Whitney?" he asked calmly.

Before she could answer Berdine appeared behind her in the doorway. It strengthened her. She ran across the room and took Jon from Addy's arms.

Mitch tried his best to ignore Berdine, but it was difficult. He kept his gaze locked with Whitney's.

"Whitney, you don't have much choice now, and

265

you know it. It would be easier if you just told me everything."

Whitney knew he had the upper hand. He had the law on his side.

"He's our son, isn't he, Whitney?" he asked gently. "Why didn't you tell me?"

Whitney's body stiffened and she looked at him with the cold look he had hoped never to see again. "Berdine, take Jon with you."

"Leave him here."

"No! If you want to talk to me then Jon goes with Berdine."

He could see she wouldn't budge.

"All right . . . for now."

Berdine crossed the room slowly and took Jon. Addy followed and they left, closing the door behind them. The silence was louder than the roar of cannons.

"He *is* my son."

"Yes, you've seen him, so there's no point in denying it."

"Why, Whitney? Why?"

"Why? How could you ask me such a thing? You didn't care when I wrote you about it and you didn't care when he was born. Why care now?"

"Those letters again."

"No matter what you want me to believe about your writing, I know I wrote. I told you I was pregnant. That's when I received your rather curt letter so I took your advice and found an 'appropriate husband.' You're not suggesting that you care now?"

"I care," he said softly, "and I never knew. When I first mentioned the child to you, you must have thought I was deliberately being cruel."

266

"The thought crossed my mind, accompanied by many others. Leave Jon alone, Mitch. He's my son and he's happy."

"He's my son, too, Whitney. That's not fair."

"Fair? Why should life be so fair to you? What did you expect?" She wanted to strike out at him, but she was afraid he would use his power to separate her and Jon and that was unthinkable.

Mitch saw her panic and fear, but he was unaware of the real cause. He watched as she turned her back to him, her hands clenched. She stood perfectly still, looking out the window with unseeing eyes.

Her obvious fear came as a complete shock to him. She had never been frightened of him before. He'd never wanted to ever see that in her eyes. Why?

He stood quietly, trying to figure it out. Then suddenly it hit him. Whitney was afraid he could take Jon away from her — that he would strike out at her through the child. It hurt him to think she actually believed he would take this kind of vengeance. He walked over and stood close behind her.

"Whitney, look at me."

Her breath seemed lodged in her chest, held by a lump of solid anguish. She knew, of course, that Mitch knew he had power and he meant to use it. She could hardly stand it. She would beg . . . or to do whatever was necessary to keep Jon. Slowly she turned around and the look in her eyes nearly undid Mitch completely.

"Whitney, for God's sake," he breathed miserably. "Do you really believe . . . you knew me before this damn war. I wouldn't have hurt you then, and I wouldn't hurt you now. How can you believe I

267

would really try to come between you and Jon? I love you. I never stopped loving you for a minute despite what that forged note said. I wish I knew how that happened but I don't. I can only tell you my love for you never changed. He's my son, too, and I'd never use him to hit back at you. Why would I want to when I love you? All I want is for us to be together . . . be a family."

He saw the confusion and uncertainty in her eyes. Love's promises had nearly destroyed her life before. Dare she believe again, trust again?

"You won't . . ." she whispered, "you won't take him away?"

"No . . . but there are conditions."

"What conditions?" she questioned warily.

"I want to see him, to get to know him. I want to spend time with him. Whitney, I want him to learn to love me, too."

He knew she wanted to resist, but she was also afraid to argue in case he changed his mind. She hated the law that gave men such power.

"If you want to be fair, Mitch, you'll admit that you relinquished your rights when you denied him."

"I never denied him. I never knew about him."

"Maybe a court would see the letter you wrote differently." She was trying to brave it out and force him away without conditions, and he was not about to concede. "What about your election? A scandal would do you a great deal of harm."

"To hell with the election! Do you really think an election is more important than you and my son? Don't fight me, Whitney. I don't want to make a battle out of this."

The subtle threat was there. He didn't *want* to make a battle of it, but he would if she forced him to it. "Look," he said desperately, "why can't we compromise?"

"Compromise?"

"Let me come . . . just a couple of times. If it doesn't interfere with you. You'll see — I won't cause any problems. I won't try to force you into anything. Try trusting me one more time."

He waited with bated breath for her reply. All was fair in love and war, he thought. If he couldn't get to Whitney any other way he would get to her through Jon. One way or the other he meant to have her back, along with his son.

"I . . . I don't know. Lazarus, Berdine, Addy, and Josiah would have to be there."

"You think I'd kidnap him?"

"You might consider it."

"No tricks, Whitney. I swear."

"I don't suppose it would do much good to say no. You'd find a way to get what you want. I'm not blind to the facts. All I can do is plead with you not to take him away. It would be too much to bear."

"I'm the one who's begging. I'll never do anything to hurt you again. Any problem we have will have to be caused by you. You've had time for Jon to love you. I've lost that. All I'm asking is for that time back. No matter how you feel about me, I think I have that right."

He watched her resistance waver, knowing he was only inches from success. Once he was safely entrenched in Jon's life he would begin a campaign to win Whitney. He waited for her answer.

Before she could speak they heard the crack of a gunshot, along with a thump and a loud shout from the back of the house.

They both ran to the door and out onto the

269

porch just in time to see a breathless Lazarus hustle around the corner.

"Lazarus," Whitney cried. "What is it?"

"Ah seed somebody at de back window jes' as ah come over de ridge. He be tryin' to git into de house. Ah be 'fraid he'd git in befo' ah could git to him so ah fired."

"Where did he go?" Mitch asked worriedly. It was then that Lazarus got the full import of his presence.

"What yo' doin' here?" Lazarus's expression was unpleasant to say the least and his hostile gaze promised Mitch a lot more than Whitney could imagine.

"It's all right, Lazarus," Whitney replied. "Mitch will be leaving soon."

"Do you have any idea who the intruders were?" Mitch inquired anxiously.

"No, ah don'," Lazarus said. "Miz Whitney said yo' leavin'."

Mitch turned to Whitney. "I will, as soon as I get an answer."

"All right, Mitch . . . one chance."

"When?"

"Next week."

"What day?"

"Monday."

"I'm not sure I ought to leave you alone like this. Whoever is prowling around has a lot of guts to try something in broad daylight. Have you had any trouble before?"

Before Whitney could answer, Lazarus cut in coldly. "It ain't yo' worry. They ain't been no trouble befo' an' there ain't gwine be anymore. Ah sleeps downstairs on de couch from now on an' ah gots a gun what speaks quick — 'sides dat, Josiah a

270

pretty good shot, too. Anybody comes 'roun' we shoots first an' asks questions later . . . anybody."

Berdine, Addy, and Josiah stood in the doorway of their cabin watching silently. Addy held Jon close. Mitch knew they were a united force and he would have to win them over. Divide and conquer was the advice of a great general and he meant to take it. Lazarus was the one he had to convince first. One at a time he meant to win them all to his side.

"I don't doubt you've been a good protector, Lazarus. But it's pretty hard for just two men to run two places."

"Ain't been no trouble up to now an' ah doan expects to have none. Miz Whitney gwine be right safe."

"And my son," Mitch said quietly. "You've been watching over him since the day he was born. I owe you a great deal for that."

There was a dual gasp from Addy and Berdine and Lazarus's scowl grew deeper. "Yo' don' owe me nuthin'. Ah done what ah could fo' Miz Whitney, not fo' yo'."

Whitney knew she had a lot of explaining to do. She was sure Lazarus would have trouble understanding. He would argue, but Whitney had little choice. Mitch would be allowed to see his son occasionally, or he would take him away. Lazarus would understand . . . he would have to. She could not lose Jon.

"You must go, Mitch," Whitney said.

"I know," he answered regretfully. "Can . . . . can I hold him first?"

"All right." She could do little else. She found it hard not to understand how Mitch must feel. "Addy, bring Jon here."

Berdine came across the yard and up the steps to the porch. She looked in Mitch's eyes as she handed Jon to him and he thought for a moment he saw a smile there. Then he felt the warmth of Jon's body pressed against his chest and the small arms came about his neck. He closed his eyes for a moment against the overwhelming pleasure that brought tears to his eyes. It was like coming home.

Finally Jon wiggled free and leaned back to look at this tall man. The son's eyes met the father's in silent contemplation.

"Hello, Jon," Mitch said, his voice hoarse with emotion.

" 'Lo," Jon replied. He had decided on the spur of the moment, as all children do, that he liked this man. "Want to see my soldiers? Lazarus make them for me."

It was poignant as Mitch realized he had missed so much and that Lazarus had taken his place, a fact that was going to change.

"I can't right now," Mitch replied, wishing he didn't have to leave. "But if I come back one day soon, can I see them?"

"Uh huh," Jon nodded. Then he wiggled again to get free and reluctantly Mitch put him down.

"Monday," Mitch said quietly.

"Monday," Whitney agreed.

"Can I bring him something? Is there anything he particularly likes? I know so little."

"Candy," Whitney smiled, remembering Jon's constant attempts to maneuver her into buying him candy. "Peppermint candy," she qualified.

"I'm grateful, Whitney."

"Just don't believe it's any more than it is. You're Jon's father, so you do have a right to see him. Remember your promise, Mitch. He stays with me."

"I'll remember. I wouldn't want him with anyone else." To himself he promised that one day, Whitney would open her heart to him again. He'd taken a big step toward that, and the word *retreat* was not in Mitch Flannery's vocabulary. Not when everything good in his life was at stake.

He went down the stairs and walked to his horse. Lazarus stood beside Whitney, and she knew that he and the others were waiting for an explanation.

"I had no choice, Lazarus," she said quietly.

"Ain't mah place to say right or wrong," Lazarus stated. "Ah knew how yo' felt befo'."

"He had the right to take Jon. I couldn't allow that so I agreed to let him see Jon at times."

"What about yo', missy?" Berdine asked.

"Little has changed . . . except one thing, I suppose."

"What?" Berdine questioned.

"I can't marry Trent Donnelley." Then she turned and walked into the house. Lazarus was about to follow her when Berdine put a restraining hand on his arm.

"Let me talk to her. She havin' a bad time. Ah thinks she need a woman now. Why don' yo' ride after him an' ask him any questions yo' gots to ask?"

Lazarus nodded and left. Berdine reached for the door handle and went inside. Addy and Josiah, eyes wide with curiosity, returned to their cabin.

Berdine found Whitney seated in a rocking chair by the window with Jon nestled contentedly on her lap, his thumb in his mouth and a heavy-lidded

273

look on his face. Whitney's face bore the trace of tears.

Berdine sat on a nearby chair and waited until Jon dropped into sleep. Then she spoke gently.

"Why yo' grievin', chile? Do it seem wrong to yo' dat a man want to see his chile? Seems to me he real carin'."

"No, I guess it's not wrong. Oh, Berdine, why did he have to come back here and spoil everything?"

"Yo' talkin' 'bout Trent Donnelley?"

"Yes."

"Yo' say yo' cain't marry him now?"

"It wouldn't be fair, Berdine. Jon is Mitch's son, and Mitch won't hesitate to say it. What would people think? Trent Donnelley engaged to marry the mother of his opponent's child."

" 'Pears to me iffen dat man wanted yo' an' de boy he wouldn' give no neverminds to what anybody else thinkin' or sayin'. Mebbe yo' could marry him, an' Mitch Flannery, he say nothin'."

"Hardly, Berdine," Whitney said bitterly. "If I married Trent, Mitch would do all he could to get his son. No, I'm not going to marry Trent Donnelley."

"Maybe," Berdine said cautiously, "yo' take up wif dis Flannery boy agin. He seem pow'ful anxious to start things over."

"No," she replied firmly. "For how long, Berdine? Until the grass seemed greener somewhere else? Until he decided he was tired of raising a child? Until he found something or someone he wanted more? No. He can see Jon . . . for now. But I must find a way to . . . get away."

"Whitney, chile. Doan yo' ever ask yo'self why dis boy fight so hard to see a chile iffen he never

274

wanted him befo'? Mebbe dey be some truth in what he sayin'. What harm would it do to listen?"

"Please, Berdine. It's too late for that." Whitney drew Jon tighter to her. "I have Jon, and he's all I need. Trent and Mitch can go on opposing each other, but I don't intend to see either one again."

"What 'bout when he come to see de boy? Yo' already say he can."

"I'll trust Lazarus, you, and Addy and Josiah to watch out for Jon. But I don't want to see Mitch."

"Ah see." Berdine did see, but for now she wisely kept her mouth shut. It seemed to her that Mitch had won the first battle. He had ended any possibility of Whitney's engagement to Trent and he had gotten permission to spend time with his son. She began to think Mitch Flannery was very clever and well on his way to renewing his relationship with Whitney. It might take a lot of time but a quiet war was being waged and she wouldn't be surprised if Mitch Flannery didn't come out a winner.

Twenty-two

Lazarus caught up with Mitch a mile or so from the house. Mitch heard the horse approaching and quickly turned around. When he saw who it was he relaxed. Knowing that Lazarus had questions to ask and warnings to give, he waited patiently until Lazarus reined in his horse beside him.

For a few moments they sat in silence, taking measure of each other's strength.

"Yo' better play yo' game careful, man," Lazarus said softly. His voice threatened only slightly, but his eyes threatened much more.

"Did it ever occur to you, Lazarus, that this is not a game for me?"

"No . . . it didn't."

"Well, it's not."

"You scared her."

Mitch smiled. "I have a feeling Whitney doesn't scare that easy. Besides, scaring her is not what I plan to do."

"Jes' what kind o' plans you got?"

"What objection do you have to me seeing my son?" Mitch countered.

"Where was yo' when she needed yo'? That ought to be reason enough. It ain't so simple. Ah tol' yo' once. Maybe ah gots to tell yo' agin."

"No, you don't have to tell me anything again.

What you need to do is listen. I didn't know I had a son, Lazarus. You didn't see fit to enlighten me on that score either. But that's beside the point. I have the right to take Jon if I want him." Mitch's voice was firm and Lazarus could see he was deadly serious.

"Yo' do dat, yo' kill her sure as yo' breathin'. Ah ain't gwine let dat happen. Ah kill yo' first."

"I said I have the right. Under the law I can do it and no one can stop me. I have the right, but I don't intend to do it. All I want is a chance to win back what was once mine."

"Ah don't understand."

"Lazarus . . . I don't want to hurt Whitney. I don't want to take Jon from her. All I want is a chance to know my son. If you had a son you would feel the same and you know it. All I want is to see him, to share his life and help him grow. I have the power of the law on my side, but I'd never use it to hurt Whitney . . . never."

"What if Miz Whitney marries Trent Donnelley? What yo' gwine do 'bout dat?"

Mitch smiled again. "Fight it every inch of the way. Take a good look, Lazarus. I'm not the poor farm boy who went off to war. I can offer Whitney and my son the kind of life we always dreamed about. Trent Donnelley couldn't offer her more. You always thought what was between Whitney and me was wrong. Well, it wasn't. I don't know what happened to our letters, maybe I never will know. But nothing—stolen letters, a war—nothing changes the way I feel about Whitney. I'm going to get them both back. Don't stand in my way, because as big as you are I'll walk over you to get Whitney and Jon back."

"Yo' thinks yo' kin do dat?" Lazarus asked, a

small smile beginning to play around his mouth.

"I'd sure as hell give it a try. I have my whole life to gain and nothing to lose."

"Dis here 'lection, it jes' one way to fight Trent Donnelley?"

"One way. I mean to be good at the job if I get it, but it's not the most important thing in my life. Whitney and Jon are."

Lazarus was hearing things in Mitch's voice that he'd never realized were there. It was confusing him. When he had first opposed Mitch, Mitch had retreated and when he expected retreat Mitch stood firm. Respect began to appear in his eyes and Mitch didn't miss it.

"Stay and protect her. She needs you. All I ask is that you give me a little time." Mitch's voice grew gentle. "I love her, Lazarus, and that's the God's own fact. I want to prove to all of you that what happened between us was good. If I had known about the boy nothing would have stopped me from being here. Think back, Lazarus. Remember, there were a lot of people real anxious to keep Whitney and me apart."

"Yo' talkin' disrespectful 'bout de dead. Miz Hope, she a fine lady an' want Miz Whitney happy."

"I didn't name Whitney's mother," Mitch said calmly. "You did. So maybe you know more than anyone else about those letters."

"No, suh. Ah doan know 'bout de letters."

"Well, it doesn't matter now. What does matter is . . . will you back off long enough to give me a fighting chance?"

Lazarus considered these words carefully. He was confused and what confused him most was Mitch's obvious sincerity.

"Ah'll think on it," he finally stated. Mitch felt a sense of relief.

"That's good enough for me. A little time, Lazarus, that's all I ask. You won't regret it."

Lazarus nodded, unsure if he was right or wrong. Mitch turned his horse and rode away. He did not remind Lazarus that they had made a bargain not too long before, but he meant to remind him and soon. Mitch felt better than he had in a long time.

When Mitch arrived home no one was there except his mother.

"Where is everybody?" he asked as he hung his jacket on the back of a chair and rolled up his sleeves to wash his hands.

"Oh, I expect them any minute. Blake and the boys stayed in town last night, probably at that hotel. Your father is about his chores and I'm trying to get enough food ready to feed a house full of hungry men. By the way," Caryn stopped working and looked at him more closely, "why aren't you still in town celebrating with the rest?"

"Celebrating," he chuckled. "The whole business has just gotten started. There's not much to celebrate yet."

"Then tell me why you look so . . . different."

"Different? How?"

"I don't know. It's like you've suddenly discovered something that pleases you very much."

He looked at her sharply. It amazed him how his mother could put her fingers on his thoughts. She noticed his glance and laughed.

"You're as obvious as the morning sun, Mitchell. Now why don't you tell me whose cookie jar you've had your hand in because it's pretty clear you like the taste."

279

"You're something else, you know that." He dried his hands and walked to the stove to lift the lid of a pot and inhale. "Umm, smells good."

"Mitchell Flannery," Caryn said laughing, "you don't get a bit to eat until you talk to me."

"You're a heartless woman. I'm starving."

"Well, you can darn well starve until you share whatever it is that's making you smile. I haven't seen that particular smile since you came home."

"Now you're telling me you know one smile from another?"

"I surely do. There's the sheepish smile, saved for when you're caught doing something you shouldn't. And the little boy smile when you really do want to get away with something . . . and there's this smile, when you have a secret you're just dying to share."

"Well . . . maybe I am, and I don't know anyone I'd rather share it with than you."

"What is it, Mitch?"

"I've been over to see Whitney. I'm trying to get her back. I don't know what kind of chance I have, but I do know I have a wonderful new advantage."

"Advantage?"

"You remember that little talk we had when I told you about Whitney's child?"

"Yes, of course."

"What would you say," Mitch said gently, "if I told you you were a grandmother . . . have been for three years. You have a grandson . . . and a beautiful one."

"Oh, Mitch," Caryn gasped as she sagged down into a chair. Her face was filled with shock at first—then she smiled. Mitch bent to kiss her cheek.

280

"He's a great boy, Mother, and I intend to spend my life with him and his mother."

"But from what I understand from all the gossip, Whitney Clayborn is engaged. She's going to marry Trent Donnelley."

"Over my dead body."

"Mitch."

"That's the only way."

"You can't just . . ."

"What makes you think I can't?" he asked with a grin. "Let me explain the situation." He went on to tell her everything that had happened from the moment he'd found out Jon was his son. "I'm not letting them slip through my fingers again."

"Lazarus doesn't sound too pleased."

"He'll come around."

"Cocky, aren't you?"

"No, just determined. I don't believe what Whitney and I had could ever be lost. Now we have a common link, and I intend to take advantage of that."

"Good heavens, Mitch, you're in for quite a battle."

"If I'm going to do it, I'd best bite off the whole chunk and try to swallow it in one gulp."

"If you don't choke. Sometimes I worry about you."

"Don't worry about me. I know what I want. In time I want to bring Whitney here. I want you to meet her. More important, I want you to meet Jon."

"Jon," Caryn said softly. "That's my grandchild's name?"

"Yes."

"Oh, Mitch, I'll pray for you. I'd so love to see him."

"You will. I promise."

"Your father and brothers are in for a very big surprise"

"Not to mention my friend."

"Blake. . . . I'm sure he's going to be surprised, too."

"Yes . . . I'm sure he is."

They heard the sound of approaching riders. Mitch and Caryn smiled at each other, then walked out on the porch to greet the rest of the family.

Trent had met with the men who supported him, mostly to assure them that Mitchell Flannery was no threat.

"The man is a nobody," Trent said firmly. "He has very little backing. His chances of winning are slim to nothing. By the time this is over no one will even remember Mitch Flannery's name."

"Of course you're right, Trent," Andrew Crocket said. "But there are plenty of precautions you can take."

Trent was still for a moment, then he smiled. "I have some papers I can use if the need arises."

"Papers?"

"They're my ace in the hole. I'll use them if the time comes. For now, don't worry. I'll beat Flannery on my own."

"What can you prove about Flannery that would swing the election?"

"Before the war he spoke out against slavery. Said the war was a mistake."

"So? The same opinion was expressed by others."

"Yes, but others didn't do what he did."

"And what was that?" Andrew asked.

"He worked for both sides. Betraying one against the other for money and his own convenience. Why do you think his closest friend is a Yankee. And why do you think he suffered so little from the war? In fact, he and his family seem suddenly very well off."

"Lord! You could destroy him with that kind of ammunition."

"If he gets in my way that's exactly what I will do. But let's not worry now. With the *Chronicle* behind me, he stands very little chance. As a mass, people are ignorant. They won't be hard to manipulate. Soon we'll have everything we want."

"Yes . . . I'm sure we will."

Satisfied that Trent was still the front-runner, most of the men left, leaving Trent and Andrew.

"So, Trent, you have incriminating evidence against our friend."

"That I do."

"Very hot stuff."

"It's meant to be."

"You'd best make sure that it doesn't singe anyone else."

"What's that supposed to mean?"

"Only that there's a skeleton in every closet. Make sure yours isn't exposed along with his."

"What are you saying, Andrew?"

"That there's always someone who knows . . . things. You see, unless a secret is only known by one . . . then it's no longer a secret. Make very sure no secrets can be uncovered about any of us that might bring the walls down."

"That sounds like a threat, Andrew."

"No, no threat. Just a word of, ah . . . precaution, shall we say."

"I'll take it into consideration."

283

Andrew nodded. He struck a match and lit his cigar. His eyes held Trent's as he slowly blew the match out. Then he left, quietly closing the door.

Trent stood in the center of the room, his anger seething. Mitch Flannery had been a thorn in his side much too long, a shadow between Whitney and him and now an even greater threat.

Well, he would eliminate one problem now. He'd waited long enough for Whitney to make up her mind — he intended to make it up for her. He couldn't afford to let her slip from his grasp. He had to find the letters he'd been searching for since he'd first 'accidentally' met her.

He breathed deeply and sighed in resignation. He had set his goals . . . neither Mitch Flannery . . . or Whitney Clayborn would be allowed to stand in his way.

Whitney seemed very close to accepting. Once she did, all she possessed would be his. The land . . . and the letters he needed.

He walked to the door. It was time to force her to make a decision. It would be simple. He had outmaneuvered more clever people. She needed a man — for herself and for her bastard son — and he could easily make her believe he was that man.

Whitney had rocked Jon for some time after Berdine had gone. He slept, but still she held him. He was her only anchor. How close she had come to losing him . . . maybe she still could. It all depended on Mitch. At that moment she felt shattered by the power he had over her. Still, he had promised he wouldn't use it . . . but Mitch had made promises before. *Trust me one more time, Whitney. I swear you won't regret it,* he had said. She had little choice but to trust him one more time. But would she regret it? She prayed not.

Her arms were numb from holding Jon, so she rose quietly and carried him upstairs to his crib. Then, flexing her arms to restore circulation, she walked back downstairs.

She had barely reached the bottom of the steps when she heard someone cross the porch and knock on the door. When she opened it Trent's broad-shouldered form filled the doorway.

"Trent!"

"You look surprised."

"Well, I am a little. I thought you'd be busy with your campaign."

"Campaigning has its place, Whitney, but on a lovely afternoon like this I couldn't help thinking of you. So here I am."

"Come in."

She seemed subdued. Had the speeches affected her so much, or was something else on her mind?

"Are you all right, Whitney?"

"Yes. Why shouldn't I be?"

"Oh, no reason. You're alone?"

"Jon's asleep, Josiah and Berdine have gone into town for supplies. Addy hadn't been away from Jon for weeks, so I told her to go along. Lazarus is out somewhere."

"Good. At least that gives us some time alone to talk, to make some plans."

"Yes. Actually, I'm glad you came, Trent." He was pleased at this, until he looked at her more closely. There was no smile, no laughter in her eyes. "There is something I have to tell you."

"I hope it's that you've finally decided to set the date. I've waited long enough to hear you say it." He tried to put his arms around her, but she

285

moved away.

"It's so difficult, Trent. You've been so kind and so patient."

"What is that supposed to mean?"

"That . . . that I can't marry you."

"You mean now, before the election."

"No, I mean that I can never marry you. Please believe me, Trent, I'm doing this for your welfare, too. It would be too costly a mistake for you. It might even jeopardize your career. You've been too good to me, and I just can't let that happen."

"I don't understand, and I don't know if I want to. Nothing you could do could jeopardize my career. You can only enhance it. I've told you that before. Whatever the problem is, I'm sure it's bigger in your mind than in reality."

"No, it's not, and it's not just in my mind. It's as real as any problem can be, and I can't walk away from it. I'm afraid it's part of my life."

"You're not making sense."

"Jon's father is here," she said quickly, as if she wanted to get it over with.

"And that's supposed to upset me? I have plenty of money, Whitney. If fighting for your son is the problem, don't worry. He'd never be able to touch you or Jon—especially if you marry me right away."

Whitney sighed deeply and clenched her fists. She hated to hurt Trent like this, but she would hurt him much more if she married him and the scandal broke. He would be laughed out of the political arena.

"It's impossible, Trent. Please believe me. Just understand that I can't marry you."

"Do you still love him?"

"No . . . it's not that."

286

"It can't be that bad, Whitney. I love you. We could be married today if you like. I would stand by you no matter what the difficulties are. Even a former lover."

The words grated on her. Did he think her wanton, that she had given herself to many men?

"He was the only man in my life before you."

"I asked you once if you loved him."

"At one time I thought I did."

"Thought? What happened?"

"He betrayed that love . . . when I told him about Jon."

"Then that should settle the matter. Tell him you're going to marry me and I have the power to fight him. He must be a coward to have turned up his heels and run. He'll run again."

"I . . . I think not, Trent."

"Who is this man, Whitney?"

"Mitchell Flannery," she said quietly. She expected anger. She expected him to lash out at her somehow to ease his pain. But he remained ominously silent. Whitney would never know of the nearly blinding rage that tore at his vitals until he wanted to reach out and squeeze her throat until she lay lifeless at his feet.

He might have done just that if it had not been for the shadowy force behind his every move. Those men would tolerate no such mistakes.

Whitney was the key to too much and he could not afford to lose any hold he had on her.

"Mitchell Flannery," he repeated slowly, trying to regain his composure. "Whitney . . . sit down and tell me everything. We could both think more clearly if all the cards were on the table."

Whitney was surprised — Trent was being so understanding.

Whitney tried to tell him the truth, never sparing herself nor denying she had made a drastic mistake. All the time she spoke Trent was sorting things out to see if he could get what he wanted without having to marry her.

He knew he had to play the game carefully. "Those letters he spoke so much about—maybe they're mixed among the ones your brother sent to your mother."

"There are only a few letters from Keith to Mother. I've read them a thousand times. There are no letters to me among them. My mother wouldn't . . ." She paused, considering this for the first time. It was a remote possibility. Her mother had always hated the idea of Whitney consorting with Mitch Flannery.

But Whitney's love for her mother was strong. She would not think ill of her, not now, when she was no longer alive to deny or confirm the accusation. Still, the germ of it remained although she was unaware of it.

"No matter," she continued, "Keith's letters have little to do with what happened between Mitch and me. I am to blame for that. Trent, I can only say I'm sorry. I never meant for this to happen. I respect you much too much to make this difficult for you. Your career would be at stake."

"Whitney," Trent said gently, smiling for the first time. "I'm sorry for what happened to you. But this man has you buffaloed into believing he's a bigger threat than he really is. I can make you another, better offer."

"You still want . . ."

"To marry you? Of course. Did you think I would love you one bit less because you made a mistake? No, believe me, you mean more to me

288

than just this election . . . much more than you know." He stood up and paced back and forth for a minute. "Whitney, you said he insisted on seeing his son?"

"Yes."

"Then believe me, if you give me time I can prove he's lying and using the child to get to you for his own protection. He's not the man you think he is."

"I don't understand."

"Well, understand this. I don't intend to let him stand between me and all I've ever wanted. If you give me time I can prove he's not good enough for you."

"Prove? What can you prove?"

"That he was a traitor to many others beside yourself. That he's the wrong man for you — and for this town."

"How? What . . ."

"Whitney, please. It's too involved for me to explain it all now. Can you give me time?"

"What is it you're proposing?"

"You said he's coming to see the boy."

"Yes, but I don't expect to be here when he does."

"No, I'm sure you don't want to be. Just say and do nothing for a while — until I have more tangible proof."

"Proof of what?"

"I'd prefer to show you because it's so complicated. Whitney, don't fall for his promises again. I don't want to see you hurt and you would be. He asked you to trust him. Well, he asked others to trust him before and they paid as well. Don't trust, but keep your silence. In the end you'll understand. You'll see him as he really is and be able to put him out of your life. And I, I'll be able to stop him from ever hurting you or the boy again."

He knew he had stirred deep doubt and confusion in Whitney by his understanding in the face of what she had told him, and by his assurance in his attack on Mitch.

But a wrath so deep and so violent seethed in him that Whitney would have been incinerated had he allowed her to feel the force of it.

In time, he promised himself, in time he would have Whitney and her precious son in his hands and would eliminate Mitchell Flannery once and for all. Then she would bend to his will. She would do whatever he wanted—he would have what he wanted and be wealthy beyond thought. Then he could concentrate on molding Whitney into a beautiful, docile, and obedient woman who would help him get whatever he wanted. The child would serve as a weapon. In time, he cautioned himself, in time. For now he couldn't let her get out of control or any closer to Mitch Flannery than she'd already been. The thought of her in his enemy's arms almost drove him to take her right now, on the floor like the whore she was.

"I know how hard this must have been on you—especially when he tried to come back into your life. But you don't have to fear his threats and neither does your son." He took her hand. "I love you, Whitney, and I'll stand by you no matter what. So let him play this little game. In the end he'll regret what he's done. Now, I don't want to pressure you into anything. All I'm saying is I want to give you a future and he wants to give you more of the past—more deceit and, in the long run, more treachery."

His voice had just the right texture—sympa-

290

thetic, understanding, and caring. He was an expert at playing to Whitney's sensitivity.

Whitney had been sure that Trent would turn on her in disgust, certain he would accuse her of deceit and betrayal for not telling him the truth from the start. In the face of his gentleness and understanding, her certainty wavered.

Trent had been nothing but good to her from the moment they had met. Why did she feel uncomfortable about his request? What kind of proof did he have that would condemn Mitch and take him away from her?

But logic told her she had nothing to lose if she did wait. She didn't want to ruin Trent's career and she didn't want to make another terrible mistake.

"He'll come here to see his son."

"Let him, but stay away from him yourself. In the end the boy will be yours forever."

"You're certain?"

"As certain as my life."

"What if the election goes against you?"

"I'll have all my evidence soon and put a stop to him before the election is over. By the time the votes are counted, Mitch Flannery will be exposed and you'll be free to make your own choices. I only hope it will be me and the life I offer you both."

"Oh, Trent, I must think. What could Mitch have done that's so terrible? I only want him to relinquish his right to Jon. I don't want to destroy him."

"We'll do it your way when the time comes. For now I think you owe me this much: stay away from him and give me time. That's all I ask."

It seemed little to ask compared to all he was

291

willing to do for her. "All right, Trent. I won't see him again. When you have whatever proof you're gathering, may I see it first?"

"Of course. That's only fair." He bent to kiss her cheek lightly and squeezed her hand. "I'm glad you told me. It gave me an opportunity to show you just how much I care. Forget the past, Whitney. We have a wonderful future ahead of . . . the three of us." He stood up. "Think things over. Just remember," he added, the opportunity to insert an insidious reminder pleasing him, "that he deceived and betrayed you once before. I wouldn't put it past him to try to use you against me. He thinks he's in love with you and so I'm in his way. Besides that, he has a driving ambition and he needs to defeat me to get to the first rung of the ladder."

Trent smiled when he saw painful memories leap into Whitney's eyes. For now this was enough. She would keep her distance from Mitch and soon he would make that distance permanent.

Trent picked up his hat and left quietly, leaving Whitney alone with her thoughts swirling in black confusion.

She wanted to run from all the memories and pain. But there was no place to go. Everything she had was in these two small cabins — the four friends who had remained with her . . . and her son.

Beside her on the table was the music box Mitch had given her so long ago when the world was a bright and loving place.

Almost against her will she reached out and lifted the lid. Soft music filled the silent room. She listened for a few minutes, then closed the lid, tears hot on her cheeks. She didn't bother to wipe them away but wept silently. After a few minutes she rose and walked upstairs.

Twenty-three

Whitney spent a very quiet weekend sharing every moment she could with Jon. All that Mitch had said, and every word that Trent had said, were burned into her mind. She had tried to search for a way out, but there was none. She had to step back from all of it and concentrate on protecting Jon.

Lazarus stayed much closer to the house than he ever had before, sending Josiah to chop the necessary wood. Berdine and Addy worked with the same careful quietness.

Berdine kept her own counsel, but she had a feeling Whitney was being torn apart. Maybe she would come to talk sooner or later.

Addy kept Berdine in sight constantly, trying to follow whatever example she set. Since no one had ever mentioned letters, Addy had never said anything. There was no link in her mind between Hope's long-ago threat and Whitney's unhappiness.

But Whitney did not come to Berdine to share her thoughts, and no matter how she tried to wish it away the inevitable Monday morning dawned. She heard a distant rumble of thunder.

To make it worse Whitney awoke with a headache, feeling sluggish. She rose slowly and went downstairs just after dawn, put the coffee pot on the stove, then wrapped her shawl about her shoulders. Still in her nightgown, bare-footed, and with her hair unbound and tousled, she walked out onto the porch to watch the sunrise.

She was certain Mitch would not come until late afternoon. That would give her time to find some place else to be while he was here. It annoyed her to feel cowardly, as if she were running away.

Lazarus had already promised that he would keep Mitch and Jon in sight and Whitney trusted him. Lazarus still did not approve of what she was doing. Well, neither did she, but one wrong move and she was afraid Mitch might do something.

The sun was a heavy orange globe and the sky was filled with breathtaking purples and reds. Pale gray and white clouds lay banked on the horizon. Whitney wondered if the promise of rain in the air would be a fact before nightfall.

She pulled the shawl a little more snugly about her against the early morning chill. Summer was coming to an end. Soon the leaves would begin to turn and the land would have that glow of color that made each day rare and important.

Memories flooded her mind, and for this brief time of quiet peace she allowed them to. In fact, she was so involved that she never realized she wasn't alone.

Mitch knew he was probably arriving before anyone else was awake, but he had found waiting for an entire weekend much too long. He was impatient to see Jon . . . and even more impatient to see Whitney.

He let his horse pick his way slowly toward the clearing and that was why his approach was almost soundless. He saw Whitney huddled on the top step and knew she was unaware of his presence. He swung down from the saddle and walked to the edge of the porch.

She looked almost child-like. Her pale gold hair looked like spun silk in the early morning light. She was deep in a dream-like state and he wondered where her mind had drifted. To her old home . . . maybe even to him.

He smiled as Whitney slowly stood up and stretched, letting her hands thread through her long hair. In the first pale rays of the sun he could see the shadowed outline of her body beneath the cotton nightgown as her shawl dropped from her shoulders. A piercing jab of hot desire caught him completely unprepared, and he could feel his body answering the call of memories that would never die.

Everything that surrounded him seemed more intense in color and sound, from the call of the birds to the breeze that sighed through the trees. He whispered her name softly, but it carried well on the morning air. Whitney gasped in shock and spun about.

"Mitch! What are you doing here?"

"It's Monday." He smiled, but she felt his eyes rake over her and drew the shawl closer, feeling her cheeks flush.

"Yes," she added hesitantly, battling the stirring in her that made her uncomfortable under his much too warm gaze. "It is, but I didn't expect you so . . . so early."

"It was hard enough to wait over the weekend without having to wait half of today too."

"Jon . . . Jon's not awake yet."

"I smell coffee. May I come in and wait?"

Her mind scrambled for reasons to refuse, but she found nothing. She had planned to be away when he arrived, but here she was, nearly undressed, barefoot, and completely off stride. "Yes, yes, of course."

She moved toward the door quickly, wanting to keep as much distance between them as possible. She'd find a way to leave as soon as she could.

The kitchen was still chilly and while Whitney poured the coffee, Mitch went to the banked fireplace and stirred it to life. Then he put a couple of logs on and watched them catch. It was as if he were part of this house. He felt the comfort along with the warmth.

Whitney handed him a steaming cup of coffee. Their hands met briefly and she withdrew hers at once. Still, the feel of her skin lingered with him. He sipped . . . and watched her. She had changed somehow since he'd seen her last.

"Whitney?"

"What?"

"Are you having second thoughts?"

"About you seeing Jon?"

He nodded.

"No," she said honestly. "I think it best that we not share the same time."

"Then I can take Jon with me?" he asked hopefully.

"No!"

"You still believe I'd do something stupid, like try to hold him or force you into something?"

She looked at him for a moment, then replied honestly. "No, I suppose not. You have nothing to gain by that. We both know that would never work."

"Then let me have him for the day. I'd like to show him to the rest of his family."

"Family," Whitney replied softly. He sensed her hurt and regretted the pain it caused. But he didn't regret his request.

"He has grandparents, uncles, they'd all like to see him."

Whitney felt unwelcome tears well in her eyes and

296

fought them desperately. He could give Jon so much more than she could.

"Come along if you choose. You'd be more than welcome."

"I couldn't do that."

"Why?"

"Stop it, Mitch. Stop trying to mend what's broken. It won't work and it can only cause more grief. I won't go. But," she added, "if you agree to let Lazarus and Addy go with you, you can take him."

"Of course I'd agree to that. But I'd much rather you came."

Whitney shook her head and started past him. "I'll go and see if he's awake yet."

Mitch caught her arm as she moved past and spun her about to face him.

"Whitney, what's happened?"

She felt the heat of his hand against her arm and became suddenly completely aware of him. She didn't want to look up into his eyes, but it seemed as if she were drawn against her will.

A sensation of raw sensual power emanated from him and seemed to permeate her body and soul. For a second hot anger scalded her. Would she never be able to kill his ability to do this to her?

"I don't know what you're talking about."

"You never were a good liar," he replied, his smile teasing.

"Aren't you satisfied yet? Or are you going to break this promise, too?"

"No, I'm not breaking this promise. I'm certainly not satisfied, but that's beside the point. What's happened since I saw you last? There's something . . . elusive. You're not running away from me again?"

"Again?" she laughed bitterly. "I wasn't the one who ran in the first place. You have what you want. Don't ask me for any more. I owe you nothing."

297

She saw flame leap into his eyes and had no time to utter a protest before his arms were around her and she was crushed against him.

"You're fighting me for no reason, Whitney. No reason except you're scared. We owe each other plenty—and that's the truth." His voice deepened with the hunger that had lain dormant for so long. "Neither of us has ever forgotten. I can feel it in every inch of you. I see it in your eyes. I can even remember the taste . . ." He stopped speaking and bent his head to capture her mouth with his.

Her first reaction was shock at the hot pleasure that coursed through her. All at once the blood seemed to rush from her extremities. Her arms and legs felt weak, her head light. Only her lips, her breasts, and her loins seemed real, tingling and pulsing. There was no thought of pushing him away, and even if she wanted to, she knew her hands would not cooperate.

For a moment she yielded, meeting his lips willingly. Then her arms went around him and her lips parted, opening the warm haven of her mouth to his questing tongue. His hands slipped down her back to her buttocks, pressed her against him, relaxed, pressed her close again with an urgent rhythm.

A soft voice from the top of the steps hit them like a bolt of lightning. Whitney tore herself from his arms, gasping for breath. Desire had darkened his gray eyes to slate.

"Miz Whitney, yo' down dere already?" Addy's voice came from the top of the stairs.

"Yes, Addy, I am. Please see if Jon is awake. If he is, dress him while I make breakfast. While you're about it, get dressed yourself. Mr. Flannery has come for Jon and you and Lazarus are going with him."

Mitch continued to watch her as the patter of feet

upstairs told them Addy was doing as she was told.

"You haven't answered my question."

"I told you there was nothing different. I just think it best that we set a time for your next meeting with Jon."

"So you won't have to be here when I come," he stated accurately.

"It will be better for all concerned."

Addy could be heard moving about, and Mitch knew it would only be minutes before she came down. There was little time to talk, but the time would come.

Whitney moved away from him, still aware that she was wearing only a nightgown. She picked up the shawl again and wrapped it about her and started for the stairs.

By the time the three of them came back down, Mitch was seated comfortably before the crisply burning fire. He'd been thinking how contented he could be to live here the rest of his life.

Whitney had gained control of her emotions—he could tell by the way she moved about as she began breakfast. Still, he also noticed that she didn't look directly at him again.

But Jon did. He toddled over almost at once and stood by his knee. He remembered this tall man.

Mitch reached out and laid his hand lightly on Jon's shoulder. "Good morning, Jon. Ready for a big breakfast?" Jon nodded and Whitney smiled.

"He's always ready for a big breakfast. If he continues to eat at the rate he does I don't know how I'll keep him in food."

"Wanna see my soldiers now?"

"Those soldiers must be his favorite thing," Mitch said, still a little envious that he had not made them or bought them for him.

"They are. The soldiers and that old jewelry box

299

of Mother's. He drags it with him wherever he goes. I don't doubt that he'll want to take them today as well."

"Of course, he . . ." Mitch stopped talking to Whitney and returned his attention to Jon who was tugging at his sleeve. "All right, Jon," Mitch said as he laughed. "Bring out the soldiers."

Jon's eyes brightened and his smile was filled with delight.

He ran up the steps as fast as his legs would take him. Mitch had to laugh at his excitement. Soon he returned, walking slowly and carrying the precious box that was almost too much for him to carry.

To Whitney's surprise Mitch left his chair and sat down on the floor. Jon placed the box between them. Mitch did not reach to touch it. "This is your show, boy, so let's see what you've got."

Jon opened the box and almost delicately, for his three-year-old fingers, he removed the well-worn figures. Only then did Mitch reach to run his fingers over the box's surface.

"It's beautiful," he said, as he looked up at Whitney.

"Yes," Whitney said softly as memories stirred anew in her mind. Whitney turned away from Mitch's gaze and began to place the plates on the table. Until the food was ready she kept her mind and her eyes away from the pair on the floor. Occasionally she heard her son's delighted giggle combined with Mitch's deep chuckle.

"Come along, Jon. Put the soldiers away. Breakfast is ready."

Jon was about to rebel when Mitch began to put the pieces away. "C'mon, sport, we can play with them later. I'm taking you for a ride after breakfast and you can bring them along. Would you like that?"

Jon nodded and the pieces were replaced. Breakfast was a somewhat quiet affair and Addy was well aware of the tension between Mitch and Whitney.

At the end of the rather quick meal Whitney rose.

"Addy, run over and get Lazarus. Tell him I would like him to go with you and Jon today."

Addy nodded, more than pleased to get out of an atmosphere in which she could hardly breathe. She ran across the clearing and erupted into the cabin, startling Berdine who was preparing breakfast and Lazarus and Josiah who were seated at the table. Lazarus leapt to his feet.

"Addy! What da matter? Miz Whitney, de boy, are dey all right?"

"Dey all right."

"Then what ails yo', gal. Yo' done scared de devil outta us."

"Mr. Flannery . . . he dere, in de house. He gwine take de boy fo' a day. Miz Whitney, she say she want yo' an' me to go wif him."

"She trust dat far she gwine let him take de boy? Maybe he don' bring him back."

"Ah 'spects dats why Miz Whitney want us to go."

"Where he goin'?" Lazarus asked, moving as he spoke. He tore off a piece of bread and sopped it in the bacon grease. Then he put two pieces of bacon on it and began to eat as he reached for his jacket.

"Ah doan know. Yo' better ask Miz Whitney."

"Damn fool mistake," Lazarus grumbled. Berdine, who had been silent, now spoke up.

"Maybe she ain't got no choice."

"She got a choice. She know iffen she say no, dat man ain' gwine be able to take him."

"Maybe she smarter than startin' trouble like dat."

"What yo' sayin', Berdine?"

"Ah'm sayin' she smart. She play like he a big fish. She give him all de line he wants. He be like

301

fightin' a shadow. She ain' gwine fight, but she ain't gwine give in either."

Lazarus looked at Berdine closely. "Seems sad to me dat two people have to fight over a li'l boy dat doan understan'," he said quietly.

"Ah knows dat. But dose two, dey done lost dere way. Ah guess it has to happen. All we kin do is stan' by her . . . an' pray."

Lazarus sighed and nodded. He and Addy left, leaving Berdine to her own thoughts. Maybe today, when she was alone, Whitney would talk to her.

Lazarus crossed the clearing, munching the last of his sparse meal, Addy on his heels. When he opened the door Whitney was already putting on Jon's coat. She was fighting tears but managing a smile for Jon. Lazarus looked across the room at Mitch who was also putting on his coat. He searched Mitch's face for one sign of treachery, but saw nothing. Mitch was well aware that not only would Lazarus watch him like a hawk, but he would be prepared to do anything he thought was necessary should he show any sign of harming either Whitney or Jon.

"Ah'll harness de hoss an' bring de wagon aroun'," Lazarus said. "Jon kin ride wif me."

"No," Mitch said, "he'll ride with me. You and Addy take the wagon. Maybe Jon will trust his box of soldiers to you."

Lazarus looked to Whitney and she nodded. He did not speak to Mitch again, but turned and left the cabin.

Whitney stood on the porch while Mitch brought his horse around, mounted, then lifted a delighted Jon in front of him. She held back her tears until the wagon and rider were out of sight. Then the unbearable quiet and loneliness overwhelmed her. If Mitch were to take Jon, this is how it would be forever. She had to hope Trent was right, because she knew she could not bear the emptiness Jon's loss would bring.

Caryn had never been more excited about anything in her life. She had been ecstatic when Mitch told her he was asking Whitney to let Jon come with him for a day. Of course, she knew it might not happen, but she had still risen early and made cookies she hoped would please her grandson . . . her grandson. She could hardly believe it.

She realized how happy Mitch had been about it, but when she broached the subject of Whitney, he was more evasive. It was a tangled, heartbreaking affair and she hoped something would happen that would change it all somehow.

She heard the riders approaching from some distance and she knew the others, who had gone about their daily chores more as a way to keep busy than anything else, heard them, too. It was only minutes before Blake appeared, followed quickly by Stuart, Morgan, and Shawn. They looked at each other with quick nervous smiles.

"Do you think . . ." Blake began.

"I hope so," Caryn replied quickly. "Can you think of any reason Mitch would return so soon if she refused?"

"No, of course not. He'd stay. He wants to enjoy his son as much as possible."

"Oh, Blake, this is so awful."

"I know."

"They're coming," Morgan said. He had drawn the curtain aside and was looking out the window. "And Mitch has got the kid with him."

A tingle of raw excitement filled the room and Caryn couldn't wait any longer. She opened the door and ran out onto the porch. It took only moments for the four men to come out behind her.

When Mitch stopped his horse near the porch he had to laugh. He could see Caryn's hands were almost twitching to hold Jon. He dismounted and lifted him down, carrying him directly to his mother.

"Well, here he is . . . Grandma."

He handed Jon to Caryn's waiting arms. As if he somehow understood, Jon hugged her enthusiastically, showing no fear of the strange adults crowding around him.

Jon adapted well to the day away from Whitney, mostly because he was spoiled atrociously. Grown men sat on the floor and played soldiers with him to his heart's content. There were games and laughter and, best of all, cookies and peppermint candy after he ate a good meal.

He walked into the heart of each Flannery man as easily as if they were all made of melted butter. But it was Caryn who knew it would be difficult for all of them, especially Mitch, to relinquish him at the end of the day.

If Lazarus and Addy were nervous it was dispelled at once. They were made as welcome as Jon, and Lazarus watched a day unfold that caused him considerable consternation. There was love flowing in this family, and it could grow into a situation that could more than confuse Jon's young mind.

How was a boy Jon's age to understand? Once he knew and maybe began to care for Mitch, it would be hard for him not to love both his parents. He could be torn to shreds. Unless . . . he looked closely at Mitch and his gaze drew Mitch's attention. For a long moment their eyes held and Lazarus knew in that short time that Mitch knew exactly what he was doing. The way to Whitney was through Jon and Mitch meant to reach her.

Lazarus also realized that Mitch had no intention

of forcing Jon to choose between them. He meant only to try and make Jon love him. The rest would be between Whitney and him. Before Mitch broke eye contact with Lazarus, he smiled and winked, conveying in no uncertain terms that he knew Lazarus knew what he was doing—and challenged him to do anything about it. Lazarus smiled. This was one battle in which he was an observer. Unless Whitney came to harm—only then would he speak. Maybe Berdine was right. These two were so clever they might just outsmart each other.

Jon sat on Mitch's lap right after the evening meal, but Mitch could already sense that he was not only tired, he was beginning to get cranky. He turned to look up at Mitch, his eyes big and questioning.

"Where's Mommy?"

"She's home, Jon."

"I wanna go home."

"So soon?" Mitch asked, reluctant to part with him. "You can stay a little longer."

Jon shook his head, his eyes beginning to fill with vague uncertainty. "I wanna go home. I want my mommy."

"Of course you do, son, of course you do." Mitch sighed. "I'll take you home. Run and gather your toys."

Jon moved with enough alacrity to make Mitch realize that Whitney was almost his whole life, and at the most he had only a small corner—a small corner that could be closed easily and permanently. It would be so easy to keep him, but Jon's fears and his tears were not a good way to win over Whitney. She already knew he had power, so the only person he could hurt would be Jon.

It was with deep reluctance that Caryn bundled him up and watched as Mitch rode away with

305

him. Lazarus and Addy followed in the wagon.

By the time the day was three quarters gone Whitney was suffering. Doubts paraded through her mind all day. She told herself she had done the right thing, only to contradict her own thoughts by swearing she would never do it again, no matter what she agreed to.

She missed Jon's bright enthusiasm, and the house felt empty and lonely without him. She had her first taste of what it would be like should Mitch choose to enforce his rights and take Jon from her forever. The taste was bitter.

She walked across the clearing to share the evening meal with Berdine and Josiah, though she certainly wasn't hungry. Berdine was wise enough not to question her—she knew the day must have been excruciating.

They talked of everything but what was uppermost in their minds, from sewing new clothes to the addition to the barn Lazarus planned to build. Whitney skirted anything emotional completely and by the time the sun was setting, Berdine watched her walk back home with deep sympathy.

Whitney paced the floor. Would he bring Jon back or not? What would she do if he didn't? Go after him, of course.

Time moved painfully slowly and Whitney's torment grew stronger. She was right, she was wrong. He was trustworthy, he was not. She would win . . . she would lose.

When she lit the lamps her hand was shaking. There was nothing more to keep her mind and hands busy. She could do little but sit before the low-burning fire . . . and think.

Her nerves were stretched to the breaking point

by the time she heard the first sounds. She leapt to her feet and ran to the door to fling it open. She could not see far in the darkness, but she strained until vague forms materialized. She almost cried out her relief.

Lazarus took the wagon straight to the barn while Mitch rode to the porch. He dismounted easily, cradling a sleeping Jon in one arm, and walked up beside Whitney. He read the look in her eyes well, but said nothing.

"He was exhausted. He fell asleep only a few minutes after we left. Show me where he sleeps and I'll carry him up and help you get him tucked in."

Whitney went ahead of him and opened the door to the room Jon shared with Addy.

She watched Mitch lay Jon gently down and remove his clothes and shoes. Her heart began to thud. It was dangerous to feel this warmth—it was just another weapon Mitch could use.

Silently they left the room and walked downstairs. Mitch knew he had no reason to stay, but he was reluctant to leave. He turned to look at Whitney, but there was no welcome in her eyes. He had little choice but to walk slowly to the door.

"I want to thank you, Whitney. I know it must have been hard on you. He's a great boy. You've done a good job with him."

"I take it he was well behaved today. You haven't seen him when he's obstinate. He can have a very wicked temper."

"He brought my mother a great deal of pleasure today. I have to thank you for that as well. Not to mention my father and brothers. When can I come again?"

"I've been thinking about it. Once a week should . . ."

"Once a week! Whitney, that's not much."

307

"Maybe later it can be more."

"Once you've really put me to the test," he was half angry and knew this was a bad time to react. "I suppose I'll have to settle for that . . . for now. I'll be here next Monday."

"No, Mitch."

"What?"

"I'll have Lazarus bring him to you. It'll be easier for all of us."

"Easier for all of us," he repeated. "You mean easier for you, don't you? What are you afraid of, Whitney?"

If he meant to intimidate her or make her back away he failed and it surprised him a little.

"Afraid?" She smiled. "Yes, I guess I'm a little afraid. I've learned a lot about fear in the past few years. I'm afraid to trust, afraid to love, and afraid to look too closely at myself because I'm not happy with what I see. I was even running from you, but that's over with now. We made our second bargain. I hope you keep it better than you did the first. You can see Jon one day a week. Lazarus will bring him, and he will stay. If you aren't agreeable to that then your reasons for wanting to see Jon are a lie, and I guess the sooner we find out about that the better."

"I want to see him . . . but I wanted . . ."

"What you wanted was lost a long time ago. Take what you can get, Mitch. I've had to. Keep your bargain . . . and I'll keep mine."

It was time to back away and Mitch knew it, but nothing had ever been more difficult. He could still taste the willingness in her kiss hours before.

He took a step toward her but something in her eyes made him stop. If he forced her now, and in the back of his mind he knew he could, Whitney might retreat to a place where he could never reach her again. She would close the door between them forever.

"All right," he said quietly. "I'll go. Lazarus will bring Jon next week. It's a long wait but I'll manage."

He left before he said something he knew he'd regret. He paused on the porch for a minute, fighting the desire to go back in. Then he looked across the clearing and saw Lazarus standing on the porch.

He smiled . . . and Lazarus returned the smile equally warmly. Neither of them was aware of the shadowed figure in the shelter of the trees some distance away.

Mitch didn't speak to Lazarus, he simply walked to his horse and rode away. Lazarus waited on the porch for some time, making sure Mitch was really gone. Then he walked back into his cabin and closed the door.

Whitney was weary. She felt as if she had fought a strenuous battle. She extinguished all the lamps but one, knowing Addy would be coming in soon. Then she walked slowly upstairs.

The lamp in her room was already lit and she slowly prepared for bed. Addy came in and Whitney heard her moving about downstairs securing everything. Then she climbed the stairs and knocked timidly on Whitney's door.

"Miz Whitney, yo' all right?"

"Yes, I'm fine. Go to bed."

"Yessum." Moments later she heard Jon's bedroom door close.

But sleep was elusive. She could hear Trent's words in her mind, and she knew he was right. She had to stay away from Mitch. The kiss they had shared earlier should have proven that. She had been caught up in the old magic Mitch could weave so well. It was pure and simple lust, and a little control and common sense would keep her on the right track.

Impatient with her train of thought, she stood and walked to the dresser and extinguished the lamp. Pale moonlight cast the room in hazy darkness. She walked to the window and looked out.

At first everything was vague — a dark cluster of trees, hazy clouds across the moon dimming its light a bit. She stood still, listening to the night sounds.

Then a soft breeze skittered the clouds away and a white glow outlined each tree. It was then that she saw him.

She gasped and stepped back in reflex. Then she realized her room was dark and no one could see inside. She drew on her courage and stepped up closer to the window again.

He was just within the edge of the trees, and he stood very, very still. His attention was focused on the house — she could tell even though she couldn't see his face. Who was he? What did he want?

She remembered that Mitch has stolen into her room so easily, and that someone had tried to break in before that. She and Lazarus had made sure the same method couldn't be used again. If it were Mitch and he had the same plan in mind he would fail.

At the same moment she sensed that the man standing beneath the trees was not Mitch. Her only real fear was that it was a threat to Jon and Addy. She had to do something and her best bet was Lazarus.

She moved across the room slowly and crept down the hall to the steps, going down carefully so she wouldn't wake Jon or Addy. If she did, both were sure to be frantic and noisy.

She laid her ear against the door and listened. There was no sound from outside so she opened it just enough to see. The clearing was empty. She stepped out and drew the door closed, leaning against it to listen again. Nothing.

She moved down the porch steps and raced across the clearing. She didn't knock, but pushed the door open, stepped in and closed it behind her.

Lazarus nearly leapt to his feet, with Josiah beside him. Berdine looked up in shock.

"Miz Whitney, what de matter?" Lazarus asked anxiously.

"Lazarus, whoever our intruder was before, he's back." She went on to explain what she had seen.

Lazarus moved quickly to the corner where his gun stood. He took it and left the cabin soundlessly with Josiah. Whitney was prepared to follow but Berdine stopped her.

"Yo' stays right here 'til Lazarus find out what's goin' on. Iffen it be somebody meanin' yo' harm yo' tie Lazarus's hands if yo' go wanderin' aroun' out dere an' he catch hold yo'."

Whitney knew she was right, but it did her already taut nerves little good to sit and do nothing.

It seemed like hours before Lazarus came back — in truth it was a little over an hour. He entered the house and both women rose abruptly to their feet.

"Lazarus?" Whitney questioned.

"Ain't nobody aroun' no mo'. Ah looked all over. But ah knows someone be standin' out dere. Dere's bushes an' twigs broke. Ah'll come an' check de house fo' yo', den ah sleeps on de couch. But ah don' reckon dere be no mo' trouble tonight. Whoever it is he knows ah's waitin' an' watchin'. Come on, Miz Whitney. Ah goes back wif yo'. Everythin' gwine be awright. Don't worry yo' mind 'bout it. Ah'll keep close watch from now on."

311

They returned to the house and after Lazarus checked it over carefully Whitney made him a comfortable bed on the couch.

But neither of them slept much the rest of the night. There were too many questions. Who was the mysterious intruder . . . . he had returned for the third time. And most important . . . . what did he want?

Twenty-four

The next month passed in a flurry of activity. Mitch campaigned heavily, often going from door to door. But he kept Mondays for Jon alone. He found more pleasure in his son than he ever could have believed possible. He did his best to ignore the fact that between Lazarus and Addy his every move was watched. Lazarus was like a silent monolith, unbending and prepared.

The Flannery family referred to Lazarus as "Mitch's shadow." Yet after the second visit he began to help with small chores and was always ready to lend a hand. To Mitch's disbelief the family began to accept him . . . even to appreciate him, and to ask him stories about what had happened to them during and after the war. Caryn was especially interested because she read much more in Lazarus's words and attitude than he realized.

She had loved Jon instantly, and nursed the secret hope that one day Whitney would let her into her life a little more. She was not sure of Whitney's feelings, but she'd seen things in Mitch and was beginning to gather the courage to pay Whitney a visit. She wasn't too sure about the reception she would get, but she meant to give it a try.

From Jon's incessant chatter Mitch learned things about Whitney. Small, sweet, loving things. He could tell how much Jon adored his mother. With

313

that realization came another. No matter what ever happened or the pain it caused, he could never separate them.

Noel and Craig had printed handbills which had been distributed everywhere and both were campaigning with all their energy. Trent had slowly become aware of this, along with the fact that the people were being swayed more effectively than he could have thought possible. Trent's hatred filled him to capacity, and he had begun to think of ways to eliminate Mitch permanently.

Kevin had spoken very little to Noel since his confrontation with Blake. He seemed to be in an introspective silence. He was reaching into corners of his mind he'd never touched before and was having a hard time coping.

Lazarus seemed to be going through a metamorphosis. His first contact with Mitch's family had sent him home deep in thought. The next two visits did very little to shore up his remaining antagonism. He found himself blending in when he knew he shouldn't be. His loyalties lay with Whitney, and he couldn't let himself forget that. Still, what he was beginning to feel toward Mitch confused him. Before Mitch's return everything was clear. He had things in perspective. He knew who to blame and why. Now he wasn't so sure. On the last visit he came face to face with the problem.

Addy had not been feeling well enough to accompany them, so Lazarus and Jon had gone alone. Lazarus knew it crushed Whitney every time Jon went and he also knew she questioned Jon subtly on every return trip. Jon's bubbling enthusiasm and his sheer enjoyment came through quite clearly.

He rode along slowly with Jon perched before him

314

in the saddle, mostly listening since the boy found the world around him challenging and asked questions to match.

"No, Jon," Lazarus said with a laugh. "Ah doan know why butterflies are diff'rent colors."

"Can I catch one?"

"Maybe later. Right now we got to get along." He started to remind Jon that his father was waiting for him but caught himself. Mitch had not yet told Jon he was his father because he wasn't sure whether it would break the bond between Whitney and him for all time. He put that out of his mind because it was too complicated.

Caryn was waiting on the front porch, as she had been every time he had brought Jon. Usually Mitch was there as well, but this morning Caryn was alone.

She watched them approach. In a short time she had fallen in love with Jon and would have done anything to hear him call her "grandmother." That, too, was still a closely kept secret.

"Good morning, Jon," Caryn called as soon as they were close enough. Jon waved with a bright smile. When they reached the porch Lazarus lifted Jon down.

"Good morning, Lazarus. It's early. Have you had breakfast? There's plenty inside."

"Yessum, ah had breakfast already. Maybe Jon hungry. He put away enough at home, but yo' know how it is wif growin' boys."

"Yes, Mitch and his brothers used to eat enough food for an army."

Lazarus looked around. It was unlike Mitch not to be there.

"Mitch is in the barn, Lazarus. One of the mares gave birth to a beautiful filly early this morning. Take Jon on out. It's quite a sight."

315

Lazarus nodded and took Jon with him, walking the short distance to the barn. The door stood ajar and they heard the sound of men's voices.

They walked inside the dim barn and followed the voices until they came to a stall near the back. They stopped at the entrance to the stall, drawing Mitch and Stuart's attention. Mitch had been kneeling next to an amber-colored mound nestled in the straw. When he saw Jon, Lazarus watched his face light up. He rose and came to Jon, lifting him in his arms.

"Morning, buddy. You ready for a big surprise?"

Jon nodded his head enthusiastically. Mitch returned to the mound and knelt down, standing Jon between his legs. "Watch," Mitch said softly. Jon became very still, his eyes glued to the new thing that seemed suddenly to come to life.

The young filly lifted her head and boy and filly exchanged looks. Then with weak, shaky movements the filly began to try and gain its feet. First the two front legs, quivering and delicate. Then the struggle to get the two back legs to obey. Finally it achieved a standing position on four wobbly legs.

Lazarus watched also, but his gaze was on Mitch and Jon. Mitch had rested his hand on Jon's shoulder, and when the filly finally stood he turned his head to look at Jon's awe-stricken face. What Lazarus saw was love, pure and honest love, and he was truly shaken about his beliefs . . . and Whitney's as well.

"She's going to be yours, Jon," Mitch said. "It'll be a while before she's old enough to ride. By that time you can start learning, too. Would you like that?"

Jon turned his face to Mitch, smiled, and nodded again.

Mitch lifted him in his arms and that was when Mitch and Lazarus's eyes met. The moment

316

stretched and the silence deepened. Then Lazarus turned and walked out of the barn.

When Mitch and his father came out of the barn later Jon was trotting contentedly between them and even from where he was Lazarus could hear the flow of questions. He smiled. If all had been as it should be Mitch would be the one giving Jón answers. But the biggest question was still in need of an answer, and Lazarus wasn't too sure Whitney had the right one either.

Lazarus kept some distance between himself and Mitch for the balance of the day. He cut wood for Caryn, helped Stuart with chores, anything to keep him away from Jon and Mitch. But with them or not he sensed the pleasure they found with each other. It was hard to keep the boundary lines defined anymore.

After supper the boys staged a mock wrestling match on the floor and Jon's boyish laughter filled the room. Lazarus rose and walked out on the porch. In a few minutes Mitch followed him, closing the door quietly behind him.

"Lazarus?"

"Nice night," Lazarus said.

"Yeah."

"Yo' ma a great cook. Ah ain't ate so much fo' a long while."

"Yeah," Mitch agreed again.

"Suppose ah oughta be gittin' along pretty soon. Miz Whitney, she worry iffen it get too late."

"He's been here later than this. Why so nervous, Lazarus? Having second thoughts?"

Lazarus couldn't deny that he knew what Mitch meant. It angered him to realize he *was* having second thoughts. He wanted time to think, and he'd be damned if he was admitting it to Mitch.

"Second thoughts? Ah doan know what yo' talkin' 'bout. Ain't my place to even have first thoughts 'bout nothin'. Miz Whitney, she want de boy back befo' too late. It my job to see he get dere."

"You won't give an inch, will you?" Mitch's grin was irritated. For the life of him he couldn't fathom why he wanted this man's understanding . . . or at least some form of acceptance. A word or two would do. "Look, Lazarus . . . I want you to do something you might not like."

"What?"

"I'm riding home with you. Wait . . ." Mitch held up a hand before Lazarus could protest. "This can't be resolved any other way. Wars are settled by people sitting down and talking—maybe it would work with us. I haven't been able to corner you, Lazarus, so maybe this is my chance to set you straight once and for all."

"Set me straight?" Lazarus's smile matched Mitch's. "What yo' wants to set me straight on?"

"Lazarus, you stood by Whitney, when she needed you most. I don't question that, I only wonder why."

"Why? Ah doan understand."

"You were a slave before the war. As far as your owners and most of society, the lowest of humanity. That was wrong and unfair."

"Sho', it wasn't fair."

"But you had a chance to get revenge, to fight back against the whites that had enslaved you. Why didn't you do it?"

Lazarus considered the question and replied, "Ah guess ah could have done what yo' say, but ah wanted . . ." He paused, slipping deeper into thought.

"You wanted what I wanted. What I still want—a chance to change things the right way. That's why

318

I'm doing what I'm doing. That's why I wouldn't hurt Whitney. That's why I wouldn't take Jon. I wanted what you wanted from Whitney and others like her—respect. And I want her love, I want my son. On top of that I want you to understand and maybe decide to give me some respect as well. Whether I get it or not I'm going to fight like hell. Lazarus . . . let me get close enough to Whitney to make her understand, to give her the life she deserves. Give me the opportunity to change her life, and I'll make it better. If I don't succeed by the time this election is over . . . then I'll let them both go. I'll get out of their lives."

Lazarus was startled by Mitch's concluding sentence and his intensity. He was also amazed that he was beginning to believe him. He'd watched the battle between Whitney and Mitch and realized even with Jon, Mitch had not taken advantage.

Lazarus was silent long enough for Mitch to garner a grain of hope that he had finally reached the one person who stood firmly between him and Whitney. He waited and prayed as he'd never prayed before.

"Yo' sho' do make it hard fo' a man to stan' his ground."

"Only if where you stand is wrong for everyone involved."

"Yo' say she be wrong. Dat Mr. Donnelley, he say yo' be wrong. Yo' both puts Miz Whitney right in de middle. Ah 'spects she need breathin' room. Maybe yo' both oughta back away."

"Lazarus, Whitney's scared. She's running away. You and I have seen a lot and so has she. But it's better to face this thing head on than to try and push it away like it never happened. Jon's proof that it did. You know what kind of a woman Whitney was, and is. Do you really believe she would have

319

given herself to me if she didn't love me? I want that love back. I'm offering you a bargain. At the end of the election, whether I win or lose, I'll get out of Whitney's life if I can't prove to you both that she loves me still."

"Yo' give up yo' son fo' good?"

"If that's what it takes. But I have to be given a chance."

"What yo' want from me?"

"Just move over." Mitch smiled for the first time. "You're too big for me to get around."

"Miz Whitney trust me. She gwine be hurt."

"Small hurt now, less hurt later."

"So yo' wants to take de boy back to her?"

"And have some time to talk to her without you breathing down my neck."

"Jes' talk? Yo' won't try pushin' her to decidin' nuthin'?"

"Just talk. I swear."

Again Lazarus was silent, weighing the pros and cons.

"Ah cain't jes' let it happen. Ah gots to explain to her. Dat way," his smile, "iffen she woan talk to yo', ah kin make sure yo' doan cause no problems. We takes de boy home . . . together."

It was less than Mitch wanted, but, he had to admit, a whole lot more than he had expected. "That's good enough." Lazarus nodded, and the two walked back inside.

Jon was seated quite comfortably on Stuart's lap, listening with open-eyed wonder as Stuart wove a tale of adventure about knights in shining armor.

Mitch smiled, remembering well the same tales from when he was a boy. He found a seat, not wanting to spoil the end of the story for Jon. When Stuart was finished, Mitch rose. He was much more anxious to get Jon home than Jon was to go.

320

"Come on, sport, it's time to go." Mitch took Jon from Stuart's lap and while he got him ready he told him he was riding home with him. This seemed more than fine to Jon, which pleased Mitch.

Lazarus bade Caryn and Stuart good night as he and Mitch left. For a while the room was silent, then Caryn spoke.

"This is the first time Mitch has taken Jon home since . . ."

"Maybe," Shawn grinned devilishly, "ol' Mitch is going to try his luck again. He isn't one to give up."

"That's for sure," Morgan said. "He's had his heart set on Whitney Clayborn for . . . how long, five years now?"

"Like father, like sons, my boys. None of you is less stubborn than your brother."

"In this case," Stuart said quietly, "I don't think it's stubbornness." His eyes sparkled as he looked at Caryn. "He's found the perfect woman. He's known true love and he wants nothing less. I can remember that feeling well."

Caryn's cheeks flushed, Stuart chuckled, and Morgan and Shawn were pleased at their display of affection.

Mitch had insisted on holding Jon on the way home, and they had not gone far when Jon curled against him and his head sagged against Mitch's shoulder. Lazarus and Mitch completed the trip in silence.

As usual, the lights of Whitney's house were glowing from nearly every window. Mitch knew that Whitney never rested until Jon was safely home.

While he dismounted and settled Jon comfortably in his arms, Lazarus walked up the steps. But the door was open long before he ever reached it. Lazarus had tried to prepare himself for what she would say when he told Whitney what was happening. Whitney smiled at Lazarus and looked past him to see Mitch carrying Jon. Without really knowing it, she somehow sensed there was more to it than just bringing Jon home.

"Lazarus?"

"Miz Whitney. Ah gots to tell yo' what ah'm thinkin' an' feelin'. They ain't been nothin' but truth betwixt us right from de start. Ah sho' ain't aimin' to lie to yo' now. An' ah takes de blame fo' all of it."

"All of what, Lazarus? What blame? You've never done anything to be blamed for." Whitney was prepared to take Jon from Mitch, trying to ignore him.

"Miz Whitney . . . ah done tole him yo' talk wif him."

Whitney took a deep breath that was nearly heart-breaking for Lazarus. She had a look of betrayal, but it passed. This was Lazarus, the sole strength of her life. She couldn't hurt him. She shifted her gaze to Mitch, then walked toward him. Before she could speak, Mitch did.

"I know his room. I'll take him up. All right, Whitney?"

"All right," she stepped aside and Mitch carried Jon up the stairs. When he disappeared, Whitney turned back to Lazarus. "Why, Lazarus?"

"Ah hoped mebbe yo' understan'. Ah know dis gwine be hard on yo', but ah knows yo' real well. Ah knowed yo' since de day yo' born. Ah hasn't never seen yo' run from nuthin', even when de war got bad. Ah thinks yo' got 'nuf courage to face this once an' fo' all. Ah'll tell yo' why." He went on to explain what Mitch had said to him. Whitney listened in silence until Lazarus stopped. She sighed deeply. She could not condemn a man who not only saved her life, but Jon's as well.

322

"It's all right, Lazarus. You did what you felt was right. I'm not sure what I'm afraid of, but I guess it's about time I quit running. I'll talk to him."

"Yo' wants me to stay?"

"No, it's not necessary. He certainly won't hurt me, and maybe if we get it over with we can all get on with our lives. I guess I've always known the final battle would be between Mitch and me."

"If yo' wants me, yo' knows where ah'll be."

"Yes."

"Miz Whitney?"

"Yes, Lazarus?"

"Mebbe . . . mebbe yo' oughta listen to how he feel. Ah seed an' heared . . . a whole lot lately. Yo' gots to think wif both yo' heart an' yo' head. Ah don' think he want to take de boy away."

"I can't let my heart tell me what to do, Lazarus."

"Well . . . no mattah. Ah'll be right across de clearin'."

Whitney nodded and Lazarus walked to the door, where he turned to look at her one more time. He hoped he hadn't made a big mistake, he thought as he left quietly.

Whitney stood looking at the closed door for some time, then she heard the sound of footsteps on the stairs. She searched her emotions and fear was no longer among them. If Mitch wanted to talk she would talk. For this last time she would have to make him understand that she meant to live her life without him or Trent. She wanted peace and meant to have it, without giving up her son.

When Mitch entered the silence grew long and heavy. They were technically only a few feet apart, but at that moment it looked like miles to Mitch.

"He sleeps like a log," Mitch said. "I undressed him and he never batted an eye."

"You didn't come here tonight to put Jon to bed."

"No, no, I didn't. I hope you won't give Lazarus any trouble about this."

"Lazarus will never have a problem with me. There's very little I wouldn't do for him."

"Even talking to me?"

Whitney had to smile. "I thought we had talked this out already. You were to see Jon, and for that you would leave us alone. You seem to have a very hard time keeping promises."

"Whitney, why don't we start by trying to forget all the harsh words that have passed between us?"

"Then where do we begin, Mitch?" she asked quietly.

"With Jon."

"Jon?" A tinge of alarm sprang into her eyes.

"He's too little to understand what it means to have relatives. But he's real pleased with calling my mother Grandmother, even though he doesn't know yet what that means or how it came about."

"Children respond to love."

"So do adults."

"What are you getting at, Mitch?"

"He's growing fast. He's curious and full of questions. What were you prepared to tell him about his father when he got a couple of years older and began to ask?"

"I . . ."

"Were you thinking that I'd sit by and let him call some other man Father?"

"There's no one for him to call Father."

"What about Trent Donnelley?"

Whitney shrugged but didn't answer.

Mitch's heart leapt, but he kept his expression under control. It seemed Trent Donnelley was not his biggest problem.

"Whitney . . . we've begun to get close. He's got

324

eyes. One day, he need only look in the mirror and he'll know. He'll know and he'll wonder why we lied to him. Neither of us is being fair to Jon."

Whitney knew Mitch was right. She couldn't deny Mitch was his father without losing Jon, and she couldn't keep up this farce without Jon seeing the truth for himself one day. That was another way she could lose him.

"I won't give him to you, Mitch."

"I'm not asking you to."

"What are you asking?"

"I'm really not sure myself. There's no turning back the clock, no way to prove that you're wrong about me. We can only go on from here."

"How do we do that?"

"By starting over."

"You say that so easily, but it can't be."

"Why?"

"You know the answer to that."

"Neither of us has the answers to that. In fact, we don't seem to have the answers for ourselves. But they're there if either of us wants to look."

"There could be an easier answer."

"What?"

"You could just go away."

"You wouldn't leave Jon. Why do you expect me to?"

Whitney sighed. "This is a useless argument, Mitch. If it's all you came to talk about then it would be best if you left."

"No, it's not all I came to talk about."

"Then what else is there?"

"There's you and me."

"No."

"I don't mean, step aside and let me move in."

"Then what do you mean?"

"I mean that we have Jon in common. I mean

325

that he needs both of us. He's worth a compromise between us on behalf of his future."

"I've been enough for him up until now."

"Have you, Whitney?" Mitch's voice was soft, so that the sting of the words would not be so painful. "Have you always felt as if you were enough? Is there no room in Jon's life for his father? He needs two of us."

"I could marry Trent Donnelley."

Mitch was quiet for a moment, trying to keep his violent reaction under control. When he spoke again his voice was calm. "Trent Donnelley will never be a father to my son. Not while I have a breath in my body. He's the only reason I would fight you for Jon. Trent Donnelley can only hurt you. And besides that, I'm going to stop him in his tracks." His smile seemed assured.

"You always had such confidence. I won't marry Trent Donnelley, but not because of your threats. I've told him you're Jon's father. I've also told him I can't marry him because you would make that fact public and the scandal would destroy his chances."

"And what did our noble fellow have to say about that?"

"Something curious."

"Curious?"

"He doesn't seem to be afraid of you."

"So much for his intelligence," Mitch chuckled.

"You find his lack of fear amusing?"

"Actually I find it rather stupid. Does he think I'm going to sit around and let him walk away with everything I love? That, Whitney, is sheer stupidity."

"Don't speak of love."

"Why not? Love is what I feel. For my son, and for his mother."

Whitney turned away and walked a few feet. Mitch watched her closely. She seemed to be very

326

much in control of herself. If he meant to throw her off stride he had failed. She turned toward him again.

"Whitney, I didn't come here to threaten you. I came because we have a wonderful son whose future is important to both of us. Listen to me. All I want is to have the freedom to help Jon grow, to share his life, to become part of both of your lives again. I'm aware of how you feel and I ask for nothing you cannot give freely. Maybe one day you'll see things differently. My family would love nothing more than to meet you and maybe visit now and then. You've had him so long, Whitney. Is it too much to ask to share him with others?"

"How simple you make it sound. First you have Jon for one day a week, then you want more and more until finally you have it all and I must stand aside—perhaps, one day, to see him walk out of my life forever. Simple . . . and more cruel than anything else you've ever done." She turned away from him again as a sob caught in her throat. She would not let him see her falter, see her weep.

Mitch crossed to her in a few long strides and gripped her shoulders, spinning her about. "You see things the wrong way. You always think of what I might want to take. Try to think of what I might want to give. I want to give Jon what you had as a child—people who love and cherish him. I want to give you the peace and comfort of knowing that I'll ask nothing of you that you don't choose to give. Please put away the doubts and fears and let Jon's world be filled with . . ."

"With more than I could ever hope to give him?"

"If you must say it like that."

"Yes . . . I must."

"Then you agree?"

"Just like that." She smiled a tired and slightly bit-

327

ter smile. "I cannot. I must have time to gather my thoughts."

"Of course you must. I'm sorry. I'm just too anxious to be part of his life." Whitney had not pulled away and that encouraged him. Old memories were hard to destroy and if she remembered the bad, she could not help but remember the good.

"Whitney," his voice was gentle, as were his hands that still rested lightly on her arms. "I don't want to hurt you anymore than you've already been hurt. I've no way of knowing, but I can imagine what you must have gone through. You've built a kind of fortress around yourself, and it's hard to tear down. You don't trust me fully for so many reasons, but don't let that keep me away from Jon. If he can learn to love and trust me . . . maybe one day . . ." His voice trailed off. Whitney's eyes were like a sky blue ocean misted with uncertainty and tears. Despite his control it touched him to the quick to see the vulnerability, the loneliness, and worse, the wariness. At the same time he was all too aware of so many other things: the soft, elusive scent of her, the spun silk of her hair, and mostly, the half-parted lips. Old memories were as just as hard for him to battle as they were for her. He remembered a sweet giving that had been his heaven. He needed to taste that again as badly as a dying man needed water. He bent his head and lightly touched her mouth with his.

An electrical current leapt between them. He drew away for a second and both realized the void between them was like a dark pit. It scared him into summoning his courage, almost as if he'd been called to battle. Even that experience was not as overpowering as this. His arms slid around her and he drew her back into his arms. This time his mouth took her more possessively.

328

He could hear the soft sound that seemed to come from the depths of her and he was lost for the moment in a renewal of the pulsing pleasure he had known so long ago.

Whitney drew back. The tears that had welled in her eyes before slipped down her cheeks. He knew with regret that he had pushed her too hard, but he could no more have helped what had happened than he could have flown.

"Whitney . . ."

She was about to speak when a sound came from the back of the house. Whitney's eyes fled in that direction and Mitch saw the subtle fear in her eyes.

"What's the matter?" he hissed in a hushed whisper.

Quickly she explained about the mysterious man. "He's been here three times. You remember, you were here when Lazarus tried to catch him. What could he want, Mitch?"

"I don't know, but I'll damn well find out. Wait here."

"Mitch, don't go out there. He may have a gun."

"We have to find out," Mitch said as he went to the door. "Put out the lamp." Whitney blew out the lamp and stood in the dark, her pulses pounding. Mitch opened the door, slipped out, and drew it closed quietly behind him. Cautiously he made his way to the end of the porch and went over the rail.

The moon was covered with thick clouds, for which he was grateful. He maneuvered step by step, inch by inch, until he came to the back of the house. He looked around the corner carefully.

The shadowy form of a tall, leanly built man stood just before a back window. He was trying to pry the window up. Mitch could hear him curse softly as his hand slipped and he set about trying again. It was obvious that whoever the intruder

329

was, he was not experienced at breaking in.

His back was to Mitch, who began to move toward him slowly, one cautious step at a time. The intruder was so completely engrossed in his efforts to get in he heard nothing, which was another reason Mitch felt he was not very adept.

At the very last second the intruder sensed another presence . . . one moment too late. Mitch leapt and they crashed to the ground. He heard the intruder's breath rush in a loud huff and straddled him. There was no need to use any more force. The intruder had had the breath knocked from him and was struggling to breathe. Mitch dragged him to his feet and forced him to the front of the house. When they entered Mitch called out to Whitney.

"Light a lamp and let's find out what he's up to." He practically tossed the still-dazed man into a chair and stood over him.

Whitney lit the lamp and turned to look at the two. In seconds her face grew pale and her hand rose to her mouth in shock.

Twenty-five

There was no doubt that Whitney recognized him, and Mitch did, too. He had not been very close to Whitney's family, but he was certain the man was her brother.

Whitney confirmed this quickly when she ran to his side and fell to her knees, taking one of his hands in hers.

"Keith! Oh, Keith, you really are alive! Where have you been? Are you well? You're not . . ."

"Hush, Whitney." Keith laughed shakily. "If I can get my breath back I'll answer all your questions."

"Why were you skulking around outside like that, trying to break in?" Mitch demanded. "I could have killed you as easy as I caught you."

"Who the hell are you?" Keith's eyes narrowed— then there was a glint of recognition. "Mitch Flannery," he said softly. "I've been hearing a lot about you around town. There've been a lot of changes, I take it."

"Keith!" Whitney was half alarmed and half angry.

"I'd still like to know what he's doing here," Keith said glumly.

"I'll bet Whitney would like to know why you weren't here a long time ago." Mitch wasn't feeling friendly either. The interruption hadn't been timely.

"Yes, Keith. Why scare us like this? Why break in where you would be more than welcome?"

"I . . . I didn't know who was here. I've seen a lot of people moving around."

"It's just Lazarus and Berdine, Addy and Josiah. Why should that matter, Keith? I've prayed for your safety. I would have been so happy to know you're alive."

"I know," Keith said, his voice growing gentle. "Whitney, we have to talk."

"Yes. Keith, you need a bath and some food. You also look like you need some rest."

"I do. I'll settle for the food now though."

Mitch had been watching Keith closely and all his instincts told him there was something drastically wrong. He also knew he would have to leave. Neither Whitney nor Keith would confide in him, that was certain. But the last thing he wanted to do was leave Whitney alone in this situation.

Whitney rose to her feet, anxiety and nervous excitement reflected on her face. "I'll go and prepare you something."

"Whitney, do you want me to go get Lazarus and Berdine?" Mitch asked. He really wasn't prepared to leave Whitney alone, brother or no brother. Keith was mixed up in something, that was certain, and he just might dump that something right into Whitney's lap.

"No!" Keith said quickly. Then he caught himself. "It's late. Besides, I'd rather no one knew I was around just yet."

"Then I'll get the food," Whitney said. "Sit back down, Keith. You look like you're ready to drop."

Keith didn't sit down even though he was more tired than even Whitney knew. Mitch studied him for a while. Before the war Keith Clayborn used to be somewhat spoiled and arrogant but he had never been in serious trouble. Now Mitch wasn't so sure.

He was as golden-haired as Whitney. Tall and, to Mitch, slightly on the thin side. He'd let his hair grow long and had a moustache and short beard. Mitch began to wonder if it had not been for a disguise.

"It's been a long time since the war ended," Mitch offered. "Whitney has never believed you were dead. Why the hell did you let her suffer like that?"

"Until the end of the war I was a prisoner. When it was over . . . I had other problems. It was impossible to get here before now. I don't see why it interests you, anyway."

"Whitney is important to me."

"Really? You don't live here, I know that. Just how and why is Whitney so important to you?"

"That's none of your damn business unless Whitney sees fit to tell you." He smiled pleasantly as he said it and Keith's face grew dark with anger.

"Maybe, since you don't live here," Keith sneered, "you ought to just run along. Whitney and I have things to talk about."

"I'm not running along. Not until I know Whitney won't have more problems knocking at her door late at night."

"What are you implying?" Keith asked angrily.

"I'm implying," Mitch said in a voice that assured Keith he was losing patience, "that there are other reasons that kept you away and let your sister believe you dead. That you, my friend, are running from something or someone, and I care too much about Whitney to see her caught up in something that can only bring her more grief. She's had enough of that."

Keith considered his words with no further anger, which surprised Mitch. He seemed to be making some decisions. "I don't mean Whitney any harm," Keith said quietly. "I love her, maybe more than you can believe. I wouldn't hurt her. That's part of the reason I haven't come until now. Do you think I'd be sneaking around trying to find a way in if I meant to hurt her? I just wanted . . ."

"Wanted what?"

"I'm afraid I can't tell you that. I don't know what you have to do with Whitney, but I don't think you're a permanent part of her life. I've been watching too long."

"That's a mistake."

"You *are* a permanent part of her life?"

"I was at one time, and I hope to be again. It's a long story."

"Look, I'm Whitney's brother, for God's sake! She's safe with me. Besides, I won't be around long. I have something to finish before I can stay."

Before Mitch could speak again Whitney returned, carrying a plate of sandwiches and a large glass of milk. She set these down on a table near Keith.

"You don't have anything stronger than milk?" Keith asked with a laugh. "I could use a little stimulant."

"I do have a little brandy."

"Good, I'll take some."

"Mitch?"

"Yes, I'll have some." Mitch was glad Whitney hadn't asked him to leave. He felt uncomfortable leaving her, even if it was with her brother. He still had a feeling trouble was near at hand.

Whitney poured two brandies and handed one to Keith and one to Mitch. Mitch sipped . . . and waited. Whitney returned to Keith's side.

"Keith, why have you not come sooner? It's been so long."

"I know, Whitney, and I'm sorry. I'll explain it to you later."

334

"At least you're here now. There's so much I have to tell you."

"I know Papa died, Whitney. I got word at Wilderness. What happened to Mother? I haven't seen her here and I've been watching pretty close. Is she staying in town or . . ."

The expression on Whitney's face was enough to tell Keith everything. A look of pain crossed his face.

"Damn," he muttered. He reached out and took Whitney's hand. For a few minutes they clung to each other in silence.

Whitney looked up at Mitch and he knew she was asking for his silence. She wanted him to go so she could talk to Keith. She wanted to tell him what had happened in her life and she didn't want it to come from Mitch. He nodded and drained his glass. He knew he had to leave them alone, but he didn't want to. The look on Whitney's face put an end to any possible argument. Still, he had to make it clear he wouldn't go far . . . and he wouldn't stay long.

"Whitney, I'm leaving you two to talk. You have a great deal to catch up on—but you and I have to finish our discussion, too. I'm coming back tomorrow." He made it a clear, firm statement meant for both of them. Mitch walked to the door and turned to look back. Keith was watching Whitney intently, but her eyes were on Mitch. He couldn't quite fathom her expression, he thought as he left.

Keith was silent for a while after Mitch left. He sensed that this man had a traumatic effect on Whitney. Before the war Mitch Flannery had not been in Whitney's social circle. How did he come to be here now . . . and why?

"How are you, Whitney . . . really?" Keith asked gently.

"I'm fine, Keith. There's so much . . ."

"I know, I know," he answered, embracing her, "but we don't have to cover everything tonight."

"You'll stay here?"

"Whitney, I can't. You always had faith in me, so please trust me now. There's something I have to do that's very important. When it's finished . . . then I'll be back to stay."

"But why? Why?"

"Because I don't want anyone to know I'm here. It could cause trouble for you. Please . . . don't ask me questions I can't answer."

"Of course I trust you. Keith, you look so tired."

"And I'm still starving," he said, reaching for one of the sandwiches. "Now, while I eat, tell me about you . . . and," he jerked a thumb toward the door, "him."

When Whitney turned and walked to the fireplace to put more wood on it, Keith's face grew still and attentive. Whitney had always shared her secrets with him. This time he began to think she had secrets she'd never told anyone. When he looked more closely, he could see the changes in Whitney. She had grown . . . in many ways, and he had a feeling not all of them had been pleasant.

He said nothing. His arrival had been shock enough for Whitney, without stirring up any more pain.

"I knew Mitch before the war," Whitney began quietly.

"Yeah, I remember him. His family worked that dried-up farm not far from us."

Whitney turned to look at him. "What do you really know about Mitch?"

"Not much. I know that the family never had anything and Mitch used to work like a horse. So did his brothers. They sure stuck together though. And I remember a few other things. Seems to me Mitch

336

Flannery held his own pretty well. I guess he got an education for himself the hard way." Keith laughed. "I do remember that Mother was beside herself when she heard about him talking to you one time. You were at a party, or the theater or something. Do you remember?" Whitney nodded. "Mother and her social standards. I also know Mitch and his brothers were some scrappers. I never traded blows with them, but I know a few who did and were the worse for it. That family could only take so much pushing." He noticed Whitney's face was pale and her hands were clenched. He rose and walked to her. "But you knew him better than I did, didn't you?" he said, his voice tender. He didn't want to upset her by sounding angry. "What's wrong, Whitney? Want to talk to me?"

"You were right, Keith," Whitney admitted. "I did know Mitch a lot better than you . . . or anyone else. At least I thought I did."

"You were seeing him?"

"Yes," her tone was almost defiant. When Keith laughed she was surprised.

"I'll bet Mother didn't know."

"No, she didn't. Why do you say it like that?"

"Whitney, come on. Mother was a snob, and a stiff-necked one at that. I loved her, but I knew her. If she had known you were seeing him she'd have locked you in a cell and thrown away the key. She was not one to let the Clayborn name be associated with anyone unless he was of proper social standing."

"She wanted what was best for me," Whitney said defensively.

"Want some honesty, Whitney? Mother wanted what was best for the Clayborn name. Whatever you got, as far as she was concerned, it had best come with money. It was easier for me than for you. There were times I wanted to say a lot more but to

337

tell you the truth she could render me speechless sometimes."

"Yes," Whitney replied softly. "Mother was very . . . commanding."

"You know, Whitney, it took me a long time to find you. I never did know what happened to you . . . or Mother. Can you tell me?"

Whitney sighed, then began to tell him about the loss of their house. She was so engrossed she was not aware of the intensity of his feeling.

"Did you save anything?"

"Very little. There wasn't much time."

"I see."

"I saved some papers and a few pictures. They were all in the box where Mother kept your letters and Father's, too."

"You have the letters I sent Mother?" His request was spoken quietly, but there was a gleam in his eyes that went unnoticed.

"Yes. Would you like to see them?"

"Yes, I would."

Whitney went upstairs, and while she was gone Keith walked from one window to the other, looking out carefully, as if he expected to see someone. There was a deep frown on his face and he gnawed his lip thoughtfully.

When Whitney came downstairs she carried a packet of letters tied in a blue ribbon. Keith went to her quickly and his hand was shaking as he reached to take them. Whitney attributed this to the fact that he was tired.

Keith took the letters, untied them, and riffled through them until he found what he was looking for. He gazed at the letter for a long time, then replaced it in the center of the pack and retied them. Then he handed them back to Whitney.

"No, Keith, you keep them."

338

"But I thought you . . . look, I must be on the move for a while. I'd rather you kept them here. I can come and collect them any time I feel I really need them."

"Of course," she replied, aware that something was wrong. She laid the letters on the table.

"Maybe you'd better put them away before you forget to . . . I wouldn't want them lost."

Keith was speaking and acting strangely and Whitney could not put her finger on what was wrong. Before she could ask him anything, Keith, who seemed aware of her discomfort, spoke up. "I plan to eat the rest of those sandwiches, and I hope you'll finish telling me about you and Mitch Flannery while I do. Put the letters away and we'll talk."

Whitney returned the letters to her keeping place and returned to find Keith sprawled on the couch munching another sandwich and washing it down with brandy. She took a seat near him, unsure of how far she could or would go with her explanations.

"So you were seeing Mitch before the war?" Keith prompted. "That doesn't tell me why he's hanging around here now. Are you still interested in him, Whitney?"

"We . . . we have things in common," Whitney began unsteadily.

"You and Mitch?" he scoffed. "Outside of the fact that we've lost all our possessions, what else could you two have in common?"

"You sound like Mother. Are possessions that important to you?"

"Me? No, I'm not a snob. The war taught me too much for that. It's just that the two of you come from different worlds."

"Not so different, Keith. You just don't . . ."

"Don't what?"

339

"Oh, Keith, how can I explain it to you? If I tell you all that happened, will you promise not to interrupt until I'm finished?"

"That sounds ominous," he laughed. "I know you, my sweet sister. There's nothing you could have done to force you to be so dour. Come on and tell me."

"All right." Keith was not in the mood for long, involved stories and she wasn't either. Maybe the blunt truth was better. "Mitch and I were lovers before the war. We had a son. He's asleep upstairs right now."

For the first time Keith was struck silent. Then he rose, crossed to Whitney, and knelt on one knee before her. He took her hands in his and studied her face closely. He saw much more there than he'd been aware of before.

"Now maybe it's time you did tell me a story," he said gently.

Whitney nodded and took a deep breath. Then she began, from the magic moments under the cottonwoods to Mitch's presence in her home when they had found Keith. Keith was quiet through it all, occasionally squeezing her hand in sympathetic support. When she finished, there was a long moment of silence. Then he stood and drew Whitney up with him. He enclosed her in his arms and rocked her gently.

"Ah, Whitney . . . sweet, sweet Whitney. I'm sorry. You didn't deserve all this."

"I guess none of us deserves this. But it's happened and there's little we can do but learn to live with it as best we can."

"What are you going to do, Whitney . . . about Jon, I mean?"

"I'm too tired tonight to even think about it. I have to have some time."

"Of course . . . have you considered . . ." He paused as if he was searching carefully for the right word. "Look, I don't mean to say anything cruel. You know I loved our parents as much as you did. They gave us all we could have wanted. But, Whitney . . . Mother might have taken those letters if she had known about you and Mitch."

"Keith!"

"Don't be a blind child, Whitney. It's true. Mother would have died if you'd even suggested marrying him."

"But Mother never knew! Not about the letters. Not until I was . . . until I expected Jon. But after that . . . there were no letters and there was very little time. The world fell apart . . . then Mother died and I had to think of other things."

"Other things? God, Whitney, you went through hell."

"It was hell for us all, you included. You were a prisoner of war for the last year. That must have been hell, too."

Keith nodded. "A little better than a year." He returned to his seat and began to eat the last sandwich. "I was part of an exchange affair."

"But Keith, after the war . . ."

"After the war I was involved in something important that made it expedient that I appear as if I never returned. Whitney, I'm asking you to trust me. I can't tell you more now, nor can I make my presence known just yet. Mitch knows and that's bad enough. I'm going to talk to him in secret soon and get him to keep quiet. I'm looking for someone, Whitney, and until I find him, my life and all those I touch would be in danger. This will all be over soon. Then we'll be family again. I wish I didn't have to do it this way, but I must. I have to depend on you to remain silent about me."

341

"But Lazarus, Berdine . . . none of them would say you were here."

"I can't take that chance. Please, Whitney."

"All right. I won't say a word."

"You will take good care of those letters for me, won't you?"

"Certainly. They've been safe for a long time. Why would you be worried about them now?"

"It's just that they're important," Keith responded. He hoped she believed it. "They're about all I've got outside of you and my nephew. Can I see him?"

"Of course." Whitney led the way upstairs and Keith tiptoed into Jon's room behind her. Since Addy had been ill she had remained in Lazarus's house so that Berdine could tend her. Whitney and Keith bent over a contentedly sleeping Jon.

"He's beautiful," Keith whispered. "I hope to be able to hold him on my knee before long. He . . . he looks like his father."

"Yes," Whitney agreed, "he does look like Mitch."

"I don't want to wake him," Keith said, reluctant to leave. He reached to brush Jon's dark hair. Jon stirred but didn't waken. "God, he's like a miracle. You're lucky, Whitney. You have something from this holocaust besides pain and death. I wish . . ." he paused. Wishing had not done any good before and it wouldn't now. He had something to finish and he had to do it before he could give any thought to finding a life of his own.

Whitney had never thought of all her problems in this light before. Jon was a blessing—a reward that far outshone the bitterness and pain. "I guess I am lucky to have him, Keith. I'm a fool not to have thought of him that way before. He did hold my life together when everything was dark."

Keith looked at her over Jon's sleeping form.

"No one can make up your mind for you, but

342

maybe you should look for some happiness and try putting the past where it belongs." Whitney sighed and nodded. "I guess we'd better get out of here before we wake him up." As they turned to leave the bed in the corner drew his attention. "Someone sleeps here with him?"

"Yes, Addy. You remember Addy?" Whitney smiled. "Mother's maid and all-around runabout. She was always so intimidated by Mother."

"Hmmm . . . yes. She would have walked on hot coals just to keep Mother from looking in her direction." He said no more, but the germ of a thought filled his head, and he promised himself an eventual talk with timid little Addy.

They went downstairs where Keith poured himself another brandy. "This one will have to do me. I've got to get going."

"Where will you stay?"

"It's better you don't know. Whitney, for God's sake, remember, not a word. Don't tell anyone about my being here."

"I won't, Keith. But you will come back?"

"Yes, but it will be at night. Don't be afraid if I tap on your door. I have to be careful. Lazarus almost blew my head off before."

"It was you?"

"Yes." He downed the last of his brandy and bent to kiss her. "I'll see you soon and . . . Whitney?"

"Yes?"

"Be careful of those letters. If anyone else should ask, they were destroyed with the house."

"All right. But why are they so important? What's in those letters?"

"You were always a nosey little girl and you haven't changed. My secret. I'll tell you sometime. Whitney . . . be careful what you decide. It's time for old memories and old hatreds to be put away.

343

I'm not saying anyone's right or wrong. I'm only hoping you'll find what's right for you and be happy."

"I'll be careful, Keith. I love you and I'm so happy to know you're alive and well."

"I'll be back. Don't worry." He kissed her and before she could say more he had slipped out the door.

Whitney walked back to the couch and sat down. Without the evidence of the brandy bottle and the empty sandwich plate it would have been hard to believe her brother had really been there.

Her entire evening had been a whirlwind affair. Mitch's words echoed in her mind, still adamant about the letters he swore he wrote. Keith's words, too, struck her. A flicker of doubt began to work its way into her mind. Could her mother have known, could she have . . . no! She would not believe it. Above all, her mother had loved her, had wanted the best for her. If she didn't want Mitch it was because she thought Whitney would suffer. She knew her mother had great pride in her family's position, but she wouldn't have stolen Whitney's letters. Not for money. Keith was wrong and when she saw him again she would make him understand that.

Her mind drifted to Keith and his urgent plea to keep his letters a secret. Why? What could be in them that could cause her brother so much consternation? She knew she had no right to do anything but keep them for Keith, but she walked upstairs and took them out of her bureau drawer.

She sat on the bed and untied the ribbon, spreading them out on the bed. They all looked exactly alike. The same strong hand had addressed them. Yes, they all looked alike . . . except . . .

She lifted one that lay in the center of the bundle. It was thicker than the others and the envelope was a bit different. She held it, wondering what was inside that had caused her brother so much relief when he saw it. She caught her lower lip between her teeth, then, as if the decision had to be carried out quickly, she opened the envelope and removed the contents.

It contained three pages of a letter addressed to Hope . . . and another piece of folded paper. She unfolded it carefully. It looked like a map, except there were no identifying words or names to describe the location. She folded the map and put it into the envelope. It would remain a mystery until Keith unraveled it for her. She re-tied the bundle of letters and put them away.

Mitch rode home slowly. It had been a very eventful night. He'd been warmed by the fact that Whitney had seemed to be listening just a little more than she had before. She had certainly been less intimidated and much more in control.

The advent of her brother's rather mysterious homecoming had put an end to the conversation. But it was a temporary end, temporary because he could see a ray of hope and he'd be damned if he'd give up now.

Remembering her brother's words made him wonder at the secrecy around his homecoming. It was surprising to think that a brother Whitney had long felt was lost found it necessary to break into his sister's home. He was after something—more than a reunion.

But Keith Clayborn was not the most important thing in his life, Whitney and his son were. He pushed Keith to the back of his mind and allowed his senses to fill with thoughts of Whitney.

She had surrendered to his kiss, but momentary sensual surrender did not change Whitney's distrust or her strong will.

He would have given his soul to know what had happened to his letters and whatever letters Whitney had written. And the letter of denial—he had not written it . . . but who did?

Of course Mitch thought of the three members of Whitney's family. He remembered a talk with her father long ago. At least he had been honest and straightforward. No, it was not her father, nor her brother; it had to be Hope Clayborn. But nothing could be done about it now. The only person who could prove his innocence was dead.

Well, he would have to rebuild Whitney's love and he had the best tool to do it . . . Jon.

He arrived home to a quiet house and found his way to bed. Awake, he planned his next steps; in sleep, he dreamed vibrant and fulfilling dreams.

Keith stole into the woods, wishing he could have stayed with Whitney. A comfortable bed would have been more welcome than the abandoned shack he had stumbled upon.

But the letters were safe. Now, all he had to do was find the name of the elusive spy, the betrayer who had played one side against the other for profit. He knew he was here. He'd searched too long and too carefully not to be sure. The only thing he didn't know was the name he was using now.

"Where are you, you bastard? I'll find you and when I do, I have the evidence that condemns you to the death you deserve," he muttered aloud.

This traitor had cost the lives of his friends, of men on both sides of the war. Keith had dedicated his life to finding him and seeing justice done.

His mind drifted to Whitney and her problems. His heart ached when he thought of his not being able to help when she had really needed him.

She had grown harder, stronger than the sister he had left behind. He remembered the missing letters. No matter what Whitney wanted to believe, Keith was certain that Hope would have put a stop to any rendezvous between Whitney and Mitch — any way she could.

If she had found out that they were writing to each other she would have destroyed the letters . . . if she could have found them.

Whitney had said they had had a secret hiding place. But someone could have known — someone afraid of Hope.

He thought of the people surrounding Whitney. Lazarus . . . . no, he would tell Whitney. Berdine . . . . no, she was too close to Whitney, too . . . Addy . . . Addy . . . why not? Addy lived in the cabin, very close to Whitney. Maybe he could find a way to watch for a moment she might be alone. If she could keep the secret of the letters she could be keeping another secret as well. It might be possible sometime in the near future to find out just what Addy knows.

Twenty-six

Blake tapped his pencil thoughtfully against his cheek while he studied the speech he was writing. It had to be especially good and he felt he was well on the way.

Resigned that, for the moment, another good sentence was not going to present itself, he laid the pencil down. Then he reached for a handbill and studied it. Noel had designed it, and he had to admit she was getting better and better. She was getting better at evading him, too. Not physically — he saw her several times a week. But she had withdrawn and stayed close to her brothers.

Since their confrontation, Kevin had been like a cold-eyed ghost. He had not spoken to Blake and kept as much distance between them as he could.

Now Blake had to go into the *Sentinel* office with his speech so he could discuss it with Craig. He stood up and stretched, then walked to the door.

The election would be over soon and he could concentrate on his own life. Courting Noel was going to be a full-fledged battle. He wished he could have talked some sense into Kevin, but obviously he had never convinced him, because there had been no reaction.

It had been two days now since he had seen Noel and he was hungry for the sight of her, no matter what her feelings were.

348

As a lieutenant in the army he had maneuvered his men and outmaneuvered the enemy more than once. Now one young woman had outmaneuvered him at every step. Besides the challenge, there was the fact that he loved her enough for both of them. Hell, he thought with a grim smile, he loved her enough for the whole damn army!

Well, he mused amiably, two days were long enough. He started for his horse and the short trip to town. Blake was a fighter, but he had no way of knowing that a bigger fight had occurred just an hour or two earlier.

Noel had been aware that Kevin was avoiding her; she just didn't know why, which bothered her. They were the two siblings who should have been the closest — they shared more than most brothers and sisters usually did. Yet it was Craig who always seemed to have the gentle word and the caring thoughtfulness. It was Craig who always seemed to understand. She was ashamed to confide in Craig. If Kevin had not found them all so terribly hurt . . . and Charlotte dead, she could have kept her dishonor to herself.

Thoughts of Kevin brought thoughts of Blake and an old hurt began to throb again. She knew how Blake felt. But she could not respond, she dared not respond. She was not worthy of his love. She felt soiled and guilty. Well, the election would be over soon and she would have no reason to see Blake again. The thought was painful, but Noel had suffered so much pain in the past she could bear this, too. How could she hope for happiness with Blake when Kevin still needed her to help fight his demons?

She finished the breakfast dishes and tidied up the house. She had always gone to the paper just before

lunch time, carrying food so they could all eat together. She was preparing the lunches when the door
opened. She was surprised to see Kevin.

"What are you doing home? Is something wrong
at the paper? Is Craig all right?"

"Yeah, Craig is fine, and there's no trouble at the
paper. I just had to talk to you, Noel."

"Something is wrong, isn't it?" she asked. His face
was tight as he crossed the room to stand close to
Noel.

"Noel . . . I've been doing a lot of thinking."

"About what?"

"You . . . me, and what happened back then."

Noel's face paled, and she turned to concentrate
on what she was doing.

"Noel, we have to talk about it. Before it kills me,
I have to know."

"No," she cried. "Why must we talk about it? It's
dead and gone. We have to forget it, Kevin."

"I thought that, too. But now I'm not so sure."

"Well, be sure. I have nothing to say."

"I think you do, Noel."

Her hands paused, trembling. She looked at them
as if they had a separate life. Then with slow delib-
eration she began to work again. Her silence was
like a wall.

"You do, Noel," he repeated softly.

"Go back to work, Kevin. Leave me alone."

"I can't do that." She ignored his words, so he
reached out and took hold of her hands. Still she
refused to look at him. "I can't do that," he repeated.

Noel struck his hand away and the look she gave
him was filled with mixed emotions. "Well, you'll
have to forget it because I have no more to say
about it."

"Noel," his voice was pleading yet gentle, "I had a
short but very violent talk with Blake."

"Blake has very little to do with us, outside of the paper."

"He has a lot to do with us. He's in love with you, Noel, and you damn well know it. It's written all over him every time he looks at you. But that's not the most important thing. What is important . . . something that I have to know . . . is do *you* love him?"

"No!"

"Your answer is too quick."

"Kevin, please. What are you trying to do?"

"Find the truth. Maybe then I can sleep. I haven't had a minute's peace since I talked to Blake. You're the only one who can give it to me, Noel." His breathing was ragged and his eyes were filled with anguish. "You've got to give it to me or I just can't live with what's going on in my head. Maybe I thought I knew what happened before. But I never looked close. I never . . . listened to you, heard anything you said. It was pure brutal grief then, but that's no excuse for my behavior now. We have to talk because I've failed you somehow, Noel. Failed you, and you're suffering every day for my cruel stupidity. You can't pay the price for me. I won't let you do it any longer, and I won't let you leave until you let go of this burden you've been carrying. At least let me share it."

She turned from him and buried her face in her hands. He hated to see her cry, but he couldn't back down now. He'd torn his mind apart, despising Blake for instilling so much doubt. If what Blake said was true he was guiltier than Noel could ever be. He took hold of her wrists. Gently but firmly he drew her hands away from her face. For a long time they looked at each other. Then he took her in his arms and held her tightly. "Now, you can tell me," he said quietly.

351

Together they relived the horror, and Kevin did not interrupt once she had begun to talk.

When Blake walked into the *Sentinel* he was surprised to find Craig the only one there.

"It's past lunch time. Where are Noel and Kevin?"

"I don't know," Craig said. "Noel is usually here by now. I hope she gets here pretty quick — I'm starved. As for Kevin, I haven't seen much of him in the past couple of days. Guess he's got a lot on his mind."

"Yeah," Blake replied dryly. "I wouldn't be surprised."

Craig looked closely at Blake, wondering if Blake meant more than he was saying. There was no sign, so he went on with his work while he talked to Blake.

"How's the new speech coming along?"

"Fine. I've got it about half written. How are things looking?"

"I took a personal poll, asked a lot of people questions. Mitch is holding his own pretty well. I think he's slowly pulling ahead."

"Sounds good. I'll bet old Trent's spinning."

"He's been working like crazy, and I'll tell you the man's good. I have a feeling if he gets elected he's going a long way."

"Not if Mitch and I can help it. I wish I knew . . . or Mitch knew . . . where he saw Trent before. We have a lot of people checking on him, but so far everything seems to come to a dead end. Mitch can't seem to place him anywhere he's been but I have a feeling it could swing things our way even more if he could latch onto his memory."

"Mitch still has a feeling it's important?"

"Yeah."

352

"Well, don't worry about it. I have a nice feeling we're going to beat old Trent Donnelley very handily."

"You're enjoying yourself," Blake said with a grin.

"I sure am. Haven't had such a good fight since I carried a gun, and this time it's not fatal or bloody."

"Don't talk too soon," Blake chuckled. "After Trent hears this speech he may just go for violence."

Blake handed the paper to Craig who began to read, then whistled softly. "Very good, very good. You make Trent sound like a threat to all humanity, and Mitch the saviour of all people."

"Not too bad if I say so myself. There are some good basic points in there that Trent hasn't discussed. I'm having Mitch present some pretty progressive ideas."

"If I ever run for office I want you behind me."

"That's a deal."

"Blake?"

"Yeah?"

"I think I owe you some kind of apology."

"For what?"

"For the way we fought you."

"You had your reasons and I respect them. The war was too fresh. It's good that we've had the chance to work together. It puts things in a different light."

"Well, I'm glad we're on the same side."

"So'm I. Craig . . . what about Kevin?"

"Kevin," he shrugged expressively, "well, he just needs more time. I guess he has a lot more to put behind him than I do. I was wounded by bullets. Kevin was hurt where the blood doesn't show. You know how much Kevin lost and how bitter he is about it. It's not easy to come home and find one sister dead, your wife brutalized until she died, and your sixteen-year-old sister in shock. Kevin was young, too. It hit him harder than if he had been wounded himself."

"That's funny," Blake said quietly. "I think there's someone in the family more wounded than Kevin."

"Meaning?"

"Meaning Noel."

"Noel had it hard. She was close to Kevin's wife and to Emma. I know it was hard on her to see Charlotte raped and murdered. But she's strong and resilient, Blake, and she's getting over it."

"Christ, Craig, are you that blind?"

"Blind? What are you talking about?"

"He's talking about what really happened." Kevin's voice came from the doorway, and both Craig and Blake turned.

"You trying to tell me something, Kevin?" Craig asked.

"I guess." Kevin seemed drained, utterly weary as he walked toward Blake. He stopped a foot or so away. For the first time he was grateful, both that Blake was around and that he loved Noel. Noel needed a man with understanding. He knew Blake would know what to do when he said what he had to say. "I left her crying and afraid. If you're smart you'll get there and pick up the pieces." He'd been right—Blake needed no further urging. He started to move toward the door. "Blake?" Kevin called. Blake turned. "I'm sorry, that's all I can say. I know it will never be enough . . . but I'm sorry. Take care of her. She needs you."

"What the hell's going on?" Craig demanded to know. Blake hesitated, but Kevin spoke again.

"I'll explain. Just go. She needs you."

Blake nodded and almost ran from the office. Craig watched in amazement, then he turned to Kevin.

"What's going on?"

354

"Sit down, Craig. It's a long story and I'm not about to crucify myself without a good stiff drink. I think I just gave Noel back her life, and that's good, because I'm the one who took it from her in the first place."

Craig remained silent. But he opened a drawer, took out a bottle of whiskey, and walked across the room to sit down near Kevin as he handed him the bottle. Kevin took a deep drink and almost choked as the fiery liquid went down. He handed the bottle back to Craig who did the same.

"Is it that bad, Kevin?"

"Hell, yes," Kevin said tiredly. "Craig, you were away. I'd been home on leave but I'd gone to get food. Things were getting rough and food was hard to come by. I had to scavenge further than I thought. Emma, Charlotte, and Noel were alone when a marauding group of animals rode through. When I came back it was already over. I found Noel holding Charlotte . . . I must have gone crazy. You see, Charlotte was broken and bloody and her clothes were torn." His eyes looked haunted as he revisited an old memory. "Noel looked like she'd never been touched. How was I to know she was so numb with shock that she'd . . . she'd changed her clothes without even knowing what she was doing? I was too far gone myself to know she was shocked so badly that she believed me when I accused her of hiding when Charlotte needed her, when I screamed at her that it should have been her instead of Charlotte."

There were tears in Kevin's voice. "I didn't know that she'd believe what I said, and because she couldn't face what had happened to her something in her died. Craig . . . God, she was only sixteen."

"She never told me."

"She couldn't."

"Me? Why? God, I'd have . . ."

"Have what? Told her everything was going to be all right. Told her stories like we did when she was a kid? There's no boogie man, Noel. Well, for her there was, and we can't change that."

"Why did you send Blake to her? He's the last man . . ."

"No, he's the best one. He loves her, Craig, and right now I'm scared even that's not going to be enough. She's afraid, afraid that . . ." he couldn't finish, but he didn't need to. Craig already knew.

"She might not forgive you for this."

"Well . . . then that makes two of us. If she can't forgive me it's because I can't forgive myself."

"Then I guess we'd better pray."

"Yeah, I guess we'd better." Both reached for the bottle.

Blake was sure he'd never moved faster in his life. His heart was pounding by the time he dismounted before Noel's house. There was no time to waste knocking. Besides, if Noel knew who it was she might not answer the door.

He had no way of knowing what Kevin had said to her or what to expect, but if Kevin had sent him it must have been pretty bad.

He opened the door and walked in, surprised when he found the room empty. He crossed the main room slowly and opened a door.

She lay on the bed, curled in an almost child-like position, asleep. When he moved a step closer he could see her cheeks were still damp with tears. She must have wept herself into exhaustion.

He sat down slowly, wanting to touch her. That, he cautioned himself, is the last thing you can do. Instead he spoke her name softly.

"Noel?"

356

She blinked her eyes open slowly, sluggishly. It took her a moment to realize where they were and who was sitting beside her. She scooted herself hastily to a sitting position against the head of the bed, her eyes wide with shock — another emotion that hurt Blake to see.

"What are you doing here?"

"Just . . . being here," he said gently.

Her eyes betrayed her understanding. She could deny it, but she knew why he'd come.

"I must go. Kevin and Craig need their lunch and . . ." she tried to move from the bed but Blake touched her arm.

"You're not running away anymore, Noel. Don't fight me. I want to talk to you."

She remained still, but he could feel every nerve quivering. "What do you want, Blake? You have no business here."

"Well, what I really want is for you to marry me."

She turned her head away, fighting tears. "No, Blake . . . no."

"Why?" he smiled. "You love me *almost* as much as I love you."

"Love has nothing to do with it."

He was pleased. She hadn't denied that she loved him, only that she wouldn't marry him.

"It has everything to do with it. Love can handle a lot of things, Noel. It's pretty strong. You should try it. You've been alone too long."

She looked at him with a direct, honest look. "I won't say I don't care for you. That would be a lie, and we both know it. Maybe that's why I won't marry you. You're a fine, strong man, Blake, and you deserve the best."

"That's what I'd be getting."

"No. Let it go, Blake. It's better if we just stay friends or better still if we part company."

Blake reached out and braced an arm on each side of her, effectively cutting off any retreat.

"Noel, my sweet innocent, I couldn't do that. Part of me would stay with you. A part I couldn't live without."

"Sweet innocent," she said bitterly. "You're a dreamer."

"Why? Because some beast attacked you, hurt you? That has nothing to do with your innocence. Noel, you know nothing of love, but I'm going to teach you."

Her eyes widened when she realized he knew her secret and filled with fear at his last words.

"Blake . . . what . . ." She tried to move, but he drew his arms closer together. Then he bent his head and lightly touched his lips to hers.

"There's a difference, Noel, and it's time you knew it. You can't hide behind guilt that isn't yours. I love you and I want you to love me. Even if it takes us a long time to know each other, it's time we got to it."

"You don't know," she said as she inhaled sharply. His lips continued to brush her cheek, kiss her ear, and move to her throat. "Stop, Blake." Her hands were pressed against his shoulders. Her struggle was ineffectual and his assault was rapidly causing unfamiliar and unwanted reactions from her nerves.

Blake prayed he was right, that Noel only needed the right person to love, to understand that the hurt and the pain could be forgotten . . . replaced with something beautiful.

He touched her lips slowly, gently tasting her.

Noel was flooded with panic, but it began to dissolve into another, equally fierce, emotion.

The kiss deepened and Blake had to muster all his control to keep from possessing her with the full depth of his passion. Take it slowly, he cautioned himself.

He could win or lose her forever—he knew he had to be right. He had to release the love she had bottled up inside. He had to let her know that loving could be good, and it could be healing.

When he reluctantly released her lips she was panting softly and his breath was ragged as well.

"With all my heart I love you," he said in a controlled voice, trying not to betray the heated condition of his blood. "Please hear me. Let me prove that you can trust me to understand. I know what you went through. But that's not love, Noel. That kind of thing is for animals. Love is a gentle, caring thing. I wouldn't hurt you, on my life I wouldn't. Let me show you that love is different, that love can give instead of take. Put your trust in me, Noel."

His voice was warm and the eyes that held hers were molten and filled with promise. She was afraid and he knew it. Yet new sensations were stirring Noel, sensations she had never experienced before. Dormant passion, long since held at bay, was struggling to life.

Did she dare give in to this? Would it be the nightmare she had known before? She teetered on the very edge and still their eyes held.

He drew her closer, longing to feel her softness against him. This time when he took her mouth with his he tasted a tentative surrender.

Noel could hear her own heart pounding, matching the rhythmic beat of his. Beneath his touch she felt herself tremble.

Her lips were parted and her breathing was ragged, then her eyes half closed as he bent his head. His parted lips found hers in a kiss that stirred something volatile in both of them, forging them together. Time seemed to hover, motionless, in this moment preordained like the blending of sand and sea.

It was enough to sap their resistance, this strong, intoxicating nectar. His mouth savored hers with a growing urgency that was echoed in her as her mouth opened and her tongue flicked against his, teasing, taunting . . . accepting. The heat of his kiss flooded her senses until a raging desire consumed the last of her will and she lost her self-control.

The awakening pleasure deep within her was strong with the promise of a fulfillment of the hunger that seemed to ravage her. Warm, strong fingers expertly loosened and discarded her clothing. She watched with half-closed eyes as if she were not a participant but an onlooker, mesmerized by the glistening bronze of his body.

All her resistance and strength were sapped as he enclosed her in a strong embrace and his open mouth took hers again. She found herself molding to his frame and moaning softly under the expert touch of gentle hands. She forgot all her darkest pain as his lips brushed her hair, her cheek, and then nipped lightly at her ear. She closed her eyes and his searing kisses traced her throat and shoulders.

Slowly, tenderly, he aroused her, stroking her breasts and then her belly. She was filled with a warm, tingling excitement.

The kisses began gently, then turned fierce as their mouths repeatedly met in mutual impatience. His lips, hot and wet, seared her breasts, and his teeth lightly nibbled the soft flesh of her belly.

She gasped, panting, breathless, and pliable beneath his caresses as time seemed to hover on the brink of eternity.

His eyes were aflame as he lowered his weight upon her, parting her thighs, and with the sound of her rapturous sigh echoing in his ears, pressed himself deep within her.

An indescribably beautiful and expanding burst of

joyous pleasure sent a splintering feeling pulsing through her. She arched against him with a fierce passion that matched his as wild ecstasy surged through their bodies, fusing them. They moved as one, the thunderous beat of their hearts blending in a drumming tempo. Both had lost touch with reality, and the world careened crazily beneath their rhythmic strokes. With fierce, naked abandon they possessed each other, spiraling up to breathless heights and then tumbling into the oblivion of completion.

For a long moment they clung to each other as if in a deep trance, neither wanting to break the spell.

Noel clutched him as if afraid if she let go she would revert to the old panic. And Blake held her, waiting until reality finally proved her wrong.

"Noel," he said hoarsely, after a time that seemed to stretch interminably. Had he been wrong? Had he pushed her too far?

He felt a dull ache beginning to grow in the pit of his stomach when she didn't answer. How could he say he was sorry if he had been wrong? It had been the most perfect moment in his life and he couldn't be sorry for that. All he could regret was any more pain he might have caused her.

"Noel, for God's sake, look at me. At least tell me you don't hate me." Maybe he had wanted her too badly. Maybe he'd not been gentle enough, patient enough . . . God, he could go crazy like this. A man's passion was hard to contain, and he was scared silly that at its peak he'd overwhelmed her.

Slowly Noel lifted her eyes to him and they were filled with tears. He caught her face between his hands and kissed away the tears, savoring the briny taste and wanting to weep himself. Because besides the tears there was a glow of warmth in her eyes that filled him with joy.

"I never knew . . ." she began hesitantly, suddenly

361

shy and unable to put into words what she felt.

"You were never given a chance to know. I'm grateful to all the gods that you've come into my life. I love you, Noel . . . if I hurt you in any way I'm sorry. It's just that I was scared to lose you, and I knew that was what was going to happen."

"I was afraid of you," she admitted.

"Afraid of me . . . or only of yourself?"

"Maybe a little of both. You made me feel things I never felt before. I didn't want to feel them or understand them. At times I almost hated you."

"Hate and love are pretty close sometimes. I don't want you to have any regrets, not now or ever. I'll give you all the time you want." He laughed softly. "As long as you promise you won't be out of my sight for one minute until the day you agree to marry me."

She laughed in response and it sounded good to him. But the laughter died and her eyes grew dark with memories.

"I should tell you . . ."

"You don't have to tell me a thing. Our lives begin here. We'll forget everything that happened before we met. Besides . . . I haven't lived the most exemplary life, and I'd rather not confess more than I have to."

"I'm sure it's not the same."

"No, most likely it's worse. You were innocent. I don't think I've been innocent since the day I was fourteen. If I want to tell the truth I've hurt a few women . . . not by brutality, but maybe by thoughtlessness. I don't ever want to hurt you. So, make an honest man out of me and marry me to keep me out of harm's way."

"You are a clever, wicked, and wonderful man, and I think I love you, too."

362

"Think!" Blake cried in mock alarm. "I've offered you my love and everything I have and you only *think* you love me? I see I must be more diligent in my pursuit. I want a definite love and I'm willing to work to get it." He drew her into his arms and kissed her until her head spun and her senses began to quiver with renewed desire.

"Blake, we should go . . ."

"Nowhere," he said positively. "Right here is the best place to be."

"It's the middle of the day," she protested weakly as his mouth began to search for her most sensitive spots.

"Best time in the world to make love. In fact, any time is the best time."

"Someone might come."

"Nobody's going to come. We know where Craig and Kevin are, and pity anyone else that walks through that door." He was caressing her body with light sensitive fingers and she could feel the languid heat flow to her limbs, leaving her weak.

"But we should . . . oh," she gasped as his lips sought the hardened peaks of her breasts and suckled gently at first, then harder as he felt her body respond. She uttered another moan of pleasure as his fingers found the softness of her and began to work magic that set her pulses racing and her body arching toward this new and vibrant pleasure. She sighed as the warmth spread from place to place following the movement of his lips.

He continued the assault for a while, then rose on his elbow to look at her. She made a tiny complaining murmur when the caresses stopped and her eyes opened slowly.

"Tell me you want me, Noel. I want to hear you say it."

"I do, Blake . . . I want you." Her whisper was

363

soft and barely finished before it was smothered by his mouth.

He kissed her again and again, fondled and caressed her until Noel's passive pleasure changed to active desire. She whimpered and wiggled and uttered little cries. Twice she tried to wiggle her body beneath his and draw him into her.

But Blake was enjoying this drawn-out titillation. Noel was real—her every sigh and cry sent a pulse of pleasure through him.

Noel was nearly weeping with frustration and excitement. She clutched Blake almost frantically, kissing every part of him that she could reach, growing even more excited by the ragged sounds of pleasure he uttered.

Soon the kisses and caresses had brought them both to a fevered pitch and when he plunged himself to the very depths of her he had to silence her cry with his mouth.

They rose to a fiery climax together and then lay gasping in each other's arms.

"My, my," Noel murmured. "Oh, my, that was delightful."

The naiveté of the remark and her tone, expressing the kind of pleasure one receives from a totally unexpected and welcome gift, set Blake laughing.

"What a compliment, my love. I couldn't have asked for anything more perfect."

Even Noel laughed. Her cheeks were pink and her eyes glowed when she looked up at him.

"To be told something is pleasant is a far cry from experiencing it oneself. Besides, *pleasant* is not the right word."

"No? What would you say?" Blake teased.

"I would say . . ." she retorted, looking devilish, "no, I won't tell you. You're conceited enough."

"But if you don't tell me, how can I change what's

wrong, or what doesn't satisfy you?" His laughing eyes met hers and held them for a long moment.

"How beautiful you are, Noel," he breathed. Love-making had made her skin flushed and her eyes glow. Blake was certain he would never forget how she looked at this moment. He kissed her again and laughed. "Now it's time to get up. The day is waning."

"Oh, now that you've had your fill you're quite willing to leave my bed," she teased with a soft laugh.

"Don't tempt me, angel. There are two points on which you're wrong. I'll never be willing to leave your bed, and if I have you every day of my life I'll never have my fill."

Satisfied with his reply, Noel rose. He watched with the utmost attention and fascination as she dressed. Only when she was finished and turned to smile at him did he remember to dress himself. As he finished he went to her and swung her against him to kiss her soundly. "Now I'm hungry."

"With such an expenditure of energy I'm sure you must be," she said smugly, then yelped as he gave her a slap on the rump. "Blake!"

"I've no doubt you're hungry as well. I think I remember a little energy of your own."

"Then," she replied, her eyes warm with promise, "if we want to store up more energy I guess we'd both better eat."

With his arm about her they walked to the bedroom door. In the doorway Blake stopped and looked back. Noel looked up at him questioningly.

"What a wonderful room. A great place," he said, looking down at her, "for a man's life to start."

They left the room and went into the kitchen where Noel began to prepare supper. They were laughing and talking together when the door opened very slowly and Kevin put his head inside to look around. The cautious look on his face made both Blake and Noel laugh. Moments later Craig and Kevin came in.

They basked in the glow of Noel's happiness, not missing a chance to take a jab or two at Blake, who found it very hard to keep his eyes from lingering on Noel.

After dinner, which, as Craig and Kevin took the time to complain, was their only meal of the day, Blake sat with them to discuss Mitch and his progress. "Or," as Kevin slyly said, "that was as good an excuse as anything to be near Noel."

"I couldn't agree more," Blake said with a laugh. "I'm sure this is some kind of a dream, and if I go home now I'll come back tomorrow to find the door locked."

"In which case," Craig said blithely, "you would most likely kick it in."

"More than likely," Kevin agreed.

"Well, then," Blake announced with a wink at Noel, "in an effort to save your home from damage I suggest you convince Noel to marry me right away."

Both Craig and Kevin seemed to be considering the idea very carefully. Then Craig looked at Noel and smiled.

"I'd be more than happy to give the bride away," he said softly. "More than happy."

"And I'll have the first dance with the bride," Kevin laughed, "and most likely get drunk."

"Oh, I love you all," Noel giggled, "and if it pleases you, Blake . . . I'll marry you as soon as this little fight we're in is resolved."

"Then I guess we'd all better work a little harder, don't you think?" Blake said. He rose and went to Noel and, despite her blushes, pulled her into his arms to kiss her.

366

Twenty-seven

Trent Donnelley's face was white with fury. He picked up the papers on the table in front of him and flung them at the three men. They flinched, but said nothing.

"All the work! And the money spent! And you stand there and tell me he's winning! What the hell do I have around me, a bunch of imbeciles!"

"He just seems to be one step ahead of us. And that newspaper! Those Andersons are vicious with those editorials. Blake Randolph is no slouch either. He and that paper are a big problem."

"That paper is half the size of the *Chronicle!* Are you telling me they have enough clout to sway people? The stupid people in *this* town? What are you doing about Mitch Flannery?"

"Everything you told us to do," one man protested vehemently. "We wanted to beat some sense into him but you tied our hands. You aren't going to stop him until you show him what you'll do to him if he doesn't get out of your way."

Trent was silent for a moment as he contemplated this. He walked to the window and drew the curtain aside, his back to the two men. Still they waited in silence. Without turning around, Trent spoke in a cold voice.

"All right. Find him. Teach him a lesson . . . a very firm and final lesson."

"You want us to kill him?"

"No. I only want him . . . convinced he'd better withdraw from the race and stay away from Whitney Clayborn. So go and find him, and make sure you convince him thoroughly."

The sound of the door closing told Trent they had gone to carry out his order. He breathed deeply, struggling to control his anger. He had taken Mitch's interference for as long as he could. Besides, the rumors that had begun to spread about Mitch and Whitney Clayborn had to be stopped. It seemed, as the men he'd sent to watch Whitney had told him, that Mitch had visited her. He couldn't let that happen again—it was much too dangerous.

He'd carefully sent a few men because he knew Keith Clayborn was alive, just as he knew Keith had contacted his family some years before. He was certain what he wanted was in the letters Whitney's brother had sent his sister . . . or some member of the family. It was imperative that he get his hands on them. He'd tried to convince Whitney to stay away from Mitch Flannery, but his reports were that she had not done so. Mitch had interfered with his plans once too often.

He walked across his library to a painting and swung it away on a well camouflaged hinge to reveal a safe. He spun the dial and worked the combination, removing three small bundles of letters and miscellaneous papers. Some he could use to eliminate Mitch Flannery. The others were evidence that he would not want revealed to anyone. Few were alive who knew about his past. One was Whitney's brother, Keith, and the other, unknowingly, was Mitch Flannery. In time he meant to remove both witnesses . . . permanently.

He separated the papers and put the largest bundle back in the safe. He could not afford their contents to be revealed. The other small bundle he put in his pocket. The time might be coming soon, and he would not hesitate to use anything he had to rid himself of the man who stood between him and what he wanted.

No one could have been happier about Noel and Blake than Mitch. When he came into the *Sentinel* office, he'd been looking for Blake who had not returned the night before. Mitch had suspected Trent's hand in it and was afraid something had happened to Blake. When he walked in Blake and Noel were seated side by side at the desk, concentrating on the papers that lay before them.

Both Kevin and Craig were at work at the press and Mitch was wondering if their feelings about Blake had eased any. He knew how Blake felt about Noel, but he wasn't sure Blake would stand much of a chance in the face of two men like Craig and Kevin Anderson.

"Afternoon, everybody," Mitch said. He was pleased as each face turned to him with a smile. From Noel he might have expected it, but when Blake was around it was rare to see smiles from her brothers. "What are you two working on?"

"Wedding plans," Craig replied with a laugh. Kevin grinned at Mitch's surprised expression.

"We are not, Mitch," Noel said merrily. "We're working on your new speech. Blake has done a fabulous job."

"I'd prefer it to be wedding plans," Blake grinned. "But the lady is a slave driver and thinks I ought to work for a living."

"What's going on here?" Mitch was puzzled—a whole lot seemed to have happened in a very short time.

"We have to get you elected pretty quick, buddy," Blake said, "because Noel's promised to marry me right after the election."

"Well, I'll be . . ." Mitch said with a grin and stretched his hand out to his friend. "Congratulations, Blake. I don't know if you deserve it, but you're getting a pretty special girl." He turned to Noel. "Can I kiss the bride before the wedding?"

"Certainly."

"Very quickly and very carefully," Blake insisted in mock jealousy. Mitch laughed and bent to kiss Noel on both cheeks.

"Be happy, Noel."

"Thank you, Mitch."

"Now, can somebody tell me how all this happened? I had a few doubts."

"A few?" Blake queried. "You're not a man to exaggerate."

"How about we finish this speech first?" Craig asked. "You have to give it in a few days. Then we'll go out and have dinner, open a bottle of wine, and tell you everything that's happened since we saw you last."

"Sounds fine to me," Mitch agreed.

They accomplished finishing and polishing the speech to everyone's satisfaction and discussed the plans for the next few weeks that would see the culmination of the race and the day of election. By this time it was near dinner time so they went out to celebrate.

The dinner party was happy and overflowed with wine to the point that Mitch was feeling quite tipsy when the time came to ride home.

He was sure Blake had no intention of riding home with him. He was much too happy to leave Noel before he absolutely had to. It was late when he took leave of his friends and started toward

370

home, quite unaware of the three men who trailed him.

Blake and Noel had chosen to walk home and they did so slowly, enjoying every minute of their time together.

"When this election's over, Noel . . . after I get you tied to me nice and tight, I'd like to take you home . . . my home, for a visit."

"To see snow?" she asked, smiling.

"Yeah," he grinned. "I just want you to see where I grew up and show you some of the things I love. Want to come?"

"Of course I do. I want to know everything there is to know about you."

"I guess we both have a lot of discovery ahead."

"It's going to be such fun. Oh, Blake, I never thought I would ever be this happy. It's like . . . like life had stopped for so long. Then you came along and you smiled at me and touched me, and it started all over again."

He put his arm about her waist and hugged her to him. "I know what you're talking about. You've just given a good description of how I feel."

"Blake?"

"Umhum?"

"Speaking of happiness, Mitch . . . he seems so . . . closed off or . . . unhappy somehow."

"I don't think he's closed off. He's just in the middle of some pretty big battles and it's taking all he's got to handle them."

"More than one battle? I know about the election but . . ."

"Look, love, I know I can tell you anything, but I wouldn't want to air any of Mitch's problems to anyone else."

371

"I know. What is it?"

Blake went on to explain the entire situation between Mitch and Whitney. Noel listened in silence, understanding completely what Mitch must have been feeling.

"It must be hard for both of them."

"It is."

"Does she love him, Blake?"

"It's not a matter of love, Noel, it's trust. You see when she got the letter, that really broke her. She had trusted Mitch completely. It's hard now to give him that trust again. In my mind she does love him. If she didn't, I think she would already be married to Trent Donnelley. Besides that, there's Jon. They both love him and neither one wants to cause him unhappiness. It's just a hell of a situation that's going to take a lot of work and understanding."

"What would it take to bring those two together?"

"I wish I knew. I'd do whatever it took. It will have to be a sudden change in Whitney's thinking or something that threatens them both."

"Unlikely."

"Yeah, unlikely."

Noel stopped walking as they reached her porch. She turned and slid her arms about his waist, feeling his warmth as he put his arms around her.

"But I know something that isn't unlikely."

"Like what?"

"It's unlikely that I'll ever let you go." She laid her head against his chest and he kissed the top of it. They were enveloped in a quiet moment of contentment. Then he lifted her chin with one finger and bent his head to kiss her. "Don't . . . ever," he whispered just before their lips met.

When the kiss ended Blake sighed and looked

heavenward. Then he chuckled. "Stands to reason both Craig and Kevin will be home soon. This election is too far away and so is our wedding."

"Abstinence is good for the soul," Noel said in mock seriousness. "Besides," she added, lowering her voice, "I want to be able to keep you with me the next time we're together."

He made a low growling sound and swung her up in his arms until the air was filled with her laughter.

"Abstinence, after a remark like that, is going to drive me very slowly insane. It's like getting a peek at heaven then announcing my residence is hell for the next few weeks. And let me warn you," he added as he stood her down, kissed her, and looked into her eyes, "I'm going to make up for it."

She laughed seductively. "I hoped you'd feel that way. If you like, you can come in for a while until Kevin and Craig get home."

"If I come in . . . . I'd better kiss you goodnight and leave while the leaving's good. I can't keep my hands off you out here. You have no idea how I'm going to get if you invite me in."

"I want you to come in, Blake," she whispered, "even if it's only minutes. I want them."

He needed no more invitation than that. He whispered her name softly and together they walked inside.

Mitch let his horse pick its own way for a while, mostly because he was just drunk enough to see things in a euphoric haze.

He was happy for Blake. Noel, as far as he was concerned, was perfect for him. The *Sentinel* and Noel's brothers had been behind him all the way and because of them what he was working so hard for might just possibly come true.

Thoughts of things that were going right in his life brought his mind to the one thing in his life that was not . . . Whitney.

The more he thought of her the more he wanted her and his condition provided ideas that he wouldn't have had sober. He turned his horse toward Whitney's . . . the three who had followed him from town were only a short distance behind.

If they were surprised that he had deviated from course there was no sign. They had plans to catch up with him when the time was right no matter what his destination.

Once his thoughts had centered on Whitney and Jon, and the night air had cleared his head just a bit, he enjoyed the idea of taking Whitney by surprise. He meant to try and talk to her again, this time without her brother's interference. Actually he had liked her brother, but preferred him to be some distance away and unable to keep Whitney from listening to him.

He continued on, forming words in his mind. Engrossed in these thoughts, he was unaware that the three who had followed him were now closing in. He reached a small clearing near a stream and his horse stopped for a minute to drink. His pursuers spread out and sprang at him from behind and both sides. The sharp click of more than one gun, and from more than one direction, finally brought him to attention.

"Stay very still." The voice came from behind him and it was a hard voice that made it clear this was no game. "Dismount."

He heard horses drawing close and from what he could tell, there were at least three, maybe more.

"If you're after money I have very little on me."

374

"Just dismount."

Mitch grew taut. They weren't after money, so obviously it was him. Why didn't they just kill him now?

"I said dismount, or would you rather we yanked you out of the saddle?"

"Easy, friend," Mitch said carefully. He dismounted and started to turn around.

"Just stay put," the cold voice commanded. Mitch stood still. "Now you're getting smart."

"What is it you want?" Mitch questioned. He was listening intently, trying to figure out how many there were.

"To give you a little advice."

"Advice? About what?"

"About makin' mistakes that cause people a whole lot of trouble. Now we're goin' to make it *real* clear to you."

Mitch was about to ask another question when a well-aimed blow to the back of the head stunned him and he dropped to his knees. Then they were on him. The beating was merciless, for they meant to do as much damage as possible. Mitch struggled to defend himself, but it was useless.

He could taste blood and the cut on his cheek was bleeding profusely. One eye was already swelling shut, blow after blow to his ribs and back brought grunts of pain, and soon he was on his hands and knees. He was kicked in the stomach again and again and could feel himself slipping. A red haze of pain was all he could see, and he could no longer fight back at all. He was still on his hands and knees fighting stubbornly to maintain consciousness when the cold voice broke through to him.

"That's enough for now, boys. I want to talk to him for a minute before you finish him off."

375

The man squatted down beside Mitch and grabbed his hair to jerk his head up. He had a gun and he tapped the barrel none too lightly against Mitch's face. "Now you listen close. I'm going to let the boys dance with you a bit more. Just so you know how it's going to be if you don't resign from this election and stay away from Whitney Clayborn. She's not interested, and we don't want any more problems. It's going to be hard on you, boy, real hard, if you decide to keep on running. I hope you understand, because next time you're going to end up dead." He stood up. "So teach him real good, boys."

Despite his struggles the trees began to swirl around him and the moon grew to a hazy ball. He didn't hear the gunshot that startled his three attackers.

"Stand where you are!"

The three stood frozen above Mitch's inert form. They looked around but could see no one. One reached for his gun, but the shot that rang out cut a crease across his hand and made him yelp in pain.

"Put him across his horse!"

The three struggled to lift Mitch's limp and beaten body and placed him across his saddle.

"Now stand back, you pieces of scum, before I blow holes in all three of you. That's what you deserve."

They moved away and the stranger stepped from the shadows, a gun in each hand. "Toss your guns into the water . . . . hurry up, my trigger finger's itchy."

After they disposed of their weapons, one had the courage to speak. "Who the hell are you and why are you interested? It's worth a lot of money if you just ride on."

"I'm not riding on, and I have more interest than your boss can afford. I have a message for him. If anything happens to Mitch Flannery . . . well, I have a good memory. I'll look the three of you up." He fired both guns so quickly that he took them by surprise. One man groaned and grabbed his shoulder, another's leg buckled under him and he had to be helped, moaning, back to his feet. "Now, get out of here, before I finish the job."

They moved as quickly as they could and soon the sound of their horses receded. The man ran to his horse and mounted, rode up beside Mitch and grabbed the reins to lead the unconscious man away before the attackers tried anything else.

Whitney crossed the clearing with Jon's hand in hers. They had gone to make sure Addy was recovering well. She was, but Berdine felt one more night would make certain.

"Ready for bed, Jon?" At the shake of his head Whitney laughed. "Well, you'd better be because after I give you a bath that's where you're going."

"Mommy, no . . . I want . . ."

"Now behave, Jon. Ever since I let you visit the Flannerys you've become a little spoiled. You've had cookies and milk. Josiah and Lazarus have played with you and told you stories. Now, it's time for a bath and bed. So let's have no arguments."

Jon wasn't agreeable, but he knew his mother's tone of voice meant a smack on the seat if he argued any further.

Whitney placed the wooden tub before the fireplace and heated water. Then she spent the next hour bathing Jon and convincing him he couldn't stay in the tub until his skin shriveled.

Once he was safely tucked in bed and Whitney had adamantly refused him one more story, she kissed him good night, turned the lamp down low, and left him with his eyes already drooping.

Downstairs she dragged the tub to the porch and dumped the water. Then she returned and began to heat water for her own bath.

A short time later, seated contentedly in the warm water, she gave herself over to the thoughts she had refused to examine before. She had to make decisions and she had to make them now, with all the honesty she possessed.

She had to decide the direction of the balance of her life. Trent had offered her all the security she would ever need, and for Jon's future as well. If Mitch had not walked back into her life would she be married to Trent by now? It was strange, but the answer could be no. She probed that subject deeper. She did not love Trent—she had to admit it. But she had loved before and all it had brought was disaster. Passion and wild emotions were not enough. Still . . . her heart began to pulse, she had loved, and her senses could not be controlled by her mind.

Mitch had walked back into her life and stirred it like a hurricane could stir the ocean. It was clear that Jon was relating to him as he had to no one, not even Lazarus. It made her realize that somehow she had wanted to keep Jon away from Mitch, as if committing him meant committing herself.

Mitch had a right to Jon—she couldn't deny that.

"Oh, what a complicated mess," she groaned. "Why don't you just decide and have done with it! Trent is the man you should marry, and just because Mitch can set your body afire is no reason to spoil the future for Jon." She was angry with herself and tried to bring her emotions under control. She would make a final decision, and that decision would be Trent Donnelley . . . for Jon's sake.

Satisfied that she knew where she was going with her life, Whitney rose from the now-tepid water and dried off. Donning a nightgown, she brushed out her hair and cleaned the tub and soiled cloths.

She knew she couldn't sleep, so she walked to the door hoping a breath of air and the calm sounds of the night might help. She opened the door and screamed in shock as Keith loomed before her. His arms were about Mitch's waist and one of Mitch's arms was over his shoulder. Even Whitney could see Mitch was not maneuvering much on his own.

"Whitney, get some hot water and tear up some cloths! Hurry! Close the door."

He staggered in with Mitch while Whitney closed the door and followed him. Keith laid Mitch down on the couch as gently as he could and it was then that Whitney got a good look at him.

"Mitch!" she cried softly and ran to kneel beside the couch. She reached out and gently touched his cheek, unaware that her eyes were filled with tears . . . or that her brother was watching her closely. "What happened?"

"Someone tried to beat him half to death."

"Why?"

"I don't know yet," Keith lied quietly. He didn't want to name anyone yet. Not until he had proof . . . but after tonight he had suspicions.

"Whitney, I'm taking his shirt off. From the way they were kicking and pounding he might have a broken rib or two. Get that water and tear the cloth into strips so we can bind him."

Whitney ran to do what Keith asked while he knelt beside Mitch and began to remove his shirt. Mitch was a large man and Keith was panting by the time he got the shirt off. Huge black bruises were already developing from Mitch's waist to his shoulders.

"I sure as hell hope they haven't punctured a lung," Keith muttered. He laid his ear against Mitch's chest to listen for the telltale bubbling sound that would tell him a lung was punctured by a broken rib. He'd heard the sound often enough during the war to know. To his relief Mitch was breathing well.

Whitney returned with the water and a bed cover which she began to tear into strips. "Let me," she urged Keith, who wasn't washing the blood from Mitch's face gently enough to suit her. She took the cloth from his hands and Keith moved over to give her room.

Mitch struggled through a red haze of pain. He tried to move, but it seemed as if his arms were made of lead and a heavy weight was on his chest.

He could barely crack one eye open, the other was swollen shut. But what he saw convinced him he was dreaming.

A white mist surrounded her, but Whitney was there. He could hear her voice even though he couldn't understand what she said. She was also touching him gently with cool fingers.

He wanted to say her name, to beg her not to go away, to tell her that he loved her, but he couldn't seem to articulate anything but a low groan. Then he drifted again into darkness.

Whitney bathed his face carefully, catching her lip between her teeth when she heard him groan.

His face was badly bruised. A cut over one eye persisted in bleeding, and his lip was swollen from a cut at the corner.

"I'll have to sew up that cut over his eye," Whitney said. She went to fetch her sewing basket.

Once she had sewn the cut and bandaged it, she and Keith concentrated on binding his ribs, because Keith was still sure one or more could at least be cracked. When they were finished Whitney and Keith stood and looked at him.

"Do you know who did it?" she asked.

"We'll have to ask Mitch when he wakes up," Keith said. He didn't want to voice his suspicions without Mitch. It was best not to say anything since Mitch might not want Whitney to know.

"We have to move him, Keith. This couch is much too small. If he were to roll off during the night he could do those ribs a lot more harm."

"Maybe between the two of us we could move him upstairs. We could put him in with Jon for a while."

"No, we'll put him in my bed."

"Your bed?" Keith was surprised.

"Yes, I wouldn't want Jon to wake up in the middle of the night and see him like this. It would frighten him to death."

"I suppose you're right," Keith agreed, but he wasn't sure Whitney's reasons were entirely what she thought them to be.

It took the two of them some time to get Mitch safely into Whitney's bed. Once she drew the covers over him she seemed more satisfied.

"He'll have to stay in bed at least a couple of days. There were three men and they beat on him pretty good before I got to them. I don't think he'll be feeling too well tomorrow."

"No, I don't suppose he will. I'll take care of him. But he needs to tell us about this. Something must be done."

"Whitney, I wouldn't say anything to anybody if I were you. Not until you talk to Mitch. He might just want to settle this affair himself."

"You think he knows who's responsible?"

"I don't know. Obviously, we couldn't talk on the way. I do know one thing."

"What?"

"He was on his way here. That's the only reason I ran across him. If this had happened somewhere else he'd be dead."

"He must tell the authorities. This kind of thing . . ." she paused, looking up at Keith. "You do know who attacked him and why, don't you?"

"I have my suspicions, but I'm not saying anything until he wakes up. Hey, how about a little more of that brandy?"

"You can change the subject all you want. You've always been an expert at evading me. Come on, I'll give you that brandy, but when Mitch wakes up he's got a lot of explaining to do . . . and he can't run away."

Whitney turned away and Keith smiled down at Mitch and spoke softly. "I wouldn't be in your shoes tomorrow for all the money in the world." He chuckled, then followed Whitney from the room.

Twenty-eight

Mitch awoke slowly and painfully. He knew he was in bed, but for the life of him he couldn't figure out how he'd gotten there. One eye wouldn't open and he hesitated to open the other for fear the light would make his pounding headache worse.

There was no part of his body that didn't hurt. Even breathing as lightly as possible was difficult.

Someone in the family must have found him, and he hoped his parents hadn't been too shocked when they saw him.

There was very little doubt in his mind about who was behind the attack, but he knew he could never prove it. If they intended to scare him away they'd failed.

He remembered the voice of the leader well, as well as his threat. He also remembered that he had been warned away from Whitney. They could go to hell.

He breathed slowly, fighting the pain it caused and wondering just how badly hurt he was and if anything had been broken. In two days he had a speech to give and he was going to give it even if it killed him . . . From the way he felt he'd come close this time. But there wouldn't be a next time. He'd drunk too much — he wouldn't do that again either. Now that he knew how vicious his opponent was he'd make sure to watch his back.

His hand lay relaxed at his side and he felt a gentle touch. Someone, most likely his mother, was checking to see if he was still alive. He turned his head slowly and used what effort he could muster to open his eye.

He was shocked. Jon, box in hand, stood beside the bed. His small hand patted Mitch's consolingly.

"Did you fall down?" Jon questioned. Mitch tried to smile, but his cracked lip hurt.

"Yeah, buddy. I guess I had a pretty bad fall."

It was then the realization struck him. What was Jon doing here? Then he looked around. He wasn't home . . . and he knew exactly where he was. What he didn't know was how he'd gotten there. He looked at Jon again.

"It's all right," Jon said confidently, "my mommy can fix it."

"I'll bet she can at that." Mitch was afraid to laugh as he lifted his hand to touch his body and found it tightly wrapped in bandages. Then he felt his face and realized how battered he really was.

"Speaking of your mother, Jon, where is she?"

"Downstairs. Her and Addy are makin' soup. Mommy says it's all you can eat."

"Probably . . . for the moment anyway."

"Why? Aren't you hungry?"

"Yeah, I'm hungry."

"Then why do you have to eat soup?"

"I could eat a steak or two."

"Then why are you gonna eat soup?" Jon insisted.

"I suppose because your mother says I am." Mitch couldn't help but laugh, pain or no pain.

Jon nodded as if he understood this completely.

"Jon . . . run down and see if your mother will come up here, would you?"

Jon nodded and turned to leave.

"Want me to hold your box for you while you go down?"

Jon handed it to Mitch without complaint, and Mitch was pleased. This was his prized possession and Mitch was very sure he didn't trust it with too many.

Mitch laid the box on the bed beside him and Jon left the room. Mitch closed his eye again, wishing the headache would go away. In a few minutes he heard footsteps. The door opened and Whitney came in, with Jon right behind her.

"You're awake."

"I'm not sure. My body's telling me I should still be asleep."

"Jon, go down and tell Addy to dish up some of the soup and bring it up."

"He don't want soup, Mommy."

"Oh?" Whitney asked with a smile. "And what *does* he want?"

"A steak . . . he told me."

"Well, you go down and tell Addy about the soup and I'll talk to him about the steak, all right?"

"All right." Satisfied he had made Mitch's wishes clear, Jon left. Whitney crossed the room to stand beside the bed and looked closely at Mitch. Then she placed a cool hand on his forehead.

"You're not running a fever. That's a good sign."

"How did I get here?"

"Keith found you. He brought you here."

"I'm grateful to him."

Whitney sat down beside him and Mitch was certain she was going to ask questions he didn't want to answer.

"I want to know what happened last night."

"I'd say from the way I must look, it's pretty obvious someone took a violent dislike to me."

"Mitch, this is far from amusing. You could have been killed."

"I don't think it's amusing either. But if they

385

wanted to kill me they could have. They were armed."

"Then they wanted to do *this* to you! Why?"

"Maybe somebody's upset over something I've said in one of my speeches."

"Stop it, Mitch. Who did this?"

"I don't know who they were."

"You know more than you're saying."

"Look, Whitney, the men who did this were violent and angry. Maybe they were just taking it out on the first man they found."

How could he tell her Trent Donnelley was behind it? She would only think he was pointing a finger at Trent out of jealousy. She might accuse him of blaming Trent to get him out of her life and out of the race. No, this was definitely not the time to tell Whitney anything like that.

"Forget it, Whitney. I'm not badly hurt, just banged up. I'll mend quick." He looked around for a moment, then back at her. "Where are you sleeping?"

"On the small bed in Jon's room."

"I'm sorry to put you out like this. If you send Lazarus for my brothers they can bring a wagon and take me home."

"Right now you need to eat a little and stay still. Keith thinks you've possibly cracked a rib."

"I don't think so. I'm just bruised."

"Don't even *think* of getting up! I can see the gleam in your eye."

"All right, I'll be good. Bring on the soup."

A few minutes later Addy came in and Jon watched in fascination as Mitch drew the line at being fed. Addy and Whitney propped pillows behind him and he managed the soup himself, once he got his breath back. He hadn't realized how hard sitting up was going to be.

Whitney and Addy left Jon and Mitch alone

while he ate, and Mitch enjoyed Jon's bright inquis-itiveness. The better part of the morning passed be-fore Whitney returned. She returned to find Mitch had swung his feet to the floor and was sitting on the edge of the bed.

"What do you think you're doing?"

"It's absolutely necessary that I get up."

"I don't see why."

"Because it might prove embarrassing if I lie here much longer."

"Oh," her eyes sparkled. "Well, I'll leave you . . . and the chamber pot is under the bed." She turned and left while Mitch grimaced at his helplessness.

Mitch's annoyance at being confined to bed was almost as fierce as his anger at the man who had put him there. If Trent Donnelley thought he was dropping out of the race over this he was sadly mis-taken; and as for leaving Whitney alone, Mitch smiled to himself. He was taking advantage of every moment he was here.

He knew Jon was rapidly growing closer to him, and he intended to capitalize on that as well.

The men who had beaten him had, in a round-about way, done him a favor. He was safely en-trenched in Whitney's house, and he meant to make good use of it.

He drifted off to sleep again and when he woke he could tell the sun was setting. Its brilliance was gone and the light through the window was a mel-low gold.

He could hear movement downstairs and the murmur of voices.

Very slowly he sat up again. Then he concen-trated on standing. By the time he was erect he was sweating. He took one step, caught his breath sharply, then another, and another. After he had walked back and forth across the room several times he felt less stiff and his breathing was easier.

387

He crossed to Whitney's dressing table and looked in the mirror.

"Good Lord, looks like I've been kicked in the face by a horse." He touched his bruised jaw and cheek gingerly. "That eye looks real good," he said, chuckling at his reflection.

He began to search for his clothes. He found his pants, but his shirt was nowhere in sight so he left the room without it.

He walked down the steps very slowly. From the sound of the voices it seemed everyone was in the kitchen.

When he came to the kitchen doorway he saw Whitney and Lazarus seated at the table, with Jon on Lazarus's lap. Berdine was standing before the stove stirring something that smelled enticing and Mitch realized he was ravenous.

Freshly made bread lay cooling on a sideboard. The whole kitchen felt warm and comfortable.

Lazarus saw Mitch first and gave a long whistle. "Yo' sho' does look bad." Mitch wasn't too sure he wasn't finding a little amusement in his condition. He was surprised at Lazarus's next words. "Miz Whitney tell us how yo' came crawlin' in las' nite. Yo' be lucky yo' could get dis far."

Mitch glanced quickly at Whitney. Obviously she didn't want any of them to know that Keith was alive and she prayed Mitch would keep silent.

"No, it wasn't easy. I'm just glad Whitney was still awake. I certainly needed help. It's surprising," he smiled, "that a woman Whitney's size can have so much strength, because I was pretty weak."

Whitney's mouth froze in a forced smile as Lazarus looked from her to Mitch. "Y'all shoulda called me. Ah would have . . ."

"Tossed me back out?" Mitch questioned.

"No suh! Ah wouldn't toss a dog out lookin' like yo' do."

"He's only tormenting you, Lazarus," Whitney said. "Behave yourself, Mitch, or Lazarus might have to toss you out after all."

"I'll behave. I don't think I could stand up to one more toss." He inhaled deeply and closed his eyes. "That smells like good beef stew, Berdine, and fresh bread. I'm so hungry I could eat a bear. One bowl of soup doesn't go very far."

"Sit yo'self down. We's 'bout to eat anyway," Berdine replied.

Mitch found a seat between Lazarus and Josiah while Berdine continued to set the table. Whitney rose to cut thick slices of bread and Addy came in from outside to help.

For a few minutes there was a cool silence. Everyone filled their bowls from the large tureen Berdine placed in the center of the table. Hot stew, fresh bread with slabs of butter, greens, and coffee made Mitch's mouth water. As he began to eat he thought of how contented he would be here with Whitney and his son if only he could get her to trust him. It seemed Jon was the only one at the table who trusted him. He promised himself that that was one thing he never intended to lose.

"Somebody sho' doan seem to like yo' face." Lazarus chuckled. "Dey done try to fix it."

"They almost succeeded, too," Mitch replied.

"Who yo' make so mad dat dey wanna do dat to yo'?"

Whitney was waiting for his answer and he knew it. "I don't know who they were, Lazarus, but I'll even the score someday. I won't be caught like that again."

"I think you had best get back in bed as soon as you're finished with your supper," Whitney said. "It's dangerous for you to move around too much, at least for another day, until we make certain your ribs aren't cracked."

Mitch might have protested, but he realized he would be relegated to Lazarus's cabin or a bumpy and painful ride home if he said he was sure his ribs weren't damaged.

"You're right, Whitney," he replied as he twisted a little as if he were uncomfortable. "I guess I'd better not push it too far."

Concern leapt into Whitney's eyes as quickly as suspicion leapt into Lazarus's. Berdine kept strategically quiet, but she was more experienced than all of them, and she knew exactly what Mitch was up to. Mitch smiled at her knowing look. "Berdine, next to my mother's that was about the best stew I've ever tasted."

"Ah'm glad yo' enjoyed it. Yo' wants Lazarus to help yo' up de stairs?"

"No," Mitch said quickly as Lazarus started to rise. "I'm sure I can make it with just a little help."

"I'll come with you and see that you're settled," Whitney said, which was exactly what Mitch had in mind. Berdine chuckled to herself as she set about cleaning up the supper dishes.

But Mitch might have overestimated his strength. There was a definite ache through his whole body by the time he'd gotten up the steps. Still, he was pretty sure one more night of rest would take most of the aches and pains away, leaving him with just the bruises and they would fade in time. He wondered just how long he could draw out his stay.

When they left the room Addy took Jon into the parlor to occupy him, and Lazarus sat quietly for a while before he spoke.

"What yo' think, Berdine?"

" 'Bout what?"

"Yo' know 'bout what. Who yo' think beat him up like dat, an' what fo'?"

"If yo' think on it real hard, Lazarus, yo' might come up wif somebody doan men dat boy no good.

390

Somebody he pushin' maybe . . . somebody whose way he be standin' in."

"How long Miz Whitney gwine keep him here?"

"Long as she wants ah 'spects. Lazarus, yo' keeps quiet fo' now. Let 'em work out dere own problems."

Lazarus sighed and got up to walk outside on the porch. It was confusing. Whitney hated Mitch, didn't she? He'd ruined her life and given her a lot of grief. Still she nursed him when he was hurt instead of throwing him out. On the other hand, Trent Donnelley was the man she was considering marrying and if he found out about Mitch being here he could be angry enough to forget it. There was still the nagging idea that Trent Donnelley was behind the beating Mitch had taken. If so . . . what was Mitch going to do about it? Yes, it was confusing and for once, he guessed, doing nothing was the best thing he could do for everybody. He crossed to his own cabin.

Berdine finished the dishes and went to her cabin as well, leaving Addy playing with Jon.

Mitch sat on the edge of the bed while Whitney checked the bandages and his eye. He had to restrain himself from reaching for her.

"You're going to have a scar, Mitch."

"Well, maybe it'll give me a dashing and mysterious air," he chuckled.

"It will most likely make you devastating to women," she replied coolly.

"Umm, it might," he said, pretending interest. He watched anger cloud her eyes and it pleased him. She could deny it all she wanted, but he still got to her somehow. Now all he had to do was lay siege to that vulnerability. "You have gentle hands. It seems I remember you were there last night. It was like seeing a vision . . . an angel." His voice was low and warm and she looked down into his eyes and was suddenly caught by their heated searching.

Whitney stepped away from him, breaking the magnetic contact with sheer will. She walked to the window and opened it.

"Whitney?" he asked as she turned to face him again. "I'm not used to being tucked into bed this early. Come and talk to me for a while. I'm in no condition to cause any problem," he added, his voice teasing her.

"Get into bed. I'll sit with you for a few minutes. At least until it's time to put Jon to bed."

"Good enough." Mitch carefully got into bed and Whitney drew a chair up nearby, but not close enough that he could reach out and touch her.

"I wanted to talk to you anyway," she admitted.

"Oh?"

"I've tried to make some decisions. It's not been easy. Jon has begun to grow fond of you."

"I hope so."

"Mitch . . . maybe it's better that he doesn't."

"Why?"

"Because," she took a deep breath, "I've decided it would be best for both Jon and me if I married Trent as soon as possible."

"You can't mean that." Mitch sat back up on the edge of the bed quickly enough to bring a grunt of pain. "Whitney, do you really think I'll stand by and let that happen? Even if you had nothing more to do with me I would do everything in my power to stop you."

"Mitch, be reasonable."

"I'm being reasonable. He can't have Jon," Mitch stated firmly. "I'll take him first . . . and I'll try to stop you."

"Why are you so selfish?"

"It's not selfish, it's your damn stubbornness! You're scared to trust me again so you're putting yourself in the hands of a man who can't be trusted an inch. Whitney, don't do this. There are reasons . . ." He stopped. He didn't want to tell her about Trent while she was in this mood. She would never believe him.

"Reasons for what?"

"Reasons to want your land first of all, for trying to get possession of it without telling you. You're a beautiful woman, and I know he must want you. But he has another motive. He wants something besides you and Jon and you're the key."

"What could he possibly want? He's wealthy. I have little to offer him."

"Are you marrying him for money?" Mitch snapped angrily. "If money's the answer I have enough to take care of both of you. You can have whatever you want."

"How dare you say such a thing! You well know that money is not what brought you and me together. How can you believe it means everything now?"

"It was love for us. Can you turn it off that easily?"

"Easy!" The argument was escalating beyond their control. "Do you know the hell I went through? Do you know I bore Jon on a dirt floor while my mother lay dying! How can you tell me that money is all I care about? It's Jon! It's all Jon!"

They were silent as the truth exploded between them. She was making whatever sacrifice was necessary for Jon and she had not been able to reclaim the trust she had had in him. But he knew the depth of his love for her and he meant to brave the shadows of hell to reclaim her.

"Whitney," he said softly, struggling for control. "Don't make a decision now. Take more time." He was sure once he had defeated Trent he could make her see things his way. Then he might be able to tell her . . . or prove to her, that Trent was behind his attack. "Surely if he loves you he'll be patient."

Whitney considered this as she looked at Mitch intently. He seemed so sincere, so sure he was right. But she wasn't sure what Mitch thought he could accomplish. Nothing could change the reasons for her decision. She heard a soft voice from the doorway and turned to see Jon.

Jon had been entertained by Addy for a while, but soon he reverted to his precious box and the well handled toys inside.

Addy picked up some mending that needed to be done and sat in a rocker before the fireplace. Jon carried the box to the braided rug before the same fireplace and set it down nearly at Addy's feet.

He sat beside it and lifted the lid very carefully. But as careful as he was, one of the soldiers caught. He tugged and pulled in childish and clumsy persistence. After a few minutes there was a faint tearing sound and the lid came open.

One of the soldiers had caught in the lining, which was already frayed with time. The soldier hung there, still tangled in the ragged edge of a small hole. Jon reached for it and for a minute it wouldn't come loose.

His struggle drew Addy's attention and she smiled. "Looks like yo' ma gonna have to fix dat linin'. Ah know it was goin' pretty soon. Yo' done played it out, boy."

Jon continued to tug at the soldier until another tearing sound loosened it. The soldier came free, but now his curious eyes spied something more interesting. The tear had pulled a corner of the lining free and exposed the edges of something wedged inside.

Little fingers reached inside to feel what was

there. Satisfied it was something mysterious and therefore intriguing, he began to work his fingers to loosen more of the lining. It refused to budge, but Jon refused to stop trying.

Finally, to Jon's satisfaction, the lining began to give. Very slowly it tore itself loose from the small nails. Time had weakened the fabric. Three inches came loose and Jon could now see that there was a very interesting bundle of papers inside.

Little by little and with much pulling and tugging, more lining loosened. Now his small hand could fit inside. The box seemed determined not to give up its treasure, but Jon was just as determined. This was a new and intriguing thing.

With another tug the entire lining on the top of the box came free and revealed the letters that had been hidden there for so long. Jon took them out and began to spread them around him. He drew Addy's attention again, only this time she frowned.

"What yo' doin', boy? Hain't like yo' to mess wif dat box. Yo' done tore out all de linin'. What yo' got dere?" She came to kneel beside him. Since Addy couldn't read she couldn't verify what she suspected, but a vague and terrifying memory was coming to life.

"Oh, Lawd . . . oh, Lawd, ah hope dat ain't what ah think it be, Jon boy," she wheedled. "Give dose letters to Addy now. Come on, boy. We throw 'em in de fire. Dey burn pretty. Come on, Jon boy, give de letters to Addy."

"No! *My* box . . . *my* papers!" Jon grasped the letters and hugged them against his chest and started to back away. Addy had always been close to Jon, but she wasn't too sure he might not throw a fit and bring Whitney down before she could destroy the letters. If Miz Hope ever knew they were found her spirit might just get vengeance on Addy and Addy was extremely superstitious. She believed

395

sincerely that Hope had the power to reach from the grave to punish her.

"Now come on, Jon boy. Ah'll give yo' a piece of dat candy yo' likes so much. Give ol' Addy de letters."

Jon contemplated this, but decided in favor of the letters. They were something new. They had writing on them, and in Jon's mind writing meant stories. Instead of his mother reading to him from the books she had read over and over, she could read a whole new story. This was more exciting. He liked new stories.

Jon was backing away from Addy, and she was afraid Whitney might appear at any minute.

But it wasn't Whitney who appeared, it was Berdine. She opened the door and walked in, then stopped, surprised at the scene before her.

"What's goin' on here?" Berdine demanded.

Addy was afraid of Hope's spirit, but she was even more afraid of Berdine's very substantial presence. She had reached the end of her rope. Addy ran to Berdine.

"Ah a good girl, Berdine," she wept. "Ah hain't never tol' no lies befo'. She made me keep quiet. She was gwine sell me away. Ah was jes' scared. Ah din want to hurt Miz Whitney, ah swear. But she was gwine sell me away."

"What yo' talkin' 'bout, girl?" Berdine grabbed Addy's shoulder and shook her slightly. "Who yo' been lyin' to?"

"Ah din't! Ah din't! Miz Hope, she made me promise."

Berdine could tell that Addy was too shaken to talk and her fear was affecting Jon who stood in wide-eyed awe.

"Stop yo' cryin', girl. Yo' scarin' de boy." She put a comforting arm around Addy's shoulder. "Now, yo'

396

settle yo'self, den yo' tell me what's got yo' all-fired scared."

Berdine watched Jon from the corner of her eye as she tried to calm Addy. He stood quietly, not too sure of whether he was in serious trouble.

When Berdine had Addy sufficiently calmed she asked her what was wrong. When Addy started to talk she couldn't stop until the whole story was out.

"Ah wouldn't hurt Miz Whitney," Addy moaned. "But Miz Hope, she gwine sell me away. She make me swear ah say nothin'."

"Hain't nobody gwine do yo' no harm, chile. Yo' has to tell de truth. Miz Hope, she gone. Cain't nobody sell yo' away no mo'. We gwine tell Miz Whitney de truth. Ah thinks it's time she knew."

"Ah has to tell her?" Addy's voice shook.

"No," Berdine smiled, "ah thinks yo' answer is standin' over dere." She pointed to Jon. "Jon, come over here to Berdine." She said the words gently and stretched out her hand. He walked over and stood beside her, still clutching his prize. Berdine did not attempt to touch the letters. She simply sat down slowly in a chair. "My, my, what yo' got dere, chile?"

"They're mine. They were in my box."

" 'Course dey yours." Berdine knew the box had belonged to Hope . . . and she knew how the letters got there. "What yo' gwine do wif dem?"

"Read them."

"Yo' cain't read, chile," Berdine laughed.

"Mommy can. Mommy can read the stories to me."

"Sho'," Berdine said quietly, "dat de best thing in de world to do. S'pose yo' take 'em on up to yo' mama an' tell her to read 'em to yo'. Ah jes' cain't think of a better time fo' dat story to be told."

Jon nodded enthusiastically. This was a much better idea than burning them. This way his mother could read a new story every night.

"Berdine," Addy protested as Jon started toward the stairs.

"It be all right, Addy. It be de right time an' de right place. Dose two together, like dey shoulda been a long time ago, an' dat boy gwine lock 'em together fo' good."

Jon walked up the steps and down to his mother's room. The door stood open and he could hear her voice mingled with Mitch's.

He stood in the doorway and watched. He had never seen his mother this angry, and he had never seen Mitch angry at all. He couldn't figure out why they were shouting at each other.

He loved his mother with all his heart, and Mitch had found a place in his affections that was slowly growing. Now he was confused.

When they stopped arguing Jon watched their faces and he felt uneasy. He spoked softly, "Mommy?"

Both Whitney and Mitch turned to look at him. They both realized at once that Jon must have been standing there for a while, and that he had heard them fighting. They looked at each other, then back to Jon.

"Jon, I thought you were downstairs playing with Addy. Did she send you up to bed?" Whitney asked gently.

Jon shook his head. "Berdine said I could bring the story papers I found and you could read them to me."

"Story papers?" Mitch looked at Whitney, puzzled. "I've heard of story books but never story papers."

"They're . . . they're letters," Whitney said. But some long past note of familiarity struck her. She began to walk slowly toward Jon. As she did, the letters looked more and more familiar. Her breath

398

caught in her throat. "Oh, Mitch," she cried. Mitch moved to her side.

A swift glance told him what his son held in his hands. "My letters," he said. "Good God, he has my letters!"

Neither of them knew how this miracle had come about, but both of them went to Jon to kneel beside him.

"Will you read me the story papers, Mommy?"

Whitney could hardly speak. Mitch reached out to touch the letters. They were a lifeline and it seemed more of a miracle that his son had somehow found them. He could ask all the questions later. For now he had to make sure they were real.

"Can I see the letters, Jon?"

Jon looked at him as if deciding, then he handed the letters to Mitch.

Whitney's eyes were glued to them, because she recognized some of her own among them and the truth finally dawned. She lifted her eyes to meet Mitch's as he tried to smile.

"Don't worry, Jon," Mitch said softly, his eyes still locked with Whitney's. "Your mother . . . and I will be happy to read the story letters to you. Very happy."

Twenty-nine

Tears filled Whitney's eyes and she couldn't speak. Mitch reached out a trembling hand and brushed one away. He wasn't even sure what to say, because he wasn't sure why she was crying.

"Well, Whitney . . . where do we go now?" he asked hopefully.

"It was lies, Mitch," Whitney sobbed. "She stole my life. The life I had planned with you. All that time she let me believe . . ."

Mitch took her in his arms, aware of her pain and shock. "It's over, Whitney," he said tenderly. "We have to put it behind us. Maybe we have to learn to forgive. She lived in another time and I guess, by her standards, she was doing what she thought best for you. It was out of love, Whitney. We have to think that."

"And us . . . all the pain. How can you forgive that?"

"Easy. I love you. I can forgive you for just about anything, except leaving me. Don't you think it's time we read Jon's story letters to him?" He kissed away another runaway tear. "I want you to read them. Just so you really know there wasn't a day that I didn't love you and want you."

"And then, Mitch? What then?"

"Then we put our son to bed and plan our future . . . together. The way it should have been years

400

ago, and the way it will be from now on."

Whitney nodded. They took Jon downstairs and found that Addy and Berdine had already gone. Neither questioned why, as both were sure Berdine must have sent Jon up to them.

Whitney found a comfortable seat next to the fire and took Jon on her lap. Tenderly she opened the first of Mitch's letters. Mitch took Whitney's letters and set them aside to read by himself.

By the time Whitney had finished reading the last letter, Jon was asleep. Her voice was thick with tears and her heart ached — for her mother's lost dreams, and then for her own.

Mitch sat quietly, watching Whitney. The glow of the dying fire was caught in the tears on her face, and he wanted to reach out to find some way to comfort her.

Whitney knew they needed to talk, to touch.

"Want me to carry him?" Mitch offered.

"I don't know if you can."

"Whitney," Mitch grinned, "I'm not hurt as badly as I let you think. I just wanted to stay here as long as I could."

He took Jon gently from her arms and carried him upstairs to tuck him safely in bed. When he came back down Whitney was seated on the floor beside the box in which, it was obvious, Jon had found the letters. She was caressing the box gently.

"What if I had never taken it from the house? If I had never saved it?" She looked up at Mitch, "I would never have known. What if she had destroyed them . . . oh, Mitch . . ."

Mitch went to her and bent to take both of her hands and draw her up beside him.

"But we do know. You have to stop looking back, Whitney. Let's pretend the old dreams are still real. We've met and fallen in love. We can have all the tomorrows we want, if we want. Do you want to

401

start over? We can begin again and build our own world."

"Yes," she whispered. "Yes, I do. Oh, Mitch, I've been so cruel, so . . ."

"No! We're not looking back, remember?" He lifted the lid of the music box and let the old familiar sound fill the room. Then he turned to her, and she walked into his arms with a new confidence. The embrace was gentle, and the first touch, when their lips met, was like their first kiss shared beneath the cottonwoods so long ago. Their mouths blended as they reached back in time to taste again the rare magic.

Whitney closed her eyes, envisioning how it had been on those sultry and passionate nights. Mitch's touch recalled the sweet fulfilling need that was slowly building deep inside her.

Whitney yearned to feel his strong, firm-muscled body against her own, and to give herself unreservedly to him. Her eyes were limpid pools of deep blue as she looked up into his. There was no doubt that his feelings matched hers—she could clearly see the depth of the fire blazing in his eyes.

"Can we return to the past, Mitch?" she pleaded urgently. "Will it be the same? Can we wash away those ugly years of separation if we're together now?"

"We can," he said, his voice was thick with passion, "and we will." He took her hand and they walked up the stairs.

Mitch closed the bedroom door behind them. In the mellow glow of lamplight Whitney turned to face him. Then she began to slowly remove her clothes. He watched in utter fascination, savoring every precious moment.

Mitch's heart leaped and started the blood surging in his veins, his long-starved passion seizing control of his body. This was Whitney—warm, responsive, capable of setting his very being on fire.

Only when she stood before him, her naked body aglow and her hair spilling about her shoulders, did Mitch move. His eyes held hers while his fingers moved to the buttons of his shirt. In a moment his brown shoulders gleamed naked. He bent to yank off his boots and soon the rest of his clothes were tossed aside.

Then he came to her and they stood, barely touching. He bent his head to taste her warm, parted lips. Slowly, he tasted, savored, and explored their willing softness. Then his mouth drifted to the soft curve of her throat and shoulder.

They sank to the bed together and Mitch rolled onto his back, lifting her with him until she lay atop him, her soft breasts pressed to his chest and the cloud of her blond hair enclosing them.

But Whitney turned aggressor now. She pressed kisses against the line of his throat, the curve of his jaw, his cheeks, then his mouth with a crushing urgency that readily conveyed their growing impatience.

Her hands slid over his body to his lean thighs and the hot blood shot through his loins and thudded through him, cauterizing his mind with a ravaging need.

Mitch turned, pulling her half-beneath him, and his mouth claimed hers again in a rapacious, twisting, devouring, and now well-remembered hunger.

His hands and lips glided over her silky flesh with the bold confidence of a man who had no doubts about himself. Whitney was swept by the bittersweet memories that plucked at the strings of her senses and responded with moaning sighs. She began to writhe in his arms, seeking that ultimate union, that moment when they would know the old promise lived. It was then that Mitch entered her, their eyes melding as he plunged with bold, fierce strokes. A tide of emotion washed through Whitney. Her whole being came alive with pulsing joy.

At first, his strokes were smooth and languid, matching her own. But soon it was not enough and became a wild, frenzied search for fulfillment. She arched against him, answering his hard, thrusting hips with a fervor equal to his.

She gasped as an overwhelming orgasm lifted them both to a place where the stars sparkled in a blinding display. She clung to him as they soared together, their lips blended in the warm afterglow of passion as they tumbled into peace and contentment.

It was the longed-for passion and yet it was new, for neither was a child anymore. It was sweeter for that, for they knew it for the infinitely precious thing it was. It could be lost so easily.

Whitney wanted to weep for what they had missed, but her heart could only rejoice in the new sweet thing that had been found.

Mitch held her close, brushing an errant curl from her cheek and replacing it with a tender kiss. "I love you, Whitney," he murmured. "God, how I love you. I was so afraid I would never get you back. I was lost for so long."

"Mitch, I'm so sorry."

He lifted his head. "I guess both of us are sorry, Whitney. I didn't mean to make it sound like you were guilty of something. You were caught in the same web of lies as I. But it's all over now."

He lay on his back and drew her snugly against him. She rested her head on his shoulder.

"Now we have everything, Whitney, everything. I have you, and Jon . . . speaking of Jon," he added quietly, "I want to tell him I'm his father."

"I thought you already had."

"No, I . . . I wasn't sure how you might feel about that. So I waited and hoped."

"When do you want to tell him?"

"As soon as he opens those beautiful eyes."

"Wonderful."

"I have a question for you now."

"What?"

"When are you going to marry me? I want to get this done right so you can't slip through my fingers again. Besides, I want to be your husband, sharing every day and every night with you. On top of that, I want to start being Jon's father."

"And I want to start being your wife," she whispered as she pressed a kiss against his warm flesh. "Oh, Mitch, I love you so much, and we have so much lost time to make up for."

He twisted so he could look down at her. "Then let's get married in the morning."

This brought her head up quickly and filled her eyes with shock. "In the morning! Mitch!"

"It's not so quick," he chuckled. "We were promised to each other for years. That's a long enough engagement for anyone."

"Mitch, I can't be ready that fast. At least I'd like to make a new dress, or do you want me to be married in an old one?"

"I'll take you wrapped in a sack," he laughed. "But I understand how you feel. How long is it going to take you to get ready?"

"I have to ask Berdine to help me . . . and . . ." Mitch groaned suddenly. "What is it? Are you in pain?"

"No," he responded with a grin. "I was just thinking about Lazarus's reaction when he finds me here in the morning. Do you think he'll let me explain before he breaks me in two? I'm in no condition to give him much of a fight."

"Lazarus has always been there to protect me," Whitney giggled. "I believe he has almost fatherly rights."

Mitch's smile faded and his eyes held hers. "I want to be here to protect you from now on, Whitney . . . as I should have been before. Do you think Lazarus will let me encroach on his rights a bit?"

"Lazarus will learn to know and care about you, too, Mitch, as he did for me. You can't blame him for how he feels."

"I don't blame him. I'm grateful to him. I'll just have to convince him we're right for each other."

"Well, Mr. Politician, if anyone can, you can."

"Speaking of politics, how do you feel about being a politician's wife?"

"Wonderfully excited. I expect great things from you, Mitchell Flannery."

"Lord, Whitney, if I loved you like a boy before, that has changed. I love you now as a man." He leaned on one elbow and gazed down into her eyes. "You're all I want . . . all I need." He kissed her deeply, drugging her senses until she put her arm about his neck and urged the kiss to deeper depths. Soon they were lost to a new building passion. They let it draw them into the wonder of the powerful thing that made them one.

Lazarus was already asleep when Berdine and Addy came in, and Berdine cautioned Addy to silence. "It best be tol' by Miz Whitney in de mawnin'. Yo' tell him now, he might jes' toss dat boy out befo' he git a chance to explain. Dose two need some time to git all dey gots to talk about straightened out."

"Yo' ain't mad at me?"

"Mad at yo', fo' what?"

"On account ah never tol' Miz Whitney 'bout dose letters."

"Ah kin understand. Yo' pow'ful scared of Miz

406

Hope. But she gone now, rest her soul, an' dey hain't nuthin' to be afraid of no mo'."

"Miz Whitney, an' Mr. Flannery, dey gwine understand?"

"Gal, if what's goin' on is what ah think is goin' on over to dat house, dey gonna have 'nuf stars in dey eyes tomorrow. Dey gonna forgive anybody an' anything at all." Berdine laughed and Addy was satisfied. As long as Whitney and Lazarus weren't angry and Berdine was laughing, her world was back to normal.

Addy found her way to bed, but Berdine sat before the dying fire for a long time. She let her thoughts roam back to the days right after the war when Whitney had struggled so hard.

Maybe, she thought, all in all, it might have been good for her. She remembered the Whitney of old and wondered if she would have really fit in Mitch Flannery's life. She had been a spoiled, willful child. Now she was indeed a woman of great depth and compassion.

It would be good for Jon as well. No one knew the brutality of society's conventions as well as Berdine did. The day would have come when Jon would have known that all of Lazarus's fatherly attention didn't make him a father. No, Jon needed Mitch as much as Whitney did and Berdine was certain that Mitch needed them even more. Otherwise he would have given up long ago.

She had once told Lazarus to remain silent, that the good Lord would work things out according to His own plan. Well, it had come to pass.

Both Whitney and Mitch had gone through hell, but it had remolded them somehow into finer people. It took the fire to burn away the chaff and make the new growth stronger.

She was content. Once again she would see happiness about them and peace reign. She closed her

407

eyes and murmured the thankful prayers she had said every night of her life.

Whitney awoke with the first rays of the sun. Dawn was just breaking and through the window she could see the dark veil of night beginning to give way.

She was curled against Mitch's body and he had one arm about her possessively, as if even in sleep something could take her away.

But Whitney didn't stir. She wanted this silent time to bask in the glow of this new beginning. She could feel the warmth of Mitch's body and she knew the rightness of it. She refused to think again of wasted years. Their lives would begin tomorrow. Tomorrow? No, they began last night. Last night they had surrendered to a torrential night of making love and rediscovering each other. Today would have its own rewards. Mitch wanted to tell Jon the truth and she wanted to help him. Then he had asked her to go home with him, and she had some trepidations. She was nervous about the reception she might get. They all knew that since Mitch's arrival she had repelled him in every way she possibly could. Their sudden "discovery" of each other might not quite be believed by those who had seen Mitch hurt before. Mitch was going to have a hard enough time explaining his battered condition to his family, much less a fiancée.

But a new idea surfaced. Mitch hadn't told her who was responsible for the attack. It was obvious that he didn't want to. Surely he wouldn't try to seek revenge himself. This idea scared her and her body grew tense.

Mitch had been awake, too, but remained quiet, content just to hold her. He knew when she had awakened and let her enjoy this peaceful time. Then

408

he felt the tenseness and knew her thoughts were not entirely pleasant. He drew her tighter to him.

"What are you thinking?" he whispered, brushing a light kiss on her bare shoulder that sent shivers down her spine. She felt so secure in his strong arms—she relaxed against him.

"I didn't know you were awake."

"I have been for a while, but I didn't want to move. It was so wonderful just holding you. You feel good, all soft and warm and curved against me. But you still didn't answer my question. What were you thinking?"

She turned so she could look up at him. "Nothing important."

"It is to me. I want to know every thought, every beat of your heart. I can't get enough of you."

"Then why waste time on random thoughts?" she whispered as she reached up and drew his head down to hers. The kiss forced everything from his mind for the moment except the loving woman he held in his arms. Then it occurred to him that she had evaded him—smooth as syrup. He released her lips slowly and reluctantly.

"Because I don't think they were so random," he insisted. "You were scared for a minute, I could feel it. Why were you frightened?"

"It's foolishness, Mitch, I . . ."

"There's nothing foolish if it frightens you. I want to know, Whitney." He held her tight and his eyes told her he wasn't about to back down.

Much against her will she told him what had crossed her mind.

"I'm not going off waving a gun and crying vengeance, if that's what you mean. There are better ways. I can win the election, for one, which would make the attack useless." He saw the relief in her eyes. "And as for my family, that's one thing you don't have to worry about. They adore Jon, and they won't be able to help loving you as well. My mother has been, to say the least, anxious. She's dying to meet you."

"Then we go today?"

"Absolutely."

"You seem to have recovered quickly," she remarked, smiling up at him. "No aches or pains?" Her hands were moving lightly over his back.

"I'm developing an ache rapidly," he said huskily. "I may need some soothing before I can get out of this bed."

"Anything to make you well, my love." She was pleased with his soft laugh as he bent to kiss her.

When they came downstairs it was late morning. The house was still empty which surprised Whitney, but only for a moment. Then she realized that Berdine had kept everyone away. They exchanged glances and laughed.

"Dear Berdine," Whitney said. "She always seems to know what's in everyone's mind. She must have known . . ."

"She saw the letters and put two and two together," Mitch chuckled. "But I must thank her."

"Shall we go and see if our son is ready for a ride?"

"Maybe Berdine has a breakfast to match that supper last night."

"Looks to me like Berdine found the way to your heart."

"The way she cooks, she's welcome there anytime."

They crossed to the other cabin, finding Jon and Addy seated at the table and Berdine filling their plates. Lazarus was noticeably absent, and Mitch wasn't ready for the answer he might get if he asked about him.

Whitney went straight to Berdine and hugged her

410

tight. Berdine smiled over her head at Mitch while she returned the embrace. "Y'all jes' in time fo' breakfast."

"I'm famished," Mitch said agreeably as he sat down beside Jon.

"Ah 'spects," Berdine murmured with laughter in her eyes as she regarded Whitney's pink cheeks.

Addy rose and came to Whitney at once. "Miz Whitney, ah gots to tell yo'. Yo' gots to fo'give me. Ah din mean to do yo' no harm." She went on to confess about her part in the deception.

"It's all right, Addy. There's no way to change what happened and it all worked out. So it's best we forget it. I've forgiven my mother because I know she loved me. I forgive you because I know you love us, too. We won't talk any more about it."

"Jon, after breakfast your mother and I are going over to Grandma's. Want to go?" Mitch asked.

Jon nodded and looked up at Mitch. "Is she Mommy's grandma, too?"

"No, she's not. She's my mother."

"Oh."

"Maybe after we get there, you and I can take a walk down to the pond. Would you like that?"

"Uh huh. Can we go fishin' like we did last time?"

"Maybe. We'll see. I have something special I want to tell you."

Jon seemed pleased to share a confidence with this man he was growing so fond of. Whitney watched and her heart filled with overwhelming satisfaction. This was what she had always wanted. Now, with all the suffering and pain behind them, the three of them could look forward to a future that promised so much more today than it had yesterday. Mitch tipped his head to look at her and smiled. He knew where her thoughts lay.

Berdine wished Lazarus hadn't left, as he was still

411

uncertain and suspicious. He would have to see a lot more before he came around to trusting Mitch. Berdine was sure he would keep a close eye on Whitney for a long time.

Mitch didn't mention Lazarus. In time, he thought, he would prove to him that he and Whitney had always belonged together. Maybe then he would give Mitch what he wanted, respect and friendship.

Breakfast was over soon, and Mitch went to the stable to saddle two horses. Whitney had chosen to ride instead of taking a buggy. Jon would ride with Mitch.

While he was gone Whitney spoke to Berdine.

"Is Lazarus angry, Berdine?"

"No, he jes' doan understan' yet. He been watchin' yo' too long to let go. One day he come round. One day he decide Mitch not gwine hurt yo' no mo'. Den it be all right. Yo' jes' be patient. Dis much has worked out, de rest gwine work out, too. Yo' gots another question to answer first."

"What?"

"What yo' gwine say to Trent Donnelley when he come here an' 'spects yo' to go wif him?"

"The truth, Berdine. It's all I can say."

"Ah 'spects yo' right. Only . . ."

"Only what?"

"Only ah doan think he gwine to take it easy. He hate Mitch Flannery nuf right now. He gwine hate him mo'. Ah doan think he be de kind of man what doan do sumthin' 'bout it. Yo' an' Mitch . . . yo' best be careful."

"Trent? Berdine, he's not vicious. What could he do . . . ?" She paused, as the thought of Mitch's attack came to her. She looked at Berdine, "No, it's not possible."

"Ah dint say it be. Ah jes' said to be real careful."

"I'll ask Mitch."

"Dint yo' already ask?"

"Yes, he said he didn't know."

"Den let it go. Let him play out dis game by hisself."

"I can't believe it, Berdine. Trent is too fine a gentleman. He's not behind this. He'll understand about Mitch and me when I tell him. He'll let me go."

Mitch came, leading the horses, and Whitney went down the steps to meet him. She never heard Berdine's last words. "Ah jes' wouldn't be too sure of dat. No suh, ah jes' wouldn't." Berdine turned and walked back into the house.

The sound of horses approaching drew Caryn Flannery to the window. It took no time to recognize Mitch, from the way he rode, and she was sure he had Jon with him. But he was riding with someone she didn't recognize. It looked like a woman . . . a woman . . . who? She caught her breath. Could it be? Could Mitch finally have what he had wanted for so long, what had obsessed him since the moment he had come home?

Hastily she dried her hands and went to the door. She knew Mitch would be amused at her excitement, but if this was Whitney Clayborn, then she wanted her to know she was more than welcome.

They rode up to the porch. Mitch dismounted and lifted Jon down and he promptly ran to Caryn, who caught him up in her arms and hugged him. Whitney could see that he had grown very attached to her. It brought tears to her eyes, because it made her think of her mother and the bitter, unhappy end to her life. It was too late for all that, but not too late to give Jon some semblance of a real family. She dismounted slowly and remained still.

Caryn slid Jon to the ground, then looked at Whitney.

"And you are Whitney," Caryn said softly. "How pretty you are. I'm so glad to finally be able to welcome you here." Caryn extended her hand to Whitney, who moved forward to take it.

"Thank you," was all Whitney could manage to say.

"Well," Caryn said, brushing a tear from her cheek. "Come in, come in." She swallowed the lump in her throat. "Here we are standing on the porch when there's cider and apple pie inside. I'm sure Mitch can eat a piece or two."

"You know I can," Mitch laughed. He put an arm about Whitney's waist and they followed Caryn and Jon into the house.

"Where is everybody?" Mitch asked.

"Oh, don't worry, they knew I was baking this pie this morning. You can count on them tramping in soon. Whitney, please sit down, sit down here and let me get you some pie."

"Let me help," Whitney said quickly. She was much too nervous to sit and be waited on.

"Best set seven places."

"Seven?"

"Yes, the four of us," Caryn replied with a grin, "and the three men who will smell that pie for a mile."

As if they heard her, the sound of male voices drifted in and the door opened, revealing Stuart, Morgan, and Shawn. They were laughing, but the laughter ceased when they realized they had a guest.

"Shawn!" Jon cried. He jumped from his seat and ran to Shawn, who swung him up in his strong arms.

"Jon! Good to see you, boy. Hey, I'll bet this pie was made for you."

414

Jon nodded happily, secure in the knowledge that everything in this house revolved around him. Whitney stood close to Mitch, who took her hand in his. "Pa, this is Whitney."

Stuart went to her. When she looked up at him she realized how much like the father the son was. He had the same sparkling humor in his eyes and was an older replica of Mitch.

"We've been waiting a long time to meet you, Whitney girl. Now maybe my son can get his life going again." When Whitney smiled, Stuart chuckled softly, reached for her, and embraced her. Then he kissed her cheek. "So I was right?"

"Yes," Whitney said softly. "You were right."

Both brothers welcomed Whitney with enthusiasm. She was pink cheeked and laughing when they finally sat down to eat the pie.

Later in the day Mitch took Jon for a walk by the pond in the hope that he could explain their new relationship and that one day soon the three of them would live together. He knew he was welcome as a friend, but would he be welcome as a permanent part of his life? Jon could think of him as a threat to his own relationship with his mother. Mitch knew he would have to use some finesse to make Jon understand.

The other three men had chores to do, leaving Caryn and Whitney alone.

"Jon is so very precious, Whitney. I'm glad you let us share his life. We have really enjoyed him."

"He can be a little devil when he wants to."

"Somewhat like his father," Caryn replied, laughing. "If one looked in Mitch's eyes at that age, one would see the devil peeking out."

"Tell me about Mitch as a boy."

"It will be our secret?"

"Yes," Whitney said merrily. "I want to know all about him, even the bad."

415

They talked for over two hours, laughing together, and Whitney listened carefully, beginning to know Mitch better than ever.

Jon and Mitch had carried their fishing poles to the pond. Not that Mitch expected to catch a fish—he was too excited to stay still or quiet long enough. But Jon was obviously enjoying himself. Then Mitch began to weave the truth into his words.

It totally amazed Mitch that Jon accepted what he said so easily. He seemed delighted at the idea that Mitch would live with them and calling him Daddy was just fine with him.

The afternoon waned and the sun set low on the horizon. Mitch sat on the grassy edge of the pond with Jon on his lap.

"Look, Jon." Mitch pointed to the sun that was slowly going down. "Going . . . going . . . gone," Mitch said as the sun sank out of sight. He watched Jon's reaction—he was awed.

"Daddy, when I get as big as you can I do that?"

"Do what?"

"Make the sun go to bed."

Mitch laughed. He'd never felt happier in his life. His son actually thought he could make the sun rise and set. It would be something to have to live up to that. He stood and swung Jon up in his arm. Then he bent to pick up the two poles.

"I guess we'd better get home. Your mother will be waiting. What excuse do we have for catching no fish?"

"The sun went to sleep and it got dark, so the fish had to go to sleep, too," Jon said positively.

Now Mitch really laughed. He was going to have to think quick to be able to keep up with his son.

When they drew close to the house Mitch could see Whitney on the porch waiting for them. He had to believe at this moment that no man in the world could be happier than he was.

When Whitney saw them she came down from the porch and walked to meet them. With his arm about her the three walked back to the house together.

Thirty

The ride home was quiet. Jon slept in Mitch's arms and Whitney rode close by. Of course, Mitch knew they had a lot of problems to solve and that Whitney still had to tell Trent Donnelley about them—but that pleased him. What scared him was Donnelley's violence; he had felt it himself and had the bruises to show for it. Was Trent Donnelley the kind who would lash out at Whitney?

What worried him also was the real reason behind Trent's attachment to Whitney. He knew in the back of his mind there was a much bigger reason than love. He wished he knew where Keith was hiding out and why. He would have loved to have gotten some ideas from him.

He put all the questions out of his mind because they had arrived home . . . home. It sounded wonderful.

Whitney put Jon to bed while Mitch took the horses to the barn. When he swung the doors open a lantern hanging from a nearby stall shed a pale light. A lantern was rarely left lit because of the fear of fire, so Mitch knew someone was there, and he was pretty sure it was . . . Lazarus.

"Lazarus?" he called softly.

Lazarus stepped out of one of the stalls. He didn't seem surprised so Mitch knew at once he had been waiting to talk to him alone. Lazarus took the reins of one of the horses and led him to a stall. Mitch led his to one opposite Lazarus and began to unsaddle it.

"You have something to say, Lazarus, you may as well get it off your chest."

"Ah jes' needs to know. Yo' plannin' on stayin' dis time? 'Cause iffen yo' ain't, better yo' go now. If yo' hurts her again . . . an' dat boy . . ."

"That boy is my son, and I don't intend to hurt him. What I do intend to do is marry Whitney as soon as possible."

"Yo' means dat?"

"I made you a wager once, Lazarus, a long time ago. Well, I'm still here, and I intend to do exactly what I said. One day you'll have to admit that this has been right all along."

Lazarus came out of the stall. His immense size made Mitch a bit skittish. He was no match for Lazarus on his best day, and this was certainly not one of his best. He waited for Lazarus to say whatever was on his mind.

"Ah been listenin', an' watchin'. Berdine tell me what she see in Miz Whitney's face. Berdine tol' me 'bout dose letters, too. Ah comes out here to think, an' it been worryin' mah mind fo' hours. Now ah gots to say it. Ah guess dose letters done prove we was wrong. Yo' makes her happy . . . den . . . mebbe ah was outta place."

Mitch could not help but grin. This was as close as Lazarus could come to an apology. He planned on pushing it as far as he could for the sheer pleasure of it. He extended his hand and looked straight at Lazarus in open challenge. Lazarus took it. They looked at each other for a minute, then both laughed.

"Lazarus, it's taken five years to do it, but by God I got you to take my hand, and to admit I'm not what you thought I was, and I accomplished them both in one night. This calls for a celebration. Come on in and have one drink with me."

Lazarus nodded and the two started toward the house. Whitney had just come downstairs from tucking Jon in.

"Do you have any of that brandy left, Whitney?"

"Yes, about half a bottle."

"Well, Lazarus and I have to drink a toast."

Whitney looked at Mitch suspiciously, but she got the bottle and poured the drinks. Mitch handed one to Lazarus, then he touched his glass to Lazarus's.

"Here's to trust, respect, and the future." Lazarus smiled back and drank.

"Ah'll go along now," Lazarus said. "Ah 'spects yo' two gots a lot to talk about."

Before Whitney could stop him he set his glass down and left. Mitch had no thought of trying to stop him. To all intents and purposes Lazarus had just given his seal of approval to his presence in Whitney's life again.

"What was that all about?" Whitney asked.

"Nothing much, just a little wager." He looked at her then chuckled. "All right, I'll confess. Lazarus has been like a wall I had to climb over if I wanted to reach you. I just climbed that wall, that's all. To tell you the truth I never felt better about things than I do now."

She looped her arms about his neck and stood on tiptoe to kiss him so fervently that he could feel every nerve responding. When the kiss ended she was smiling.

"So you feel good, do you?"

"I have to admit, you feel better," he chuckled.

"Do you always get your way, Mitch Flannery?"

"I try, I try. Wonderful things are worth fighting for."

His arms drew her closer and this time the kiss was more heated. Pressed against him, Whitney returned his kiss with enough enthusiasm to leave him breathless.

420

"Ummm," he murmured, "it's a long way home."

"I suppose," she said, looking innocent, "you'd be awfully tired by the time you got there."

"Not to mention my poor horse," he agreed.

"I imagine you wouldn't mind sleeping on the couch."

He eyed the couch with a raised eyebrow. "It's pretty narrow. Just think of how my poor bruised body would feel by morning."

"You have a suggestion?"

"Well, you have a nice big bed upstairs," he began.

"Uh huh," she encouraged.

"And you're so small."

"Uh huh."

"That should certainly leave a little room."

"And what if Jon should find you there?"

"Doesn't he sleep with you when he doesn't feel well?"

"Yes, sometimes," she answered, looking puzzled.

"Well, just look at me. He'd understand that completely. I need comforting, woman . . . . I need you."

"I wouldn't think of sending your poor abused body out into the dark night," she said softly. "That body means a lot to me." She drew his head down for another deep and hungry kiss. This time there could be only one end to it, and they both knew it. Without another word he swept her up in his arms and walked up the stairs.

They had time, precious time, and they took all of it. They undressed each other with lingering fingers, caressing, memorizing every line, every curve of sweet-tasting flesh.

Lips soon replaced hands and soft murmurs of love filled the quiet room. After a long while, when their joyous lovemaking had exhausted them both, they slept in each other's arms.

* * *

The next morning Mitch woke to find the bed empty. He rose and dressed quickly. The days were too short to waste them in a bed that didn't have Whitney in it.

He walked down the hall and gently opened the door to Jon's room. He was still curled deep in his blankets, sound asleep. Good. It would give Whitney and him a chance to talk and make plans. He, for one, would try for a quick marriage.

He started down the stairs, but at the top he stopped. Voices came from below and both of them were familiar. One was Whitney and the other was Trent Donnelley.

Whitney had awakened just at dawn, too happy and excited to sleep any longer. She rose, checked on Jon, and went downstairs. Her plan was to make breakfast and carry it upstairs. She was sure Jon would wander in and find Mitch and her and they could have some time, just the three of them, to get Jon used to having Mitch around. She didn't want Jon to feel jealous or left out. It would be fun . . . . it would be a beginning.

She moved around the kitchen making the meal as quietly as she could. Sunlight flooded the room before Whitney picked up the tray and started toward the stairs.

Before she put her foot on the first step a knock sounded on the door. She smiled. Lazarus, Berdine, and Addy must know Mitch was still there. They were knocking to keep from surprising them.

She set the tray on a stand and walked to the door, opening it wide as she spoke. "Good morning, it's . . ."

"Good morning, Whitney," Trent said casually. "I haven't seen you in nearly a week. I thought I'd stop by and talk about our future. I hope you've decided

422

about the wedding and don't want to put it off until after the election."

"Trent," Whitney began, surprised at her own calmness, "I'm glad you came. I have something very important to talk to you about."

"Our wedding?" Trent smiled. "What could be more important than that?" He walked inside and she closed the door and followed him into the parlor.

"I'm afraid it's not our wedding. Trent, I'm not going to marry you. I've made up my mind—new and extenuating circumstances have changed everything."

"What circumstances?"

"I told you before that Mitch is Jon's father."

"Yes, and I told you it made no difference."

"But it does, Trent."

"Why? He ran off and left you when he found out you were carrying his child."

"That's what I thought, Trent. But . . . it seems that's not what happened. Please, will you let me explain?"

"All right, I'm listening."

Whitney took a deep breath, then told Trent about the terrible mistake she had made and how she had misjudged Mitch. It had been her mother who had intervened, hiding the letters she and Mitch had written to each other. "It was such a terrible and tragic thing, and if the hand of fate had not allowed my mother to hide, rather than destroy, the letters, I might never have known."

"And that changes everything?" Trent was fighting to control his anger.

"Of course it changes everything."

"You're not being fair to me, Whitney."

"I'm sorry, Trent, I never meant to hurt you. But marriage must be . . . well . . ."

"You mean you must love whoever you marry and you don't love me. But passion and love shouldn't be mistaken for each other."

"It was not just passion, Trent," Whitney said firmly. She put her hand on his arm. "I don't want us to be enemies, Trent, and maybe that would have happened if we had married. In the end it would have made neither of us happy."

"And you believe you'll be happy with him?"

"I am. Jon has grown to care for him, too. After all, he is Jon's father."

"And he would have taken him from you. Are you sure this isn't your only reason? That you don't still believe he deserted you? He wants his son—and to defeat me."

"I don't really believe that anymore. Mitch never tried to do anything but be with Jon."

"You've regretted it before, you're going to do it again. He's not the man you think he is."

"I don't believe that either. But one way or the other it's up to me to find out. I've made up my mind and it's final."

"Then there isn't much left I can say, is there?" Trent asked quietly. He walked to the door, then turned to look at her. "But you'll regret it, Whitney. You'll be sorry Mitch Flannery ever came back to Holly Hill." He opened the door and left, leaving Whitney with a sudden chilled feeling as if somehow his threat could harm those she loved. For one moment she was frightened, then she heard footsteps on the stairs.

Mitch had heard only the last few words of the conversation, then the closing of the door as he started downstairs. Trent was much more of a threat than Whitney could imagine, and Mitch meant to be there in case Trent had a violent reaction. He was sure Whitney had told him the truth—he was also sure Trent Donnelley was not the kind of man to take any kind of rejection easily. Especially if Mitch were part of it.

When he walked into the room, he thought he saw

fear etched on Whitney's face. It fled too fast for Mitch to be really sure.

"Whitney, what is it? What did he say?"

"You heard?"

"Only the end, a few words. He left before I could come down. What happened? I didn't know you expected him."

"I didn't. But maybe it's better that he came. This way there can be no problems. I told him I couldn't marry him, that you and I were together."

"I'll bet he took that well."

"Actually, he did. He only said that he was certain I would regret it."

Mitch put his arms around her. "You won't regret it, Whitney. I almost lost you. I don't intend to do anything to jeopardize your love again. I've got a family any man would envy, and I won't lose it."

"Then I don't think we have anything to worry about," Whitney replied as she moved tighter against him and her eyes grew warm and inviting. He could not resist kissing her deeply. When the kiss ended Whitney was smiling.

"I was bringing you breakfast in bed."

"You're spoiling me."

"As much as I can. I thought we'd hear the sound of little feet soon, and we could have some time, just the three of us."

"I'm not above being enticed back into bed."

"Too late. If I'm not mistaken I hear those little feet right now." She laughed at Mitch's mock scowl as he released her. She walked to the stairs as Jon jumped the last two steps into her arms—all three of them were laughing.

Mitch smiled, but inside the fear gnawed at him that they had not seen the last of Trent Donnelley. He had given up much too easily. They would have to be very careful from now on. It was one thing to attack him, but being close to him, Whitney and Jon might be jeopardized as well. He would do anything in his power to protect them. He knew that Trent might know that as well. If Trent wanted something that Whitney had, and Mitch was sure he did, then nothing would stop him from going after it. He wished he knew what it was. If there was just some way to find Keith he might have the answer, but Keith seemed to have vanished.

Trent rode along slowly, trying to control the seething anger that ate at him. Mitch Flannery had spoiled his plans for the last time. The beating had obviously not stopped him, so it was time to play his last card.

Damn that Keith Clayborn, he thought. All his sources told him he was alive and that he had half of the pieces needed to complete the puzzle. He'd gotten close to Whitney for just that purpose, but could not get his hands on the letters Keith had written home. He was sure what he wanted was there.

He'd had Whitney's house, the area around it, and the old plantation site watched, but there had been no sign of him. He had been certain Keith would contact his sister just to get the letters back, and when he did Trent would have had him, if it hadn't been for Mitch's inopportune appearance.

Trent could have gotten the letters himself, but Mitch was a roadblock. And that huge black, Lazarus, had been too close to attempt a break-in. Now he had to resort to desperate measures. He would get rid of Mitch Flannery first. Then, if he had to, he would force Whitney to give him the letters. If that angered her brother and he came after him, so much the better. He would kill the last person, besides himself, who knew where the puzzle led.

With Mitch gone and Keith dead, Whitney would have little choice but to do what he wanted — other-

426

wise her son could be used to bend her will. As for Lazarus . . . despite how watchful he was, there would be a way to eliminate him.

Trent rode straight into town to his office. He removed the papers from the safe and sat at his desk. Hours ticked by while he very carefully altered them. When he was finished it would be clear to anyone who read them that Mitch Flannery was indeed a double agent—a spy who had preyed on both sides for profit. The wealth Mitch had accumulated would be the most damaging evidence against him.

Once Mitch was arrested Trent would see to it that the town was stirred to the boiling point, leading to a mob that would effectively take Mitch Flannery out of his life forever . . . in fact, Trent chuckled, out of life altogether.

Once he was satisfied that the papers were incriminating enough, he left his office and walked to the *Chronicle*.

He found Andrew Crocket and Douglas Banks in deep conversation. Douglas, the owner and force behind the *Chronicle,* was an ambitious and cold-hearted man. He had made his money from the war by smuggling contraband from England to the South and selling medicine and clothing at a very large profit, none of which found its way to the Confederacy.

A self-made newspaper man, he used his wealth and his paper like a club. He was a tall, thin man who gave the impression of a body whose spirit was already dead. His skin was an ashen shade, his eyes were pale gray, and his hair was gray. A gray man who could deal a bloody and merciless blow whenever and however he chose.

"Good afternoon, gentlemen," Trent said.

"Trent." Andrew smiled a half smile, but his eyes were narrow and watchful. "Are you ready for your speech tomorrow night? I hear Mitch Flannery is speaking at the social center. The man

427

is running you a pretty stiff race."

"Don't let it worry you, Andrew. I'll take care of Mitch Flannery."

"I hope you get around to it pretty soon," Douglas said. "The man is gaining ground every day, and that blasted rag, the *Sentinel,* is more support than I thought it would be. If you can bring down Flannery, I can use their association with him to finally rid myself of the Anderson brothers and that paper of theirs."

"Don't get in an uproar, Douglas," Trent remarked complacently. "I've run across some evidence that will not only put Mitch Flannery out of the race, but will have him arrested and most likely hanged."

"Evidence? What kind of evidence?" Douglas was immediately alert. "And what kind of criminal act could the esteemed Mitchell Flannery have committed that the town would want to see him hanged?"

"The war hasn't been over long enough that the sting of defeat doesn't still hurt."

"What has that to do with our problem?"

"What would incense the citizens more, or the law more, than a Union sympathizer? One who decided to wear the uniform of both North and South to betray his own . . . and for profit, I might add."

"Lord, Lord," Douglas muttered. "I'd love to have some proof of that. I'd bury him, by God, I'd bury him."

Trent reached into his pocket and withdrew the papers. He tossed them across the desk to Douglas, who reached for them avidly. Trent smiled, still unaware that Andrew was watching him quietly through narrowed, knowing eyes.

Douglas opened the papers and read, drumming his fingers on the desk as he did so. Trent just sat quietly, sure his work had been done carefully. He was just as sure this ammunition would eliminate

428

Mitch Flannery, leaving the way clear to Whitney and her secrets.

Finally Douglas sat back in his chair with a satisfied smile. "Where did you get all this proof?"

"Does it matter?"

"Not a whit. I'll write my first editorial tomorrow, just in time to be read before he gives that speech. Your words . . ."

"No," Trent interrupted. "I want them to be your words, not mine. If you claim them as an attack by me, the people will take them as such, just another political attack. But if an astute newspaper man like yourself has dug up all this evidence, they'll most likely not only believe you, but sympathize with me. It should put the election in my pocket."

"You're very clever."

"I'm also quick to use an opportunity. Get him arrested, print the evidence, scream to the top of your lungs for justice. All for the life of the man who caused the deaths of our young men in gray and gold. You do that, and I'll stir the right element in town to drag him out and lynch him."

"Don't worry," Douglas said as he rose, "I'll start on this right away. We'll have a blazing editorial for tomorrow evening's paper that'll finish Mitch Flannery." Douglas left the room, carrying the papers. It was only then that Trent turned to Andrew.

"You've been very quiet, Andrew."

"What is there to say? You're an effective opponent, all right. Flannery will certainly know he's been in a fight. You're also very clever, letting someone else shoot the gun you loaded. No one will ever be able to point the finger in your direction."

"If I'm going to get what I want I can't afford to have fingers pointed in my direction. I have to get Flannery out of my way, and permanently."

"Tell me, Trent, where did all this 'evidence' come from?"

"What difference does that make?"

"None," Andrew shrugged. "Not really. Just curious."

"Let's say I've had this evidence for some time."

"Because you knew someday you might need it?"

"Possibly."

"You're formidable, my friend."

"Yes," Trent agreed, "I am. Andrew, if you've thought otherwise, if you thought me weak enough to be played with, manipulated, you were wrong. I know you're a power here." Trent smiled a smile that was deadly. "But one day I'll be a far greater power. It would be folly to forget that, for, as you've just said, I'm a formidable opponent."

Andrew Crocket had always had the confidence that went with his power. He'd always thought that one day he'd pull the strings necessary to create a puppet in power. Now he had just begun to understand that the power was being deftly taken from him. It was the first time in his life Andrew Crocket had ever been afraid of another man . . . but Trent Donnelley was a man without a conscience, and that made him a man to fear.

Keith had second thoughts about leaving the letters with Whitney. If anyone guessed that was where they could be, Whitney would be in danger. He knew there were only two men left who knew what had happened. Himself and the mysterious man he pursued.

He'd followed him as far as Holly Hill and he knew he was somewhere near. He prayed that maybe the man he sought didn't know him by name either.

Still, the more he thought of the letters the more worried he became. He had stayed away and allowed everyone to believe he'd been lost in action because he knew he might lead someone to Whitney. Maybe sending the evidence to Whitney had been just as dangerous.

Keith had a safe hiding place, one that put him in a position to watch the comings and goings, yet near enough to Whitney that he could watch over her.

He'd spent the afternoon quietly out of sight, waiting until nightfall so he could go to Whitney, retrieve the letters, and try to prevent any harm to her.

He was thinking of her, of their parents, and all that had been lost. He knew Whitney was still filled with grief as well and when this was all over he meant to bring together what was left of his family. Him, Whitney, and her son, Jon.

He stood in the darkness and watched cloudy streaks drift across the yellow moon. Then he began to make his way quietly through the woods toward Whitney's house. He moved carefully, but it took him only a few minutes to realize there were others around him. He had narrowly missed one. Were they looking for him? His heart began to pound. Or were they watching whoever came and went at Whitney's? Could it be possible he had been discovered before he could find his quarry? Whitney was in the middle as long as the letters were in her possession. He had to get them.

Whitney and Jon were home alone for a few hours, as Mitch had to ride into town and see to the preparation of the speech he would give the following night. He wanted Whitney to go along, but she, Addy, and Berdine were making Whitney's wedding dress.

"I'll be back before it's too late. I know," he said, "I can't stay here. You're afraid people will talk, and it'll affect the election, but I'm coming back to make sure you and Jon are safe. Then I'll go along home quietly."

"I'll bet you will," Whitney laughed.

"All right," his laugh blended with hers. "So you'll

have to throw me out. But it'll only be for a while. Then I'll be here to stay."

"Mitch, what if you lose this election?"

"Not a chance."

"But what if you do?"

"Then, my sweet, I'll marry you and be the happiest farmer in captivity."

"Then, it doesn't mean . . ."

"Whitney, the election is important, but I told you before. You and Jon come first. You'll always be first. Believe me, I could be quite satisfied raising crops . . . and a family, here with you. Don't ever worry about my priorities. It'll always be you and Jon . . . always."

"I do love you, Mitch Flannery."

"Keep that thought in mind until I get back. I may need a little proof to get me by."

"I'll be glad to prove it over and over again until you get tired of me."

At this Mitch laughed outright and swung her against him for a hearty and enthusiastic kiss.

"Go ahead, keep proving it until I get tired of you. Might be a hundred years before you manage it."

Whitney stood on the porch and watched him ride away, then returned to her chores.

Some hours later she was tired and surprised that the day had gone so fast. She fed Jon his dinner and a little while later she put him to bed. As time went on, she began to think Mitch had gotten tied up and couldn't get back, so she decided to get ready for bed.

She had just turned the parlor lamp down low when she heard a soft rap on the door. It could be Mitch . . . but it could be someone else. She went to the door.

"Who is it?"

"Whitney, it's me, Keith. Let me in." His whisper could hardly be heard.

She opened the door and Keith entered, closing the

door quickly behind him. "Keith?"

"Shh, I don't want anyone to know I'm here. Whitney, you need someone to protect you."

"What is it?"

"Someone's watching your house. I had to slip past them. Do you have any idea who?"

"No. Why would anyone want to watch me? I have nothing of value."

"Never mind, maybe it was just my imagination."

"Are you hungry? Are you staying?"

"No, I've come for something."

"What?"

"The letters I wrote Mother. I've changed my mind. I'd really like to have them with me."

"I'll get them for you, but I wish you'd tell me what's going on. You're not given to flights of fancy and I have a feeling it's not me they're interested in. Keith, I only want to help you."

Keith spoke as sincerely as he could. "Would you believe me if I told you it was much safer if you didn't know? I'll ease your mind on one thing. I worked for special services. What we're looking for is a traitor, a double spy. He's responsible for a lot of deaths. When I find him then I'll be able to come out in the open and live a normal life. I must find him, Whitney, because I'm the only one who can. If he gets away . . . then a lot of men have died for nothing. Some of those men were my friends."

"I'm so sorry, Keith. Of course I understand. Do your letters have something to do with it?"

"Yes, but it's too long a story to tell now. I've got to get out of here. There are a lot of clues I have to trace down." He grinned. "And I do my best work after midnight."

"Keith, please be careful."

"I will. I'm pretty safe. Everyone thinks I'm a war casualty. That's going to make my man pretty sure of himself. When he gets overconfident he'll make a slip, and when he does I'll see that he pays for what he's done."

"I just don't want you to pay."

"I won't."

"Do you think your man is someone who lived in Holly Hill?"

"Maybe. He was a soldier, I know that. Most likely had a career that put him in close proximity to the front lines and men who could slip him back and forth. He wore whatever uniform was necessary at the time. Originally he might have been a Confederate. Either way, he played both sides. He also came out of this war with a lot of money — a lot of blood-stained money."

"Keith . . ."

"There's not time, Whitney. We'll talk when it's over. Put the light out." She did so and moved to the door with him. He kissed her lightly and vanished into the night.

Whitney stood in silence. The evil thought that had entered her mind was pushed aside. No matter how much wealth Mitch had come home with, she would never suspect him. She would never believe such terrible things about him. She loved him and she had promised to forget the past and she meant to do just that.

Thirty-one

When Mitch walked into the *Sentinel,* all three of the men working there looked up. Blake whistled softly, then walked toward Mitch.

"What the hell happened to you? You look like a horse stomped you. And where have you been for two days? You had everybody frantic."

"Sorry, I ran into an obstacle. In fact, you might say three obstacles."

"Some of Trent's men?"

"I'd say, but I couldn't prove it. In fact, I have no idea who found me. All I know is one minute I was out and the next . . ." He shrugged, not wanting to tell them where he had recuperated, or who had brought him home.

"You'll look good giving that speech tonight," Blake said with a laugh.

"Might be a good thing," Craig added, "if you subtly referred to your opponents. You don't have to name Trent. Sometimes implication is good enough."

"I don't know. He's too clever for that. He'll have plenty of witnesses to prove where he was. Then he might imply that it's just a clever move on my part, and that I'm looking for sympathy."

"What are you going to do about this?" Kevin questioned.

"For now, beat him in the election. Then, who

knows, it might be possible to convince old Trent he made a big mistake."

"You know who they were?" Kevin asked.

"No, but the threats they threw at me were all about quitting the election and staying away from Whitney."

"That's Trent, all right," Blake said angrily.

"Well, let's put it out of our minds for now. I can handle it later. Besides, there's a good side to all that's been happening. Blake, how would you like to be best man at my wedding?" For a minute Blake looked at him in such utter shock that Mitch had to laugh. "It seems," he added quietly, "that those lost letters have been found. It's a long story."

"Well, we have a few hours. Suppose we stop for lunch and you can tell me about it. I can't believe it. The last I knew Whitney was going to marry the opposition. How . . ."

"Come on," Mitch laughed, "all three of you. In case you've lost your faith I'll tell you how miracles can still happen."

All four of them left the newspaper and walked across the street to a combination bar and restaurant — a gathering place for men who wanted to talk, drink, and eat.

They found seats, ordered food and drink, then Blake turned to Mitch. "All right, now, let's get on with that story."

While they ate Mitch explained that in some remarkable way the letters had not only been intercepted by Hope Clayborn, but secured in Jon's precious box that he had carried around for all this time.

"Amazing," Craig said. "Why do you suppose she kept them if she hated you so much, Mitch?"

"I don't know. Maybe, deep down, her hate was really fear. Maybe she couldn't understand her feelings and kept them in case she changed her mind . . . or

436

in case Whitney found out some other way. Then the letters could just . . . appear."

"You're so soft-hearted, Mitch," Blake said, "giving her the benefit of the doubt."

"No, I'm not giving Hope anything. But she was Whitney's mother and Whitney loved her. I can't vilify her. Whitney has had enough and this isn't the time to dwell on the past."

"You're right," Craig agreed. "It looks to me, Mitch, as if the future's bright for you. The election looks good and with Whitney and Jon you've got just about everything a man could want."

"That's exactly the way I feel. Whatever has happened can be put where it belongs—in the past."

"I guess it's time," Kevin said quietly, "to do just that."

"And I think it's time to get back to work," Craig added.

When they returned to the office Mitch asked about Noel.

"Well, she usually brings lunch," Blake said, "but with the election only a couple of weeks away, she's taken it upon herself to talk to the ladies."

"Why? They can't vote."

"Mitch, old boy, have you any idea what effect a woman can have on her husband? Maybe she can't vote, but some of them carry a lot of weight in their households even if the gentlemen will never admit it. Besides, there's something stirring up the country and I wouldn't be surprised if that law didn't change one day."

"Maybe you're right," Mitch laughed. "Women like Noel and Whitney have pretty good heads on their shoulders."

"So let's hope Noel can sway a few votes. Sometimes it's only one that counts."

"Noel's pretty sure you have him licked, Mitch," Kevin asserted.

"I hope she's right. But we'd better not celebrate too soon."

"Yeah," Blake agreed. "You better make sure you have that speech down pat. You've only got two more after this—then it's up to the voters."

Mitch agreed and the four settled down to work. Craig and Kevin had been in the process of setting type for the next day's paper. Blake was engrossed in an article he was writing. Mitch took the speech he had already memorized and tried different tones and inflections, deciding the points he wanted to stress and where he should add humor. He was so engrossed that he was the last one to look up when the door opened. When he did he was stunned.

Noel stood just inside the door, a newspaper clenched in one hand and her face so pale she looked as if she'd seen an apparition. Kevin was the first one on his feet.

"Noel! What's the matter?"

"This is terrible, terrible," Noel cried. "Mitch, you've got to put a stop to this!"

"Put a stop to what?" Mitch asked anxiously. "Has Trent done something ugly?"

"It's worse than ugly. This time it's an outright accusation. Trent Donnelley didn't write it, Douglas Banks did, and he says he has absolute proof."

Mitch walked to her and took the newspaper. As soon as he saw the headlines of the editorial his face went gray and his teeth clenched.

"LOCAL POLITICIAN, HERO OR TRAITOR," Mitch read slowly. "Douglas says there's doubt as to how loyally I served the Confederacy and where the money I have came from. He suggests I have shady things in my past that I'm trying to hide, and he has proof that he's bringing to light soon. What the hell is he talking about?"

"And what kind of proof could he have?" Blake asked, puzzled.

438

"Proof of what? What's he aiming at? He's calling you a traitor, Mitch," Craig shouted.

"A traitor!" Mitch snarled. "I served as honorably as any other Confederate soldier. I've half a notion to shove this newspaper down his throat!"

"Maybe that's the reaction he wants, Mitch," Noel said calmly. "It would be better to fight fire with fire. Make it clear tonight that this editorial is a bunch of tripe and you'll have a bigger and better reply in an editorial in the *Sentinel* tomorrow. Hit back, and ask him to show his proof. Tell him to fight you in the open instead of hiding behind vicious headlines."

"Maybe you're right. I better make a few changes in this speech," Mitch agreed.

"I'm wondering," Blake said with a dark frown, "just where Andrew stands. I know he supports Trent, but there's something more here, and I smell old Trent in there somewhere. The man hates you for a whole lot of reasons, Mitch, and he's going to a lot of trouble to bring you down."

"What can he say or do? This is another ploy to confuse the voters. Just say *traitor* and everyone's up in arms," Mitch argued. "No matter what I felt personally about slavery, I fought with my friends and neighbors. I would never have betrayed them."

"Well, as Noel said, we'll just have to fight fire with fire. You battle it out with him tonight, and we'll run an editorial that'll shut him up. You say there's nothing he can do to harm you and that's good enough for us," Craig said. "The race is getting hot and Trent Donnelley's running scared."

"I'll do my best," Mitch agreed. He went back to work on the speech, but he kept picking up the newspaper as if he couldn't quite believe it.

Noel was watching Mitch closely—he seemed angry and maybe a little uncertain. She couldn't control her premonition that this was only the tip of the iceberg, that Trent Donnelley and his friends had a lot more mud to sling. She was too good a newspaperwoman not to know that even though you brushed it off, some of the mud would cling, even if it was only in people's minds.

She made up her mind that when the speeches were finished tonight and she had written her editorial for tomorrow, she might just drop around and see Douglas at the *Chronicle*. If he had any kind of proof at all, even a minor incident, she might be able to make him angry enough to tell her. It was worth a try.

"Mitch, is Whitney coming tonight?" Noel queried.

"Yes. I suppose she'll arrive at the last minute. Look, Noel, maybe it would be better if you didn't mention this to her just yet. I don't want her upset about what might be a tempest in a tea pot."

Noel looked at him closely. "Or is it you don't want her to be worried about you?"

Mitch grinned. "Perceptive."

"She's going to be your wife, Mitch."

"I certainly hope so."

"Then she has a right to know."

"I suppose you're right, Noel. But Whitney and I, well, we've just begun to enjoy each other. I don't want anything to spoil it. This will blow over, it has to. There's no truth in it. Give me a few days and I'll tell her myself."

"I wasn't going to tell her something like this. It's up to you, not me."

"Thanks, Noel."

"I'm in love with Blake," she said gently. "As a woman in love, I know how Whitney would feel if you tried to spare her by taking problems on by yourself. If you love her, let her share everything."

"After the speech I'll talk to her."

Noel smiled and Mitch went back to his preparations. He sat over the speech without really seeing it. Something in the back of his mind jangled, but he

440

just couldn't quite figure out why. It was as if a ghost of a memory was coming to life, but he couldn't place it. Something so simple, yet it eluded him. Oh well, maybe if he didn't fight it so hard all the time it would come to him. In the meantime he had to concentrate on his speech. He put all other thoughts aside and returned to work.

Whitney sat with Mitch's letters in her lap. While Jon had taken a late afternoon nap she had read them again. She was allowing herself this quiet time to reminisce, to place old memories in perspective. Then she would put the old bitterness away for good. Thankfully, she and Mitch had reclaimed what should never have been lost.

At last she rose and put the letters away. When she walked downstairs she felt for the first time in a long time that she had some control over her life.

When the door opened and Berdine came in she could see a new kind of contentment in Whitney's eyes.

"Yo' feelin' fine, girl?" Berdine asked with a smile.

"Yes, Berdine, I'm feeling fine."

"Lazarus like to know jus' what yo' wants to do tonight."

"Well, if Lazarus will hitch up the buggy for me and Jon, I'll get an early start into town."

"Yo' gwine take Jon to de speakin'?"

"Yes, I want him to see Mitch and hear what people think of his father. It will give him pride in his father and that's what both Mitch and I want."

" 'Spects yo' right. But yo' knows fo' sho' Lazarus, he gwine want to ride into town wif yo' an' Jon. He don' feel right yo' takin' dat trip alone."

"Berdine, it's not that far. Jon and I will be fine. Are you sure Lazarus just doesn't want to miss all the excitement?"

"Wouldn' be surprised. Maybe he curious 'bout what Mitch Flannery gwine say."

"I hope it goes well, Berdine."

"Yo' doan think it will?"

"Oh, of course. It's just . . ."

"Jes' what?" Berdine walked closer to look in her eyes. "Somethin' stirrin' in yo' mind?"

"When you put it like that, well, yes. I just have a feeling something is unfinished, as if . . . oh, it's foolishness, Berdine. I'm nervous and excited. My life has changed a lot in the past few days. I'll be fine. Just tell Lazarus to hitch up the buggy. I'm sure Mitch will ride home with us."

"All right, ah go tell him. Maybe yo' oughta think some mo' 'bout him goin' along."

"Now don't be a worrywart, Berdine. I'll be fine. Like I said, Mitch will ride home with us."

Berdine nodded and left, but she still didn't feel comfortable about Whitney and Jon making the trip to town by themselves. There was little she could do about it and there was actually no reason why they shouldn't go. It would still be day when they left and Mitch would be with her coming home. Berdine tried to shrug off her discomfort, but it lingered vaguely in the back of her mind.

When Jon awoke it was late afternoon and Whitney fed him, then bathed and dressed him carefully in his very best outfit. Jon was, to say the least, excited. First, he was thrilled to be going into town, which meant he would buy some candy, but second to see Mitch give a speech. Not that he knew what a speech actually was, but his mother seemed to think it was something very important.

As usual, his excitement prompted plenty of questions, and by the time they were ready to leave she was quite exasperated and eager to turn him over to Mitch.

When they went out onto the porch, they saw Lazarus, who had brought the buggy — and an argument.

"Miz Whitney, it ain't right. A lone woman kin run into all kinds of trouble. It be best iffen ah goes wif yo'."

"Nonsense, Lazarus. It's not that long a ride, and I'll get there long before nightfall. Now just stop worrying. Jon and I will both be fine."

Reluctantly Lazarus handed Whitney up into the buggy. Then he lifted Jon to a seat beside her and stood in the center of the clearing and watched them ride away.

Whitney felt wonderful. The waning daylight was exceptionally beautiful and she was going to see Mitch. Even Jon seemed contented as they rode along. The road could barely be called that — it was dirt, with ruts in many places. The woods on either side were thick, and huge trees overhung the road in several places, making shadows.

There was enough breeze to make the ride comfortable and they moved along at a nice trot.

"Mommy?"

"What, Jon?" Whitney replied, sure another unanswerable question was about to be asked.

"Is Mitch . . . Daddy . . ." he began, sounding confused.

"Yes, Jon . . . he's your daddy. What were you going to ask me?"

"Is Daddy going to live with us?"

"Would you like him to?"

"Yes." The answer came so straight and clear that Whitney had to smile. "Mommy, will he fix my box? It's broken."

"I'm sure he will, sweetie, soon."

Jon seemed satisfied and was about to speak again when his attention was drawn to the roadside. Whitney let her gaze follow his and was suddenly frozen in fear.

They rode out from each side of the road. One

reached out and gripped her horse's bridle, bringing it to a halt. Five of them . . . and Whitney knew there was little point in putting up a fight. She had to think.

"Why do you accost a lone woman and child on the road?" she demanded. "If it's money you're looking for, you'll be sadly disappointed."

"Pretty thing like you don't need to worry about money," one said with a laugh.

"All right, Jake, stop it," a second man snarled. "No harm to her and the kid, remember."

Whitney was scared more for Jon than for herself. Who would do a thing like this? And why?

"What is it you want? Let me pass. Let go of my horse's bridle."

The man who had spoken second rode close to the buggy. Whitney could see the color of his eyes — a cold, deadly blue.

"Now you just be quiet and no harm will come to you. Cause me too much trouble . . . and I just might have to separate you."

His words struck sheer terror in Whitney but she remained quiet. She put her arm around Jon and drew him close.

"Now, Jake here is getting into the buggy and we're going for a ride . . . to a new destination. Cause any problem and the kid gets the worst of it. Understand me?"

Whitney nodded, too afraid to speak. The man called Jake tied his horse to the back of the buggy and climbed in beside her. He seemed to enjoy her discomfort and pressed his leg against her. He saw rage leap into her eyes and chuckled softly.

They drove into the trees for some distance, then Jake drew the buggy to a halt. He climbed down and the others stopped their horses close beside them. Now Whitney was beyond terror. If it had not been for Jon she might have resisted, but she couldn't

444

endanger his life any more than it already was.

"Get out of the buggy and bring the boy with you," commanded the man who seemed to be the leader. She couldn't do anything now, but she would watch for an opportunity. She got out of the buggy and lifted Jon down. He clung to her, wide-eyed.

"Hand the boy to me."

"No," Whitney said, clutching Jon tighter.

"Look, we have some riding to do so don't give me any trouble. Give the boy to me or I'll have to take him."

"You won't hurt him?" she pleaded.

"Not as long as you behave."

"I'll do whatever you want."

"Then give me the boy."

"Why are you doing this? Why?"

"Be good and don't ask questions. In a week or so you'll be free and no one will be the worse for wear."

She knew somehow that none of these men was the real force behind this affair. But why would someone want to kidnap her and Jon? No one had a thing to gain.

"Are you gonna move, or do you want to settle our problem here?" His voice had taken that cold, deadly tone again. Trembling, she handed Jon up and he put him on the saddle in front of him.

"Mommy . . ." Jon protested.

"Jon," Whitney said with a sob in her voice. "Please be quiet, dear. We're just going for a ride. Mommy will be with you."

Jon tried to keep from crying, but Whitney knew he was afraid. She grew even more frightened when she was ordered to ride with Jake, but she kept her control and walked over to him. He lifted her onto his horse and Whitney remained stiff as they rode away.

They traveled for almost two hours, then stopped in front of what looked like a one-room cabin of sorts.

It was very roughly made and, she was sure, offered no comfort at all.

When they dismounted Whitney rushed to Jon and took him in her arms. They were pushed inside the cabin and the door was pulled shut. In a moment she heard the lock click. She sat down on a rickety wooden chair, holding a very frightened Jon on her lap.

Mitch couldn't figure out why Whitney hadn't come. It was nearly time for him to go to the hall, he realized, pacing the floor nervously.

"Look, Mitch, women are notoriously slow," Blake offered. "Go on ahead and I'll wait here. Maybe she's just coming straight to the hall. Noel, Craig, and Kevin can save her a seat. No matter where she goes, one of us will meet her and make absolutely sure she gets to the hall."

"All right, all right," Mitch replied. "So I worry too much. You're right. I'll go on, but if she comes here, tell her to hurry."

"Don't worry, I will," Blake agreed. "Now get going before you're late."

Mitch left with Noel and her brothers. By the time they reached the hall it was already beginning to fill. Mitch was greeted warmly and his hand was shaken heartily by enthusiastic townspeople. More than one mother looked hopefully at this tall, handsome, and still single man as a prospect for a daughter, and Mitch was just as aware of the flirting smiles and inviting gazes of the young ladies. He smiled, too, but his mind was on Whitney.

While Noel and her brothers settled in their seats Mitch made his way to the back room where he would stay until he was introduced. He was joined there by Matthew Tyler and several of his friends. They discussed the next two weeks' strategies, and

Mitch listened carefully to their ideas. Less than a half hour later a young man stuck his head through the open door.

"Hall's full, gentlemen. I was told to come back and tell you it's time."

Mitch shook hands with Matthew and the others as they left the room. The applause when he walked out was heartening, and he felt elated until he scanned the audience and found Noel, Craig, and Kevin. The two seats next to them where Jon and Whitney were to sit were still empty.

Noel saw his smile fade for a moment, then reappear. But it wasn't the same smile. Craig leaned close to her.

"I wonder where Whitney is. This is unusual and it might get Mitch off stride."

"Want me to go check?" she whispered back.

"No, wait a little longer. She might be on her way."

Noel nodded and they listened to the preliminary speeches meant to rouse the crowd in preparation for Mitch. Still there was no sign of Jon and Whitney, and they could sense Mitch's concern as he kept looking in their direction. Finally Noel made a decision. She told Craig she was going to check, then she mouthed the words at Mitch, who nodded. He watched her leave and wished he were going with her. He couldn't shake the feeling that he should be, but it was too late. He was already being introduced. He stood to a cheering ovation and walked to the podium. After a few minutes of acknowledging the ovation he raised both hands, palms outward, to calm the crowd. When they finally grew silent he began to speak.

Noel nearly ran toward the office, but when she got there Blake was still alone. He'd been reading the *Chronicle*'s defamatory editorial again, and he looked up when the door opened, expecting to see Whitney.

"Noel, what are you doing here? Did Whitney get to the hall all right?"

"No, she never came. Mitch is really nervous so I came to see if she'd gotten here yet."

"This is really strange. You don't think something could have happened to them on the way in, do you?"

"God, I hope not," Noel breathed. "I don't think Mitch could go on with the campaign if that were true."

"Maybe I ought to ride out and see. If she's had a problem I'd run into her along the way."

"You don't suppose Jon is sick or anything? That would be the only thing that might keep her away."

"That or a little interference from Trent Donnelley."

"You don't think . . ."

"I hope not. But I'm going to find out. Look, Noel, maybe you better go back."

"No, I'd rather go with you. We can go back to the hall first and tell Craig and Kevin where we're going. The Tylers would gladly lend us their buggy, I'm sure."

"All right. Maybe if there's a problem you can help. Let's go."

Mitch saw Noel re-enter the hall with Blake behind her, but no sign of Whitney and Jon. He was worried, but his speech was in full swing and he couldn't break the momentum. He saw Blake and Noel in brief conversation, then they left. He was impatient now for the speech to be over so he could find out what was going on.

Noel and Blake raced to the buggy and were soon on their way. They rode slowly, aware that if Whitney had run into trouble her buggy might be off the road. Blake drove while Noel watched carefully, but there was no sign.

They drove into the clearing between the two houses, but there was no sign of Whitney. When

Blake jumped out and lifted Noel down they ran to Whitney's house, but it was dark.

"We better go see who else is around," Blake said.

Noel followed him across the clearing and stood beside him as he pounded on the door. Josiah answered, looking surprised to see them.

"Yes, suh?"

"Josiah, is Lazarus or Berdine here?"

"Sho' is. Come on in."

Lazarus had been seated before the fireplace on a low wooden bench whittling another toy for Jon. Berdine was in a rocker nearby with mending in her lap. Both looked up at Blake and Noel, amazed they would be here when they should have been with Mitch. Lazarus rose slowly, already suspecting something from the look on Blake's face. Lazarus had seen Blake often and Mitch had talked of him and Noel enough that he had no trouble knowing exactly who they were. He'd even seen the articles Noel had written, and Whitney read them to him when she was teaching him to read. He liked Noel at once and would have given her a warmer welcome if he hadn't suspected serious trouble afoot.

Whitney's house was dark and she obviously wasn't here either. Blake could feel his heart begin to thud as the full realization hit him.

"Lazarus . . . ?"

"What y'all doin' here?" Lazarus questioned, afraid he already knew the answer.

"Where are Whitney and Jon?" Blake asked, his voice full of fear.

"She done gone to town hours ago. To de speakin'. Her an' Jon took de buggy . . ." Lazarus stopped. There was no use avoiding the truth any longer. "Dey din get dere, did dey?"

"No, they didn't," Blake replied. "Worse yet, there's no sign of them along the road. Lazarus, this is no accident."

"Somebody took 'em," Lazarus muttered, his anger beginning to grow. "Dat Trent Donnelley."

"We don't know and we can't do anything if we can't prove it. We have to find her."

"Blake, how are you going to do that? It's so dark out there. You have to wait until morning," cautioned Noel.

"I know. In the meantime we have to go back and tell Mitch. Good Lord, he'll go crazy. He'll go after Trent."

"That's all the ammunition Trent needs."

"Mitch'll kill him," Blake said through clenched teeth.

"He can't do that. It'll destroy any chance he has against Trent."

"I know. But we have to tell him . . . then we have to control him, and that's not going to be easy."

"Ah knowed ah shoulda gone wif her. Dis nebber woulda happened."

"Lazarus, you can't blame yourself. It's not your fault," Noel insisted.

"Ah felt sumthin' was wrong. That sumthin' was gwine go wrong. Even if she dint want me to, ah shoulda gone wif her."

"Jon," Addy cried. "Dat po' baby, he be scared. Ah always been dere when he scared. Oh, mah po' baby!"

"Hush, chile," said Berdine. "Moanin' an' cryin' ain't gonna do us no good." She looked at Blake and Noel. "Y'all are right. Y'all gots to go back an' tell Mitch. An' y'all gots to keep him from doin' sumthin' he gwine be sorry fo'. First light, Lazarus gwine out an' start searchin'. Y'all and me, we knows dey done dis to git back at Mitch . . . mebbe stop him from runnin'. Iffen dat so dey ain't gwine hurt either of 'em. An' sometime soon someone gonna come to Mitch and tell him what dey wants. Den he know fo' sho'. Comes dat time we knows fo' sho' who to go

450

after . . . den we lets Lazarus an' yo' men track 'em down. Mitch gots to play smart. Dat de only way he gonna protect her."

"Berdine is right." Blake had to agree, even though he didn't want to. "I guess we'd better get back and tell Mitch. God, I hate this. I'd like to have my hands around a certain somebody's neck."

"Yes," Noel said softly. "And if any harm comes to Whitney or Jon . . . Mitch will do just that, election or no election."

"Yes," Lazarus said, "an' iffen he don't do de job right, ah'll do de rest. Dey better pray dat chile an' Whitney be awright, or dey won't be no place to run dat we cain't find 'em."

"I'll be out at daybreak, Lazarus," Blake said. "We'll start a search that an ant couldn't get through. We'll find them."

Lazarus could only nod, his mind already on what he would do to the men who had taken Jon and Whitney.

"Come on, Blake," Noel urged. "We have to get back. Mitch will be finished speaking and he'll be worried. We have to tell him."

"In the morning, Lazarus," Blake reminded.

"Yassuh, in de mawnin'. Come befo' light. Ah wants to be searchin' by dawn."

"All right."

Noel and Blake left. On the ride back both were silent for some time. Noel spoke first.

"Blake, why do you think they took Jon and Whitney?"

"To keep Mitch in line, what else?"

"Why would they take them two weeks before the election? If he agreed to what they want and got Whitney and Jon back, he could still run."

"You're right. I hadn't thought of it that way. It looks like they want him to do something now. But what?"

"I don't know. Let's hurry, Blake."

He urged the horse to a faster pace and before long they had reached the outskirts of town. They tied the buggy outside the hall and went in, but just inside the door they stopped cold.

Mitch stood on the platform, an expression of anger and disbelief on his face. The crowd was stunned. The aisle was empty except for three military men dressed in Union blue and the town constable, who turned to Mitch and began to speak.

"You're under arrest, Mitchell Flannery, for betraying your army as a spy against the Confederacy and the Union, and for being a traitor to this country."

Thirty-two

Mitch had delivered his speech well, even though it was hard for him to keep his attention from the empty chairs. Halfway through, Andrew Crocket and Douglas Banks knew that the speech was much more effective than they had thought it would be. Andrew leaned close to Douglas.

"It doesn't look as if your editorial scared the gentleman much."

"No, it doesn't. Maybe this can't be taken care of in print," Douglas Banks replied.

"What do you mean?"

"Let's get to Trent. It's time we put an end to this Mitchell Flannery thing once and for all, before it's too late."

"So Trent does have more proof?"

"That he does, and tonight's the time to use it. Want to come along?"

"Where?" Andrew asked.

"Why, to the proper authorities, who else? I'm a law abiding citizen. When I know a traitor's in our midst, I have to do my civic duty."

"Your . . . your civic duty? Lead on, this is most interesting."

The two men left quietly and made their way to Trent. When they explained what was happening, Trent was eager to turn over the papers, but he was still reluctant to go with them. He didn't want his name associated with what was about to happen. More important, he didn't want attention focused on his life—present . . . or past.

It took Crocket and Banks very little time to reach the Union offices still in control of the city. Major Paul Ryan had been asked by Mitch to help him find the man responsible for the burning of the Clayborn plantation. In the process he had come across some unexplained items, among them unsigned reports from an obvious spy.

Was what Ryan was now reading true? He found it very difficult to believe about Mitch Flannery, but the incriminating papers lay before him. He had no choice. At least, he would have to arrest Mitch and look into the matter. He, of all people, knew that sentiments ran high. A man guilty of what Mitch was being accused of would be in great danger—especially if people thought he was trying to turn a dark past into a political coup.

"This is highly incriminating evidence, gentlemen. Are you both certain?"

"Major Ryan, you have in your midst a traitor who is trying to hoodwink you again," Douglas announced. "Before this news *accidentally* gets out and the man finds himself lynched, I suggest you put him under arrest."

Major Ryan was not particularly fond of either Douglas Banks or Andrew Crocket, but he couldn't ignore evidence like this. He had to arrest Mitch.

"All right, in the morning . . ."

"No!" Andrew said sharply. "The man is influencing the people at this moment. They have a right to be spared that, and you have an obligation to arrest a traitor as quickly as possible."

Major Ryan breathed a sigh of capitulation. "You're right. But there will have to be a trial so the man has a chance to account for himself."

"Of course you do," Andrew said smoothly. "In fact, I think the young man might be safer behind bars . . . just in case the news stirs up trouble."

Major Ryan looked coldly at both men. "There had better not be anyone stirring up such trouble. The safety of this town is my responsibility as well."

"Then I suggest, Major Ryan," Andrew said icily, "that you had best be about your duties before the people of this town begin to think you're sympathetic to this traitor. That alone could stir up plenty of trouble."

Major Ryan knew a threat when he heard it. He also knew the threat could quite easily become real. He could have a general uprising on his hands.

He snatched up the papers, folded them, and put them in his pocket. Then he called his orderly.

"I need two troopers to come with me," he commanded, "in ten minutes, out front."

"Yes, sir." The orderly left, and both Andrew Crocket and Douglas Banks turned to leave. They had put the wheels in motion—now they had only to sit back and watch the pot boil.

Major Ryan sent one of his men for the town constable. He had to make everything as legitimate as possible. Union soldiers were tolerated, but that was tenuous, to say the least. When the constable joined them Major Ryan explained as quickly as he could. The news suited the constable, who had been in Trent's employ for some time. He would most likely lose his position should Mitch be elected, so a chance to sabotage the Flannery campaign was most welcome.

They walked to the hall and entered just as Mitch concluded his speech with a solemn promise to build Holly Hill into a town that would rival the best in the nation.

People began to applaud, many rising to their

455

feet. Mitch was suddenly aware of a number of things, the most noticeable being Whitney's absence and the men who were slowly walking toward him.

As Major Ryan and his group walked closer the applause began to die. Everyone seemed to sense that something momentous was about to take place. In a few moments the entire crowd was silent.

Major Ryan would have preferred to call Mitch aside and carry out his mission, but the constable was anxious to cause Mitch as much grief as possible.

"You're under arrest, Mitchell Flannery, for betraying your army as a spy against the Confederacy and the Union, and for being a traitor to this country."

A shocked gasp rippled through the crowd. Craig and Kevin pushed their way out of the crowd to Mitch's side. They hoped two loyal townsmen like themselves would help Mitch convince everyone this was a lie.

Mitch was stunned and stood for a moment in sheer disbelief; then he moved between Craig and Noel toward his accusers.

"What kind of a game is this? That bit of garbage is a lie and you know it. Major Ryan, what's going on here? I thought you didn't take political sides, that you were here to keep the peace."

"Look, Mitch, this is not political. I have a job to do. These charges have been pressed . . ."

"By the local paper, I presume?" Mitch snapped.

"Evidence has been laid before me."

"What kind of evidence? What am I accused of?"

"Mitch, don't cause me any trouble. There are too many people here for me to be explicit. I'm sure you understand. It's best if you come with me."

Mitch looked around him. Except for Craig, Kevin, Noel, and Blake, who had just pushed their

456

way to his side, and his parents, he was surrounded by a sea of curious faces that could turn hostile at any moment.

"I suppose you're right. I guess this is the only way I can clear it up."

Major Ryan nodded, relieved. But Mitch was thinking about something else. He turned to Blake. "Where are Whitney and Jon?"

For a second neither Blake nor Noel could speak. It was difficult to strike another blow when Mitch had just been dealt such a severe one. But Mitch had read their faces and grew pale.

"Where is she?" he hissed harshly.

"Mitch, let's get out of here so we can talk," Blake pleaded.

Mitch reached out and grasped Blake in a brutal grip. "Where is she?" He tried not to shout, but desperation gleamed in his eyes. Suddenly his world seemed to be coming apart. He couldn't be locked in jail if Whitney and Jon were missing. He had to know. His relentless gaze held Blake's.

"I don't know," Blake said quietly. "No one knows. She and Jon left the house to come here. They just never arrived."

"Come on, Mitch," Major Ryan warned, "we've got to take you . . ."

Mitch turned on him. "Major Ryan, I'll give you my word I won't run away. You've got to give me some time. Whitney and my son are missing. I've got to find them."

Paul could see that Mitch had no intention of going to jail until he had done what he had to do. But Paul had no choice. He couldn't let Mitch walk away or the town would be in an uproar. He took his pistol from his holster. "You have to come along with me . . . now."

"You going to shoot me, Major?"

457

"Don't force me, Mitch. I'm here to keep the peace and I'm going to do just that. I'll shoot you if you force me to."

Their eyes met for a long minute, and Mitch could see that Major Ryan meant what he said. Mitch couldn't allow himself to die here—he had to find out what had happened to Whitney.

"All right," he said softly, "I'll go." He turned to Blake who spoke up quickly.

"We'll move heaven and hell to find them and get you out of there. Mitch, what could they . . . ?"

"I don't know, but we have to find out. Major Ryan is right, we don't want trouble here. It could turn nasty. See Judge Marshall, see if something can't be done to get me out. In the meantime, we've got to find Whitney. It all has to be connected somehow—it's planned too carefully. Accuse me, then use Whitney to keep me quiet. Blake, move!"

Blake nodded. He motioned to Craig and Kevin, took Noel's hand, and made his way from the crowd. Mitch went ahead of Major Ryan and his men, his mind racing. He knew he was a threat to Trent, but Trent wanted Whitney as well, so why would he take her? To keep him quiet? Or was it that Whitney herself had something he wanted? That was possible . . . the question was . . . what?

When the cell door was slammed shut and the lock turned, Mitch felt a sense of helplessness such as he had never felt before.

Blake, Noel, Craig, and Kevin gathered in Judge Marshall's office with Mitch's worried parents and he listened carefully to all they said.

"Mitch has little to fear. We all know what kind of man he is. He's not guilty and a trial will eventually clear him."

"Before or after it ruins his reputation?" Blake asked angrily.

"If the trial can be held before the election, clearing his name can be the best way to win. People who believed the lies will feel guilty, and those who didn't will be more supportive than ever. If Trent Donnelley is behind this, as you feel he is, then he'll look like a fool for creating such a farce."

"You don't know Trent Donnelley like we do," Craig said. "He must have more cards he hasn't played yet, and that scares me."

"Besides that, Mitch thinks Whitney's disappearance is connected somehow," Noel offered.

"But how? He certainly doesn't need her to cause Mitch any problems. He's already got his hands full," Judge Marshall countered.

"Well, we have to do something," answered Blake. "We have to get to Whitney, and we have to get to the truth as well."

The four left the judge's house.

"Let's go back out to Whitney's," Noel suggested. "We have to stop running and settle down to make some plans. I'm sure all this confusion is just what Trent hopes for."

"You're right. We've been running around like chickens with their heads cut off," Blake agreed. "We have to get ourselves together if we're going to help Mitch at all."

Kevin spoke quickly. "The best help we can give him is to find Whitney and Jon. If Trent intends to use them as a tool against Mitch, he's chosen the right one."

"That still doesn't make sense. The timing is all wrong," Blake argued. "If Trent planned to use Whitney and Jon against Mitch he would have waited for the last minute and forced Mitch to withdraw from the race. Somehow I get the feeling

459

there's a hell of a lot about this whole situation that we just don't know."

"Then maybe someone else has a few pieces we can fit into our puzzle," Noel suggested.

"Like who?" Craig questioned.

"Berdine maybe, or Lazarus," Blake offered. "I'm sure Whitney confided just about everything to them. Maybe if we all put our heads together we can come up with an answer."

"Wonderful idea," Noel agreed.

"Noel, maybe it would be better if you stayed here," Blake said.

"Blake!"

"Now wait a minute," he replied, laughing. "I just think you can do more here. You can go to Mitch and talk to him. If we all tried to, it might cause a problem. You've a good nose for what's going on. Move around and listen. Tell Mitch we're going out to get Lazarus and Josiah and start a hunt and we won't leave a blade of grass unturned. Maybe you can settle his mind and get him thinking."

"I suppose you're right," Noel agreed.

If Blake was surprised at her easy acceptance it was overcome by their rush to get started. "Then we'd best get going right now. Lazarus and Berdine and the others will surely be waiting for word from us. They have no idea what's happened here tonight. Not to mention Mitch's parents. They'll be worried to death."

Noel watched her brothers and Blake ride away, then she walked to the jail and went inside.

Blake, Craig, and Kevin rode fast, so there was little time to talk. When they came into the clearing, lights glowed from Lazarus's home. None of them was too anxious to tell Lazarus and Berdine that there were more problems, but there was nothing else they could do.

Blake knocked and the door was opened almost immediately by Berdine. It was obvious she had been waiting. Her eyes were filled with curiosity.

"No, Berdine, we don't know anything more about Whitney's disappearance. But we've got some bad news to add to it." He went on to explain what had happened to Mitch and how he had been put in jail. "Where's Lazarus?"

"He couldn't sit still no mo'. Dark or no, he took him a lantern an' set out to search. He in a black mood. Ah feel sorry iffen he catches up wif dem."

"I don't see how he can," Craig said. Berdine looked at him with controlled curiosity.

"This is Craig Anderson and his brother, Kevin. They own the paper that's been supporting Mitch." Berdine nodded and turned her attention back to Blake.

"He kin iffen anybody kin. Lazarus know dose woods like de back of his hand."

"Then maybe we ought to get horses and lanterns and go help him," Kevin suggested.

"Yo' all get yo'self lost in 'bout a minute," Berdine said convincingly. "Best wait 'til Lazarus come back or 'til it get light."

"She's right," Blake sighed. "I don't want Lazarus to have to be searching for us. Besides, when I go back to Mitch I want to be sure to have something to say, and right now there's nothing."

"Mitch must be miserable," Kevin said, "not knowing where Whitney is and helpless to do anything about it. It's like both things were planned to happen at the same time."

"I wonder," Blake began with a puzzled frown.

"Wonder what?"

"We've been looking at this only from Mitch's

461

point. What if his arrest was just to get him out of the way? What if whoever it is wants something from Whitney and they were sure Mitch would be too big an obstacle. After all, if he married Whitney, he'd be right there to protect her."

"What could he want that Whitney would have?" Craig asked.

"I don't know," Blake admitted. "It was just a thought. Something doesn't fit. Arresting Mitch now was just too opportune, and taking Whitney on the same day. It just doesn't fit," he insisted.

"Y'all gentlemen sets down, an' ah gets y'all sumthin' to drink. Lazarus come back befo' day since he 'spects y'all to be here."

The three sat, uncomfortable with the prospect of endless waiting and the inability to find an answer to what was going on.

Nearly an hour later Lazarus came in. He was not surprised to see them, and he was exceptionally quiet while they explained everything.

"So Blake thinks there's some connection between taking Whitney and Mitch's arrest that we don't know anything about. That's what we have to find out," Craig said.

"We needs a whole lot of answers," Lazarus said calmly. "Ah think we oughta be movin'."

Blake thought Lazarus was calmer than he should have been, or even had been a few hours before from what Berdine had said, but he said nothing. He just watched him closely. Josiah, who had come in with Lazarus, seemed to want to keep to himself completely. He helped himself to some food that had been warming on the hearth and went to a far corner to eat it.

Lazarus, too, took some food and sat at the table and began to eat. It was too casual, too smooth for a man who was supposed to be as angry as he had

462

been. But Blake also knew that whatever Lazarus was thinking, he wasn't about to share it with any of them — and that was what worried him.

"Lazarus, did you search far? Did you find any trace?"

"Ah had a pretty hard time. Too many clouds, so ah din't get too far. Ah followed buggy tracks to a place where dey was off de road. It were too dark for me to tell how many men, but ah kin say fo' certain it was mo' den one."

"So it was well planned?"

"Had to be. How many times we rode on dat road, Miz Whitney an' me an' de boy. Nobody try nuthin', nobody had reason. So now, who think maybe she come along dat road alone?"

"I don't know. How would anyone know?"

"Cain't . . . lessen dey been watchin' fo' a while. So now ah asks myself, why somebody been watchin' so close?"

"And you got an answer?"

"Mebbe ah did."

"Want to share it?"

"Mebbe ah gots de same idea yo' gots. Somebody hankerin' fo' sumthin' she gots dat maybe she doan know nuthin' about."

"Like what?"

"Ah said ah doan know. But mebbe Mitch Flannery, he know sumthin'."

"Mitch? Mitch would never do anything to hurt Whitney or Jon. He's frantic with worry."

"He say he wrote to her an' after a time dey finds dose letters. Yo' thinks mebbe dey be sumthin' in dere dat he want to stay a secret?"

"No," Blake said thoughtfully "What things would Mitch have to hide? Or . . . what things would someone else have to hide, someone who could trust the secret to Whitney as well."

463

"Dey be a lot of things sent to Miz Whitney befo' de war get bad. From her daddy, her brother, an' Mitch. She save some things. Trouble is we don' know what to look fo'. So ah guess we keep thinkin' on it an' at daybreak we gets out an' finds our answers."

"But dammit, Lazarus . . . who wants these secrets kept?"

"We finds dat out come de minute we find Miz Whitney. An' when we do," his voice was quiet, "ah gonna make him wish he ain't nebber been born."

For the first time Blake began to realize that Lazarus's calmness was not calmness at all. It was violent fury held in check by a very strong will.

"Lazarus, you can't take the law into your own hands."

"Sometimes de law gits played wif an' nobody pays."

"This time we'll make sure that doesn't happen."

"Fo' now we jes' gots to worry 'bout findin' Miz Whitney an' de boy."

"Lazarus . . ."

"We gots to git goin', Mistah Randolph. Yo' best gits some rest. Mawnin' gwine come right quick."

Blake sighed in exasperation. There was no way to reach Lazarus. He was deeply dangerous and didn't want to understand. He hoped to find some answers before Lazarus did.

When Blake and her brothers were gone, Noel hurried to the jail and requested permission to see Mitch. In a few minutes his cell door was unlocked and she walked in.

"Noel!" Mitch turned from the window when he heard the door. In a few steps he crossed the cell and took hold of her shoulder. "What's happened? Have you heard from Whitney and Jon? Has anyone found them? Where . . ."

"Mitch, please."

"I'm sorry," he said, releasing her. "It's just that I've been going out of my mind."

"I know how you must feel. Mitch, Blake has an idea."

"An idea? What kind?"

"He thinks maybe there's more to this."

"Go on," Mitch urged.

"He thinks someone wants something from Whitney and you had to be gotten out of the way so she would have less protection. If you married her they could hardly get near her. It was killing two birds with one stone, so to speak. In the end, you would have been gotten rid of, too."

"Too?" The word was filled with a new terror. "Whoever it is means to kill her when they get what they want and me . . . I'll be found guilty and most likely hanged. Damn! I wish I knew where all that so-called proof came from. And who's really behind all this? I thought it was Trent Donnelley, out to get Whitney. But what would Whitney have that he would want? None of this makes any kind of sense."

"Blake, Craig, and Kevin have gone out to join Lazarus in an all-out search for any trace of Whitney and Jon. For now they can't do anything to you. A trial will take at least a few days."

"A few days! How can I sit here calmly for a few days when Whitney and Jon are somewhere needing my help? Noel, I've got to get out of here!"

"It's so well guarded. How can we do that? There's no chance, Mitch. You'll have to trust us to do everything possible."

"It's not trust, Noel. I couldn't live my life if

465

Whitney and Jon weren't part of it. I must get out of here."

"I'll talk to Blake. We'll do what we can."

"Just get me a weapon somehow. I'll do the rest. Please, Noel, try. Get me something."

"All right, Mitch, I'll try."

"Tonight."

"Mitch!"

"Tonight!" he insisted.

"Be reasonable. If I go out and come back tonight they'll surely search me. Tomorrow. I promise I'll try tomorrow."

She knew the long night would be agony for Mitch, but she also knew she was right. They wouldn't be fooled by two visits in one night and would suspect she carried some sort of weapon.

"What could Douglas Banks and Andrew Crocket have against you? Why would they want to destroy you? It isn't just the election—there's something more."

"I don't know what it could be. I don't know either of them that well, except as political opponents."

"There's so much that just . . . doesn't make sense."

"Noel . . . just find me a weapon and get me out of here. I'll take care of all of this as soon as I'm free."

"All right, Mitch, I'll do my best."

Mitch bent to kiss her cheek. "Thanks. You said Blake and your brothers were going to Whitney's?"

"Yes. If there's any kind of trail at all, they'll find it." She tried to assure him, and he allowed it to look as if he really believed her.

"You'd better get going."

"All right. Mitch . . . I'm sorry about this."

"I know." He tried for a smile, but it was weak.

Noel turned away and called for the guard. In a few minutes she was gone and the iron door again clanged shut between him, freedom . . . and Whitney.

The cell was small—no more than eight feet by eight feet. There was only one narrow, barred window, and Mitch had stood looking out of it into the darkness long enough to know he could see nothing from there.

He paced the floor like a caged lion, battling the fear that gripped him. What if he were too late to save Whitney and his son? He realized he would give up anything, everything, just to have them in his arms again. He wanted to lash out at something, somebody. But he had no name, no face, nothing but a shadow to rage against.

He was so deep in his own blood-red thoughts that at first he didn't hear the sound. He stopped pacing and listened carefully.

"Ssssttt." It was like a sharp hiss and came from the darkness beyond the window. He started toward it, then paused, wondering if he was walking into some kind of trap. The sound came again, followed by a soft voice whispering his name.

Mitch moved to the window quickly. It was a voice he recognized. He glanced back over his shoulder toward the door that led to the constable's office. It was safely closed. He grasped the bars of the window and looked out.

At first he saw no one. Then a vague form, darker than the darkness about him, slowly moved closer to the window, just as he heard the voice again.

"Mitch?"

"Yeah," he whispered. "Keith, what are you doing here?"

"I might ask you the same," came the humorous reply.

"How did you know I was here?"

"I have ears around town. This has caused a lot of excitement. I need some information. I might know a few things you'd be interested in."

"And I know something that might interest you, too. Someone's kidnapped Whitney and Jon."

"What?"

"Look, they're more important than I am, Keith. You must know very inch of land around here. If anyone could find them, you could."

"True."

"And I want to help."

"How can you do that? It seems to me your cell is rather breakproof."

"I have someone bringing me a gun. I'll be out."

"When?"

"Tomorrow, I hope."

"Look, Mitch, I have an idea I'd like to try on you."

"What?"

"They're labeling you a traitor, a double spy."

"I know."

"It's said they have proof."

"Impossible."

"Oh, it's quite possible. I've been looking for the man who played double agent."

"Well, you're looking at the wrong man. I was never a spy."

"I know that, but you make a good scapegoat. He knows someone's hunting him, so he threw you to the wolves."

"I don't understand."

"You're not guilty."

"So?"

"So there was a lot of proof."

"Make your point."

"If," Keith said patiently, "the proof was provided, just who the hell do you think provided it? Who else would know?"

Mitch grasped what Keith was getting at. "Whoever gave them the proof is the bastard who played traitor in the first place."

"Well, well, well, so the dawn finally comes. I need a name to go with that little piece of information."

"I don't know. The only ones who know are Andrew Crocket and Douglas Banks. They contacted Ryan."

"Then you're right. We've got to get you out of here. I have a suspicion, my friend, that it's a lynching they have in mind. Look, I'm going out to Whitney's and see what I can find. I'll be back tomorrow. If you can't get out by then . . . then I'll have to see to it myself."

"Why not right now?" Mitch demanded. "For Christ's sake, Keith, get me out of here now! I've got to find Whitney!"

"We'd tip our hand and you'd never see Whitney. I have my own ideas about why Whitney was taken. In fact, I have what they want from her. It's all connected. We find one, we'll find the other."

Before he could speak again the door to the office opened. Mitch knew that in that same split second, Keith was gone. He was angry and frustrated. The constable came to the cell door. He wore a gloating smile and if Mitch could have gotten near enough he would have strangled him.

"You got a visitor," the constable said.

"I'm in no mood for visitors," Mitch growled. "Unless it's someone with an apology and the key to this door."

"Ah, no, no, my friend. We're gonna have a

469

hanging. Right now, it's time to entertain."

Mitch looked toward the open doorway and when his visitor came in, Mitch knew the truth. The pieces fell neatly into place.

"Hello, Trent, come on in. We have a lot to talk about."

Thirty-three

The night grew deeper and darker, and Jon became frightened. He huddled on Whitney's lap and she crooned softly as she rocked him. She was as terrified as he was, but she couldn't let him know it.

They'd been in this dark and dirty place for hours and she wondered if they intended to leave them here until they died. What did they want? Obviously it was not to hurt them — they could have done that any time. Who was behind this? It was obvious that the men who had left them here had been under orders. Hadn't the leader warned the dreadful Jake that someone had said neither of them was to be harmed? Whoever her jailer was, what did he want from her?

The sound at the door was so sharp and sudden that Whitney jumped in surprise. Jon stirred in discomfort, but didn't wake. The door swung open and the leader walked in.

He carried a lantern and hung it on a nail. Whitney was not about to give him the satisfaction of hearing her beg, so she remained stoically silent.

"I'm sorry about how uncomfortable this place is. I've brought some blankets. There's an old wood bunk in the corner. You can let the kid sleep there." He motioned to a shadowed area and Whitney no-

471

ticed the bunk against the wall for the first time. She hesitated to put Jon down even after he had spread the blankets. Maybe he wanted Jon away from her for a reason. He turned to her. "I said put the boy down. Unless you want me to do it for you." He started toward her, knowing she would resist.

"Don't you touch him," she said coldly. "I'll lay him down." She rose, stiff from having to sit holding Jon for so long. Even at three he was a heavyweight. She walked to the bunk and laid him down, patting him and humming softly until he sank back into deep sleep. Only then did she turn and face her jailer.

"What do you want with me? Why have you done this?"

"I have orders," he answered, as if that ended the matter. He shrugged. "I don't want a thing from you. But my boss does, and he's used to having his way."

"Who's your boss?"

"That's really none of your business. What you need to think about is telling me what I want to know."

"What a coward he must be," she sneered. "Can't he do his dirty work himself?"

"Don't push me, lady," he warned. "What you think of the man who pays me doesn't interest me a bit. I just do my job."

"I suppose if you were told to kill us you'd do it."

"Don't doubt it for a minute," he muttered. "You and that kid don't mean a thing to me, so you'd better be careful you don't make me real mad."

Whitney breathed deeply, stricken by his unemotional response. Jon's life hung in the balance.

He read her expression with satisfaction. She would do whatever he wanted. He couldn't resist

472

hitting her with another mental blow to weaken her resistance. "You're a real pretty lady. It's a shame you weren't home when we raided your plantation. I was feeling pretty good that night and we might have danced a jig or two."

Whitney's face went white and she clenched her fists. The pain was enough to stun her momentarily. "Why?" she gasped. "Why did you destroy my home?"

"We weren't supposed to. My men were likkered up and got carried away. We were looking for the same thing then that we're looking for now."

"What in God's name could be so important that you would destroy so much? What kind of a man is this boss of yours that he'd be so brutal?"

"A man who knows what he wants and won't stop at anything to get it. Too bad we missed it that night. But it don't matter now. You cooperate and give me what I'm lookin' for, and I'll set you and the boy free."

Whitney was leery. She was sure if he got what he wanted she and Jon wouldn't have a chance. Surely Mitch and his friends had missed her by now. She had to hold out as long as possible. There would be a search. If she didn't survive, at least she would thwart all their efforts. They had destroyed her home, and in a roundabout way, had killed her mother. She was not going to surrender one more inch of her life to whoever this man's boss was.

"I have no idea what you or your boss could possibly want from me," she said with a stubborn tilt of her chin. She might have expected many things, but not what he said next.

"First off he thinks your brother, Keith, is still alive and he's here. He wants to know where he is. Second, you have some letters your brother wrote home. He wants those, too."

473

"Keith?" she said, thinking fast. "But Keith was reported missing a long time ago. Everyone has given up hope that he's alive. He wouldn't have come home and not told me." She wasn't actually denying Keith was home.

She watched his face and knew she had not fooled him for a minute. He waited.

"As far as letters are concerned," she continued desperately, "all my family's effects were destroyed in the fire you — and the beasts who follow you — set."

"You're quick . . . and clever. I'm not getting angry . . . yet. We know your brother's alive and that he's here. You know where he is."

"But . . . I . . ."

"Don't interrupt. I want this to be very clear. We searched thoroughly before the fire. We know you took those letters with you. Now, think this over and while you're doing it, remember that your son will pay the price if you're gonna be stubborn. You just might force us to kill him first, just to prove a point."

"No," she moaned, fear gripping her heart.

"Then think about it. Your brother and those letters . . . or your son."

Her heart was pounding so hard she could hardly get her breath. Words wouldn't come. Her lips were stiff and her mouth dry.

"That's horrible! You can't mean that," she choked.

He gripped her arm brutally, jerking her close. She looked up into eyes without pity. "Just see if I don't. It's all up to you. Just remember that." He released her and she stumbled backward. There was no doubt in her mind that he meant exactly what he said.

He left, locking the door behind him. He was confident that if she was given time to worry about

474

what he had said she would tell him what he wanted. All it would take was a little more time.

Whitney sagged down on the chair, unable to believe what had happened. Who was this "boss" who knew so much about her, Keith, and the letters? Keith had come and gone in the night. As far as the letters . . . who would know?

But Whitney was not a woman to surrender so easily, not when Jon's life was at stake. Adversity had always brought out the best in her; this time it made her more determined than ever to find a way out of this dilemma.

She was grateful that the lantern had been left. It gave her a chance to look around. She moved slowly, searching for any method of escape, any crack in the wood walls . . . any weapon. Near the furthest corner of the far wall, she found that one panel of board was loose enough to pry it apart and look outside. It was possible, she thought, that with enough time she could loosen it enough to slip out. But would she have that time?

Surely her captor would be back soon. She did not have the letters, and she had no way of knowing Keith's whereabouts. She had to depend on her own courage and ingenuity to find an escape. She'd looked into her captor's snake-cold eyes and knew he would not stop at killing a child.

She searched the room. There had to be something, some way. Her eye fell on a loose piece of board protruding from beneath the bed on which Jon slept. She bent to pick it up. It was heavy, and a good two and a half feet in length. It would make a sturdy club.

She held it up. Her captor was strong, and he was armed.

For a moment her courage wavered. But she had only to look down on Jon's sweet sleeping face. His

475

trust in her was consummate. She was willing to do anything to keep him safe. She gazed at the thick board, all that stood between her and Jon and sure death. Suddenly it seemed much too light and too small.

Whitney turned to look at the door. It opened inward. So if she stood behind it she might have one chance to strike as he came in.

Once the decision was made, she took the lantern as far from the door as she could and hung it so the area behind the door would be as shadowy as possible. Then she stood behind the door . . . and waited.

Every second seemed like hours. Fear coursed through her constantly as she imagined she would fail and both Jon and she would die . . . or worse, she would fail and he wouldn't let her die for a long time. She began to sweat and tremble. She pinned her gaze on Jon and prayed for enough strength to do what needed to be done.

Time ticked on and on, and she wanted to scream as her nerves were stretched taut. Then she heard footsteps. Someone fumbled with the lock and she prayed he was alone. The door swung open and for a minute it was between them. Then he took a step toward the bunk. Whitney came from behind the door, raised the club, and brought it down on his head with all her strength. She heard a low grunt and he sagged to his knees. She raised the club and struck him again, watching in horror as he collapsed completely.

Whitney pushed the door almost closed. She knew he was not alone. She looked out through the crack of the open door. Less than fifty yards away three men sat near a low-burning fire. She could hear their voices and soft laughter. She hesitated to imagine what they might be laughing about. At least they didn't seem to have any idea that their plans had gone wrong.

She had two choices: pray she could open the crack in the wall board enough to get out . . . or leave by the door.

Could she move quietly enough through the shadows so she could avoid being seen? She took one precious moment to think, then made her decision. She went to Jon's side and wrapped the blankets around him. Then she lifted him gently and walked to the door. Taking a deep breath, she stepped out into the night.

Trent smiled at Mitch and sauntered into the cell. "You can leave us now," he said to the constable.

"But, Mr. Donnelley . . ."

"I said," Trent interrupted coldly, "you can leave us now."

The constable pulled the cell door shut and reluctantly turned to leave.

Trent took a slender cigar from his pocket and clamped it between square white teeth. He lit it casually and blew a stream of smoke. All the while Mitch said nothing. He simply leaned against the wall and crossed his arms.

"You've been a nasty problem, Mitchell Flannery," Trent said pleasantly.

"Not as nasty as I plan to be," Mitch said with the same tone.

"I don't see that you're in any position to make threats."

"That's not a threat, it's a promise."

"You're in no position to make such promises either. In fact, you have no position at all."

"I'm where you should be. After all, we both know who the real traitor is, don't we?"

"So you do remember?"

"I didn't until you walked in the door. It was in a jail cell that I saw you the last time, but not the first time." Mitch chuckled mirthlessly. "I saw you on both sides, in both uniforms."

"Well, you know that and I know that, but no one else is ever going to know it."

"Don't be too sure. I've made a lot of friends in this town. Maybe the trial won't go as you hope."

"Trial?" Trent looked innocently surprised. "What trial?"

"Come on, Trent. No one's going to convict me without a trial. You aren't thinking of asking me to keep my mouth shut?"

"No, I certainly don't mean that. I want you to talk. Loud and clear, so no one will misunderstand you."

Mitch looked at Trent through narrowed eyes. There was much more to this. The last thing Trent should want would be for Mitch to be able to talk.

"You want me to tell them I'm guilty?" Mitch laughed. "That's something you'll never hear."

"Oh, I wouldn't be too sure about that."

"Trent, why don't you just clear out of here? It might be a good idea if you left town entirely, because when I get out of here I'm coming to find you."

"Well, I guess I can't clear out until I tell you just why you're going to do exactly as I say."

"You're wasting your time and mine."

"Maybe . . . but I'm not wasting Whitney . . . or your son's."

Mitch inhaled sharply. The desire to kill Trent where he stood was so strong it nearly overwhelmed him. But he knew he'd be playing into Trent's hands.

"If you harm a hair on her head I'll kill you if it's

478

the last thing I do."

"Harm her? Don't be ridiculous. Once you're out of the way permanently I intend to enjoy Whitney very much."

"Don't count on it."

"I do. You see, Mitch, I'm going to let you do away with yourself. You'll tell the judge tomorrow that indeed you are a spy and a traitor. Because if you don't," he threatened, "then you'll never see Whitney or your son alive again." His smile was wickedly triumphant. "And don't bother to attack me or there'll be no one to send word to set them free. They'll surely die."

"You're a heartless bastard," Mitch raged. "You'd harm an innocent child. For what? Just to get back at me?"

"I'm not here to answer your questions. You have an ultimatum. By this time tomorrow night you'd better call the constable and make your confession. If you don't, by dawn the day after tomorrow," he observed with a shrug, "you'll wish you had, believe me." He smiled a smile that made Mitch shudder with rage. Then he opened the cell door, stepped out, and closed it. His eyes held Mitch's for a minute and Mitch knew he meant what he said. Trent called for the constable, who came at once to lock the cell again.

"If you want to talk to me anytime tomorrow, please don't hesitate to send someone. I'll be most anxious to hear your *opinion* about what I've told you. It might facilitate matters if you send for the judge at the same time."

As Trent walked away, the gloating look on his face was too much for Mitch. He slammed against the door, gripping the bars until his knuckles were white. "Trent, damn you!" Trent's receding laughter was all he heard before the door closed.

Rage shook him and worse was his utter helplessness. He had one chance. If Noel brought him a weapon he would find his way out, just as he would find a way to get back at Trent.

He walked back to the window, wondering if he might be lucky enough to find Keith still there. He called out softly, but no sound came from the darkness. Mitch sank down on his bunk slowly, trying to control his panic.

He struggled for rational thought. If Trent had taken Whitney, then she knew him for what he was. Then it meant . . . no matter what Trent told him, that he planned to kill them. Mitch not only had to get out, he had to find Whitney and Jon before Trent's orders could be carried out. He didn't even want to think about what could happen if he failed, or what his chances of success might be.

Trent walked out of the jail feeling better than he ever had. Everything he'd ever wanted was nearly in his hands. Once his men got the letters from Whitney and he had permanently rid himself of Mitch, the way would be clear. He would have it all and the amusing thing was Whitney would never know he'd done it. Once Mitch confessed he would see to it that a crowd would gather and be whipped to a frenzy and lynch him before anyone could stop them. He would win the election, have the lady, and have all the time in the world to collect the ultimate prize—the one that would give him the rest of his dream.

He popped the cigar back in his mouth and walked to his buggy. This was one night he planned to sleep real well.

Noel stood in the window of the *Sentinel* and watched Trent leave. As he drove out of sight she was puzzled. Why should Trent Donnelley be visiting Mitch? The idea of talking to Douglas Banks became even more appealing. The hour was late but she no longer cared. She left the office, hoping that one word, one idea might come from a confrontation with Douglas Banks.

Blake, Craig, and Kevin were already prepared to move when Lazarus came for them. None of them would have been able to sleep a wink even if they'd tried. They were glad to be on the move.

The sound of Lazarus's footsteps on the porch brought Blake to the door.

"Y'all be ready to go?" Lazarus asked.

"We've been waiting for you."

"Den let's git movin'."

"We've been trying to figure this thing out."

"Ah been doin' dat fo' hours. Ain't no way fo' us to answer nuthin' 'til we find Miz Whitney. We best git along now. It's a ways to where dey yanked de buggy offen de road. We ain't got no idea how far it gwine be after dat."

"You a good tracker, Lazarus?"

"Passable. Ah kin trail a snake over a rock. We gwine find dose boys. Den we gwine git some answers."

"Right, let's go."

The four of them mounted their horses and rode away. Berdine stood on the porch and watched them leave. She said every prayer she knew for them. Berdine didn't frighten easily. She had seen and lived through too much for that. But now she was afraid for a child who didn't know yet the bitter lessons life could teach. She didn't go back into the house until they had completely disappeared.

Blake, Kevin, and Craig followed Lazarus until they reached the place where the buggy had left the road, then they followed the trail to the empty buggy. It looked so deserted that for a minute Blake just stared at it, knowing how frightened Whitney must have been . . . and Jon. The thought set his teeth on edge. Men who preyed on women and children would stop at nothing, and he and those who rode with him would be just as merciless when . . . and if, they found them.

The hunt grew slower. They moved at a snail's pace as Lazarus sought signs to indicate the way the abductor had gone. But three hours later the trail seemed to be lost. They came to a stream with a heavy enough flow of water that tracks would quickly be washed away.

"Which way would they go, Lazarus?" Craig queried. "It's clear they didn't cross here."

"We'll have to split up," Kevin observed.

"Dat be best. Mistah Craig, yo' an' yo' brudder go down stream. Me an' Mistah Randolph go up. One hour. Dey sho' to leave de watah by den. Yo' finds anything, one stop an' watch an' de udder come back fo' de rest."

"Sounds good," Craig agreed. "Come on, Kevin, you watch one side, I'll take the other. They might have doubled back on us."

That's what was scaring Lazarus, that some of them had left a trail just faint enough to trace while two or more others had doubled back in a completely different direction.

They moved away from each other, going up stream slowly, watching each bank for any sign of horses leaving the water.

Again it was Lazarus's sharp eyes that found the first clue. He drew his horse to a halt and peered at the ground carefully. "Fo' hosses lef' de watah here. Y'all ride on back an' git de udders befo' dey goes too far."

Blake didn't ask any questions, he just rode away.

He knew that Lazarus knew how to track better than any of them. It had occurred to him that Lazarus would have made a good commanding officer.

When the three returned, Lazarus had checked the area carefully. He'd traced the tracks for a short distance to make sure they weren't being tricked. It seemed clear that they didn't think anyone could be tracking them. Another thing was clear and brought a half-smile to his lips. He had roamed this area all his life, having been only seven when the Clayborns bought him, and even though the plantation was nearly two thousand acres, he knew every inch. He had fished every stream and hunted every acre. In the back of his mind lingered the memory of a cabin he and Keith Clayborn had built when Keith was a child. Keith had been very impressed by the idea and he used to call it his hideaway. Lazarus was sure he had never told anyone else, not even Whitney. Lazarus was certain that the cabin was where Whitney's abductors had headed. Obviously they had found it deserted and decided to use it.

When Blake rode up beside him Lazarus said, "Ah gots kind of an idea dat ah knows where dey might have taken dem." He went on to explain about the cabin.

"Great," Kevin said. "Now we don't have to be so careful. Let's ride in and . . ."

"Mistah Anderson," Lazarus said quietly, "yo' doan suppose dey was tole to let Miz Whitney an' de boy go any time?"

"No, of course not."

"Den iffen we rides in like dat dey gonna kill her sho' as yo' breathin'."

"How far is it?" Blake asked.

"Some distance dat way," Lazarus replied, pointing.

"Then let's ride as fast as we can until we get

close. I don't know how many of them there are, but there are four of us. If we're quiet, we might just be able to get the drop on them."

"Dat a better idea," Lazarus agreed. "Let's ride. Ah'll let you know when we gets close 'nuff dat we has to be quiet."

They rode for the better part of an hour before Lazarus halted again.

"Ah doan think it gwine be safe to ride hard no further. We can walk our horses quiet fo' a spell, den we gwine to have to walk."

No one had any argument with this so Lazarus took the lead again and the three followed as quietly as they could. They were moving so slowly it seemed an interminable amount of time had passed before Lazarus stopped again. His voice was low and barely reached them. "We tie de hosses here. Dat cabin just over de nex' ridge."

They dismounted and followed Lazarus, who moved through the trees like a silent shadow.

After a few minutes they saw the cabin. Lazarus squatted on his haunches and the others gathered near him. They knew their voices would carry on the night air so they spoke in whispers.

"Dey's three 'bout dat fire," Lazarus remarked. "But de do' to de cabin is open little over half way, so dere might be one or mo' inside. What kind of man would need fo' men to guard a woman an' chile?" Lazarus's voice was heavy with disdain.

"How are we going to handle this, Lazarus? If we grab the men outside, the ones inside will see us. They could pick us off."

"Ah knows. Dis gwine take some careful work. Here's what we does. Ah'm gwine sneak round behind dat cabin. When ah gets close to de corner, yo' three works yo' way to dose three 'round dat fire. Ah'll give a signal an' we all move at one time. Ah kin be inside befo' dey know what's happenin' an' ah kin trust yo' three kin handle dose others."

"Sounds like a good plan to me," Blake said.

"Hell, it sounds like the only plan we have," Craig chimed in.

"You're right about that," Kevin agreed.

"Lead on, Major Lazarus," Blake grinned. "You're the commander here and as for me, I don't think we could have a better one."

Lazarus nodded and felt a swell of pride at these men who so casually put their lives in his hands. "Watch fo' mah signal," he cautioned.

He seemed to vanish in the night as the three kept their eyes glued to the darkest corner of the cabin.

Everybody's nerves were stretched to the breaking point. Blake found himself gripping his rifle so hard that his hand was almost numb.

It seemed like a century before they caught a quick glimpse of Lazarus nearing the back of the cabin. Only then did they begin to edge toward the three men who sat unsuspecting by the fire.

When Lazarus reached the corner of the cabin he paused, looked in their direction, and raised his rifle slightly as a signal.

"Here we go, boys," Blake murmured.

All four moved simultaneously and seemed to materialize out of the surrounding blackness. The threesome before the fire looked in paralytic shock at the rifles leveled at them.

At the same moment Lazarus fairly leapt at the cabin door, kicking it the rest of the way open. A man lay face down, unconscious or dead.

When he stepped out of the cabin alone Blake felt sick. Surely Whitney wasn't dead . . . and Jon . . .

"Hold 'em, Craig," Blake cried, his voice thick

485

with rage. "If one of them blinks an eye, shoot him." Blake raced to Lazarus's side, trying to read his expression. "Lazarus?"

Lazarus looked at him. "Dey gone. Dere's a man inside. He be on de floor unconscious. Miz Whitney an' de boy . . . dey both gone."

Thirty-four

Whitney had stood in the darkness, holding Jon close and praying he wouldn't make a sound. She edged her way toward the corner of the cabin and the deeper shadows. Step by step, inch by inch she moved. The men were laughing—were they surmising what their leader was doing in the cabin? The thought only made her more angry and determined.

She caught her lower lip between her teeth as she set each foot down very carefully. She couldn't run as she wanted to, as the sound would draw their attention.

She felt as if her heart was going to stop at any moment. She reached the corner and stepped around it into the blackness. Only then did she begin to breathe, but she couldn't waste a second. She still moved slowly, making sure she didn't snap a twig. She had no idea where she was, or how far she was from safety, but she preferred the wilderness to being taken again.

When she felt she had covered enough ground, she began to run. It was useless even to attempt to steal one of their horses. They were too close to the men and she would have to put Jon down to do it, and that she would never do until she got him somewhere safe.

She ran until the sharp pain in her chest and the trembling of her lip told her she could run no more.

She sagged against the trunk of a huge tree and for the first time she wept.

Jon slowly awakened. The strange place, the dark shadows, and his mother's tears were more than he could understand. His voice was a plaintive cry.

"Mommy?"

Whitney drew him tighter, "Hush, Jon. Please, baby, please. You've got to be very quiet."

"Why, Mommy? Why are we out in the dark? I'm scared."

"I know you are, love, but it's going to be all right. All you have to do is be very, very quiet. It's," she thought desperately, "it's like a game . . . like hide and go seek."

"I don't want to play, Mommy. I want to go home."

"So do I, Jon, and if you stay quiet we'll go home. But we have to walk and it might take a long time."

"Where did those bad men go?"

"That's who we're hiding from, Jon, and we don't want them to find us. Now, do you think you can be Mommy's big boy and try real hard to be brave? We have to walk for a while and we can't talk. Can you do that?"

His voice was shaking and he was frightened and insecure . . . but he answered *yes*.

"Are you cold, sweetheart?" Whitney put him down and folded the blanket so she could wrap it around him like a cloak. He clutched it with one tiny fist and Whitney took hold of the other hand. She knew he wouldn't be able to walk far, but it would give her a moment to rest her weary arms.

"Mommy?"

"What, Jon?"

"Where's Daddy?"

"I don't know right now, honey, but you can bet he's looking for us."

"I wish he would come and carry me."

"Well, if he doesn't find us, suppose we go and find him. Then he can give you a ride home on his big black horse. Would you like that?"

"Yes."

They walked along slowly. The ground was uneven and the darkness made it difficult to walk.

Whitney had to match Jon's much shorter steps, try to keep him from stumbling, and watch the terrain at the same time. Still they kept moving, and Jon struggled along with a lot more courage than Whitney could ever have imagined.

She was about to tell him so when a deep rut in the ground caused her to trip. She thought she had regained her balance when the earth seemed to open up in front of her. She had not seen the edge of the ravine and she tumbled forward. She tried to release Jon's hand as she fell, not wanting to carry him with her. She twisted and rolled and as she neared the bottom her head struck a protruding rock and darkness overcame her. At the bottom of the ravine she lay still and quiet.

Jon had only fallen a short distance when Whitney let go of him. His tiny body didn't continue to fall and he watched as his mother rolled downward. Then she lay still. Jon moved slowly down, frightened and worried about his mother. When he reached her he sat down beside her and took hold of her hand. "Mommy?" he said in a whispered sob. "Mommy, wake up. I'm scared. I want to go home."

Whitney didn't answer and Jon was near panic. He began to cry. Then a noise drew his attention. He looked up to see a huge form silhouetted against the night sky. The man started down toward him.

When Keith left Mitch he hadn't gone far. He

needed time to think. Things were definitely not going the way he had planned, and Whitney and Mitch were both in serious danger. He needed to change his plans, and quickly. He wished he knew the one name that could make sense of all this, but he didn't. Now Whitney and Jon were in danger so he had to find them and get them somewhere safe so he could finish what he'd started.

He sat in the darkness and tried to channel his thoughts constructively. If someone had taken Whitney and Jon near their home, maybe he could find them.

He made a decision to get Mitch out of jail and work with him. It would take two of them. Of course, he would explain everything to Mitch, but it was time he did that anyway, now that he knew Mitch was not the man he had been tracking.

He settled his course of action quickly without discussing it with the one man in town who had been his contact all this time. There was no time for arguments. He knew quite well, even if Mitch did not, that the man they were dealing with would not hesitate to get Mitch out of the way, and he was pretty sure how he would try to do it. He had to get Mitch out of jail before morning, or the next night might see him dead.

Keith was well armed with a rifle and two pistols, and his horse was tied beneath the trees some distance from the back of the jail. But he would have to get another horse if they planned on getting away, and he set out to rectify that situation at once.

It was well past midnight when he brought the second horse next to his, tied it carefully, and began to make his way to the jail. At this hour there would be no more than one guard. After all, they didn't want to protect Mitch, they just wanted to keep him from getting away.

490

The streets were nearly deserted as he slipped from shadow to shadow. This would be the last thing they would expect.

In the shadows of the jailhouse he pressed his ear to the door to see if he could hear any sound from inside. There was none.

Mitch lay on his bunk, his arms folded under his head. Sleep was an impossibility. He could not push away the vision of Whitney and his son caught in Trent's web of deception and remaining in his clutches for the rest of their lives. He wanted to see Jon grow up, and he couldn't bear the idea of Trent and Whitney together.

He thought of how clever Trent had been. Whitney would never know he was behind all that had happened and once he was gone . . . the thought crashed against the walls of his mind and left him weak. He wanted to shout his anger, to lash out at something, but there was nothing he could do. He was fighting a losing battle against despair. He had to find a way out of this situation, because he was certain that tomorrow would be the last day of his life if he didn't.

He thought of everything Trent said. If he didn't do what Trent wanted, Whitney and Jon would pay. He knew in the long run only one man could come out on top and it would be Trent.

Unable to lie still any longer, he rose and walked to the window, gripping the bars with both hands. "Keith Clayborn," he muttered in a harsh, half-angry voice, "where in the hell are you?"

"Right behind you," came the humorous reply. Mitch spun around to see a smiling Keith turning the key in the lock and swinging the cell door open. "Want to come and give me a hand? I think we have some cleaning up to do."

At first Mitch was stunned by Keith and the open

cell door. But it didn't take him long to grasp the opportunity as Keith laughed and led the way out. They walked past the unconscious guard and slipped out quietly to the horses. In a half hour they had ridden far enough that Mitch felt it was safe to stop.

"All right, Keith, I think it's time we talked. A whole lot of things have been going on that I don't know anything about. It's endangered Whitney and Jon and I think it's time I knew."

"You're right, Mitch. I'll tell you everything—just let me finish."

"Go ahead."

"It started about a year before the war ended. The South was desperate. We needed just about everything. Some pretty big deals were made with northern contraband runners, and most of the negotiating was done by a man named Lyle Berton . . . a man who worked, or so we thought, on both sides, but for us. We found out later he was working for himself. He promised us a large cache of guns, ammunition, and medical supplies that we needed desperately. The only catch was it had to be paid for in gold. Sacrifice was made that few would understand. Anything made of gold was melted down. Women surrendered everything, including their wedding bands. Finally enough gold bars were gotten together and several good men were to escort it to a place where it could be traded. Two maps were made to fit over each other. One consisted of boundaries and line and the other had the names. You had to have both." Keith paused for a minute, his mind focusing on the tragedy that had set him on this course. "The gold was buried and one of the maps was entrusted to Berton and the other to my commanding officer. Berton was to slip over the lines and make the deal. Once the supplies were furnished the maps would be turned over. Only Berton wanted the gold for himself. He

492

betrayed Colonel Raymond and all our men with the dirty bargain that we were all to be killed. When he was dying Colonel Raymond turned his map over to me because he knew what had happened. He told me to escape if I could, and destroy the map if I couldn't. I did escape. Colonel Raymond also told me who to contact if I managed to get away. I sent the map home to my mother with instructions to keep it a secret and never give the map to anyone, even if I was reported dead. I would rather have seen the gold lost forever than in Berton's hands.

"Then suddenly the war was over. But there were some of us who couldn't forget that men had died because of a traitor. The only problem is, I didn't know what he looked like. It took a long time but we traced Berton here, then he seemed to vanish. I knew he knew about me, and I was sure he would come for the letters one day."

"And Whitney has the letters?"

"Yes. Only she didn't, still doesn't, know what she has."

"You took a hell of a chance with her life, didn't you?" Mitch said with a dark frown.

"It was a time when we all were taking chances. I never thought Berton would figure out where the letters were, at least not until I found him and killed him."

"And Berton is Trent Donnelley," Mitch stated.

"I know that now."

"And he's got Whitney."

"I know. I'm sorry, Mitch. I never meant to get Whitney mixed up in this. I had her turn the letters over to me but Trent doesn't know that. He's trying to get something from her that she knows nothing about and couldn't give him even if she did."

"God, we've got to find her. If she won't, or can't, say anything, he'll never believe her. He might . . ."

Mitch couldn't finish the sentence, because he knew that a man like Trent Donnelley wouldn't stop at anything, even using Jon as a weapon against Whitney. Keith was thinking the same bitter thoughts.

"Mitch, even if we go to his home, he still has the upper hand. He won't tell us where Whitney and Jon are."

"I'll beat it out of him."

"Maybe, maybe not."

"Damn it, Keith."

"I know. Look, your friends are looking for Whitney now. Why don't we go there and see if they've found a trace? If we find Whitney and Jon first then we've disarmed Trent completely. Then," Keith's voice grew hard, "we can beat that map out of him, and I assure you it'll be my pleasure."

"Good idea," Mitch replied as he nudged his horse ahead.

"Let's get going."

They rode as fast as their horses could go. When they neared Whitney's home they stopped, checking the area to make sure there were no unwelcome visitors. But there was no sign of any strangers and only one light burned in Berdine's window. They rode down to the house.

Berdine was surprised to see them, and told them the story as quickly as possible. Keith was quiet for a few moments.

"If they took the wagons into the woods and went on horseback, maybe they weren't going as far as we thought."

"I don't know what you're getting at," Mitch said.

"Damn if I don't remember . . ." he seemed to be in deep thought. Then he snapped his fingers.

"It's a chance, but maybe they're holding Whitney on her own property, in a place no one knows about."

"Like where?"

"Like an old cabin Lazarus and I built. No one's been there for years. Hell, no one knows about it. I'll bet Whitney doesn't even know where she is."

"How long does it take to get there?"

"We can make it in about an hour, hour and a half."

"Then let's get going."

Keith didn't answer, just followed Mitch to the horses. Mitch was in torment during the long ride, and he sensed that Keith was harboring the same fear. They could be wrong and wasting hours of precious time. To keep his mind off that possibility he focused his thoughts on Trent Donnelley and the price he was going to pay if any harm came to Whitney and his son. He would hound him to the gates of hell if he had to.

Keith reined in his his horse and Mitch stopped beside him. "What's wrong?"

"It's been years since I've been up here. I know the cabin is around here, but . . . I'm a little disoriented." He kept looking around. "Besides, there used to be a path, now it's pretty overgrown."

Mitch was beginning to get nervous.

"A path," he repeated. He dismounted and began to move slowly on foot. Keith did the same. It was then that he heard a soft sound. Was it someone crying? He paused, listening carefully. It seemed to be coming from the ravine just ahead. Mitch ran to the edge of the ravine and looked down. The sight turned his heart cold. Whitney lay at the bottom, much too still, and Jon was beside her crying in terror.

"Keith!" Mitch yelled as he began to move his way down. The moonlight bathed Jon's upturned face and his tears glittered like silver.

"Jon!" Mitch called as he grew nearer. Jon's heart

leapt with joy. It was a voice he recognized. He raised his arms as Mitch came to a halt beside him and reached down to pick him up and hug him close.

"Daddy," Jon sobbed. "Mommy won't wake up."

Keith was now beside him and Mitch thrust Jon into his arms and fell to his knees beside Whitney, gathering her gently into his arms.

"Whitney," he murmured in sheer agony. Her face was ghastly pale in the white moonlight. He held her close and was relieved to feel the steady beat of her heart.

"Mitch! Is she . . ." Keith could not bring himself to say it.

"No, she's not dead. She's hit her head on something."

"If we can find that cabin at least we can make her comfortable. Jon needs to be taken care of, Mitch. He's shaking like a leaf."

"Okay, let's get out of here. Are you sure that cabin's near?"

"No," Jon exclaimed, trying to wiggle free. "That bad man's there. I don't want to go there! I want to go home."

Mitch had lifted Whitney tenderly in his arms, and he and Keith looked at each other. Obviously Whitney and Jon had been held practically under their noses—and just as obviously, their captors were still there.

"How the hell did she get out of there—and get here?"

"Mommy carried me." But Jon was not satisfied with this. "Then she let me walk by myself. But she fell, and I couldn't get her to wake up."

"It's all right, Jon," Mitch soothed. "We're taking you and Mommy home." His eyes turned to Keith. "Then we have a score to settle."

Keith nodded and they made their way up the hill with Whitney and Jon.

Whitney seemed to rise through a black mist. She was lying on a bed and for a moment she was confused. Then the terror returned full force. She remembered falling and Jon . . . Jon! She cried out for him and struggled to open her eyes and sit up. Had they been found? Or had it all been for nothing? Strong hands held her as she fought through the haze of panic.

"Whitney, Whitney, love. Don't be afraid. It's all right. You and Jon are safe. You're safe. Whitney, can you hear me?"

Whitney blinked and struggled to focus her eyes on the dark figure that hovered over her. Then his face seemed to slowly take shape.

"Mitch," she said, with a relief that was almost painful. Then she was in his arms. He held her against him, crushing her to him and whispering her name against her hair. When she looked up at him her face was wet with tears. Gently he kissed them away. Then his mouth found hers in a kiss both sensitive and healing. Her lips were damp with tears and he tasted the brine mingled with the sweetness that was Whitney.

"I thought I would never see you again," she said.

"I know, love. For a while there I was doubtful myself. But it'll all soon be over. Whitney, I wasn't here to protect you because I was in jail."

"Jail? But why? Who . . . ?"

"It's a long story and right now there are a lot of people worried about you. Berdine and Keith are downstairs. I'll carry you down and we can explain everything."

"Mitch . . . who's behind all this? Those men were

497

following someone's orders. Who, and why, did they want Keith's letters?"

"We'll explain it all, Whitney, but . . ."

"Who, Mitch? You know, don't you?"

"Yes, I know."

"Then tell me. I have a right to know, too. He almost took Jon's life."

"Not to mention yours," Mitch said. Her eyes held his relentlessly. "All right, if you must know now. It was Trent Donnelley."

Whitney was so shaken she couldn't reply.

"Let me take you downstairs. Your brother can confirm that Trent was behind everything. He has a long story to go with it that might surprise you."

"I'm not doubting you, Mitch, it's just that . . ."

"That you've been deceived."

"Yes, I guess so . . . no, it's not that. It's that I *let* him deceive me."

"Well, you're about to find out that he deceived many others, too. In fact, the man outfoxed two armies."

"I guess I'd better go down and hear all of this." She tried to get up but suddenly felt weak and dizzy.

"Don't try it, love. You've got a nasty bump on your head." He bent over and lifted her in his arms. She nestled her head on his shoulder as they left the room.

As they reached the bottom of the step Keith, who had been telling Berdine, Addy, and Josiah what had happened, stood up and was ready to speak when the door opened.

All Whitney saw was the man who had abducted her. She cried out in alarm, then buried her head in Mitch's shoulder. This couldn't be happening, she sobbed silently. This man could not have found them so quickly. If he and his three men were armed Keith and Mitch could never subdue them.

498

What Whitney did not see was that the man's arms were bound and standing in the shadows behind him was Lazarus. He gave the man a rough push and came in behind him. It was then Lazarus saw Whitney in Mitch's arms.

"Miz Whitney," he stammered, his voice shocked. "We all was scared half outta our minds 'bout where yo' was." He laughed. "Seems dis here boy doan know where yo' go either."

"How she did it I'll never know, but she managed to get away," Mitch explained.

"Not befo' she give dis boy a couple smacks on de head dat gonna give him a bad headache fo' while."

"Where's Blake?" Mitch asked.

"Him an' his friends, dey makin' de udder three comfortable in de barn. It good y'all here. Dis boy got a heap o' talkin' might interest yo'. Seems he know 'bout a whole lot o' things it's best yo' knows." Lazarus's eyes lingered on Keith. "Mistah Keith, it good to see yo' home. Ah knowed yo' wasn't dead. Ah felt like Miz Whitney did, ah would have knowed."

"I suppose you would know, Lazarus," Keith smiled. "You and Whitney were in my mind all the time. I'm sorry I couldn't let anyone know where I was."

"Ah kin see why. Dis fella had quite a story. Ah thought ah'd best bring him back an' tell y'all de truth."

"A lot of things need to be cleared up," said Mitch. "Putting it all together ought to be enough to rid us of Trent Donnelley once and for all."

Suddenly Blake, Kevin, and Craig walked in.

"Those three are safely taken care of," Blake said. "They won't be causing us any trouble." He paused, noticing Mitch and Whitney for the first time as well as the stranger, who stood near Berdine. "Mitch . . .

499

how . . . Whitney, too. How did this happen?"

"I think you'd all better sit down," replied Mitch. "This is going to take some time—first to get the whole story straight, then to figure out what we're going to do about it." He carried Whitney to a comfortable chair.

Lazarus pushed his prisoner to a chair some distance away. "Yo' be real still, 'cause if you decides to make a move you're jes' gwine give me a chance to do somethin' ah been wantin' to do. Understand?"

The man eyed Lazarus's huge frame. Even with his hands untied he'd be no match. With his hands tied it was sure death. He nodded.

Keith was the first to speak and the others gathered around. He told the same story he had told Mitch. Then Whitney described how she was abducted and learned that these were the same renegades who had burned her home. Mitch was last, and all the threads of the story were finally put into place.

"You think our friend and his pals will talk if we drag them in to the authorities?" Blake questioned.

"Oh, he'll talk. They'll all talk," Lazarus said with a frigid look at the bound man. "Ah'll ask 'em real nice." The man gulped. He didn't care about Trent Donnelley's hide any longer—he was too worried about his own skin.

"We'd better see Major Ryan before we go any further," Keith said. "We need some authority behind us."

"Major Ryan? Why him?" Mitch asked.

"Who do you think my contact in town has always been? He's kept me pretty much up to date on what's been going on. I had no way of knowing who my man was, so there were very few I could trust."

"It'll take a while to get things sorted out with the good Major," Mitch said quietly. Whitney cast a suspicious look at him as did Keith. But Mitch smiled. "I have a little unfinished business that can be taken care of while you're talking to the Major. Might save a whole lot of trouble."

"No!" Whitney said quickly. She knew exactly what Mitch had in mind. "You're not going after Trent alone."

"I have a score to settle, Whitney. Trent Donnelley has meddled in our lives for the last time. He came to see me in jail and told me very clearly that he'd harm both Jon and you if I didn't confess I was the traitor. He would have destroyed you without thinking twice. I'd like to watch his face when he finds out it's all over."

"Don't try to make this sound so casual," she replied. "Once he sees you're free, he'll know. He'll kill you, Mitch!"

"I don't think so, Whitney," Keith responded with a grin. "But I'll bet he'll wish that hanging had taken place before Mitch is through."

"This is no laughing matter, Keith," Whitney insisted. "Now that you know the kind of man Trent is, you know he's still eager to kill Mitch. You just can't go in there. I won't let you," she pleaded, close to tears.

Mitch stood and drew Whitney aside.

"Listen to me, Whitney. That man tried to ruin me, tried to kill me, and worst of all, he tried to use you and Jon. We both know he would have killed the two of you without a thought. I can't let him get away with that. The rest of them are going into town. I'm going after Trent Donnelley."

"To bring him to justice?"

"If that's the way he lets it be."

"And if he doesn't?"

"Then I'll do what has to be done. One way or the other, I'm not giving him even the slightest chance to get away."

"Mitch, I'm afraid. He's dangerous."

"Not anymore, love. His claws have been yanked. When Major Ryan gets Blake's report and these men Lazarus caught have done their talking, Trent Donnelley's finished."

"There's no way I can talk you out of this?"

"No," Mitch said firmly. "You can talk me into or out of anything in the world except capturing the man who threatened you and Jon."

"Then," Whitney said softly, "promise me you'll stay safe and come back."

"That's a promise. I'll be back here by midday tomorrow." He bent to kiss her lightly.

"I'm going with you, Mitch," Keith offered. "Lazarus, Blake, and Noel's brothers can take care of everything here. I want that other map."

"What's going to happen to all that gold?" Blake asked. "It's Confederate money really."

"But the war's over," Keith replied. "There is no Confederacy. The money should go to the town . . . but either way, the military will take care of it."

"How much is it worth, Keith?" Craig queried.

"Three quarters of a million."

Kevin whistled softly. "No wonder Trent was so hot to get his hands on it."

"No wonder he wants the property, too," Keith added. "You see, the gold is buried there . . . somewhere."

"Then that's why Trent wanted my land," Whitney said, "and that's why he . . . oh, what a fool I was."

"No, Whitney," Keith consoled her, "that man was clever enough to fool two armies. You weren't alone."

"Well, I guess we'd better get going," Mitch said, turning to Blake. "You can handle everything?"

"Sure. We'll take these four in to the major and make sure he knows the whole story. Noel's going to love this. I can just see tomorrow's headlines."

"Speaking of Noel," Mitch said, "she was going to bring me a gun in the morning and help me get out of jail."

"Then I'd better get over there. It's getting close to dawn," Blake replied.

"Good idea," Mitch agreed.

Blake, Kevin, and Craig, along with Lazarus and Josiah, took the bound man and went to gather the others and head for town. Mitch again turned to Whitney, "I love you, Whitney Clayborn, and it's time we started the life we promised each other a lifetime ago."

"Yes, hurry back, Mitch. Remember that I love you . . . that Jon and I both need you. Don't let anything happen to you."

"I won't. I have too much to live for." He drew her into his arms and kissed her deeply, holding his hunger inside for the moment when they could be truly together.

Mitch turned away and left the cabin before he lost the will to go at all. When the door closed behind him Whitney sank down in a chair.

"Oh, Berdine."

"Ah knows, chile," Berdine said comfortingly, "but it gwine be awright. We prays . . . an' it gwine be awright."

"I hope you're right, Berdine . . . I hope you're right."

Trent woke to bright sunlight and a feeling of intense satisfaction. The world had a rosy hue. By this time tomorrow he would have three quarters of a million dollars and be firmly established on his first step to political office. Whitney Clayborn and all the land she owned would be his . . . and he would be rid of Mitch Flannery once and for all. He couldn't remember a time in his life when he felt better.

He rose and called out for a servant. A few minutes later he was surprised and annoyed that no one had yet answered his summons. He opened the bedroom door and called out, "Brewster! I need hot water to shave. Hurry up!" He listened, but there was still no sound. He was truly annoyed. This was his special day and he didn't want to waste a minute.

He went back into his room, put on his pants and boots, and grabbed a shirt as he headed for the door. Somebody's head was going to be on a plate for this. He buttoned his shirt as he walked downstairs. He found no one in the kitchen and now a subtle alarm began to tingle along his nerves. He walked to the doorway of the living room and froze. Mitch Flannery was seated with a pistol in his hand and a smile on his face.

"Good morning," Mitch said pleasantly. The words were spoken casually, but the look in Mitch's eyes was deadly serious.

"How did you get in here?" Trent asked, thinking rapidly.

"Easy. But that's not important," Mitch said mildly. "I have a question or two. When you've answered them to my satisfaction, you and I have . . . a few things to discuss."

"Obviously someone helped you break out of jail," Trent said curtly. "I'd suggest you get out of here. I don't intend to tell you anything."

"Break out?" Mitch asked, chuckling dryly. "Well, you're right about that. But you're wrong about your second statement. You see," he added softly, "Whitney and Jon have been found and four of your men are, at this minute, telling Major Ryan a very interesting tale of murder and treachery . . . and a lot of gold."

504

Trent's face went gray, but he remained silent.

"You mean you have nothing to say about that?" Mitch's smile faded as he rose from his chair. His eyes gleamed with a depth of anger that Trent could actually feel. "Come on, Trent, you've got all those magic words. Tell me how you would have killed a woman and child. Tell me how you betrayed all those men who died. Tell the truth for a change."

"Damn you," Trent hissed through clenched teeth. "You can't prove anything."

"I can prove a lot," Mitch countered. "I want that other map."

"Map? What the hell are you talking about?"

"The map," Keith said from behind Trent, "that you sacrificed a lot of lives for. The map that matches mine."

Trent didn't need to turn around. He knew who was standing behind him. He also knew that Mitch had found out more than he thought he had. But he was not a man to give up so easily — not for something he wanted this badly.

"Go to hell. I'll see you dead first." He swung halfway around so he could see both Mitch and Keith.

"Look, my friend," Keith observed, his smile like ice. "My buddy here is dying to get his hands on you. You have a choice. Tell us what we want to know and we'll take you in peacefully. Otherwise . . ."

Trent seemed to consider this — his conceit and confidence only made Mitch angrier. Keith or no Keith, Trent was not walking away from this. Trent moved slowly toward a chair by his desk as if he were debating what Keith had said. At the last second he leapt toward Mitch, who threw his gun aside and leapt at the same time.

Mitch's body slammed into Trent and flung them both across the desk. They then rolled to the floor.

505

Knowing the degree of Mitch's anger, Keith backed away, reasonably certain of how the battle would end.

The weight of Mitch's body, plus the intensity of his fury, overwhelmed Trent. Mitch never felt the few blows Trent was able to land. Mitch punished Trent with fists that seemed to be made of iron. Trent had little strength left, and Keith was half smiling until he realized that Mitch didn't intend to stop until Trent was lying lifeless at his feet.

"Mitch!" Keith said in alarm. Trent was now almost unconscious, Mitch's hands around his throat. "Mitch, let go!" Keith moved toward him, but it was as if Mitch never heard.

Keith had to forcibly tear him from Trent's inert body. Mitch was panting and shaking.

"It's over, Mitch. That's enough."

"I should kill him for what he's done."

"Let's let the law take care of it. You've got more important things to do."

Mitch turned to Keith as full sanity returned. "Yes, I guess you're right."

Whitney paced the porch, anxiety etched on her face. It was long past noon and no word had come. She was desperate with fear. The door behind her opened and Berdine joined her.

"Yo' ain't et nothin'."

"I'm not hungry."

"Yo' gits yo' son frettin', too. Best yo' come in an' git him settled so's he can eat."

Whitney seemed to ignore her. "Berdine, I can't do anything 'til I know what happened! We all know how dangerous Trent is, and Mitch went after him alone."

"No, he din't. Yo' brudder went wif him. Dey be two of dem an' dat man only one. Yo' gots to have

506

faith. He say he be back, den he be back."

"He said by midday. It's almost two in the afternoon. Surely it's all over by now. Mitch might be . . ."

"Goin' on like dis ain't gwine do no good."

At that moment the door opened again and this time Jon appeared. "Mommy?"

"Come here."

He came out onto the porch and Whitney knelt before him to give him a hug. "Everything's all right, Jon. Why haven't you eaten your lunch? Berdine made you something very good."

"I want to wait with you."

"Wait," she repeated softly. Would they just be waiting . . . waiting until someone brought word that Mitch was dead? She was so frightened, and she knew her fear was disturbing Jon. "All right, go and eat your lunch and when you've finished you can stay out here and wait with me."

He was reluctant, but finally agreed. Berdine took his hand and led him inside. Whitney stood and scanned the surrounding area. No sign. Every minute that ticked away tore at her very being.

She heard a horse approaching. She held her breath, hoping, praying. Then, some distance away, she saw him. She would have known his broad-shouldered form anywhere. She raised her arm in a gesture that was half a wave and half an expression of pure joy. By the time Mitch brought his horse to a halt Whitney was flying down the steps. In a moment she was in his arms, laughing and crying at the same time until his kiss silenced her.

Epilogue

Morning broke with a brilliant sun shedding light over the small house nestled amid the trees. Birds heralded the new day and a soft breeze carried every sound to the sleeping pair. Whitney woke slowly and lay very still. She had never been so contented in her life.

She nestled against Mitch's warm body and relished the way he reached for her, even in sleep.

She thought back over the past few weeks that had seen Trent Donnelley's conviction. She was glad that the military had taken him away to serve his sentence elsewhere. She would not have wanted it carried out in Holly Hill.

The gold had been found and turned over to the United States government, which promptly returned a nice sum to the town. Mitch's election had guaranteed them that the money would be spent for the benefit of everyone.

But the event that would live in her heart forever was their wedding. Mitch had chafed at the thought of waiting a week or two before they could marry, but he was nearly speechless at the wedding and glad they had waited. It seemed as if the entire town had turned out for the celebration and Mitch could not keep his eyes off his beautiful bride. He had sworn there never had been one as beautiful, and that he'd have waited another six years if he'd had to.

Jon and Mitch had taken to each other as if the separation had never happened. Mitch had repaired Jon's precious box and he and Lazarus had finished filling it with small, hand-carved soldiers and horses that would eventually become family heirlooms.

Today they would stand beside Noel and Blake as they took the vows that would join them in marriage. Although Craig was the eldest, Kevin had pleaded to be the one to give the bride away. He was delighted to see Kevin whole again and know that Kevin and Noel had regained their closeness.

While she had been partly in a dream state, Whitney was unaware that Mitch had awakened. Her delicate presence, even though she was lost in thought, had brought him from his dreams to something infinitely more appealing.

He lay still, enjoying her caress as her fingers lightly traced the hard muscles of his arms and the breadth of his chest. But his body was responding in a way that would let him pretend sleep no longer.

He tightened his arms about her and Whitney looked up into eyes filled with such warmth that she grew meltingly warm inside. Love was written so plainly on his face, and she drew his head to hers in a deep, lingering kiss.

His hands began to search for more delectable spots and her muffled giggle made him whisper in her ear. "What's funny, woman? You stir me up—then you laugh at me."

"I? Stir you up? Never."

"Love," he laughed, "you can stir me up just by breathing." His arms bonded her to him, and he sought her mouth in a deep kiss that promised so much more. It was then that the sound of small feet padding in made Mitch groan, and Whitney tried her best to muffle her laughter. Jon appeared in the doorway, his gaze curious. Mitch smiled and motioned him in. He raced across the room and climbed up on the bed to pounce into the warmth between his mother and father. They had romped like this often and it was Jon's favorite time. His little mind was already forgetting how it had been when it was just him and his mother. Mitch had become important in his life, and he accepted him with a growing love that often filled Mitch with tender emotion.

They listened to Jon's chatter for a while and then acquiesced quickly to his desire to see if Lazarus and Berdine were awake. He got down from the bed and ran out, promising to come back quickly.

"Not too quickly," Mitch muttered as the door swung shut. He reached for Whitney again.

"Mitch, I have to tell you something."

"Later," he said as his mouth took hers.

"But, Mitch," she gasped, "it's important."

"It can wait. There's nothing more important than this." Her hands pressed against his chest and brought him to a stop.

"Will you listen to me? You'll be pleased, I think."

"I'm listening," he said, but his hands were creating havoc.

"Not with your full attention."

"You're asking the impossible. At least I'm listening with half my mind."

"Mitch, you know when I had Jon I named him Clayborn, because I thought . . ."

"That I didn't want him. Whitney, I'll always regret that."

"Well, don't, because yesterday I had his last name officially changed to Flannery."

Mitch stopped moving and gazed down into his wife's eyes for a long moment. "I never thought I could love you more. Whitney, that's the greatest gift you could give me."

She breathed softly as he kissed her again. "But I think there's more," she whispered.

"More? What more could there be?"

"Well, if Berdine is right, and she always is, Jon should have a brother or sister in almost seven months."

"Ah, Whitney," Mitch said tenderly. "I always regretted that I wasn't with you when Jon was born. You've given me so much, but this . . . this is more than I could ever have wished for. I love you, Whitney Flannery . . . with every breath I take, I love you."

"And I love you, my dear husband. But we've got to get up."

"Why?"

"Because we're expected at a wedding and there's lots to do."

"Later," Mitch murmured. He drew Whitney to him and for a while they forgot all but the brilliant and consuming love they shared . . . and had promised to share forever.